RAVE REVIEWS FOR THE DONOVAN NOVELS BY W. MICHAEL GEAR:

"What a ride! Excitement, adventure, and intrigue, all told in W. Michael Gear's vivid, compulsively readable prose. A terrific new science-fiction series; Gear hits a home run right out of the park and all the way to Capella."
— Robert J. Sawyer, Hugo Award-winning
author of *Quantum Night*

"A marginal colony on a living world—where human life and human will are tested to the limits. An intriguing and inventive new work from Michael Gear."
— C. J. Cherryh, Hugo Award-winning
author of *Downbelow Station*

"Gear kicks off a new sf series by weaving a number of compelling characters into the narrative, including bold heroine Talina Perez and Donovan itself, a planet teeming with danger and delights in turn. The mix of stolen identities, rapacious greed, and treacherous landscape propels the reader forward. . . . Fans of epic space opera, like Rachel Bach's *Fortune's Pawn*, will happily lose themselves in Donovan's orbit."
— *Booklist*

"W. Michael Gear creates a fun and colorful setting on a planet full of interesting fauna and cunning, deadly animals."
— *RT Reviews*

"The novel's prose is as razor-sharp as Donovan's toothy beasts, its characters deftly defined. The enveloping narrative gallops along at a fierce pace."
— *SyFy Wire*

"A thrilling tale of high-stakes survival on an alien planet."
— *Dread Central*

PARIAH

DONOVAN: BOOK THREE

W. MICHAEL GEAR

DAW BOOKS, INC.
DONALD A. WOLLHEIM, FOUNDER
1745 Broadway, New York, NY 10019
ELIZABETH R. WOLLHEIM
SHEILA E. GILBERT
PUBLISHERS
www.dawbooks.com

First Paperback Printing, March 2020
1 2 3 4 5 6 7 8 9

I AM DELIGHTED
TO DEDICATE *PARIAH*
TO
THE GEAR FAN CLUB: BOOK SERIES
FIRST NORTH AMERICANS
FOR THEIR
CONSTANT ENTHUSIASM AND ENCOURAGEMENT.

AND TO
THERESA HULONGBAYAN FOR MAKING IT ALL HAPPEN.

ACKNOWLEDGMENTS

The good folks at DAW books made *Pariah* possible. Hard to believe that our relationship goes back to 1986 when I introduced myself to Don Wollheim at a conference, and he told me how much he'd enjoyed the Spider books and personally welcomed me to the house.

My special thanks to Sheila Gilbert, to Betsy Wollheim, and the rest of the DAW staff. They've made me feel welcome from start to finish.

Also, my deepest appreciation to Theresa Hulongbayan and the Gear Fan Club on Facebook at www.facebook.com /groups/54987233824/. I can think of nothing more pitiful than a writer without readers. For all of you who have followed the Donovan books to this point, thank you all and read in health.

7 July 2102
Off Neptune transfer point

Tamarland Benteen had never been on the run like this. Sure, he'd been chased. Hunted like an animal through back alleys and sewers. Some of the finest security teams in Solar System had been hot on his tail with orders to kill on sight. But never like this. Not with the stakes this high.

No safe haven awaited him at the end of this flight. No sanctuary with fine wine, succulent food, or luxurious beds, immaculate rooms, and sparkling female companionship.

This was the end of the chase. Here, on this ship. The last chance. And he was so close to escape. He'd made it to *Vixen*. Assumed his identity of Corporate Advisor/Observer.

Tam watched the clock ticking down from where he sat in one of the conforming chairs in the small astrogation control. Second by second, hope built that he would actually make it before Radcek's agents stopped the countdown and surrounded the ship.

Scrolls of holographic data—projected in various colors meaningful to *Vixen*'s officers—unreeled in the air before each station. The tension continued to build as the survey and exploration ship's field generators came online.

I'm going to make it.

Words couldn't describe the sudden surge of joy that burst through him. Euphoric. Possessed of the urge to laugh. And cry. Escape now lay but heartbeats away.

In his central command chair, Captain Tayrell Torgussen addressed the photonic com. "Neptune Control, this is *Vixen*. We're one minute from inversion. All systems go."

"*Roger that,* Vixen. *You are cleared for inversion. We'll see you in another four years or so. Godspeed. Good luck. Happy spacing."*

Inverting symmetry required the control and focus of energy that squeezed a vessel out of time-space, out of the universe. Benteen didn't understand how the generated fields created an interdimensional bubble. He'd been told that the fields were so incompatible with the laws of physics, the universe itself spat the ship out of time-space.

Even the physicists weren't sure they had much of a hypothetical handle on where a ship went. As long as *Vixen*'s reactors generated a field that inverted symmetry, the vessel would remain "outside."

The moment the reactors were shut down, symmetry reverted to "normal." According to the hypothesis, the ship's matter, "our" physics, could no longer exist in that dimension, and like a bubble of air that had been forced underwater, it rose and "popped" back into our reality.

Symmetry? Multiple universes? Travel based on descriptive and probability statistics? As far as he could tell, the difference between interdimensional physics and black magic was that one started with a P and the other with a B.

Chairman of the Board Radcek had the entire Solar System alerted, searching for Tam. Even as Benteen ran that unpleasant thought around the inside of his head, his implant sent a chime through his thoughts. Message? From whom?

Fear returned in an instant, tensing his nerves, pumping through his veins.

Benteen flicked on the photonic com that channeled through his implant. The image projected before his eyes was a news shot: Artollia Shayne as she was paraded into a Corporate board of inquiry at the Hall of Justice, her hands cuffed behind her. Artollia was accompanied by a phalanx of lawyers. Not that it would do her any good. Chairman Radcek and his henchmen would orchestrate the entire proceeding. The depth of Artollia's machinations had been discovered; she'd been flanked, ambushed at the last moment, and set up for the fall.

Corporate politics wasn't a game for the timid. Those who lost considered themselves lucky if their only censure turned out to be exile or incarceration. Benteen suspected that Artollia—having come as close as she had to unseating Radcek—would pay with her life.

"*Tamarland? Hope you're getting this,*" Artollia's head counsel's voice accompanied the images of the courtroom. "*Whatever you do, under no circumstances should you return to Solar System. I'm sending a short-burst photonic encryption, starting now.*"

A red dot flashed in his holo, indicating that the compressed photonic code had been received by his implant and placed in memory.

The red dot flashed off. The image faded.

Benteen tilted his head back into the astrogation chair's cushion and closed his eyes. She'd already risked more for him than she should have. Had somehow wrangled at the last instant to assign him to *Vixen* when she could have used his life as a bargaining chip. That bit of loyalty had been above and beyond call despite the intimate aspects of their relationship.

"She knew they were onto us," Benteen whispered as the countdown continued.

The miracle was that he'd made it this far. And, in only minutes now, he might make it all the way.

Escape.

For the last couple of days it had seemed impossible. Yet here he was.

It had been too good to be true when a reservation under a false identity placed him on an express flight to Neptune where Corporate marines had met him at the shuttle hatch and escorted him to *Vixen*'s airlock.

By the time he'd been directed to his quarters aboard the exploration ship, word had broken of Artollia's arrest on charges of corruption, sedition, extortion, and murder.

By removing him, facilitating his escape, she'd ensured that no one could interrogate Tamarland Benteen about his actions on her behalf. All that blood, all that murder and death. He might have been Artollia Shayne's most potent weapon, but with Callypso Radcek's victory, Tam Benteen would now become Solar System's most hunted and feared criminal.

Tam had no trouble imagining that familiar and mocking smile as it curled Artollia's delicate lips.

Yes, you won again, didn't you, my love?

"*Vixen,* do we have a go?" Torgussen asked the ship.

"*All systems are go,*" the ship's AI replied in its reasonable voice.

Benteen glanced around the astrogation center with its controls, workstations, and the holos displaying endless data. Once this would have been called the bridge. Now it accommodated Captain Torgussen, Engineer Wang Chung Ho, and First Officer Seesil Vacquillas. Each sat at his or her station, eyes fixed on the scrolling data and tuned into their implants.

Second Officer Valencia Seguro was down below, monitoring the ship's physical plant where water, hydroponics, and atmosphere were located. The scientific and survey team should be another two decks down, watching in the lounge monitors that gave them the last glimpse of Neptune and the distant sun as *Vixen*'s reactors began spinning energy fields around the globular ship.

For the next two years *Vixen* would be Tamarland Benteen's home, his entire universe. At the other end of the monotony, processed food, and claustrophobia, lay Capella III—commonly called Donovan's planet for the man who'd died there. *Vixen*'s mission consisted of comprehensive mapping, survey, analysis, and sample collection before initiating the two-year voyage home. Her scientific team was to determine if the planet's resources justified the cost of exploitation, and, critically, if human habitation was even possible.

Figure, all in all, that Tam had maybe five years before he had to face Corporate justice—assuming they even still cared by that time. Surely Radcek couldn't stay in power that long.

The external monitors showed space wavering and distorting around *Vixen*.

"Ten seconds," Vacquillas called. ". . . Five, four, three, two, one."

In the monitors the black-and-star-frosted fabric of space turned pearlescent gray. Shiny, flowing and translucent. Then blank.

"Inversion," Torgussen called. "Status?"

"Reaction stable," Vacquillas told him. "Inversion complete."

"Good work, people," Torgussen said softly. "Looks like we made it."

I win! I made it! Tam wanted to shout out loud. Raise a defiant fist and bellow, *Fuck you, Radcek!*

Like the professional he was, he let none of it show, but shifted in his chair, calmly asking, "Is that all there is to it? I thought I'd feel something. A sense of difference. I mean, we're outside of the universe, right? Like we just vanished from space."

"Advisor Benteen," Vacquillas told him, "we might be outside of our universe, but we're carrying our own little bubble of it locked inside the field generation with us. Sorry, but it's kind of anticlimactic."

He forced himself to take a breath. Back in Solar System they'd be pulling Artollia's organization apart, searching out every one of her operatives, clients, and benefactors. Radcek was ruthless when it came to the destruction of his . . .

"What the hell!" Torgussen straightened in his chair as the monitors flickered, shimmered, and flashed with the image of stars against velvet black.

"I don't get it," Vacquillas muttered under her breath. "The reactors just shut down, reverting symmetry. All systems are reporting normal, just as if we'd completed the entire two years in transit. Chronometer reads zero elapsed time since inversion."

"Neptune control, this is *Vixen*. Do you read?" Torgussen addressed the photonic com. The unit's entangled photonics allowed him real-time communications with the navigational station at Neptune control. He should have received an immediate response.

"Neptune control, this is *Vixen*. Do you read?" Torgussen repeated. "We've got a malfunction, Neptune control. Inverted symmetry failed. Do you read?"

Benteen leaned forward, curious about why there was no reply, wondering, immediately, if Corporate Security was behind the failure. That somehow, some way, he'd been fingered as Artollia's key agent. The man she lovingly called her scorpion. Perhaps Neptune control was under orders not to reply as a marine patrol cutter closed to effect his arrest.

A sinking sensation in the gut brought a weary smile to his lips. *Well, shit.*

"It always came with risk," he told himself softly, waiting to hear the Corporate hail for the *Vixen* to stand to and be boarded.

"*Vixen*, do we have a malfunction?" Torgussen demanded.

"*Negative, Captain,*" *Vixen*'s voice assured. "*Analysis of all systems indicates a successful inversion of symmetry. Mathematical algorithms analysis indicates that all statistical probabilities have been met.*" A pause. "*In short, sir, analytics indicate that we're right where we're supposed to be.*"

Torgussen looked puzzled. The journey to Capella took a little over two years as the mathematical and statistical equations ran in the qubit computers.

Tam Benteen sure as hell didn't have a clue about how *that* worked. More black magic.

And then he really got a good look at the monitors that showed the star field, the swirls, splotches, and patterns of frost-like light that smeared the midnight background. Nothing looked familiar. He couldn't quite place the patch of near total black that looked like a hole in the stars. Certainly not the Coal Sack. Nor did the Milky Way, brighter, more misshapen, seem quite right. He struggled—having often oriented himself by the heavens—to find the first fricking familiar thing in this new immensity. No Big Dipper, no Orion, no Southern Cross. He stared at an entirely new starscape.

"This is nucking futs," Vacquillas growled as she flipped data bits back and forth where her hands interacted with the holo display and her implants. "We should have red lights all over the board. Everything's reading optimal. No abort to the field generation, no fluctuations in the reactors. Nothing."

"I'm getting the same thing," Ho added from his station. "Nothing's offline. The only weird reading is an eighty-eight-percent fuel consumption."

"Eighty-eight percent?" Torgussen swiveled in his chair. "That's impossible. It would have taken years to consume eighty-eight percent. Gauge malfunction?"

"My board diagnostics don't indicate a malfunction," Ho insisted.

"Okay, so we inverted, it failed, and we popped back into Solar System," Torgussen insisted. "What went wrong?"

"You tell me." Ho growled. "Maybe Neptune control telemetry can give us a clue. They would have been watching right up to the last second."

Torgussen tried again to raise Neptune control on the photonic com, heard only silence in return. "They're still not answering. Seesil, get an astral fix. Maybe we popped a couple thousand klicks from our original position."

Finally. This would solve his mystery.

Vacquillas did, flicking her fingers to bring up the star charts for Solar System. Then she ordered: "Superimpose *Vixen*'s position and locate."

The stars wavered, seemed to expand and then shrink as the ship's external sensors projected their observations against that of Solar System.

"No match," *Vixen*'s voice informed. *"Checking star charts now."* A pause. *"Location established. Capella system. Six point one five light-hours from the primary. Twenty-one degrees, seven minutes, thirty-two seconds inclination."*

"Impossible!" Torgussen cried, standing from his chair to stare as *Vixen* superimposed the star charts with the masters recorded during *Tempest*'s initial survey of the Capella system more than a decade ago.

"This has got to be wrong," Ho snapped. "We barely inverted symmetry."

"Running additional analytics now," the ship told them.

"I gotta go check this." Vacquillas stood, taking her holo with her. "I'm headed to the observation dome. I want to see with my own eyes."

"Yeah, go," Torgussen told her, gaze fixed on the rolling screens of data.

"I don't get it. What's the problem?" Tam asked. "So, we're there. So what?"

"So, Advisor, it doesn't work that way," Torgussen insisted. "After years of hypothesis testing, we're barely beginning to grasp the theoretical roots of navigation in inverted symmetry. Put in the simplest of terms, once a ship has inverted symmetry, its location is a matter of statistical probability. The longer the ship is outside, the more time it has to appear in any given place, or nowhere at all. But we know that if you run a series of mathematical equations and statistics, they somehow set the initial conditions for where the ship will or will not appear. Sort of like the way quantum mechanics function in our universe. *Vixen* is programmed to run the same mathematic probabilities that *Tempest* ran when she discovered the Capella system. Assuming those initial conditions, and running those same descriptive statistics, we should come out at the same place after the same amount of relative time: two years ship's time, in whatever dimension, universe, or wherever the hell *Tempest* went."

"But we're missing the two years. What we call transit time," Ho said. "Which is a problem."

Torgussen added, "And if anything goes wrong during the transit time, the ship is supposed to default back to Solar System by immediately running the math backward."

"Which *Vixen* never had time to do," Ho added.

"But I still don't get how running a series of statistics can get us from point A to point B across space."

"Yeah, well, we really don't have a handle on that. No one does. Maybe, eventually, the brainiacs will work it out. In the meantime, you're just going to have to accept that it works, and when we initiate the program, we usually get where we want to go. As to the mathematics necessary to get from Solar System to Capella, it takes a 10^{23} power quantum qubit computer to compute, which means it's an insoluble problem to figure it out by hand."

"It still doesn't make sense," Tam muttered under his breath.

"Neither does photonic entanglement and a plethora of other observed phenomena in the universe," Ho replied.

Valencia Seguro's face formed on the holo. "Cap? I'm in observation with Seesil. Got the fricking star chart. It's impossible, but we're in Capella system. Everything matches, right down to the primary's stellar emissions and spectra. Background constellations, everything right where it oughta be. Just like *Tempest* reported them."

Torgussen shook his head violently back and forth. "Damn it, Val, I take your word for it, but it's just freaking impossible."

"Yeah," she told him. "We're supposed to believe we jumped thirty light-years from Solar System, and we did it in a fraction of a second."

"Which means something's really wrong," Ho added darkly from the side. "Where'd our two years and eighty-eight percent of fuel go?"

"You're right." Torgussen rubbed his jaw. "That energy had to go somewhere."

"Okay, that's just about what it would take to invert long enough to get us to Capella. But the transit time . . ." Ho gave up and blinked in confusion at his screen.

"What do you want to do, Captain?" Vacquillas asked from her holo. "Spin up and try and invert back home? See if we can run it again backward? If we've cracked instantaneous travel, it'll be worth a vacuum-sucking fortune to The Corporation slicks and their profit margins."

"Cap, we don't have the fuel," Ho added.

Torgussen shot a wary look Tam's way, as if to judge his reaction.

That brought a spear of amusement to Tam Benteen's heart. Artollia had placed him here under false pretenses. He was no more a Corporate bureaucrat than he was a fish. Wouldn't Torgussen and his crew love it if they knew he was facing a death sentence back in Solar System?

He said, "Captain, if we're really here, in Capella's orbit, my advice is that we look around, proceed with our mission, and collect our survey data. As I understand it, the exact math that brought us here will run backward, which means whatever happened to get us here instantaneously will be just as likely to happen again on the way back, right?"

"Hypothetically that is correct," Torgussen answered warily.

Not that Torgussen would buck his decision. Tamarland Benteen's title was Advisor/Observer. Once past the semantics, he was in charge. Chances were that if *Vixen* inverted again and reappeared immediately outside Neptune orbit, Corporate Security would be waiting for him.

And it wouldn't be pleasant.

2

Her night vision acutely sensitive, Talina Perez ghosted down the dark street. With care she skirted the few cones of light cast onto the graveled avenue. In the thrill of the chase, her charged muscles allowed her to almost flow, each movement liquid and powerful. Her clawed feet barely made a whisper of sound as she searched the houses that lined either side of the road. She slowed to listen and inspected each of the doors.

Doors were fascinating. Such clever things. And latches even more so. They existed as puzzles. And here, in this next pale white dome, she found just what she sought.

She melted into the shadows as a young woman stepped out of the dome-shaped dwelling. Closing the door behind her, the woman skipped down the stairs and hurried off down the street, then took a right and vanished between two of the stone buildings.

Easing forward, Talina tested each step lest it collapse under her weight. With a tentative try, she managed to undo the latch, watched the door swing inward in silence.

Warm air drifted out, filled with the scents of alien foods, hints of chemicals she couldn't identify, and the moist odor of human.

She paused, taking one last careful look up and down the street. Nothing moved. She extended her collar, the membrane picking up the finest of auditory vibrations. The only sound came from the faint whisper of voices from nearby dwellings.

Talina entered, vision adjusting to the bright light within. The scent led her through the main room with its curious furnishings, past the kitchen with its interesting smells. She had to maneuver just so to pass her bulky body through the narrow doorway, and there, in a cage-like bed, lay the newborn. It was on its back, legs bowed, arms out and bent at the elbows. A wrapping partially covered the tender skin. Fine hair—pale and almost golden—crowned the round head. As if it sensed her, the infant shifted, opened blue eyes to stare up in curious wonder.

Talina felt a flare of color roll through her, white and fluorescent pink. A statement of satisfaction.

She could sense the infant's life, the beating of its heart, the warm blood in its veins. Such a marvel this soft and tiny creature was. Its harmless little hands opened and closed. The feet kicked up and down on the mattress.

As more color flared, the infant's face bent into a smile, and the little mouth began to leak saliva as it uttered a happy "Gooo. Daaaa." It reached up as if to touch, fingers fluttering. Delight filled those oddly focused blue eyes.

Had the creature no clue?

In that moment, Talina experienced a jolt of disgust.

No! This is wrong.

Even as she recoiled, her mouth opened and she reached down. Could taste the infant in the crib. Experienced the rapture as her jaws closed on the fragile little life. Heard the wail of terror as her teeth clamped down. The cry cut off as bones snapped, and that small body crushed in her jaws.

And then she was outside, in the dark street, running. Around her, the town remained quiet. She was reveling in the taste of the infant—so different from anything she'd ever devoured. Curiously sweet and barely more than a morsel, its fluids were running down her throat, into her digestive . . .

"Fuck me! No!" Talina shrieked as she bolted upright in her bed. At her cry and movement, the lights flashed on in her bedroom.

Talina gasped for breath. Her heart hammered hard at her chest as if to explode her ribs. She reached up, running a hand over her face and clawing her long hair back.

Worst of all, she could still taste the infant. The memory of it thick on the back of her throat.

Dream. It was all a dream.

No, it couldn't have been.

The imagery, the smells, the sensations. They'd been lived.

She felt the quetzal in her gut resettle itself.

"You piece of stinking shit," she told it, awake enough now to know the dream's origins.

Which did little to lessen the horror.

For whatever reason, the demon quetzal had made her relive the night it had sneaked into Port Authority and eaten Allison Chomko's baby girl. Talina had tracked down and killed that same quetzal. In the bloody final confrontation, Talina had been contaminated by the killer's fluids. Shared its blood.

She could feel the beast inside her. Though Raya Turnienko—the town's only physician—assured her that no malignant quetzal was growing in her gut. As eerie as that would be, it wasn't much better that she was infested with the quetzal's molecules: Donovan's analog of DNA. Turnienko and the chemist, Lee Cheng, were still trying to understand how those alien molecules managed to interface with Talina's brain.

"You really are disgusting," she told the creature.

Mistake. The word formed in her mind.

"Yeah, you and your kind seem to be prone to that, huh?"

In retaliation, her quetzal's mate had come seeking revenge. That had been a tough fight. Left her dome in ruins. The man in her life, Cap Taggart, had been crippled. And days later, someone had murdered him in his hospital bed.

"Guess neither one of us came out on top," she muttered to the beast. Checking her implant, she discovered the time was two thirty-three in the morning.

Lightning flashed through her dome's bedroom window, and the first spatters of rain hit the roof.

An image flashed in her mind: A pot, Mayan in origin, colorfully painted and decorated with images of Maya gods. One, a feathered and bedecked human figure with a large nose, was shown in profile flanked by hideous beings, looking maimed and infected.

She knew that pot. Remembered it from when she was a girl. She had reached for it, only to watch it fall from the high table . . .

"No!"

Talina blinked, trying to clear away the memory. The falling pot left her with a sense of terror. Started her heart pounding. That had been one of the worst days of her life. The pot had been priceless. Freshly excavated from a newly discovered Mayan tomb in Chiapas.

Worse, she still had the aftertaste of eating that little girl. "There are times when I really hate you," she told the beast inside her.

The quetzal squirmed in her gut, whispering, *Good*.

Cheng, Turnienko, and the microbiologist, Dya Simonov, had no clue about how to purge her of the alien molecules.

"Meanwhile, I'm a freak," Talina whispered as she dressed. She shut off the light. Could see fine without it thanks to the infrared and ultraviolet receptive cells that had grown in her retina. Proof that having a quetzal inside wasn't all bad.

Thunder boomed, and the rain increased. Which was why the quetzal had been so active in her dreams. Quetzals liked to hunt during storms.

She paused in her kitchen for a glass of mint tea, then took down her rifle, checked to ensure a round was in the chamber, and slipped her rain poncho over her head. Outside, she locked her door and glanced up and down the wet, dark street. Images from the dream flashed behind her eyes.

Allison Chomko's old dome was there, two doors down. Talina's quetzal would have prowled right here, checked this very door, though the dome was empty back then.

Yes, the beast whispered.

"All that, and it was a bust. Thought you were going to learn something about us by eating that baby. And all you got was shot."

We didn't know.

"Ignorance is a bitch, isn't it?" She slung her rifle and padded down the street; rain tattooed an irregular rhythm on the poncho hood.

Talina cut across town to the aircar field gate, her night vision finding the guard awake at his post. Smit Hazen had just survived his eighteenth birthday. He was fifth ship, arrived on Donovan as a gawky, tow-headed boy. His father had died that first year, and Smit had grown up without any illusions about the world on which he lived. Even as she approached, he was using night-vision goggles to scan the aircar field just behind the tall fence with its locked gate.

"Hey, Smit?" Talina called as she approached the guard post and stepped under the roofed enclosure.

"Hey, Tal. Middle of the night. What are you doing up?" The young man lowered his goggles.

"My quetzal wouldn't let me sleep."

"Yeah?" He glanced sidelong at her. "It's the kind of night they like. So far the only thing moving is a herd of chamois. About fifteen. They were hugging the bush out past the farmland."

"Seem nervous?"

"Naw. Still, that doesn't mean squat." He lifted his goggles again, looking out past the security light that illuminated the grounded aircars glistening in the rain.

"Okay, stay frosty."

"You got it, Tal."

Something in the wind and rain turned her steps toward the Mine Gate on Port Authority's north end. There, the main avenue ended in a large gate through which the heavy haulers could pass. Beyond it, the haul road vanished into the darkness.

Wejee Tolland, a dark-skinned man with Australian aboriginal ancestry, could have stepped right out of the outback. His curly red-blond hair was squashed down under his rain hat; the man's flat nose and strong jaw were balanced by the prominent brow that made a shelf over his eyes. "Hey, Tal," he called as she splashed into the illuminated area around the gate.

"How's the night?"

"Wet." He stepped out from the shelter of his little shack and gestured beyond the fence. "Something's got my back up. Hard to say. I smell it every so often when the wind's right."

"What do you think?"

"Quetzal," he told her. "People tell me I'm nuts, but I'm only three generations out of the red center."

She sniffed the night wind, her own sense of smell acute. Another of her quetzal changes. And, yes, when the wind eddied there it was, that familiar musk. She'd smelled it often enough after she'd killed the beasts.

Stepping up to the high gate, she peered through the falling rain that slanted silver in the floodlights. At the edge of the pool of light, the bush—made up of scrubby aquajade, sucking scrub, and muskbush—had a washed-out look. Water shone in the graveled surface of the haul road. She sniffed the air again, caught that faint whiff, and almost immediately her mouth started to water. She winced at the bitter, almost overpowering taste of peppermint, like concentrated extract dripped on her tongue.

"Yeah, quetzal," she agreed. "Just out beyond the lights."

"Been a while," Wejee noted, shifting his rifle. "What? Almost a year since we've had one prowling around?"

"'Bout that." She accessed her com. "We've got a quetzal out in the bush north of the mine gate. Be frosty, people."

"Roger that," repeated in her ear bud as the other guards checked in.

Inside, her quetzal tensed, expectant. She'd felt that same nervous excitement just before her quetzal's mate had tried to kill her.

"So," she mused. "Another of your relatives?"

"What's that?" Wejee asked, wary eyes on the bush, his rifle raised under the protection of his raincoat.

"Talking to my quetzal," she told him. Half the town thought she was nuts, the other half considered her infected and quasi dangerous, but everyone knew about her quetzal.

"What's it say about this one?"

"Relative."

"Ah." Wejee gave her a knowing grin as he stepped back under the shelter of his guard shack. "You know, back on Earth my people put a lot of stock in family and kinship. On how we were related to each other and what obligations we had. Gave us a clue as to how we were supposed to act toward each other."

"Yeah, well, this is Donovan. Last time one of my quetzal's kin showed up, it crippled Cap, came within a whisker of killing me, and I dropped the bucket from a front-end loader on its head."

"Remind me never to claim you as kin." Wejee lifted his night glasses and scanned the brush line. "What are we gonna do about that quetzal out there?"

"Hunt it down in the morning."

No. Her quetzal sent a spear of displeasure through her, followed by an intense pain. Once, it would have left her prostrate—had almost gotten her killed the first time the beast had punished her that way. Talina had learned to mute its effect.

"What's your buddy doing out there? Come to hunt?"

Changing.

"Yeah, right. Whatever that means."

Wejee watched her with curious eyes. "What's it telling you?"

"Not to kill the quetzal."

"Well, sometimes you gotta go with the spirits, Tal."

"Last time I went with the spirits, Wej, people died." Which left her with the memory of a terrified infant girl crunching between quetzal jaws. Trust a quetzal? Not a fucking chance.

Come sunrise, she was going to kill it.

In her gut, the quetzal sent another stab of pain through her stomach in response.

3

Almost everything about Tamarland Benteen bothered Dr. Dortmund Weisbacher. The renowned planetologist cogitated on that thought as Benteen took the central chair at the conference room table on the crew deck aboard *Vixen*.

The conference room was combination meeting, work, and study area. A sort of command center, social space, and seminar room where research, survey, and data crunching were supposed to take place. Each of the walls had holo projection capabilities, and through their implants, the survey team could access and display their research data as well as interface with *Vixen*'s AI.

Dortmund had fought hard to get his posting to *Vixen*. He'd finished his second PhD in conservation management ecology at the age of twenty-six, then spent the rest of his life battling his way through academic politics to eventually chair the department of planetology at Tubingen University's Transluna campus. His papers on conservation biology and management, long-term terrestrial management ecology, theoretical planetology, and re-wilding had made him one of the most influential conservation proponents in Solar System.

When the preliminary data on Capella III had been released, he'd immediately understood not only the planet's importance, but dedicated himself to the cutthroat Corporate politics necessary to get appointed to the next survey ship. Capella III would be the final battle that would see the evolutionists broken and discredited.

He'd been instrumental in expanding and reinvigorating the re-wilding program on Earth, insisting that entire ecosystems be set aside, and ruthlessly managed them to propagate original native species, even if it meant supplementing and isolating entire populations.

In the process, he'd had to fight the evolutionary

biologists—colleagues who mistakenly insisted that, yes, an incredible number of species had slipped into extinction in the last twenty thousand years, but that the Earth was irrevocably changed. Their creed insisted that the remaining species had to adapt to modern conditions, that investing vast sums of money to maintain what was essentially a vanished ecosystem was folly when it couldn't exist without intensive human management. They asked: Was it truly a "wild" ecosystem if humans were culling every invasive species, protecting resurrected species like rhinoceroses, mammoths, and tigers from epizootics by means of dome-enclosed savannahs and endless vaccinations?

Dortmund had to be first to Capella III. His comprehensive report would establish the benchmark. Upon it, policy for the management of Capella III's pristine biosphere would be implemented. Here, finally, was a world to save.

Getting the position had cost him friendships, the chairmanship of his department, his husband of ten years, and every SDR to his name, but, thanks in part to Boardmember Artollia Shayne, he'd bribed, harangued, threatened, and finally wrangled the appointment.

And he'd do it all again if he had to. He would become both the Linnaeus and Darwin of a whole new world.

He just wasn't sure he had the best team he could have for the job. Had it been up to him, he'd have chosen much more qualified individuals.

Dr. Kobi Sax, the xenobotanist, had won her position by default. She'd conducted the initial analysis of the first "plant" specimens brought back by *Tempest*. She'd published the initial reports on Capella III's biology, histology, and metabolic pathways.

His zenobiologist, Dr. Shanteel Jones, had supervised the Cambridge/Harvard team that had described the preserved microbes, tissue samples, and animals collected by *Tempest*. The results had been controversial and disappointing to some scholars, but Jones had political clout.

Lots of planets and moons had life. Mostly simple reproducing organic or silicone-based cells. In many ways, Capella III was both fantastic and unique: a full-blown biology on par with that found on Earth, including complex higher organisms. While they were fundamentally different from terrestrial species in chemistry and evolution, the limited observations made by *Tempest* indicated a plethora of higher organisms. And best of all, the chemistry was organic, or carbon based. The study of Capella III's life was going to make a monumental contribution to science, and Dortmund Weisbacher's influence on that science would be every bit as immortal.

Unless this new advisor, Tamarland Benteen, turned out to be an impediment. So far, the man hadn't shown the slightest respect, let alone appreciation, for Dortmund's position.

In the conference room, Dortmund sat to Benteen's right, a cup of coffee clutched in one hand, the other extended on the table. The geologist, Lea Shimodi—a PhD from University of Tokyo and a Corporate puppet—sat to his right, followed by Kobi and Shanteel. Across from them sat Captain Torgussen, First Officer Vacquillas, and Second Officer Seguro.

Tamarland Benteen, his own cup of coffee in hand, leaned forward. The man appeared to be in his late thirties, as if one could tell given genetic therapy and med. He didn't come across as a Corporate bureaucrat. Anything but. The guy was muscular in a way that spoke of action rather than hormonal augmentation. Something about that hard stare hinted at some deep-seated danger. It was the way he looked at a person, as if determining whether to ignore, manipulate, or dispose of him or her as an obstacle.

And then there was the curious last-minute substitution. Advisor Maxim Grant had been originally detailed to *Vixen*. A survey supervisor, he'd had previous experience, mapping two star systems for their resources. Grant had actually had his belongings aboard when he was suddenly recalled, ordered back to Neptune Control, and *Vixen* had to wait almost a week for Benteen to be delivered before she could space.

Dortmund had tried to get a feel for the new Advisor during the rushed hours before *Vixen* inverted symmetry, but Benteen had summarily curtailed each and every conversation. The way he'd done it was unsettling. Cold. Not just disrespectful, but dismissive. As if Dortmund Weisbacher wasn't shit on the man's shoe.

As Dortmund studied Benteen, he thought, *If he's a trained Advisor, than I'm a monkey's uncle.*

The saying had been a joke in his undergraduate genetics classes that stemmed from some unknown antiquity. Some hinted it went back to Darwin himself.

"I'm going to call this to order," Benteen began, his voice hard and flat. "Everyone knows that something odd happened on our transit to the Capella system. You've all discussed it, know what it means. What was supposed to take two years was instantaneous. I've listened to the crew's arguments for an immediate return to Solar System as soon as we can generate the fuel for the reactors."

Torgussen took a deep breath, started to say something, then relented as Benteen shot him a warning glance.

"An immediate return would be a mistake," Dortmund said as much to establish his authority as anything else. "After all, we're here. Capella III is the reason we came. Our concern isn't the ship, it's the data. What we discover on that planet is going to change science, rewrite our understanding of—"

Benteen snapped, "You'll get your chance, Dr. Weisbacher. *Vixen*'s plotted a course to get us to Capella III within the next couple of weeks. All in all, we got lucky. We could have popped in clear across the system and been looking at months to match Cap III's orbit."

"So, what do you want us to do in the meantime?" Torgussen asked.

Benteen turned his cold gaze toward Dortmund and his people. "I want you to take the next couple of days and provide me with an operational plan. I know you've got priorities that were determined back in Solar System. Locations you've plotted on the maps where you want to visit and collect samples. I need that list prioritized. If you could do just one thing, what would it be? Then work your way down from there."

"How clad in stone is this list going to be? Might change our priorities once we're in the field," Shanteel said.

Benteen turned his emotionless and steely eyes on her.

"Operational flexibility isn't a problem as long as I'm aware of what you're doing and why."

At Dortmund's side, Lea Shimodi said, "I don't know if you were fully briefed, but my mission statement gives me a certain amount of autonomy and latitude in my reconnaissance of the planet. My job is to evaluate Capella III for its exploitable resources. Corporate prioritized geology over all other concerns not related to crew and ship safety."

Dortmund ground his teeth. Corporate always prioritized profit over everything else. Mine it first, study it later. Didn't the bastards ever learn?

Benteen took a sip of his coffee, level gaze meeting Lea's. "Fine with me. We've got two shuttles. My assumption is that one was for geology, the other for the biologists."

"What about security?" Torgussen asked. "*Tempest* had a casualty, after all. Outside of the shuttle pilots there's three crew for each landing party. Only two of them are security trained."

"Split them up. One armed guard per shuttle."

Dortmund said, "We went over this back in Solar System, but I must drive the point home yet again. This is a pristine planet with a unique biome. We cannot afford to introduce any contaminants into this ecology. Absolute category five quarantine and hazard protocols *must* be observed at all times."

"Even when one of the indigenous life-forms ate a person last time humans were on the planet?" Shimodi asked. "You ask me, that was a pretty big violation of the quarantine protocols."

"Not to mention that they buried the guy on Capella III." Vacquillas had a wry smile on her lips.

Dortmund raised a cautionary hand. "Yes, yes, but that doesn't mean that we should compound the problem. People, let me stress. We've only got one shot at getting this right. Our own history back on Earth is rife with ecosystem after ecosystem crashing because of the introduction of pathogens, invasive species, predators. . . . Well, the list is endless. And that's on a planet with a shared evolutionary ancestry. People, we're talking about a totally unique, isolated, planetary biome. A simple, unguarded moment, a sneeze, could unleash a holocaust of destruction that will devastate this world in a matter of years."

Benteen replied, "Doctor, that's your concern. Run it like you see fit. My understanding is that everyone's been trained in biohazard management and quarantine protocols. We don't want to make Capella III sick, and we don't want to bring anything nasty home with us, either."

"Glad we agree," Dortmund said darkly, and got an icy look in return.

"Now that that's all happily established"—Torgussen shifted in his chair—"what's our time frame? I'm assuming we're still looking at six months for the survey and data collection?"

"What's your estimate to regenerate the fuel reserves?" Benteen shot back.

"A little over two months to one hundred percent in the tanks," Seguro answered. "That's assuming the normal scavenging rate for hydrogen and oxygen was correctly calibrated by *Tempest*'s crew. In the next couple of days we'll have collected enough data to refine that figure given Capella's solar wind and the system norms."

Dortmund saw the tightening of Benteen's expression, as if the news was somehow displeasing. What was it about the guy? As if this whole situation was somehow distastefully inconvenient.

Benteen narrowed an eye as he fixed Dortmund in his hard stare. "We're here to establish the baseline when it comes to information about Cap III. To ensure that, I'm happy to give Dr. Weisbacher and Dr. Shimodi as much latitude as seems prudent to achieve those goals."

Dortmund felt his heart skip. Of all the scenarios he'd played out in his imagination since Benteen had come aboard, this was the least likely that he'd entertained.

"Thank you, sir," he told the Advisor with a slight nod, and flashed a look at his team. Everyone was smiling. Especially Shimodi, but she'd have to be watched.

Torgussen said, "While no one doubts the value of the Cap III survey, what just happened, instantaneous transfer from Solar System to the Capella system, is of even greater importance to The Corporation. *Vixen* just cut *years* off the transition time, and the answer to why lies hidden somewhere in the ship's mathematical programming. Getting that information back to the engineers in Solar System is our single biggest concern. Sure, we were slotted for six months, and let the scientists do what they can in the time it takes to refuel, but as soon as the tanks are full, we should space."

Shimodi shook her head. "Unacceptable. My mission guidelines are for six months at a minimum. Three months is barely enough time to run a planetary scan, let alone establish even a baseline survey of the geology."

"With instantaneous travel," Seguro shot back, "you can be back in no time. The key to that lies in this ship's deep com. Something special the engineers and programmers wrote into the code. If we had the fuel, I'd vote to power up, invert, and get *Vixen* back to Solar System immediately. Dump the data, refuel, and you're back here. Just like that."

"But we don't have the fuel," Benteen said, "which makes it a moot point."

"We're arguing for minimizing the mission," Torgussen replied reasonably. "Listen, each of these ships is programmed differently. Each run we make is an experiment. No one understands how inverting symmetry works, or how statistical navigation functions. The explanation for *Vixen*'s instantaneous transition lies hidden somewhere down in her qubit core. I'm not trying to be dramatic here, but it could be the key that unlocks the entire universe for humanity."

"Getting that data back is critical," Vacquillas agreed.

"And it will still be in the qubit com in another six months or however long it takes us to finish our studies," Dortmund protested. "That bit of delay won't hurt—"

"In the meantime, you could be condemning some ship and crew to years of transition," Torgussen declared. "Don't you get it? We need to get this information back before another vessel goes out."

Benteen's lips quivered, a calculating look in his eyes.

Dortmund, again, had that uneasy feeling, as if he were in the presence of a lurking spider.

"We'll finish the scientific survey," Benteen said with finality. "The ship's data can wait."

Seguro cried, "But, you don't—"

"I damn well do," Benteen snapped. "And more to the point, I have the authority to make the decision." He pointedly glanced at Shimodi, and then Dortmund. "I'll be expecting your priority lists."

With that, the Advisor stood, and still holding his coffee, strode out of the room.

"I don't fucking believe this." Vacquillas knotted her fists on the table. Seguro and Torgussen were staring uneasily at each other.

"It's just a delay," Shimodi said reasonably. "In the end, you'll get *Vixen*'s data back. And once there, it'll take the engineers and programmers months to analyze everything in the core. I'll deliver a complete geological report, and Dr. Weisbacher's team will rewrite zenobiology. We'll be immortal."

"Precisely," Dortmund told Torgussen. "You and your crew will be remembered in the same light as the captain and crew of the H.M.S. *Beagle.*"

Vixen's officers were glancing back and forth, looking slightly perplexed. "Never heard of it," Seguro muttered under her breath.

"Old sailing ship on Earth, as I remember." Torgussen had a disgusted look on his face.

Dortmund smiled to himself as he stood. Sure, everyone remembered Darwin and the *Beagle*. There wasn't any point in telling Torgussen and his officers that no one remembered the names of the captain or his officers.

4

"Y ou're headed into the bush to find a quetzal? You're out of your fart-sucking mind," Trish Monagan declared as she squinted skeptically toward the horizon. Mist rose in the morning sunlight, making a haze above the distant treetops.

"You could go back and have a cup of tea with Step Allenovich while he flies the drones. Hungover as he is today, he'd enjoy the company."

"If I was smart I'd be lazing around in bed and sleeping late."

Talina grinned to herself. The only way Trish would miss a hunt like this was if she was bound to a stone pillar with chains or locked in a dungeon's deepest and darkest cell.

Capella's morning light shone golden, emphasizing the various greens and blues of the Donovanian bush.

Trish shook her head as she followed Talina off the haul road and into the stands of aquajade and thornbush where the three-toed quetzal tracks led.

Tal shot a glance her companion's way. Trish wore a chamois-hide shirt and pants; she had a pinched and troubled expression on her face. The dusting of freckles on her nose and cheeks, in addition to her auburn hair, set off Trish's wary green eyes. She'd shifted her rifle from its sling to an easy carry, ready for a snap shot.

One of the drones whirred softly through the air as it scouted ahead. Around them, the chime—as the locals called the musical song created by the invertebrates—rose in the morning air.

Talina sniffed, catching the faint fragrance of quetzal on the humid morning. "Asleep in bed, huh? Then why are you out here with me?"

"'Cause, like you, there's times I don't have the sense God gave a rock."

Trish's green eyes had that glitter of deep-seated worry;

the breeze played with her hair where it lay on the shoulders of her quetzal-hide coat. Trish served as Talina's able lieutenant. The young woman's parents had been second ship, and Trish was one of the few survivors of the first generation of children to be born on Donovan. She'd been orphaned at the age of twelve, and Talina had more or less taken on the role of guardian and mentor.

Talina looked up at the high clouds, their edges rimed by Capella's morning light. "My quetzal says not to kill it."

"The last time one of your quetzal's relatives came for a visit, it ambushed you in your house. Came within a neutron's hair of killing you."

The chime changed, its harmony subtle, but different in tone. Talina slowed, altered her grip on her rifle, and felt the quetzal in her gut shift. She carefully searched the aquajade, sucking shrub, and thorncactus. Though the latter wasn't really a cactus, its thorns were just as dangerous. The damp, almost perfumed odor of Donovan's vegetation filled her nostrils.

The thing about a quetzal—and from the tracks, this was a big one—was that it could perfectly camouflage itself. Blend in so seamlessly that people had unknowingly stepped on the things.

With care, Talina scented the breeze. The morning light cast shadows from the vegetation that mottled the ground in patterns perfect for hiding a quetzal.

As the thornbush turned its branches her way, Talina carefully eased forward. She could smell the licorice scent of the sucking scrub, and the milder peppery odor of biteya bush.

A fastbreak darted off into the maze. That brought a slight sense of relief. The creatures wouldn't move if the quetzal were within attack range.

"Pus in a bucket," Trish whispered. "I hate hunting quetzals. 'Specially in the bush like this."

"Yeah." Talina swallowed hard. "You could go back."

"Hate to have you eaten, Tal. Means I'd be in charge of security, and I don't want the job. Too much stress. I might find myself out in the bush hunting a damn quetzal." A pause. "Why the hell are you so sure this one doesn't want to kill you?"

Talina raised her rifle, slowing as she noticed a patch of deeper shadows behind an aquajade tree. Exactly the sort of place a quetzal would go to ground. She studied it through her rifle's thermal scanner and found nothing.

"Something's changing," Talina replied when she got her heart rate back to normal. "We don't understand quetzals any better than they understand us."

"Well, damn, let me think here. Wait. Yeah, it's coming to me. Large alien alpha predators, cunning, with tooth-filled jaws and really sharp claws. Capable of blending into the environment, can run a hundred and fifty kilometers per hour for short distances. And what was that last part? Oh, of course. Silly of me to forget. Been known to eat people. Frequently."

"So? We put quetzal on the menu ourselves. Not to mention we kill them for their hides. Steaks and leather. Sounds kind of like a balanced equation."

Talina tensed as a flock of scarlet fliers sailed overhead. Where in the hell had that drone gone? She accessed her com. "Step? You still got us on your scanner?"

"Yeah, Tal. We're running a pattern ahead and to each side. Nothing yet." Stepan Allenovich's voice came through her ear bud.

"So, what's changed?" Trish asked, stepping wide around a questing branch of thorncactus.

"Maybe nothing. Maybe something." Talina raised her rifle, swept the thermal sight across the screen of vegetation into which the trail disappeared. "Life on Donovan communicates by molecules. The quetzal that infected me ate Allison Chomko's baby girl. Not because it was hungry, but because it figured it was going to absorb everything the kid knew. Same thing happened when those quetzals ate Rebecca and little Shantaya down at Mundo Base. Kylee said the quetzals were trying to 'learn' their victims. That her whole relationship with Rocket was an experiment."

"Some experiment," Trish muttered, swung around, and snapped her rifle to her shoulder as something small dashed off to her left.

"Might have worked if we hadn't driven Rocket out of Port Authority, if that two-legged piece of shit, Deb Spiro, hadn't shot him just for the pleasure of killing something."

Trish said nothing in response. The rift in their relationship, created by her part in Rocket and Kylee's exile from Port Authority, remained a sore subject.

"What if it was all a mistake?" Talina asked. "Going all the way back to when Donovan was eaten by that first quetzal? The guy had stepped out from the survey ship to take a leak, right? What if that first quetzal just wondered what in hell that two-legged thing was? So it grabbed old Donovan around the midriff, chewed him up, and swallowed, thinking it was going to absorb Donovan's molecules and thereby understand what this strange new being was."

"Must have been a hell of a surprise when Donovan's crew blew the damn thing in two."

"It may not have even had a chance to realize that humans don't have TriNA, that quetzals can't absorb information from our tissues. They have a hard enough time digesting our proteins."

"That goes two ways."

The vast majority of Donovanian plant life, when ingested, either killed a person dead or passed through the human gut without providing any benefit. The Donovanian plant cell, with its silicone structure, was too resistant to acids or endogenous human flora and fauna. Dya Simonov was working on enzymes that would enable people to eat more of Donovan's plants.

Animal proteins on Donovan—while still not as digestible—provided enough nutrients to justify the effort to procure and devour.

And then there were the heavy metals that made most life on Donovan toxic to consume. The planet had been likened to a ball of metal: mercury, zinc, cadmium, lead, lithium, scandium, and even more exotic metals permeated everything.

People ate a lot of garlic, and chelation therapy was considered a prophylactic.

And that was *before* Donovan's various deadly creatures tried to devour any unwary soul who set foot outside Port Authority or Corporate Mine.

Because of the hostile environment, the planet bred a hardy, independent, and often violent breed of men and women who took the settlement of interpersonal spats to an extreme. Dying of old age on Donovan was as much a statistical rarity as Dan Wirth's crooked roulette wheel paying off on red twenty-two.

As Talina liked to say, "Welcome to Donovan."

She smiled as she considered the inherent risk of just getting out of bed in the morning.

So, here she was, hiking ever deeper into the bush in search of a clever man-eating predator that might or might not be on a peaceful mission. All she had to go on was a "gut" feeling provided by an alien, and the sense of guilt she'd felt ever since Rocket's death. As if, somehow, she'd let the little quetzal down. Not to mention the girl it had been bonded to.

You failed, the quetzal in her gut whispered.

"Asshole," she growled in reply.

She carefully scrutinized the thicket of aquajade through which they passed. Felt the thorncactus as it scraped along her boots. Not for the first time, she wondered what the quetzals thought about humans tanning and wearing their colorful hides. Back on earth, cows, horses, and goats had never minded, but quetzals—everyone assumed—were different.

Even as she thought it, the quetzal tensed inside her. Her hearing, so acute since she had been infected, caught that faint altering of the tremolo as the chime reacted to something in the bush.

She stopped, raised her rifle to her shoulder. Vision sharp, she searched.

"Tal? Trish? Got a hot spot about fifty feet ahead of you. Be ready."

Talina caught sight of the drone as it cut into view, slowed, and dropped to hover a couple of meters above the tops of the scrubby aquajade trees.

"Yep. Quetzal. Can you see the drone?"

"Roger that, Step. Keep an eyeball peeled in case I'm wrong about this."

"If it were anybody but you, I'd label what you're doing a quick way to suicide. My call is to use the drone to drop explosives on top of it and pick up the pieces later."

"I'm for that," Trish whispered, loud enough Talina could hear her from behind as well as through the com.

"Yeah, well," Talina said with a sigh, "wouldn't be the first time my judgment was in question."

Her quetzal was so excited the thing felt like it was vibrating behind her stomach.

"Cut it out," she growled. Fuck, it wasn't like she wasn't scared enough for the both of them.

"Don't shoot."

"Yeah, you'd like that, wouldn't you, you little creep? Let your molecules go home to roost in one of your kin. Is that how you achieve immortality?"

She started at the thought. What the hell? Was a quetzal just a TriNA molecule's way of living forever?

The beast in her belly gave off that chittering response Talina equated with amusement.

She continued to scan the thornbush as she advanced step by step, rifle up and at the ready. Her heart was pounding out that old rapid cadence so familiar from a hundred hunts like this. Her finger hovered in the air over the trigger. She might have less than a second to aim, fire, recover, and fire again.

And if she went down, Trish was right behind her.

Nobody on Donovan she'd want backing her more than Trish. The woman had ice in her veins when it came to a situation like this. And she damn near never missed. Especially up close when the adrenaline was burning through a person's veins like fire.

Talina sidestepped a questing sucking scrub that ran a branch out to feel her boot.

Took another step.

"Tal? Got it on visual," Step said calmly in her ear bud. *"It just dropped its camouflage. Turned bright white. Man, it's standing out like a beacon in all that blue-green and brown. Like it wants to be seen."*

Talina saw. There, ahead. Maybe twenty meters. Patches of white in among the blue-and-teal-colored leaves and stems.

"See it?" Talina asked.

"Got it," Trish said through a husky whisper.

The quetzal in Talina's gut was shifting uncomfortably. By God's ugly ass, she wished she could trust it.

"Hey, quetzal?" she called. "Here we come."

"Don't think they talk our language," Trish growled.

"But if it comes to shooting, you drop to a knee, Tal. I don't want to take you out by accident if you leap into my line of fire."

"If I gotta be shot, I'd rather it be by a friend," she murmured, trying to find any shred of humor as her fear quotient rose.

The damn quetzal was just standing there. Talina took the last step past the brush to find the thing on the other side of a small clearing. As she did, the familiar rush of saliva flooded her mouth. The concentrated peppermint taste made her wince.

At her appearance faint patterns of yellow and black bled into the quetzal's snowy white, a sign of fear. It stood on its powerful hind legs, the toes bunched, claws sunk into the clay soil. The tail was raised, ready to lash out if the beast had to flee. The forearms were tucked close to the thing's breast, the wicked claws curled inoffensively out of the way. Instead of spread wide, the neck's expandable collar was down, signaling no threat. The saurian head was lowered, tilted, those terrible serrated jaws closed. Three hard black eyes were fixed on Talina, and a nervous clicking sounded from deep in the animal's throat.

Talina's quetzal continued to vibrate. A series of emotions tickled around the margins of her limbic system.

No more than five meters away, the big quetzal slowly took a breath and sent a harmonic exhale through the vents behind the back legs and at the top of the tail.

Trish sounded like she spoke through clenched teeth when she said, "Now what?"

"Yeah, good question, huh?" Talina kept staring at the creature through her rifle's optics. It hadn't moved.

She had to do something; the beast in her gut was whimpering and twisting around.

"Be ready, Trish." Talina took a deep breath, and slowly lowered her rifle.

The quetzal remained motionless.

Fuck this. The tension was killing her. She took a step forward, saying softly, "We haven't shot. Your move."

At her words, the quetzal uttered a gargling sound. A thousand colors burst out in patterns across its hide. Fantastic crimson, royal blue, teal, and a fluorescent deep purple.

"Sorry. We don't read quetzal." Talina had to keep swallowing as her mouth watered.

"Trish?"

"Yeah?"

"If this is going to work, I've got to share spit with this thing."

"That's nuts!"

"You know how quetzals do it."

"You'll be halfway down its throat before I can kill it."

"Only if it goes wrong."

"Talina, don't!"

But she was taking another step forward, letting the rifle hang inoffensively in her right hand.

If I survive this, Raya's going to have me on psych meds for the rest of my life.

But the Wild Ones—the humans living out in the bush—had brokered peace with quetzals. Kylee had lived with one for years.

"What the hell do you want?" she asked the creature as she stopped less than a meter in front of it.

Talina fixed on the three eyes, tried to see the intelligence behind them. Her quetzal kept purring inside her. She wanted to spit, kept swallowing the rush of saliva. Then, unable to think of anything else, she expectorated a pool into her left hand and offered it to the quetzal.

In an instant, the creature's tongue flicked out like a cured-leather rope. She'd bitten a quetzal tongue before, knew how hard and tough they were. It barely skimmed across her wet palm.

The tongue snapped back like a whip. The quetzal's jaws worked, the head tilted in an almost human gesture of interest.

"Yeah, there's a bunch of different quetzals' molecules there," she told it. "The two I killed. They think you're kin. Then I shared spit with one out by Briggs' place. Some is from Rocket. He was a friend of mine. The rest are his kin."

The quetzal chattered in response, and the tail flipped lazily back and forth.

"Tal, you're out of your mind," Step's voice said in her ear bud. She could hear the drone's faint buzz overhead. Half of Port Authority was no doubt watching.

"Not dead yet," she replied, wishing her heart would stop hammering and the cold sweat of fear would recede.

The quetzal made a croaking sound, extended its tongue nearly a meter beyond the jaws, and waited. Again it croaked, as if urging her to do something.

"Yeah, yeah, I know." Talina wiped her mouth. "You bastards don't know this, but humans find this disgusting as all hell."

She spit into her hand, offered it again. The blazing white quetzal ignored it. The beast's three eyes peered at her, questioning, perhaps wondering if she were an idiot.

The tip of the extended tongue wiggled like an angry worm.

"What's this all about?" Trish asked anxiously from where she'd taken a position to one side, rifle still shouldered and aimed at the quetzal.

"Wants to trade saliva."

"The infamous French kiss?"

"Yep."

"You gonna do it?"

"I *hate* that shit!"

"Talina?" a woman's voice came over the com.

"Yeah? Dya, that you?"

"I don't have to tell you what's at stake here."

Shit! If it were anyone but Dya, Tal could have told them to go suck a fart. Dya had been forced to abandon her eldest daughter Kylee to the quetzals—the woman almost broke down in tears at the mere mention of it.

"For the cause," she said irritably, took another step forward, and opened her mouth. She squeezed her eyes closed, unable to watch. The quetzal's tongue probed her mouth, flicked off her teeth, cheeks, and tongue. It seemed to suck up the saliva, and then a new peppermint flavor—overpowering and astringent—flooded her mouth.

As quickly it was over.

Talina made a face, turned her head, and spit. "Bloody sucking snot, that's fucking rude!"

"I don't believe you just did that," Trish declared from behind her rifle.

"Yeah, I'm just a laugh a minute."

The quetzal had gone quiet, peering at her with a new

intensity. Again it inhaled, blew a harmonic out of its rear vents. Opening its mouth, collar extending slightly, it flashed a chevron pattern of taupe and burnt umber.

Whatever the hell that meant.

Talina stepped back, watching it warily. "So . . . what's next? We all retreat to Inga's, drink whiskey, and sing 'Coming Together Under the Bower'?"

"Don't know that quetzals are musical," Trish growled, her eye still glued to the optical sight.

Chittering, the quetzal lowered its head until the jaw barely touched the ground. Maybe it was a bow. Or perhaps a gesture of submission. Then, carefully, it backed up a step. Then another. One eye looked up at the drone, the other two never leaving Talina.

With a final loud clapping of the jaws, it turned, slipped off through the brush, and disappeared.

"Step? You on it?"

"Yeah, Tal. It's headed west at a quick walk. The thing knows we're watching. It glances up at the drone every so often. It's staying white. Like it wants us to know where it is."

Talina took a deep breath, made a face at the taste in her mouth. A feeling of triumphant satisfaction emanated from the quetzal inside her. Not that she took the beast's feelings as anything but a ploy.

"It's still headed away, Tal," Step reported. *"Straight line, and on a path that will keep it away from the claims. It's like it's going out of its way to avoid any contact."*

She glanced at Trish, rhetorically asking, "So, what the hell just happened here?"

Dya's voice over the com said, *"A wild quetzal came in, traded molecules, and is leaving. No one's dead, and the quetzal's still alive. That's a first for Port Authority."*

"You didn't get French kissed," Talina groused.

"No," Dya replied. *"But Raya, Cheng, and I are just aching to get some of those new TriNA molecules you've got on your tongue."*

Talina shook her head, reading the dismay in Trish's expression. "Okay, we're headed back to the Haul Road. Assuming we don't get eaten by a bem, slug, or skewer. Meanwhile, everybody stay frosty. Doesn't mean this wasn't a diversion and another quetzal or two haven't tried to sneak in for lunch."

"*Roger that,*" Step answered. "*Got the rest of the drones deployed. Gates are closed. We've got eyeballs on the motion detectors, and the farms are on lockdown.*"

Talina led the way, retracing their path, following where their boots had scuffed the damp clay. The image flashed behind her eyes: Mom's kitchen back in Chiapas. Talina's child-small fingers, reaching up for the beautiful pot with its fascinating figures. She barely touched it, the surface smooth, the colors so vivid. And then horror as the pot teetered, began to fall in slow motion . . .

Talina angrily jerked her head. What the hell? Why had her brain dug that up from the past?

Trish, eyes scanning to all sides, rifle at the ready, asked, "I mean, how did you know it wasn't going to attack? Just from smelling it outside the gate? How does that work?"

"I haven't a clue, Trish."

"And talk about being creep-freaked, putting its tongue in your mouth?"

"It's how they share information, though lord knows what my quetzal molecules are telling it. Besides, it could be worse."

"How's that?"

"Quetzals could share information through urine or feces."

"Oh, yuck."

"Yep. And as soon as Dya gets her swab, I'm off to Inga's to sterilize my insides with her meanest whiskey."

"Right. Not even quetzal spit could survive that."

5

Tamarland closed the door to his personal quarters, walked to his small desk, and rotated the chair out. It swiveled on an adjustable pivoting arm that allowed it to be stored under the knee recess.

The room didn't measure more than four by five paces, which included the bed, small bath, and toilet, as well as storage space for his clothing. Not that he had much, just his tactical weapons case and a few changes of apparel. His exit had been so precipitous that he'd only taken what he could carry.

Seating himself, Tam shielded the room, ensuring that he was in complete privacy and couldn't be recorded. Then he leaned back and accessed the compressed message he'd received in the moments before *Vixen* inverted symmetry.

He wasn't surprised when Artollia Shayne's remarkable features formed in the image projected from his implant. Befitting her power and position, her physical appearance was that of an exotic beauty with high and almost triangular cheekbones, tan eyes that mesmerized, a delicately formed nose and full mouth. Now those lips were smiling in a way that betrayed no humor. One of her petite brows arched into a V.

"Hello, my lover," she told him, her voice honeyed and sensuous. "I have but a few moments before they defeat the security and charge in to arrest me. I've thought of suicide, but rather than take that last victory from them, I'm planning on laying some traps of my own during the trial. Like landmines sown into Radcek's path. I won't live to see the effect they will have, but I'm hoping that you will, my scorpion."

She tilted her head in an intimate gesture. "If you received this, it was because you've made your escape. My apologies for the manner in which I had to extricate you from the fray. But knowing you as I do, you'd have insisted on some final act of defiance. Dramatic as your action might have been, it would have been pointless. You'd have ended up just as dead. And had they taken you alive, they would have employed advanced psychiatric interrogation and dissected your remarkable brain and personality in the process.

"I would spare you the pain, invasion, and the humiliation of having your living brain cut apart like that. Seeing bits of your personality being gawked at by the behavioral scientists, let alone broadcast by the media. What makes you so remarkably ruthless and cunning shouldn't be served up as gaudy entertainment by a few specialists in abnormal psychiatry."

Her seductive smile and twinkling eyes were for him alone as she added, "A woman in my position shouldn't succumb to such failings, but I have a special place in my heart for you. Don't call it love, but I need to know that you survived. We're two of a kind. I would never have made it this far without your acute cunning. Sharing your thoughts and company was every bit as fulfilling and stimulating emotionally and intellectually as it was physically when our bodies were locked together in sexual ecstasy. In another age, we'd have made the perfect marriage."

Her laughter filled with bitter irony. "That is to remain our secret. But then, I know you can keep a secret. Unless, of course, Radcek should capture you. Another reason for spiriting you away. I don't want his technicians pulling those salacious bits from the deepest recesses of your mind. He'd use such maudlin sentiment as justification of my unworthiness."

She narrowed a crafty tan eye. "No, my darling scorpion, I want you to live. You're one of my landmines. I want you safely out of the way for the time being. Radcek will fall. It's inevitable. My gamble is that you'll be returning five, perhaps six years from now. My ruthless weapon from beyond the grave, slipping back into society, creeping through the cracks and hiding under the stones until you can sting each and every one of my enemies to death. And when you do, I want them to die knowing you act on my behalf.

"And your own, of course. I may be saving your life for

the time being, and hence, deserve your consideration and at least a modicum of loyalty, but you know that had I not ordered you to *Vixen*, you'd be dead, too. Knowing that, they are even more your enemies than mine."

He felt a flutter of sadness in his heart. Damn, what a remarkable woman.

Then she leaned forward, pupils glistening and black in a sea of tan, a devilish expression on her exotic face. Seeming to fix on his gaze, she formed her lips into a kiss, inhaling as she did so.

"Live for me, my scorpion. Upon your return, make them pay."

And with that, the holo ended.

Tam Benteen sat back, his heart rate accelerated, the blood pounding in his veins.

A thousand memories flooded him, times they'd shared. The way she had looked at him over a candlelit supper. The occasion she'd been present when he executed one of her rivals, her eyes had almost glowed with excitement. Or the special way she'd convulsed in the throes of orgasm as her exertion-hot body had burned against his. The cunningly satisfied look as she'd listened to information he'd provided on a fellow Boardmember, each bit of data unlocking yet another secret.

Taking a deep breath, Tam stood, the chair automatically swinging back under the desk on its swivel.

She was betting that in the years he was away, Chairman Radcek would fall. That in that time, the warrant for Tam's arrest would be dropped, or at least be considered a lower priority. That, at best, he might walk off the returned *Vixen* a free man, or at worst, he had five or six years to concoct a plan that would allow him to slip past any security officers waiting to detain him.

Counting on the latter, he could already see ways to make his escape. Upon *Vixen*'s return, he could disable the communications, and as soon as symmetry was normal, he could drift away on one of the exploration shuttles. Once far enough from *Vixen,* he could slip sunward and eventually dock at a station. From there, it would be a simple matter to pick up one of his various IDs and ride back to Transluna in comfort.

"But that's years in the future," he told himself.

Did he dare trust Shayne? As a Boardmember she had certain protections that a man like Tamarland Benteen did not. Radcek's psychiatric techs wouldn't be allowed to use advanced interrogation. They were prohibited from cutting her skull open and picking around in her brain, stimulating memories, like they could in his. Who wanted to create the precedent that a Boardmember's secrets might be exposed to the public? Certainly not Chairman Radcek, no matter how powerful. Nor would the other Boardmembers take kindly to the notion.

The power elite might play a deadly winner-take-all game, but they insisted on sticking to the rules.

Tam's take? Shayne was telling the truth. She wanted him to stay alive, make his return, and pay the bastards back with mayhem. Correctly, she also figured that while his loyalty to her might not survive the years, the knowledge that her enemies would kill him remained as a motivator. And what the hell, he really was good at what he did. He had been her foil, the sharp wit against which she tested her plans.

"Damn, Tam," he told himself. "Five years is a long time. Stretch it out to six, and it's even longer. Get back, slip through the net, and who knows who you'll find waiting on the other side? Maybe another Boardmember like Shayne. And maybe next time, you'll ride his or her coattails all the way to the top."

And that, he figured, was something to live for.

6

Talina sat with her butt braced against a counter, arms crossed as she watched the holo projection in Lee Cheng's lab. Overhead, only one of the original lights remained working, while handmade bulbs blown at the glassworks, with filaments made from locally mined tungsten, supplied the rest of the room's illumination.

Raya Turnienko, Dya Simonov, and Cheng clustered around the table, gazes rapt on the image projected before the lab's back wall.

"Fascinating," Dya whispered, one hand fingering the long locks of blond hair that hung over the shoulders of her canvas shirt. Anything having to do with quetzals obsessed Dya Simonov. She rarely let it show, but the woman tortured herself over the fact that her daughter Kylee chose quetzals over humans down at Mundo Base. That somehow she'd failed as a mother.

On the projection, Talina watched three molecules. Each reminded her of a short length of three-stranded S-twist rope. They began unwrapping into separate strands. As they did, the filaments—molecular strings—were wavering, looked to be searching around in the solution into which they'd been injected.

"The TriNA molecules that are unwinding are three of your quetzal molecules," Cheng told her. "The one on the upper left is from the strain we recovered from your original infection. The second is from Rocket when he shared saliva with you at Mundo Base. The one at the bottom is one we recovered from this morning's encounter."

"Lucky me. I just love being a source for your entertainment pleasure." As she said it, Talina felt her quetzal shifting inside her, apparently as rapt as the rest of them.

"Enjoy it, you piece of shit," she growled. "Maybe the solution is finally here that will allow us to finally get rid of your pestilent ass."

Dya couldn't hide a smirk. Raya Turnienko, however, seemed to miss it. The physician's tall and thin frame might have been spring steel, tense, and almost quivering. Her mouth puckered tightly in her flat Siberian face. Fully half of the blood samples Raya had taken from people living on Donovan now exhibited TriNA molecules that survived in their bodies.

No one had a clue about what it meant, let alone what the long term ramifications might be. Raya—as the only physician on the planet—ached to know. Back in Solar System it would have been as easy as submitting a sample to a biochem lab. Within seconds, the complete atomic composition, structure, and geometry of the molecules would have been mapped and cataloged.

The scanning microscopy equipment for such analysis now sat in a shed out back, tarped and waiting for replacement parts and a technician who might know how to both fix and operate the thing.

Lee Cheng fingered his round chin, small lips compressed; his eyes were half squinted, fixed on the image as the strands, like blind worms, slowly separated from their mates, dividing the molecules into three threadlike lengths.

"Must be some trigger," Dya noted. "Some signal to cause them to initiate separation. We can leave a single molecule in solution for weeks, and it just sits there. Put two in from the same strain, they sit. Put in a second strain, Rocket's for instance, and they separate and recombine."

"What do you think is the trigger?" Talina asked.

"Might be a small molecule, something with a specific architecture and structure. Perhaps an analog to our microRNA. Could be something as simple as vibrations. Photons? Who knows?"

In the projection, the molecular filaments wiggled sinuously around, seemed to orient, and sorted themselves before beginning the intricate dance of weaving themselves together again. Within minutes, three new TriNA molecules had assembled themselves.

"Remarkable." Cheng had a knowing smile on his lips. "None of the filaments reassembled with any of their original partners. Each joined one apiece from the other two."

"Definitely non-random," Dya said. "When two partners might have recombined, they shifted away from each other."

"Much more organized than DNA," Raya agreed. "It's as if these molecules are smarter."

Cheng nodded. "That's what we've come to suspect. That TriNA is coding much more sophisticated information than DNA, and doing it on purpose . . . Wait a second, what's this?"

Talina and her companions leaned forward as the three TriNA molecules in the image again began to unwind into separate strands.

"That was quick."

"What are they doing?" Dya wondered.

The room was silent as the nine separated strands again wiggled, switched, and wove. Like tiny bits of animated cat hair, they again rearranged, once again twisting themselves together into three separate spiral molecules.

Cheng glanced at his companions. "They did it again, folks. Perfectly sorted into a completely new arrangement. Not a single repeated pairing."

"Each strand has now been exposed to every other strand." Raya frowned at the image. "Every potential combination has now been explored."

"We suspect that sections of the TriNA are dedicated to the storage of certain kinds of information," Dya reminded. "The three filaments are each in contact with the other two. Communicating."

"That's a huge information dump," Talina noted uneasily. "You think that's why that quetzal was so insistent on me going out there today?" The implications sent a shiver through her. "I mean, what we just saw here? Damn. These molecules are doing the same thing in that white quetzal, aren't they? Comparing information?"

Dya arched a slim eyebrow. "Tough to think of, huh? That you might have just downloaded a year's worth of intelligence on your body, thoughts, actions, and physiology to some strange quetzal. That as soon as Whitey gets back to the pack, they're all going to be studying what it means to be Talina Perez."

Talina accessed com. "Two Spot? Is our drone still following that quetzal?"

"'*Firmative, Tal. He's moving fast forty klicks out, still on a westerly course. Still white. Hasn't made a move to give us the slip.*"

"What are you thinking?" Raya Turnienko asked.

"About grabbing my aircar, flying out, and dropping a seismic charge on his ass before he can report to his buddies on ways to kill me."

Cheng chuckled. "That's my Talina. Always ready to shoot first and ask questions later."

"It's too soon to be killing quetzals," Dya said softly, her gaze on the TriNA as they began separating again. "Anyone want to make bets that they're going back to their original configuration? Maybe to compare notes?"

"No takers," Cheng answered. "Yep. See how they're separating?"

The quetzal in Talina's gut seemed remarkably satisfied, but then the molecules in her body would have been doing the same thing she'd just been watching on the screen. Sharing information, recombining with the new quetzal molecules. But getting what kind of instructions from them?

Talina knotted a fist, pressing it into her stomach.

"What's wrong?" Dya asked, perceptive as usual.

"You know, I really hate having this thing inside me. It's bad enough when it screws around with my dreams. Half the time it wants me to kill someone, and half the time I get the feeling it's laughing at me."

Turnienko turned. "But you still have control, right? No episodes like the night when it paralyzed you with pain?"

"For the most part I think I've got the little bastard on a choke chain. And, yeah, yeah, I know I've got better vision, hearing, strength, and all the rest. I still want this shit out of my body."

Cheng sighed. "Tal, we've tried. I think, like it or not, you're our test case."

Talina gestured at the holo where the TriNA had reassembled into the original three molecules. "Okay, so we've just seen a huge data dump, right? Hey, people, come on. We don't know what the hell they just 'discussed.' Could be a plan to take over my body and use me to blow up all of Port Authority, or to walk down the avenue shooting people like they were rats."

Dya's lips flattened into a line, sudden frost in her blue gaze. Talina fought the impulse to wince. Once, long ago, she'd shot Dya Simonov's husband down just like that. On someone else's orders. She'd tormented herself over it ever since.

Turnienko said, "Tal? We'll keep an eye on you. We promise. Half the population tests positive for TriNA in the blood. We're going to have to deal with this, figure out what it means."

"I think what we've just seen is a big chunk of the puzzle." Dya was still studying Tal through veiled eyes.

"And, by luck of the draw, you're the guinea pig," Cheng chirped happily. "I've got faith in you, Talina."

But from the expression on Dya's face, it sure wasn't unanimous.

7

Inga's tavern, officially named The Bloody Drink, served as the heart and social center of Port Authority. Originally it had been contained in a dome, but as the establishment needed space, and being on a mining planet, the room had been expanded underground. Now a section of the west wall was tarped off where another excavation was chunking out the heavy clay soil to create additional room for a kitchen. The canny Inga Lock was adding hot-cooked food to entice her patrons.

Not that it would put Millicent Graves and the cafeteria out of business, but it offered another option to the locals, and would certainly pay Inga for the time, effort, and cost of the expansion.

Talina wearily descended the wooden stairs that led to the stone-paved floor. She'd have her drink in hopes it would cleanse the bitter taste from her mouth. After that she was headed home to make up for the sleep she'd missed the night before.

Lines of chabacho-wood tables, benches, and chairs were occupied, showing that Inga was doing a booming business. But then the shuttle from Corporate Mine had landed no more than a half an hour previously and disgorged its crew to enjoy the benefits of four days in PA.

As Talina's boots rapped out on the wooden steps, people turned. The hubbub in the room stilled, all eyes turning her way. She could feel the change in mood.

Shifting the rifle on her shoulder, she glanced at the familiar faces, not sure of the expressions. Some wary, others perplexed. More than one suspicious. Still others were almost hostile.

That latter sent a jolt through her, and her quetzal shivered against her backbone.

She nodded cautiously to the few who muttered a greeting or tipped a hat her way. And the unforgotten feeling returned to settle like a weight on her shoulders. She'd seen this, felt this lack of trust before. Back when she was Clemenceau's enforcer.

The old familiar unease tickled along her spine as she strolled down the aisle, her eyes automatically scanning for threats. Her vision was sharpening, edging into the ultraviolet and infrared. Every sound came to her ears in crystalline clarity.

". . . not the same anymore."

"How the hell can we trust a woman that tight with a fucking quetzal?"

"The thing had its tongue in her mouth, for God's sake."

Heart pounding, Talina kept her expression flat as she reached the front of the room and turned toward her chair. Of course they didn't understand. But, damn it, these were her people. The ones she'd fought and bled for. That they didn't trust her? That was like an iced blade through the heart.

And she knew the moment it had happened. She'd protected Rocket—helped the little quetzal make his escape. And then she'd shot Deb Spiro down in the street. Not that Spiro was particularly beloved. People wanted her gone. It was the way Tal had done it. Like magic.

And worse, someone was sitting on her stool at the end of the bar. A wry smile came with recognition as she strode up.

She told the scarred woman in the black pantsuit, "Your ass is in my fucking chair."

Corporate Supervisor Kalico Aguila pulled her thick black hair back. A tracery of pink scars crisscrossed the delicate skin on her hand as she did so. Then the woman shot Talina a sidelong glance through crystal-blue eyes. "So, who is it, exactly, that you fuck in this chair? Most of us reserve a bed for that."

"You gonna move, or am I going to move you? It's really not the right day for witty repartee."

"So I've heard." Kalico slipped out of the chair and into the next, pulling her glass of wine across the marred surface of the bar. Talina had made most of those dents, generally pounding on the chabacho wood with her pistol butt to get the room's attention during some meeting.

Talina lowered her rifle to rest on the floor with the muzzle against the bar and seated herself, calling, "Inga! Whiskey backed by stout, please."

"You got it, Tal!" the buxom blond bartender called back and reached for the blown-glass mug she reserved for Talina.

"So. Had an intimate encounter with a quetzal this morning, I hear." Kalico glanced back at the room where conversation was slowly returning to normal. "Far be it from me to tell you how to run your affairs, Tal, but you'd have made a lot more people happy if you'd just shot the damn thing. Some are starting to wonder which side you're on."

"That's too absurd to even dignify." She took the glass and mug Inga handed her, asking, "How's my credit?"

"You're still up by ten and a half, Tal." And, slapping a towel over her shoulder, Inga started back down the bar to where Hofer was bellowing for whiskey.

Talina took a big swig of the amber saint. Not one of Inga's best barrels. In relief, she swished it back and forth around her mouth. Thought better of throwing her head back and gargling, and choked it down. Then she enjoyed her first sip of the rich black beer.

Kalico watched, amusement writ large, then added, "So what really happened today?"

"That quetzal, Whitey's what they're calling him, came for an exchange of molecules. Once he had it, he left. Apparently headed back to the deep bush. What he learned? What it all means? I don't have a clue. Nor does Raya, Dya, and Cheng. What did happen was an encounter, in the bush, and nobody died. Call that a first."

Kalico fingered one of the long scars running down the length of her jaw. "Lot of hatred for quetzals around here."

"It's a cliché to call it a big misunderstanding. To insist that when that first quetzal ate Donovan, it was a FUBARed attempt at first contact. That we're going to make a breakthrough and discover that all this blood, death, and hatred was a mistake, that we can live side-by-side in peace and harmony."

"You really buy that?"

"No pissing way. Too friggin' simple. If—and I say it's a big flipping if—we can ever figure out the molecular language, we're going to be looking at layers upon layers of complexity. Think about how long it took us to figure how to talk to a bottle-nosed dolphin. Then throw individual motives, passion, and self-interest into the mix, and there's going to be no singing 'Coming Together Under the Bower' moment of eternal human-quetzal brotherhood and bliss."

Kalico laughed. "Please, control yourself. I can't stand the starry-eyed optimism."

Talina took another shot of the whiskey. Enjoyed it as it hit her stomach like a warm balm and momentarily displaced the dominating presence of her asshole quetzal. And thank God she wasn't having flashbacks of that damned Mayan pot. That had been the worst day of her young life.

"So, how are things at Corporate Mine?"

Kalico smiled thinly, the action rearranging the pink scars on her cheeks. "Forest's stopped for the time being. Farm's producing. Mine's operating at sixty percent efficiency. We could be pumping out more, but the smelter's the bottleneck. If we had the power, we'd be running it twenty-five point five hours a day."

"Notice that you've brokered a peace with Dan Wirth. You and he come to terms?"

"I think they coined the phrase way back in the twentieth century: mutually assured destruction. Like two tigers we circle each other, knowing if we ever went at it, that whoever survived, it wouldn't be worth the mauling it would take to win." Kalico made a face. "But he's still got someone inside. Someone close to me and clever enough I haven't figured out his or her identity."

"I should have shot good ol' Dan the day he stepped off the shuttle from *Turalon*."

"That was then. This is now."

Talina ran fingers down the sides of her whiskey glass, remembering the day Dan Wirth first set foot on Donovan, how Capella's sunlight gleamed on his recently shaved scalp. "True. Smart bastard that he is, he's funding public works. Hired a crew to demolish the old education dome and build a better academy for the kids. Says that after he builds a school, he wants to build a real courthouse, codify a legal system."

Kalico gave a derisive snort. "One that he controls."

"That's the thing about corruption. He's putting enough back into the community that he's managed to build a fair amount of good will. Even Shig and Yvette are mollified for the moment."

Kalico sipped her wine, gaze unfocused. "The cunning of the psychopath. He's absolutely brilliant when it comes to playing the game. He knows just how far he can push your libertarian values and how to use them against you. Master that he is, he's woven himself into the fabric of Port Authority. You're the only person who could remove him."

"I'd have to shoot him to do it."

"That's right. But if you're going to, don't take too long." Kalico hooked a thumb in the direction of the other patrons. "They're not behind you like they once were. Your purity has been tainted by quetzal. You might still be a legend, but you've become an unpredictable one. And all the things that make you great? All the stories and deeds? Walking out of the forest with Cap Taggart when you should have died? Sticking up for that little quetzal? Felicity's death? Even shooting Deb Spiro when she had you dead to rights? Is that because you're really a hero? Or did you sell your soul to the devil?"

"That's nucking futz."

"Is it? In another age, back on Earth, they'd have branded you a witch. Burned you at the stake. Called that quetzal in your guts 'demonic possession.'"

Talina washed her distaste down with another swig from the whiskey as Kalico added, "It's not the same world as it was the day when *Turalon* landed. A whole new social dynamic has evolved with the *Turalon* people. The population's doubled. New folks, like Dan Wirth, have unbalanced the old status quo. New fears—especially after *Freelander*'s arrival—now prey on the peoples' peace of mind. And into that mix, you declare that you've got a quetzal inside you, and then you start sticking up for the beasts instead of killing them."

"So you think I'm turning into a social leper?"

"Not yet. But if I could give you a warning? Be careful."

"Uh huh." Talina squinted at her now-empty whiskey glass. "I was there at Mundo Base. Didn't believe it at first, either, but that little quetzal, Rocket, was bonded to Kylee

Simonov. And when Lieutenant Spiro shot it, she killed Kylee, too."

"Thought Kylee was still alive down there, living in the forest with the quetzals."

"Maybe. Not sure I'd want to make a serious wager about that. But alive or dead, Rocket's death broke that little girl's mind. Left her catatonic. Think it through. For all those years the people at Mundo lived peacefully without a single quetzal attack. The day they threw us out the quetzals ate two people. Kylee told Dya and me, 'The experiment is over.'"

"Yeah, Dya told me the same thing. Did you know that every night when she leaves the hospital, she checks with Two Spot to ask if Kylee called in? She's still convinced her kid's going to walk out of the forest someday and call on that radio we left."

"Poor woman almost breaks into tears at the mention of Mundo and quetzals. Blames herself. As if it were somehow her failure. But hey, I was there. The kid was broken. Nothing Dya could have done."

Kalico shrugged. "The day Kylee calls on that radio, I'll start believing in miracles again."

Talina took a big swallow of her stout. The first soothing fingers of the alcohol were massaging her brain. What a day.

"They wouldn't turn on me," Talina muttered. "As much as I've done for them? Hauled their asses outta the bush when they were hurt? Fought their fights for them?"

"People change," Kalico said wryly. "A year ago would you have said that you and I could sit here over a friendly drink? Remember me? I'm the cold-assed bitch who was going to put you up against a wall and have you shot as a common criminal."

People change.

Down in her gut, Talina's quetzal curled and chattered in that irritating manner that indicated that the little demon was just biding his time.

8

The call had come in the middle of Dortmund's sleep cycle. Just Captain Torgussen's calmly worded announcement through the com: "*Attention, please. Scientific personnel are requested to assemble in the conference room in fifteen minutes. We have an important development that requires your analysis.*"

Dortmund stumbled out of his bunk, the lights blinding him as they illuminated the cramped room. At least he had it to himself. Little more than a closet, the quarters were anything but plush, and served only as sleeping space.

He pulled on coveralls, slipped his feet into shoes, and passed the hatch to the main corridor. Climbing up a deck, Dortmund struggled to pull his dream-scattered wits together.

In the conference room he found Captain Torgussen and First Officer Vacquillas, each standing with a cup of coffee in hand and staring across the table at a holo projection that covered the far wall.

"What have we got?" Dortmund asked as he yawned.

Before the captain could reply, Shimodi, Sax, and Jones came stumbling in, hair in disarray, robes tied around their bodies.

"We'll wait for the Advisor," Torgussen said, narrowed eyes on the holo. "No sense in telling this more than once."

"Telling what?" Benteen asked as he appeared in the doorway.

To Dortmund's disgust, the man was fully dressed, looked completely alert, not a hair out of place.

The Advisor stepped up beside Torgussen to stare at the holo. "What are we seeing?"

Torgussen reached out, using his finger to indicate an area that began to expand. A faint dot of light grew brighter, larger, and finally morphed into a planet, its cir-

cumference marked by the darker line of the terminator.
To its right, a smaller dot, white, could be seen.

"That's Cap III," Torgussen began. "To the right is its
moon. Now, watch."

Again the image expanded in zoom. The faint outlines
of continents, seas, white patches of clouds could be seen
on the dayside. The moon finally zoomed out of frame.
Another small dot, faint, gleaming, could be seen hanging
just above the planet's surface.

"Looks like a station," Benteen said.

"Does, doesn't it?" Torgussen agreed. "We're at the extent of our optics, people." He indicated the gleaming dot.
"That's not in *Tempest*'s report. Whatever it is it's orbiting
the planet. A station? Some sort of satellite? Hard to say.
From the trig, we estimate it's about five kilometers in diameter."

"Any emissions?" Lea Shimodi asked.

"We tried a photonic hail," Vacquillas told her. "No response. Ho thinks he's getting a very weak radio signal;
he's retuning the survey array toward it as we speak."

"Asteroid?" Shimodi wondered. "There's a lot of junk
in this system."

"But it's a couple more AUs out," Torgussen reminded.
"And what are the chances that Cap III could have captured an asteroid in a perfect orbit just in the short time
since *Tempest* was here?"

"If you will excuse me," Dortmund said. "As fascinating
as an asteroid might be, I don't see why, with the exception
of Doctor Shimodi, you needed to wake me from a—"

"Captain!" Wan Chung Ho's face formed on the holo.
The man's eyes were gleaming with excitement, a curious
smile on his small mouth. "I've got the whole array tar-
geted on that satellite. Sir, it's no satellite. It's a ship!"

The implications were too stunning to believe.

"Whose?" Torgussen said, voice choked. "I mean, dear
God, humans are the only spacefaring life we've ever . . ."

"You mean someone else is here? Another spacefaring
race?" Vacquillas gaped at the image. "And we're going to
be the ones to make that first contact?"

In the holo, Ho's expression displayed his sudden unease. "Look, I don't know what the hell this means. I've got a locator beacon."

"What do you mean, a location beacon?" Torgussen demanded. "Photonic?"

"No, sir. Not photonic. Not hyperlink or microgravity. It's a radio frequency."

"And?"

"And I've sent a query, sir." Ho made a face. "It's traveling speed of light, so it will be a couple of days before it pings the target and we get a reply."

"I don't understand," Benteen snapped. "What's this mean?"

Shimodi faced him. "*Tempest* didn't record any ship in orbit. It's not ours. If it's not ours, not human, it has to belong to another spacefaring species. Some sort of lifeforms that we've never encountered."

"Um, Doctor Shimodi?" Ho interrupted. "That's what doesn't make sense."

"Explain," Benteen asked irritably.

"Well, we won't know for a couple of days yet, but I think it's from Solar System." Ho looked uneasy.

"Why?" Torgussen asked.

"Well, if it's aliens, they're using the same kind of locator ID we do in Solar System. I mean, it reads the same as a Corporate ID, but, sir, there's no such ship listed in the catalog."

Vacquillas lifted a curious brow. "If it was Corporate, it would have responded to a photonic or hyperlink hail, wouldn't it?"

"You'd think," Torgussen agreed, his eyes on the magnified dot of light. Watched it vanish as it was eclipsed behind Cap III's bulk.

"Who in hell uses radio?" Ho wondered. "I mean, that's right up there with smoke signals. We're talking ancient."

Torgussen shot a glance at Benteen. "My advice, Advisor, is that we monitor the situation. Get closer. See if it responds to our radio hail. If it is Corporate, it will recognize our code. If it's really an alien ship, chances are it will pass our ping off as noise."

Dortmund glanced at Shanteel Jones, his pulse beginning to race. "So, Doctor, we came to catalog a higher order of life, and perhaps we're to be the ones to meet the first spacefaring race we've ever encountered?"

She swallowed hard. "Leaves you half creep-freaked, doesn't it, Dort?"

Benteen turned, his cold eyes curiously amused. "Don't leap where angels fear to tread, Doctor. Alien means just that. They might greet us with open arms, maybe they'll ignore us completely, or they might shoot a nuke and blow us right out of space."

"What makes you so suspicious?" Dortmund asked sourly.

"Just who I am, Doc. Just who I am."

9

No one slept. The implications of the ship orbiting Capella III were overwhelming. It didn't matter that its locator— or what they assumed to be its locator—was in Corporate code and appeared to be a registration number. Fact was, *Vixen* had a record of every Corporate registration going back one hundred and fifty years. No such ID had ever been recorded. Nor could a ship of that size have been built, say, by a station, and spaced here. Solar System was too highly regulated. The Corporation controlled everything. Someone would have known.

Since the vessel couldn't be of human manufacture, the only other viable hypothesis was that it was alien. Humanity had been searching the heavens for centuries in search of another spacefaring culture. Had listened, looked, and tried different detection technologies, and found nothing.

A flurry of hope had built as life was discovered in pockets around the solar system and on several of the planets visited by exploration vessels like *Tempest* and *Vixen*. But none had the kind of higher organisms that *Tempest* had recorded on Donovan. None of the life-forms discovered to date built anything, let alone space ships.

And now a ship orbited that very planet.

Could it be Donovanian? Had *Tempest* somehow missed the culture that had produced it? Perhaps an underground civilization or something in the seas?

Tamarland Benteen sat back in his chair in the conference room and listened to the science team as they kicked different hypotheses around. All of this was fine, exciting as hell—and if it turned into a first contact with alien spacers, it was sure to gain so much notoriety it would get him killed upon his return to Solar System.

"Might have come from one of the outer planets in the Capella system," Kobi Sax suggested. "Maybe they noticed *Tempest* was at Cap III and came to investigate."

"The outer planets? They're rocks," Lea Shimodi responded. "Nothing that could support a spacefaring civilization. Cold, frozen, metal balls. Note the cold and frozen part. Think methane and CO_2 snow. That sort of cold."

"The kind that couldn't support any kind of life as we currently understand it," Shanteel Jones countered.

Dr. Weisbacher had been staring pensively at the image of the shining dot where it remained projected on the back wall. "If it does turn out to be alien, we must be very careful. Our own planet's history is full of cautionary stories of disasters precipitated from a clumsy or arrogant first contact, and that was among fellow humans. Not to mention the diseases."

"Assuming we have anything in common with them." Shanteel Jones, like Dortmund, had her eyes on the dot. "We're making a lot of assumptions that they'll react like primates. That they'll be curious. Could be that they'll react like a hive of bees or a colony of ants. Ignore us completely unless we do something to force them to take notice. We might not even register as meaningful in their realm of perception."

"That's hard to swallow." Lea Shimodi flipped her shoulder-length blond hair back. "Hello! Space ship here! Different beings aboard. Hard to ignore."

"Again, you're assuming terrestrial mammalian curiosity," Jones shot back. "Hive mentality, fish mentality, or bacteria for that matter, perceives the world in an entirely different manner than mammals. Is it food, or not food? Is it dangerous, or not dangerous? If the answer is no on either count, it's meaningless."

Sax arched an eyebrow. "Nor is it unreasonable that they see the universe as 'Us' and 'Not Us.' Anything 'Not Us' is no more interesting than a passing rock."

"Hey, some of us think rocks are pretty damned interesting." Shimodi crossed her arms and glared.

Tam noticed that Dortmund was absent-eyed, an almost glazed smile on his face. "Doctor? Mind sharing what you're reviewing on your implants?"

The planetologist waved it off, his hand trembling with excitement. "Making sure we have a recording of everything said. This is one of the greatest moments in human history. We teeter on the verge of the monumental. Every aspect of what we do and say here is going to be studied for centuries."

Dortmund's eyes cleared. He looked around the table. "Think, people. Purport yourselves accordingly. Every movement, every thought, must be channeled to this single epic achievement."

He paused, eyes going glassy again. "Remarkable. Absolutely humbling. Fate has chosen to place us, we few, at this hinge point of the human experience. From this moment forward, everything is going to be different."

Tamarland fought to keep his expression blank. The fool sounded like he was having a religious epiphany. His face sure beamed the part.

What the hell? Does he think he's some kind of messiah?

Oh the other hand, if that ship out there really were alien, the God-struck planetologist was right. If and when they ever made it back to Solar System, every tiny detail of this mission was going to be scrutinized with an atomic microscope—especially the people involved.

Oh, sure. Running to avoid having his brain dissected, and what happens? He has to be in the ship that stumbles upon some alien intelligence. Sure it was exciting. How could it not be? But why did it have to happen to him?

10

Dan Wirth stood in the middle of the avenue, thumbs tucked into his belt, feet braced, as he watched the crane lift the heavy chabacho-wood beam. One of Lawson's crew was at the controls and carefully lowered it into place atop the sawed-stone walls. The workmen called to each other as they eased the ends of the square-hewn beam into the recesses.

The morning was remarkably bright and warm. Dan could smell Donovan's unique perfumed air. In the distance the faint musical sound of the chime could be heard in the fields beyond the perimeter fence.

He'd slept alone last night. Allison, his woman, had spent the night in her room at The Jewel with a client. Wild One named Rand Kope. The guy had hit town the day before. In exchange for a walnut-sized ruby as red as petrified blood, he'd opted for a whole night.

These days Dan never slept well alone. Hard to say why. It wasn't jealousy. He hoped that Allison was giving good old Kope the ride of his life. No, it was something about having a warm body beside his. But for a gem that size and quality? Damn straight, he'd deal with the occasional solitary and sleepless night.

And then there was Allison, something different about her. Something he'd started to note a while back. She'd cut back on the drugs, lost that dreamy-eyed ambivalence he'd taken for granted. The woman seemed harder now, more focused.

As long as she kept to her place and threw herself into the sex with that same old vigor, he could care less.

Atop the new building, the workers attacked the chabacho beam with drills. In the background he could hear the nail guns as the interior walls were framed.

"I fucking don't believe it," Dan whispered to himself.

"I'm building a goddamned school. Oh, Father, if only you could see me now. What the hell would you think?"

"Talking to yourself?" a voice asked from behind. "That's the first sign of a guilty conscience. Ah, but wait, we all know that you're a murdering, back-stabbing son of a bitch."

Wirth allowed himself a bitter smile, and turned. "Ah, Officer Trish Monagan. Out and about early, I see. Such dedication to duty. Just knowing that you're making your rounds, keeping us all safe from ourselves, sends rays of joy beaming through my heart."

She was giving him that look of total loathing that he so loved. Fact was: She had absolutely nothing that could be used as evidence against him, and it drove her clap-trapping crazy.

"What? No reciprocity for such a kind greeting? One would think that you might bear me ill will. And on such a glorious morning. Look at that golden light Capella is bestowing upon us. Such a marvelous day, though I do believe that the thin cumulus might portend a shower or two this afternoon."

"You really leave me sick and disgusted, you piece of shit."

"Me? Hey, I'm building a school, Officer Monagan. Last I heard, you were out in the bush, escorting your old friend and mentor Perez out to meet and socialize with a marauding quetzal. Why, you should hear the stories! Word is that not only did they have the most amicable of relations, but Perez shared more than a little tongue with the beast."

He raised hands in mock surrender. "Not that I mind, you understand. My own girls share tongue with some of the most amazing partners. Of course, they charge for it. But then, perhaps Perez and her quetzal are still in the formative stages of their new relationship. It adds to the intrigue, saving more complex lingual explorations for a future date."

To his absolute delight Monagan almost vibrated with rage. He liked the way her jaw muscles knotted under the smooth skin of her cheeks. Anger added to her complexion, accenting the dusting of freckles on her nose. The young woman's eyes were now green slits.

"Talina was right. Should have shot you the day you landed."

"Indeed, and where would Port Authority be today?" He fingered his chin. "Let's see. Half the town would be out of work. Not just because of my new house, but there's the addition on the rear of Betty Able's. And wait, didn't I loan Inga Lock the money to build her new cafeteria? Not to mention the *Turalon* exiles I hid. You know, the ones who'd have been rounded up and spaced back to Solar System and near certain death. Can we count the hours of entertainment I provide not just the locals, but those hardy souls who come for R&R from Corporate Mine? Oh, and there's the prospectors I've grubstaked. The civic improvements I've covered out of my own pocket."

He smiled, gestured grandly, and added, "And let's not forget what rises before your eyes: a school. A real academy. Can't believe Shig and Yvette let those poor kids attend class in that old leaky duraplast dome for as long as they did."

Trish was shaking her head. "It's a scam. All of it. Camouflage. You're a predator, Wirth."

He kept his winning smile in place, all the while wondering what it would feel like to place his hands around her firm young throat and squeeze. Watch those green eyes go wide. Feel her blood pulsing against his hands as he choked the life out of her. They always thrashed. That was part of the joy. Then the pupils would go wide, the gaze unfocused. The thrashing would weaken into twitches, and the lungs would stop pumping.

"What?" she asked suspiciously, obviously seeing something in his expression.

"Permutations of another time and space. Call it visions of an alternate reality. That's the thing about the multiverse. We never know what's limited only to this universe, and which fantasies might be playing out in a dimension parallel to this one."

Her lips twitched. "Yeah. I'm enjoying fantasies of my own right now. Right in the center of my pistol sights as I gently press on the trigger."

"Beware, Officer. Others have considered what you have just described. It might just be the curious laws of the universe, but I'm still here, and they are not."

"Yeah, yeah," she told him, hand resting suggestively on

her pistol. "Just out of the goodness of my heart, I'll tell you how it is: One of these days, I'm going to take you down. But when I do, it will be because I've got you dead to rights. Talina made me swear I had to do it that way after we rid ourselves of Clemenceau."

"Police and their rules. Almost makes me pity you. Almost." His plastic smile still in place, he gave her a salute. "Have a most pleasant day, Officer."

He watched her walk off, back straight, the mad virtually leaking out of every pore.

"Everything okay, boss?" Art Maniken asked, appearing at Dan's side as if by magic.

"Just a friendly chat with Officer Monagan. The officious little slit stopped by to share her hatred. I feel for her, got all that impotent rage bottled up on the inside and no way to let it out."

"You watch her, boss. We get careless, and one of these days she's gonna get something on us that'll stick."

"Maybe." Dan waved at the school. "Moves and countermoves. That's all that politics is. We're past the tough part. The casino's paying, we've got an interest in Betty Able's, got liens on half the property in Port Authority, and interest in the oil wells and half the small mining claims.

"Now we're building a school. And it's defensible. The sweet kiddies can learn in a safe and secure environment. You see, it's always the family types you gotta worry about. Those self-righteous, holier-than-thou housewives and their glassy-eyed creed of family before all. Those women? The ones like Sian Hmong? Amal Oshanti? Friga Dushku and Dya Simonov? They're the really dangerous ones."

"I'd put my money on Talina Perez, Supervisor Aguila, and Trish Monagan. They've proven that they'd kill you without looking sidelong at you first, boss. And you saw Perez take down Deb Spiro. You ask me, there ain't a more deadly person on this planet."

"Think, Art. You want to survive in this world, you've got to pay attention. Talina Perez was like a god. Everyone's hero. The woman who shot Supervisor Clemenceau. The woman who saved countless lives and shot down how many quetzals? She faced down Aguila and survived for weeks lost in the bush. A walking, fucking saint." He lifted a finger. "Right up until the moment she protected that half-pint quetzal in the hospital. She lost it all the moment she took on those housewives about getting rid of the freaky little beast."

"Still, Perez and Aguila—"

"Bah! Them I can deal with. They know the game. When to act, and when to back off. No, it's the housewives and that toilet-sucking dedication to their bratty little kids. They think there's a threat to their happy little community? That some action is putting their precious families at risk? Threaten to harm a hair on their little rug-crawling darling's head? That's when they march down the street in righteous indignation, pick up the pitchforks, and goad their lazy husbands and the government into stringing a guy up by his balls."

Dan shook his head in weary acceptance. "While we're worrying about Perez, Aguila, and Monagan, those bitches are braiding a hangman's noose and building a scaffold. Next thing you and me know? We're swinging in the wind while they're clapping the dust off their hands as a job well done."

"But, boss—"

"Never, ever, threaten a mother's children or her happy house. In that order of priority." He gave Art a forced smile. "Which is why we're building a fucking school. Puts us on a whole new footing with 'the families.'"

"You really think this will work?"

"Well, if it doesn't, I guess the next thing we're building is a nursery. And if that doesn't do it, what? A prenatal center?"

Maniken studied the dressed-stone walls. Atop them, Hofer was directing his workmen as they began screwing lag bolts into the heavy beam. "I heard you're paying Hofer a fortune to build this thing."

Dan chuckled, slapping his muscular enforcer on the shoulder and turning him toward The Jewel. "It's not costing me a cent. That's the thing about Hofer. I can pay him any damn thing I want to. He's the horniest guy on the planet. And he's so damn hard to deal with, the only women on Donovan who'll put up with him are the whores.

That means that every single SDR I put in his pocket is headed right back into mine, either from the gaming tables or what he pays the girls."

"You're a clever man, boss."

"Damn straight." And while he might have dismissed Talina Perez as a threat in Art's presence, fact was, he'd had all of his people dropping bits of poison in the well.

And bless Perez for the fool she was, having that holovid of her letting that quetzal stick its tongue in her mouth was like sharpening the very knife he was going to use to slit her throat.

11

The damn dream possessed her. Back in her mother's kitchen in Chiapas. Talina had been maybe five or six. She could still see the heavy kitchen table, the wood dark, worn with age. She could smell the odors of chili, recado, and cilantro. Red Saltillo tiles covered the floor.

And there had been the beautiful bowl. Freshly excavated from some Mayan lord's ninth-century tomb. The ceramic vessel had been left by his head, its sides decorated with images that celebrated the resurrection of One-Hunahpu and the defeat of the Xibalban Lords of Death who had cut off his head and hung his skull in a calabash tree.

Beautiful. Priceless. A stunning find that her mother had taken home to better record prior to curation in the museum.

Talina could see it as clearly as she had that day she'd reached up, wanting to touch and hold the beautifully painted bowl. So light, the colors so brilliant. She could feel her fingers slipping along the smooth surface, feel the pot slide away from her grasp. Toppling off the end of the table, it fell . . .

She blinked, images flashing behind her eyes. In an instant, she was running through dense bush, every sense alert. She could smell prey, some hopping thing that was made of all legs. No name for it, just the image, the knowledge of it, and the fact that she was hunting it.

She was close now. Inhaling its scent as she eased between the aquajade trees. An instant later, something snapped past her head. A loud crack. Then came the feel of air patting her head.

Bullet. Run!

Her vision blurred at the sides, and she came to appreciate the three-eyed triangulation, the superior depth of field as she ducked and darted among the aquajade trees.

The memory faded, leaving Talina gasping and panting, sweat beading on her skin.

She cried out, sat up in bed, and stared out at the morning light beaming through her bedroom window.

"Fuck this shit," she growled, climbing out of bed.

She was standing in the shower, her head splitting. Her mouth had that foul taste, her tongue like a piece of wood.

Hangover.

Funny, she could remember . . . Yes. She'd closed Inga's last night. Vaguely she remembered Step Allenovich had walked her home. Something about people couldn't be trusted anymore.

"What the hell are you doing, Tal?" she asked herself as water ran down her head. "That's three nights in a row."

Truth was, alcohol helped. It deadened the presence of the demon quetzal in her guts. Let her sleep the whole night through.

But like this morning, it wasn't enough anymore.

"Getting worse." She palmed off the water and stepped out into her bedroom. "I am not going to live like this."

So, was it Whitey's doing? Something about the TriNA he'd given her? Maybe some molecular time bomb to make her go crazy?

An image flashed, vivid. Kylee's laughter. A sudden memory of her. Blond hair flying about, her incisor teeth looking too large behind her pink lips. Blue eyes sparkling with humor. In the background Mundo Base rose on its central tower.

Plants. What looked like squash. They were in the farm area.

"Kylee. Damn." Talina fought her way back to the world, struggled to towel herself off.

Why the hell couldn't she keep a cogent thought in her head?

Her stomach queasy, she fought the urge to throw up.

She needed to eat, and she forced down a big plate of beans, poblanos, and crest meat seasoned with ancho and annatto.

The edges of her vision rippled with waves of color from infrared to ultraviolet.

Kylee, dressed in a blue smock, reached out, seemed to be petting Tal with a small hand. "You're my best friend."

Talina shook herself. The words had been crystal clear.

She glanced around her empty house. Knew she was alone.

"Fuck this." She slipped off her stool, fastened her old black uniform with its various patches, and pulled her rifle from the rack.

Outside, she squinted in the light. Capella burned down with a passion. When had it gotten to be midday? Muttering to herself, she stalked down the avenue, hardly aware of the people she passed.

There had to be a way to get the damn molecules out of her body.

At the hospital, she stopped, flashed back to the night when she'd faced down the mothers who wanted Rocket gone. She was there, living it. Trish standing off to the side, telling her to get Rocket . . .

Ought to just shoot the bitch.

Sian Hmong was in her face, eyes burning. Shaking a finger within inches of Talina's nose.

The hiss came from down deep. What the hell had Sian ever contributed to Port Authority but the fruit of her womb? The woman's only saving grace was as a breeder. A friggin' two-legged baby machine. She couldn't even shoot a pistol, let alone . . .

"Either you get rid of that quetzal, or we'll do it for you!" Sian's voice seemed to heterodyne in Talina's skull.

And the pistol was in Talina's hand.

Then she was back in her mother's kitchen. Horror filled her as the beautiful bowl tilted off the table, falling, turning in the air. She could see the bright images of One-Hunahpu and the hideous Lords of Death. The *Way* glyph mocked her with its three internal divisions and meanings. Instead of hearing a hollow *pock* when the bowl hit the floor, she jerked at the sound of a gunshot.

The pistol recoiling in her hand brought her back.

She gaped, stared stupidly at the avenue. People were stopped dead in the street, staring. The entire world seemed to be on hold.

What the hell?

Talina looked down at the pistol. Felt the familiar grip. The faintest threads of smoke rose from the barrel.

Dya Simonov burst out the door behind her, a look of surprise on her face. She took in Talina. The pistol.

"I heard a shot. Was that you?"

Talina ground her teeth, shoved the pistol back into its holster. "I . . . Damn. I think I just shot Sian Hmong. It was so clear. Just like that night."

"Shot her where?"

"Right here in the . . ."

Talina took a breath. "Listen. You've got to help me. I mean, this is new. The visions. They're like real. I'm a quetzal. Then I'm not. I keep seeing Kylee. Hunting things in the bush."

"You drunk?"

"I friggin' wish. It's the only way I can keep that little shit in my gut under control."

"God, Tal. You look like hell."

"Hey, everything okay?" Step asked, appearing at her elbow. "What was that shot about?"

"I don't . . ." Talina shot a worried look at Step. "You sure it was me?"

"Listen, I was following you up the street. Then you stop outside the door here. You start looking back and forth, as if talking to somebody. Then, like a flash, your pistol's out and you've sent a shot right into that shipping container over yonder. What gives?"

"I shot Sian Hmong."

"Sian? Why? She's harmless." Step was watching her with skeptical eyes. "Not to mention that she's not here."

Tal was aware that old Artie Manfroid, Port Authority's oldest citizen, was watching from the side, his grizzled face looking appalled. Quetzal crap! The story would be all over town within an hour. Not that everyone hadn't turned to watch at the sound of a gunshot.

"She was with the others. Amal and Friga. Bernie Monson had a broken arm. Wouldn't set foot in the hospital so that Raya could set it. They were afraid of Rocket." Talina reached up, grabbed a hank of her hair to keep from reaching for the damn pistol again. "And I took Kylee, Rocket, Dya, and Talbot back to Mundo that night. Which is why Spiro shot him."

She made a face. "Fuck! It's all my fault."

"Talina," Dya said softly. "Come on. Let's go inside and get to the bottom of this."

"What the hell came over me? I mean, it was so clear. I was back there. That night." She knotted a fist. "But, damn it, I didn't shoot Sian. I *wouldn't*."

But she just had. The fact that a new bullet hole could be seen in the shipping crate was pretty conclusive.

Talina gave Step a worried look, then Dya, and licked suddenly dry lips. Fear tickled like frost down her spine as she looked down at her hand. Remembered the feel of the pistol in her grip. The bucking recoil and bark of the shot.

But I did. Would have, if she'd been standing there.

Time seemed to stop, the world sharpening as her vision clarified in the IR and UV ranges. An "otherness" possessed her. A feeling of dissociation from her flesh. Step reached out and steadied her as she wobbled unsteadily on her feet.

"Come on," she heard Dya say. "Let's get her inside."

Talina shook loose of Step's hold, saying, "Hey, I can still walk. It's not like I'm an invalid or something."

The last glance she had over her shoulder was of the street, the people still standing there, watching silently as she passed inside the hospital doors.

12

Supervisor Kalico Aguila sat at one end of the conference table in Port Authority's admin dome. A mint tea steeped in her cup as she studied the people around the table.

She should have been down at the mine. It wasn't like she didn't have more than enough on her plate. Especially since the mucking machine in the Number One was giving her mechanics fits.

Shig Mosadek—who'd radioed down to ask her to attend the meeting—was in his mid-fifties. She had come to cherish the small brown man with a pug-nosed round face as one of the most remarkable men she'd ever known. He barely topped five foot three—even in his boots. Shig's ragged mop of unruly black hair earned him another couple of inches, but not enough to matter. He was dressed in a simple fabric shirt woven of local textiles.

Friga Dushku, one of the townswomen, had discovered that by pounding claw shrub branches with a hammer, she could separate the long fibers. Then, once boiled, they created a fine filament that could be spun into thread. Overnight Port Authority had created its first textile industry.

Still the hot new thing, the fabric had caused Shig to give up on his old chamois-hide shirts and pants. The stuff was lighter and more airy than hide, and almost as tough.

Kalico had come to value Shig. Hard to believe that once upon a time she had fully intended to have him shot for conspiracy, theft of Corporate property, and rebellion.

Same for the tall, ash-blond woman who sat to Shig's right. Yvette Dushane, also in her fifties, topped six feet. Austere, hard-eyed, and imminently practical, Dushane saw to the day-to-day management of Port Authority. Kalico thought of her as the nuts-and-bolts go-to person when it came to land, labor, or resource procurement.

Next to Dushane sat Dya Simonov. The attractive blue-eyed blond xenobotanist had proven herself as the leading authority on Donovan's plant life, its chemical and medicinal uses. She also understood quetzals, having lived with the one that had bonded with her daughter, Kylee. At least until Deb Spiro shot it.

Now Dya asked, "So, Supervisor, do you have any idea of when you'll be sending my husband back?"

"Mark's out in the forest running a survival training exercise. Shouldn't be more than four or five more days. He keeps complaining about being too long away from that new baby."

"The fact that you let him wait until Su gave birth was very kind. We appreciate it. You can tell him that we're all fine and missing him."

"Of course. And your own infant?"

"Three months now. Doing well."

Across from Dya sat Trish Monagan, tough-eyed, with a grim expression on her face. Now she met Kalico's thoughtful stare and lifted an eyebrow.

Kalico allowed a wary smile to escape her lips. Monagan had always been something of an enigma. She might have been Talina's second-in-command, but something about her was off-putting. The young woman rubbed Kalico the wrong way with her bucolic air of superiority. Part of it could be explained by the fact that Monagan had never been off planet.

"Okay, so we've got some new information on quetzals. Shall we get started?" Having lost twenty-one of her precious personnel to Donovanian wildlife in the last year, Kalico was interested in anything that changed the dynamic when it came to people and deadly beasts.

"Thank you all for coming," Shig said thoughtfully as he studied his own cup of tea. Something green.

They all ached for coffee, but the trees—carefully nursed in the greenhouses outside of Port Authority—were still years from bearing.

"So this new quetzal has somehow compromised Talina?" Kalico asked, glancing down at her quetzal-hide jacket where it glistened in sheets of flowing color with every movement she made.

She'd been horrified the first time she had seen piles of excrement where a quetzal had eaten four human beings, shredded their clothes, and gone on to infiltrate Port Authority. In the year since, she'd lost additional people to quetzals.

Unlike the bush that surrounded Port Authority, Corporate Mine was in thick forest. Only once had she and her people managed to track down and kill a marauding attacker, and her jacket was crafted from a piece of that very beast.

The rest had melted away into the forest.

"How's Talina?" Kalico asked.

"Sedated." Dya fiddled with the holo projector she'd brought. "Raya's keeping an eye on her."

"She imagined she was killing one of the local women," Trish told her. "Some hallucination. Discharged her pistol into a shipping container. Just lucky that no one was in the way."

Yvette said, "Not to mention that it's inconceiveable, even in a delusion, that Tal would actually shoot Sian. She's one of the teachers at the school, a mother of three. That's just not the Talina we know."

"Speak for yourself," Dya said, voice clipped.

Kalico remembered that Talina had shot the woman's husband on orders from Clemenceau.

"The fact is"—Shig rotated his cup of tea—"that something's wrong with Talina. I figured she was in trouble when she started spending every night in the tavern. Tal has always enjoyed her stout, but in moderation. Step said she could barely walk that night when he saw her home."

Dya said, "My guess is that she was self-medicating. Alcohol was damping the effects the quetzal molecules were having on her system. Or so she thought."

Kalico asked, "How is this working? These molecules. What are they doing to her physiologically?"

Dya flipped on the holo projector. "From the beginning, we've known that the basis for Donovanian life is a three-strand deoxyribonucleic acid. Chemically it's the same as our DNA."

Shig asked, "Does this imply that Donovan and Earth organisms share some common origin? Seeding? The hand of God, alien intelligence, or purposeful action like the old stories would insist?"

Dya gave him a wry smile. "Sorry. Like so much in science, it's a matter of universal and basic chemistry. Ultimately, the most efficient molecule for the compilation and transmission of information is the basic deoxyribonucleic acid strand. Think Occam's razor. Some chemistries, molecular structures, and shapes are simply more efficient solutions to problems in a given environment than others."

"How so?" Yvette asked.

"Deoxyribonucleic acid, which makes up our DNA and quetzal TriNA, is the most efficient way to encode all the information necessary for life. The molecule's perfect for the job. Easily replicable, the helix design is relatively durable, and it compresses to maximize storage space. The two base pairs, purines and pyrimidines, when patterned, allow infinite combinations in a small space."

"So we have the same genetic material?" Kalico asked.

"But a different structure." Dya used the holo to show the standard DNA double helix that reminded Kalico of a spiraling ladder.

"Next we have TriNA." Dya projected an image where the groove in the DNA had been filled with another strand. "The difference between DNA and TriNA is that third strand. The downside is that the Donovanian molecule is stiffer than our DNA. Replication isn't as simple as it is for DNA. TriNA depends on a different polymerase during replication that bends each of the pentose sugars one hundred and twenty degrees along two atomic bonds. That allows the base pairs to bond with two other strands instead of one. Following practice, we label the strands A, B, and Z. One from each progenitor. Can't really say they have three sexes since Donovanian life doesn't exhibit sexual dimorphism. Makes sense given that Donovanian life developed from trilateral symmetry."

"So, is it better?" Yvette asked.

"Different. The payoff is an increase of information storage of three to the third power multiplied by the number of base pairs. And the molecules are smarter. What we're seeing suggests that they communicate with each other in an exponentially more sophisticated way than DNA does. And that, in itself, is mind-boggling."

"Okay," Shig noted warily. "What does this have to do with Talina?"

Dya arched an eyebrow. "Roughly a third of the population of Port Authority and all of the Wild Ones test positive for TriNA in their blood. My daughter bonded with a quetzal. When the quetzals took her after Rocket's death, she admitted she'd been an experiment. My call, backed by Raya and Lee, is that Talina's an experiment, too."

Kalico went cold in her gut. "You're telling me that Talina's compromised? Being used by intelligent molecules?"

"I'm not sure I'd use those terms."

Shig was looking worried. "How does an alien molecule, no matter what its intelligence, affect Talina this way? I mean she says the thing talks to her. It's changing her body."

"Ultimately, it's deoxyribonucleic acid that we're talking about." Dya leaned back, expression thoughtful. "Just like DNA, TriNA unzips, controls the formation of all the different RNAs. Keep in mind, the underlying chemistry is the same. RNA, be it Donovanian, or terrestrial, has the same morphology. RNA functions the same way in our cells as it does in Donovanian cells."

"Thought Donovanian cells were different." Yvette was frowning into a distance only she could see.

"They are. They're prokaryotes. Don't have a nucleus. Don't have ribosomes, either. Instead they have analogous structures that function like Golgi bodies, ribosomes, and the rest. But forget structure. It's the underlying chemistry that's the same."

"That doesn't answer my question," Shig said. "How is it actually manipulating Talina?"

Dya took a deep breath. "We're still working that out, but the operative hypothesis is that the TriNA is interacting with Talina at a cellular level. We know that she's grown optical cells that allow her to see in the UV and IR ranges, that her musculature and stamina have been enhanced. She claims the 'quetzal inside' has learned to manipulate the language cognition centers of the brain at a basic level. That it is doing so means it is communicating through RNA that stimulates those specific neurons."

"Do you know how crazy that sounds?" Kalico asked. "We're talking billions of specific cells."

Dya pointed at the TriNA molecule projected above the table. "That molecule can process three times the information your own DNA can. We estimate there may be a million TriNA molecules in Talina's body. And, unlike your DNA, they recombine with each other, sharing information, before returning to reconstitute the original molecule to integrate what they've learned. Given that kind of computational ability, maybe figuring out how to run a human body isn't that difficult."

"Shit," Trish Monagan muttered.

Kalico asked, "Can TriNA combine with DNA? Is that how it's doing it?"

"No." Dya pointed to the third strand. "Remember that while it's chemically the same molecule, TriNA uses a different polymerase that bends the base pairs one hundred and twenty degrees out of alignment. You might get a short segment of TriNA strand that might bind through a Hoogstein bond in human DNA, but that would be it."

"Unless we start exchanging polymerases, too," Yvette noted.

"Won't matter even if it does," Dya said. "The codons won't come close to matching up."

"That's all fine, but what about Tal?" Trish asked. "She going to be all right?"

Dya tapped her fingers rhythmically on the table. "We can't make any predictions at this point. It would help if we knew what the quetzal in her wanted. Rocket and Kylee lived for four years in a symbiotic relationship. Until Rocket's murder, Kylee was fine."

Dya paused, jaws knotted, and took a calming breath. "That was one quetzal and one little girl. Talina has the molecules from a host of different quetzals interacting inside her. We're just going to have to wait and see."

"Anything you can do to exorcise them?" Kalico asked.

"Not yet." Dya pursed her lips.

"Hey!" Trish leaned forward. "This is Tal we're talking about. I know you've got history with her, and, yeah, Tal hasn't been the same since she got infected by that damn quetzal. But she saved this whole colony. Most of us owe our lives to her."

"Easy, Trish," Shig said with a benign smile on his face. "Your tamas is showing."

"No Buddhist crap," Trish shot back. "I just want to be

sure that Dya takes what's wrong with Tal as seriously as we do."

"Oh, you can be sure I do, Officer Monagan." Dya gave the woman an icy stare. "You see, my children, Su and her children, Damien, Sallee, and Tweet? My whole family? Just like me, they, too, test positive for quetzal molecules. Not to mention the rest of the Wild Ones. So, whatever is happening to Talina? In the end, that could be the future for every human on this planet."

13

The call to the conference room—once again—came in the middle of Dortmund's sleep cycle. What was it about *Vixen* and its crew? Did nothing happen during the hours when he and his team were awake? Or did the spacers purposefully wait until everyone else was asleep as a means of demonstrating their mastery of the environment? Perhaps a sort of snub? A means of putting the scientists in their place?

Nevertheless, he sighed, dressed, and made his way to the conference room where, again, Torgussen was staring at the holo projection. The mysterious ship orbiting Capella III could now be seen clearly on the optical image.

Commensurate with his status as head of the scientific team, Dortmund stood resolutely at the captain's side as the others crowded in. He enjoyed a moment of gratification when Advisor Benteen seated himself off to the side.

"What have you got, Captain? Especially given that you've interrupted our sleep yet again." Dortmund emphasized his statement by squinting at the projected image.

"We think it's ours," Torgussen said by way of introduction.

"Ours?" Dortmund asked, barely aware as Shimodi, Sax, and Jones took seats at the table. He remained standing by the captain.

"Human. Not alien. At least, it is built the way we build them." Torgussen pointed. "Those two counter-rotating sections that look like stacked discs on the forward aspect? The topmost contains the cargo bays and storage, the second is the living quarters. That big round ball beneath them contains the reactors and generators. The pods on the sphere's sides are the reaction engines for in-system maneuverability. Our call after studying the engineering is that we're looking at a ship from Solar System."

"Why didn't they answer a photonic hail?" Benteen asked.

The Advisor's hair was pillow-mussed. He should have been as sleep-muddled as the rest of them, but to Dortmund's surprise, the man's eyes and expression were as sharp as ever.

"For the moment, I have no answer," Torgussen told him with a shrug. "We've even blasted the thing with a directional photonic signal. Should have triggered every sensor on board. Same with hyperlink and microgravity. Nothing. All we get is a radio-emitted locational beacon every thirty seconds. It's like that bucket's dead in space."

"So the mystery's solved?" Dortmund asked, feeling a sense of desolation building in his chest. "Our aliens are just another ship from Solar System?" He swallowed against the building frustration.

Damn it! Who are these three-thumbed fools? Drifting around out here, playing games. That's a pristine planet down there. My planet!

Torgussen rubbed the back of his neck. "Dr. Weisbacher, I don't know what to tell you. Looks human, it's built with our engineering, our technology, but the thing's huge. Bigger than anything built to date in Solar System for interstellar travel. To have made such a vessel would have required the shipyard at Transluna. It would have taken a year or more to build along with a massive reallocation of resources, and sure as hell we'd all have heard about it."

"And if it is from home, why didn't it answer a hail? Someone should be on board, monitoring the systems, correct?" Benteen asked.

"That, Advisor, is the central question. And why's it emitting a navigational warning? Ships have had AI since the mid-twenty-first century. Even if the crew had abandoned it for dirtside, the ship should have been talking to us from the moment we reverted symmetry and started scanning the system."

"So, maybe it's not human after all," Shanteel Jones said softly. "Listen, there are parallels in technology, right? Can't we assume that basic laws underlay engineering? Metals and ceramics are limited by their very nature in how they can be formed to withstand stresses. How many ways can a starship be built? Just like so many of the Donovanian life-forms recorded by *Tempest* have terrestrial analogs: things like limb length corresponding to a Fibonacci ratio; comparable morphology; all built on organic chemistry; and with basic RNA. Occam's razor."

Torgussen countered by asking, "Then what are the statistical chances they'd broadcast on the same frequency? That they'd use Solar System navigational code? Because that ship out there is broadcasting its location and ID just the same as if it were sitting in a Jupiter orbit. Right down to the required interval."

"But only on radio?" Benteen stared warily at the dot on the holo. "As I understand it, they should also be sending out on hyperlink and photonic."

"Yeah," Torgussen admitted. "And even if it were abandoned, the ship's AI should have immediately responded to our ping."

"There are improbabilities in the universe," Shimodi reminded. "It's a really big place."

Benteen said, "The thing had to have arrived after *Tempest* left the Cap III system, right? No way they could have missed it being in orbit?"

"*Tempest* had the same sensor array we have. They couldn't have missed that navigational beacon. No, if we're really in the Capella system, this ship arrived sometime after *Tempest* inverted on the way home. It's the only explanation."

"You tried a photonic hail to the planet? Maybe they took their com dirtside with them."

Torgussen crossed his arms. "Not yet, sir. We thought we'd see what your orders were first."

Dortmund kept coming back to the aliens. "You say you'd know if a ship that size had ever been built in Solar System?"

Torgussen gave him a flat stare. "You're a planetologist, Doctor. Would you know if a second moon had been discovered orbiting the Earth?"

"Don't be silly."

"I'm not. If that ship had been built anywhere in Solar System, I'd know about it. But it's here, broadcasting a Solar System navigational beacon on an obsolete technology. So, you tell me, Doctor."

"Parallel evolution and technology, it has to be." Dortmund felt the rise of excitement.

"How's that, Doctor?"

"Photonic coms go back to the twenty-first century. It's a simple technology. If that was a human ship, they'd have the technology. Shanteel has to be right. We're looking at an alien vessel built with similar technology to ours."

Torgussen warily asked, "Just how, exactly, do you know this?"

"By thinking rationally. As you say, anything this size built in Solar System would be in the registry, not to mention common knowledge among the spacing fraternity to which you belong, Captain. We know it has arrived in the last ten years, a period during which The Corporation was planning the *Vixen* mission. So why would they have sent us if they'd already dispatched that huge behemoth? Additionally, even if the crew was dirtside, they would have left someone on board. And if this ship was one of ours, the AI would have responded to our hail. The only viable conclusion is that no matter how improbable, that ship did not come from Solar System."

"Which leaves aliens," Shanteel finished.

Dortmund felt a wash of relief run through him. "People, consider. Whatever kind of life we're dealing with—but for some traits like photonics—their technology is remarkably similar to ours. Eerily so. All of which leads me to wonder if they haven't been observing us. Perhaps for a long, long time. Maybe that's why their technology is so similar to ours. They copied it."

"I don't follow." Torgussen was watching Dortmund through skeptical eyes.

Dortmund shrugged. "I'm just trying to anticipate all the possibilities. Maybe they've observed us from afar. Have seen our gross technology, things they could infer from visual observation at a distance, like the general shape of our deep space vessels. Maybe things like photonics, which operate at an atomic level, are unknown to them."

"Aren't you grasping at straws here?" Lea Shimodi asked. "I mean, come on."

Dortmund saw it all unreeling in his head. "Who are we to know their motives yet? Maybe they observed *Tempest* when it made its call here. After it spaced for Solar System, our aliens placed this ship here. What better place for us to find it? In neutral territory? Yes! Perhaps as a way of making contact without putting themselves at risk."

He blinked. "Dear God, how incredibly clever! They know how volatile and dangerous we are. But here, at Capella III, they leave the startling proof that they exist. A statement that says, 'See, you are not alone in the galaxy. When you are ready, we will make official contact, and by then you will be so used to the idea it won't come as a destabilizing surprise.'"

His heart beating, Dortmund continued before the others could interrupt. "Remarkable! By doing it this way, we can't feel threatened. They've kept themselves at a safe distance. Nor will we be frightened by their superior technology. That ship out there says, 'See, our technology is not a threat to your safety. Were our motives otherwise, we could have just come and conquered your Solar System.'"

Dortmund swallowed hard "I wonder if that means they've been monitoring our stories. I mean, all the way back to the twentieth-century radio show when the Martians supposedly invaded Earth. They understand the trope that deep down, humans fear other intelligences."

"I call that over the edge, Doctor," Torgussen told him.

Dortmund noted that even Shanteel had a skeptical expression on her face.

"People," Dortmund told them, damping down his enthusiasm, "perhaps I'm indulging wild speculation. Nevertheless, we're about to embark on a new world. We have a ship in orbit around Cap III that looks like it could have come from Earth, but didn't. If we assume it's impossible that it came from Solar System, then the only alternate hypothesis is that it came from an alien culture."

Benteen was watching him through stony eyes that sent a shiver down Dortmund's back. What was it about the man?

"What about the radio beacon?" Torgussen retorted.

"We have to keep an open mind about a great many things in the coming days. The old dogmas need to be shattered, discarded as potentially meaningless in this sudden and unexpected circumstance. We need to embrace the impossible."

"Nice speech," Torgussen told him. "Sounds like a lot of

work for an alien race. Building a big ship like that. Leaving it in Cap III's orbit for us to find. If they know us well enough to employ our navigational codes, why not a broadcast that says, 'Greetings, humans. You are not alone'? No threat in that."

"Don't be naïve. There's always a threat, implied or not." Benteen was studying Dortmund, an amused smile playing at his lips. Might have been a cat watching a mouse. "Let's go back to assuming that it's human. Maybe manufactured by some rogue station by mysterious means. What's it doing here? I mean, why Cap III?"

"For the resources," Shimodi said.

Dortmund wondered: Dear God, didn't the man understand what was at stake here? And Benteen was supposed to be the *Advisor*?

Shimodi continued, "Capella III may be the wealthiest concentration of rare-earth elements, metals, and fine-grade clay in the galaxy. If the preliminary survey samples withstand our scrutiny, Capella III could be the richest find in human history. This one planet may contain more exploitable resources than are found in the entire Solar System."

Braced by his passion, Dortmund jabbed a finger at Benteen. "Sure, it's rich. But it's up to us to ensure that Capella III isn't turned into a waste like so much of Earth was. Unlike some airless and frozen moon, we're talking about a remarkable ecosystem and a stunning variety of life. Our job, *Advisor*"—he couldn't help but emphasize the word—"is to ensure that the ecosystems are preserved and protected."

He ignored Shimodi's irritated smirk, but found himself unsettled by Benteen's response to his tone of voice. Despite no change of expression, something inside the man seemed to coil like an angry cobra.

What the hell? Didn't Benteen know who he was? What it took to rise to the top of his profession? To become a department head at Tubingen?

Benteen's voice remained calm. "So they would only have come for the minerals? We might have stumbled upon an illegal mining operation?"

Dortmund gave the man a dismissive shrug.

Shanteel Jones said, "That's just part of it. No telling what we're going to learn from the planet's wildlife."

"Pharma, alone, could be worth billions once we start to get a handle on the plant life," Sax agreed.

"All in good time," Dortmund cautioned. "We're here to design a protocol that protects the planet while at the same time allowing us to carefully access some of its wealth."

Shimodi pointed. "If that ship's really one of ours, they're here as looters. Maybe some rogue Boardmember who's managed to keep that ship off the books? Some criminal element? If that's the case, we're going to have to take action."

Benteen nodded, expression veiled again. He turned his attention to Torgussen. "Since the ship didn't reply to your initial hail, and since we don't know who or what it represents, I want no further communication with it. Bring us in silently. Passive surveillance only."

Torgussen nodded.

Benteen added, "On the chance that we have stumbled upon a rogue operation, I want you to use the utmost caution. People discovered in the commission of illegal activity will often do anything to avoid the consequences. I remind you, we are on our own, without backup, and a long, long way from home."

Dortmund gestured toward the holo projection, a slow rage building in his blood. "If anyone has dared to corrupt that planet, its ecosystem, or, God forbid, hasn't taken the appropriate measures to mitigate their impact, I swear, I will see them broken! Do you hear?"

That was *his* planet! The first of its kind in human history, and he'd be damned if he'd see it ruined. Not by Shimodi, and certainly not by a bunch of looters.

Or, better yet, pray it was aliens.

14

C uriosity filled Talina as she stalked through the forest twilight. She had been watching the little girl for days now. Dappling her skin with the unique greens of the alien vegetation, she'd hidden among the oddly spaced plants in their unusual rows. But then, the aliens did many odd things.

She had watched and learned.

Now, for the first time, the child had wandered away from the adults and other children. Distracted by three young roos, the child had followed them into the tree line, and then into the forest margin.

In shadow, the girl's hair had gone from golden to yellow, and she stared around with wary eyes. Yes, she knew that she shouldn't be out of the others' sight. Inhaling the damp air, Talina could scent the girl's change, that slight shiver of fear.

Even so, the girl completely missed the skewer, looking as it did like an old root.

Talina crept closer.

Now the girl had fixed her attention on a cluster of invertebrates, their chime harmonic as they rotated in a breeding circle.

The skewer was no more than ten meters away, its smell like vinegar. Heavy on the air.

Talina, her body held parallel to the ground, eased up behind the girl. She was small, not much larger than Talina. Her body had a slight glow, warmer than the surrounding air. But then, it was morning, the heat still several hours away.

Talina edged closer, froze as the girl turned her attention from the invertebrates to the fluttering of a scarlet flier. The avian had been drawn by the distinctive breeding chime, expecting to find an easy meal. Instead it stopped short, fluttering in the air, the colors of panic running across its hide as it tried to determine the little girl's nature.

As it did, the little girl took another step closer to the camouflaged skewer.

In that moment, Talina dropped camouflage, stepped around the little girl and placed herself between the girl and the predator.

The girl froze, terrified. Mouth gaping.

Turning, Talina lowered her head, hissing at the skewer. The predator immediately dropped its camouflage, extended the grasping pads, and flourished its thorn-like spear as it backed slowly away.

Talina glanced at the little girl, flipped her tail playfully, and uttered the closest sound she could to laughter.

"You saved me!" the little girl cried. "But you're a quetzal!"

Talina lowered her head, her three eyes fixed on the girl's awed expression. Again she made the chittering sound. Then she leaned up against the girl, bumping her gently with a shoulder.

"You're a kid. Just like me." She laughed, reached out, patting Talina's shoulder. As she did waves of white, pink, and orange rolled across Talina's hide and her collar membrane flared out.

"My name's Kylee. What's yours?"

Talina tightened her throat, wondering how the humans could make such sounds. Her utterance came out as a roar as she vented air to the rear.

"You're like a rocket! You take in air and shoot it out the back with a roar! I'm going to call you Rocket!"

Talina glanced back into the darkness under the trees. Her vision, so much better than the little girl's, easily picked out the two adult quetzals that blended with the shadows.

Yes. The first stage had been—

"Hey, Talina! Wake up."

Tal blinked, visions of forest, blond hair, and sky-blue eyes fracturing like a dropped ceramic pot.

Shards, like dancing sprites, clattered across a Saltillo-tile floor. One triangular fragment, dominated by a *Way* glyph, seemed to catch her eye. *Way*, pronounced *"wh-eye,"* the Maya glyph for the spirit possessed. For the Dreamer.

"What the . . . ?" She glanced around the familiar hospital room. Piss in a bucket if she hadn't spent enough time in this room to know it inside out.

"What happened this time? How'd I get here? Am I shot, stabbed, or wrecked?"

Raya Turnienko was staring down at her. "Another one of the hallucinations. What was it this time?"

"The day Rocket met Kylee in the forest outside of Mundo Base." Talina tried to reach up and rub her forehead, but her arm was immobilized. Looking down, she found straps holding her securely in the bed. "What the hell?"

"You remember putting a bullet through Sian Hmong? Turns out it was just a shipping crate. Not that that was particularly reassuring for Sian and her family."

"That's nuts!"

"Yeah, well the story's all over." Raya leaned down to emphasize her words. "Tal, most of the town thinks you've lost it. That you can't control yourself. The decision's pretty much unanimous. They want you restrained."

"How long's it been?"

"Couple of days. Dya and I have kept you sedated. Mark just got back from Corporate Mine, so Dya took the day off to spend with him, Su, and the babies."

Talina took a deep breath. Images kept playing in her memory. In them, she kept seeing Kylee through Rocket's eyes.

"So, everyone thinks I'm a quetzal, huh?"

"Not exactly a quetzal. Just infected with one."

"What do you think?"

Raya gave one of those unconvincing shrugs. "Honestly, I don't have a clue as to what's going on in your head, Tal. I'm a physician, Dya's an agricultural microbiologist with a minor in psychology, and Cheng's an industrial chemist. We've barely figured out the chemistry of how the TriNA interacts with your cells. We haven't a clue what it means, or what the molecules want. Hell, for all we know, each molecule wants something different from its counterparts."

"Raya, that really sucks."

A faint smile rearranged her flat face.

"When can I get out of here?"

"Don't know, Tal. That depends on if and when you can control the quetzal thoughts. The fact that you thought you were shooting Sian? That you pulled your pistol and discharged a round? Does that sound like the old Talina Perez we've all known and respected?"

Talina squeezed her eyes shut. Yeah, she remembered. Just like the day she confronted Deb Spiro in the street in front of The Jewel. It wasn't her. Just the action. Beyond her control.

"Maybe you're right, Doc. I mean, I never liked Sian. She's not exactly my kind of person, if you know what I mean. We might not have seen eye-to-eye over Rocket. But I'd never, ever shoot her dead. Not if I was in my right mind."

"Good. Since you're sane for the time being, how about a little supper? Millie brought over a plate of crest and beans. I had her throw in some extra chili for you. If I unstrap you, you promise to give me warning if your vision starts to change?"

"Yeah, sure, Doc." The images of Kylee were still floating in the back of her mind. "What time is it?"

"About nine. You were the last patient on my list. So, eat. I'll give you a sedative and get you buckled in for the night. We'll tackle this whole quetzal thing again in the morning."

Raya's quick fingers began unbuckling the straps.

15

The question of the ship perplexed Tamarland. He sat in the *Vixen*'s observation bubble and stared out at the unfamiliar stars. Everything about his presence on the survey ship was at once unsettling and at the same time advantageous.

The universe bless Shayne, she'd removed him from the clutches of Radcek's terrible retribution, and dropped him smack into a situation for which he had no previous experience.

A month ago, his current circumstance would have been unthinkable. Now, as if he'd been batted out of reality, he was thirty light-years from Solar System, a hunted man in charge of a Corporate expedition into the unknown. All of it seemed preposterous. Especially the mystery ship.

His sense of self-preservation, however, had triggered that deep-seated wariness that had kept him alive over the years. His strength was in planning and implementation. Whatever was awaiting him out there, politics were at the bottom of it, and Artollia's scorpion was nothing if not adept at political gamesmanship. All of which had prompted him to order Torgussen to adopt a stealthy approach to Cap III and the mystery ship.

Additionally, he'd caught the captain on the sly, ordering him: "Any additional intelligence that comes in on that ship or planet, you and your officers consider it privileged information. My eyes only, understand?"

Torgussen had studied him for a moment, lips pursed. Tam suspected that the captain was considering the strange set of circumstances that had landed Tamarland Benteen on this mission in the first place. Was no doubt drawing false conclusions and misinterpreting Tam's presence on *Vixen*. Which was fine. Let the man think he was The Corporation's special agent. Let him think anything he wanted, so long as it added to Tam's authority and power.

"It's your call," Torgussen had told him, saluted, and strode off down the corridor.

Saluted, no less. The action of an inferior to his superior.

Tam chuckled dryly at the irony.

He was staring out at this new and fantastically thick band of the Milky Way, blotched as it was with black smudges of dark matter. It was beautiful, brighter than that seen from Solar System, and a patch of orange that was shaped like a lizard glowed against a star-smeared background. Old nebula?

A hesitant voice said, "Advisor?"

Tam turned to see Lea Shimodi at the hatch. The geologist's face seemed even thinner given her chin-down posture. She had her hands clasped before her, uncertainty in her light brown eyes.

"What can I do for you, Dr. Shimodi?"

"I thought we might talk. I could come back later if this isn't—"

"No, that's fine. Come in. Have a seat."

He'd already noticed that she carried herself well. Appeared to be in her late twenties, her spare body just enough out of proportion from the current fashion to indicate that she'd never bothered to undergo the makeover procedure. If anything, the slightly too wide hips, overly waspish waist, and un-augmented breasts imparted a sense of authenticity.

"What's on your mind?"

"You're going to have trouble with Dortmund."

Of course he was. The man was a snobby, egotistical prig carried away by his sense of importance. "What's your take on the guy?"

"I don't dispute that he's the master of his discipline. Perhaps the foremost planetologist in the last fifty years. The man has a truly formidable intellect with a string of publications that stretch back forty years. He has practically reinvented the discipline with his theory of management ecology. Time and time again he has crushed the evolutionists and saved conservation biology from being dismantled. His students worship him, and he has his political following as well."

"A particular Boardmember?" Here, at last, was a battleground he was familiar with.

She seemed to hesitate. "Boardmember Shayne, I think. And particularly with the conservation ecologists. Have you spent any time on Earth lately? Been out to the re-wilded areas?"

"No. Wait." He thought back. "They're trying to rebuild wilderness areas, right? Reconstituting extinct species through recovered ancient DNA. Lot of argument about adding genes to species that couldn't survive in the new re-wilded areas."

"Dr. Weisbacher won that round. His argument was that re-wilded areas could slowly be managed back to their natural state, that it was transitional to use lab-modified animals to establish the initial ecosystem, then slowly replace them with what he considered genetically pure organisms until the original gene pools were once again fit for those environments."

She raised her hands. "The point of all this is that Dortmund is a true believer. A sort of messiah. Willing to appear compromising on the front end, he's going to keep whittling away at the edges until it's his way or nothing."

"No humans have screwed with Capella III." He gestured at the transparency. "Unless that single ship's been able to decimate the planet in the last ten years."

"Capella III is Dortmund's holy grail. He sees it as pure, uncontaminated by humanity. That's why he's so dogmatic about hazard protocols. Sure, to a point, I agree with him. On the other hand, I'm not living in a fricking safe suit for the next six months every time I'm down planet. I'll take reasonable precautions against infection and contamination, but if I want to breathe the air, I'm breathing it."

"You're technically independent. Running your own show. So, why bring this to me?"

"If Capella III is as rich as we think, it's going to be developed. In writing his management plan, Dortmund and his team will throw every obstacle in the way that he can think of. He's not just committed to keeping Capella III as his own shrine, it's a holy crusade. To the point that if he has to burn and raze Jerusalem and become a martyr to save it, he will."

"He thinks his study is going to rewrite biology. I had to look up the H.M.S. *Beagle*. Even I've heard of Darwin. You heard Dortmund that day."

Shimodi nodded. "Great. Let him be the new Darwin. I just need to know which side you're on. Keep Capella III as a laboratory of alien biology, or exploit its resources? I mean that's why you were substituted at the last minute, right? Because the Board has a specific agenda?"

Tam laughed. "Nope. I'm neutral."

Again her gaze narrowed. "Then it's that ship out there. I was watching. When it comes to that ship, you've never so much as blinked an eye. It's like you knew it was going to be there."

"Nope." He lifted his hands innocently. "Like I said, I'm just here to oversee the expedition. You do your job, Weisbacher can do his. If he starts to get insane, I'll step in."

She seemed unconvinced. "What if that ship out there is really illegal?"

"You don't buy that it's an alien?"

"Nope. It'll be human. But did you see that crazed look Dortmund got trying to sell the alien idea, and then his outrage that someone could be screwing with his sacred little world?"

"I did."

Her smile was anything but humorous. "I tell you, Advisor, you've got a mad messiah on your hands. Don't say I didn't warn you."

16

There were advantages to being a psychopath. Especially the cold, antisocial kind like Dan Wirth. The guy just didn't feel guilt. As far as Talina was concerned, that wasn't such a bad thing. She'd been drowning in guilt for years. Guilt over the acts she'd committed under Clemenceau's orders. Guilt over shooting Pak and Paulo down in the street that day. Guilt over the times she'd gone to the rescue of someone out in the bush—and got there too late. Guilt over Cap's murder and the fact that she'd never found his killer. Guilt over Rocket's death that day at Mundo and what it had done to Kylee. Guilt over the fact that Felicity had been blown up in Talina's place.

"Yeah, a whole universe of guilt. I should have been born Catholic and Jewish."

But she'd been born Maya. Her mother might have had a Catholic overlay, but at heart she still believed in the Lords of Xibalba, in the Hero Twins, and *Wakah Chan,* the great Tree of Life. In that Spirit World, pain, death, and blood were balanced with beauty, life, and joy. That was the cosmic balance that Talina had sucked in with her mother's milk.

Why, then, the guilt?

As she sped south in the dying night she looked off to the east, searching for some sign of morning's first light. Her aircar was down to a thirty-six percent charge. Her compass reading was on the money. With her augmented vision she could see the trees passing below—a vast expanse of deep forest, the roof of it mounded by the interlocking tops of mighty trees.

To the east, finally, the first faint graying of dawn was touching the horizon far out over the Gulf.

And, of course, now there was guilt over what she had done to Raya. While she hadn't physically hurt her old friend, strapping her down on the bed and leaving her in Talina's place was in many ways a worse betrayal.

But, damn it, she'd had to do something, and Talina Perez wasn't the kind of woman who'd let herself be immobilized with restraints, drugged, and locked away in the hospital to helplessly await someone else's discovery of a cure.

If she'd turned into a mad-dog danger to the community, she'd damned well remove herself. Run for the bush, and either figure her way out of the mess, or die trying.

Fortunately, she knew the only place on Donovan where that understanding might be found.

As rays of Capella's first light poked above the horizon, Talina caught sight of her destination. A darker rectangle hacked out of the endless trees, the ruins of Mundo Base couldn't be mistaken.

She corrected her course, circled the compound, and studied what lay below. In phallic defiance, the great tower thrust up where it had punched through the middle of Mundo Base's circular dome like a *lingam* and *yoni*. Most of the surrounding buildings remained intact. The band of terrestrial trees—though dwarfed by the high canopy of chabacho, stone wood, mundo, and southern aquajade— marked a stark boundary for the agricultural fields they surrounded.

Talina made her descent, touching down in the weed-filled yard before the old storage shed. Only a twenty-eight percent charge remained in the power pack. Not even enough to get her to Corporate Mine if she had to make a run for it.

Mundo Base had always been a place of refuge for people fleeing Port Authority. She'd just never figured it would be hers, fleeing from her own people.

"Yes."

"Oh, shut up," she told the demon quetzal in her gut. "You and your kind, it's your damn fault in the first place. Piece of shit."

She felt rather than heard the now-familiar quetzal laughter.

It's screwing with my mind. Triggering thoughts. Making me see what it wants me to see.

Or they were. She had molecules from at least five different quetzals inside her. Two of the quetzals wanted her dead. No telling what the Briggs quetzal wanted. Rocket was bonded with Kylee, and Talina thought of him as a friend. And Whitey? What the hell did he want? Seemed to her, she had had everything under control until good old Whitey spit in her mouth.

That had to be the catalyst for her descent into madness. Or possession. Or whatever the hell this was.

She pushed her aircar under the shed's cover and used one of the old solar panels left behind after Mundo's abandonment to hook up the trickle charger. As old as the panel was, it would take days to top up the power pack. Not that Talina had anywhere to go for the time being.

She shrugged into her pack as morning's first light caressed the rows of corn, beans, squash, cucumbers, garlic, broccoli, and other terrestrial delicacies.

Mundo had been established to be an experimental agricultural station. It had been a breadbasket until Deb Spiro shot Rocket and pissed off the quetzals. That, coupled with the lack of repair, had led to the base's desertion.

Talina tapped her pistol butt for reassurance, made sure her utility belt was secure, and grabbed her rifle. After she checked out the wreckage where the dome had collapsed, she strolled down past the last of the buildings and into the fields.

The chime was different down here. Unlike Port Authority's, it had a more symphonic sound: deeper, more resonant, mindful of a concert hall reverberation. But then the invertebrates here were entirely different species than those up in the savannah country she was used to.

Breakfast consisted of green beans, tomatoes, blueberries, cherries, and blackberries. All ripe for the picking. The quetzals might kill her for trespassing, but no fart-sucking way was she going to starve to death.

Water wasn't a concern either. All of the cisterns were full. Unlike ground water, rain water wasn't contaminated by heavy metals.

Overhead a batch of scarlet fliers descended on the field, searching for invertebrates.

Was it real, or did she delude herself into believing the part of her that was Rocket was delighted to be back in his home? Here, the little quetzal had spent his best days with Kylee. And she with him.

A pang almost brought a tear to her eyes.

"So, what now, Talina? Nobody here you can be made to shoot. You're a pariah, looking for answers."

Following the raised causeway south, she walked through the deciduous trees to the pines that marked the end of the human incursion into Donovan's vastness.

Here, just inside the forest, Kylee had told Dya and Tal to leave. Beyond was forest.

The quetzals inside her began to thrill.

"So, come on, you bastards, let's get this over with one way or another."

And so saying, she walked fearlessly into the forest's dim shadow, all the while wondering if she was still going to be alive come sunset.

17

F or once, the call came when Tam was actually awake. He'd buried himself in the reports and notes from *Tempest*'s initial survey of Capella III. Trying to understand the science and planetology left him confused, wishing he'd had a chance to snare an implant back in Solar System that would have allowed him to synthesize the terminology and math.

Yeah, right. As if he'd had any clue where he was headed. Or that he would have had the sense to download an implant even if he had known.

One thing was sure, the holographic images of the planet were truly awe-evoking. The stuff that looked like plants ranged in color from blue to turquoise, to teal, to green, to viridian. Nor did the plants look quite right. And they moved! Branches and leaves would follow a person as they walked past.

Then came the various organisms that Tam assumed were animals. Everything seemed to be in marvelous color. Right up until one of the holos showed what appeared to be a rock. Only when probed by a long stick did it suddenly move, two tentacle-like arms shooting out. As they did, the cameraman leaped back and the rock dropped its camouflage. Three eyes appeared.

"Don't know what to call it," the cameraman said in the voiceover. *"Some kind of predator. Whatever it is, it's a bastard evil monster."*

And then there was the tape of one of the crewmen, a fellow named Donovan. Apparently unconcerned, he walked out to the perimeter, the edge of the shuttle wing visible in the holo. Wearing yellow coveralls, he stepped up to a bush and was apparently about to urinate. As he unfastened his fly, the ground seemed to flow, rise, and take form.

Whatever the thing was, it went from invisible to a wild flash of crimson. A neck ruff popped out like a sheet, violet, mauve, and orange bands flashing in intricate patterns.

Donovan stood gaping, paralyzed.

And then the thing shot a triangular head forward in a lightning move. Serrated jaws snapped shut around Donovan's head and shoulders. The thing jerked him off his feet; clawed front legs pinned his sides. Bone, muscle, and flesh were sheared as the beast bit Donovan in two. Tossing its head back, the creature began swallowing. The bulge moved slowly down the throat, expanding the ruffed neck.

Seeing that bulge move down, knowing it was a man's head, neck, and shoulders, sent a tingle of horror through Tamarland like he'd never felt before.

Even as the monster took its first bite, shouts could be heard. A man and woman appeared at the edge of the frame, rifles lifted. Taking aim, they fired bursts. In their panic only about half the rounds had any effect, the rest splintering the vegetation.

The monster leaped as if stung, whipped around. Its tail slashed through the brush, flattening plants. Yellow and black—almost electric in vivid color—flashed across the creature's hide. It fixed three gleaming black eyes on the shooters, and charged.

By luck the woman's simultaneous burst caught the beast full in the head. Explosive rounds tore the skull apart, blasted bits of bone and tissue into the air.

Even then the thing slammed to the ground just short of her feet.

Tamarland stared in amazement as the holo showed close-ups of what was left of the creature.

"Sir?" a voice interrupted.

Tam pulled himself back to the present, turned, and found Valencia Seguro at his doorway. "Yes, Second Officer?"

"Captain would like a word."

Tam paused the holo, got to his feet, and followed Seguro up a deck to the AC. Torgussen sat in the command chair, Engineer Ho at his station to the side.

"Advisor," Torgussen greeted. "Sorry to bother you. In the last couple of days we've managed to close enough distance that we can get a good image at maximum magnification. Thought you might like to see."

"Thanks, Tayrell." Tam stared at the image on the screen. "Is that . . . ?"

"We've cleaned it up with a fractal program, Advisor." Ho made an adjustment, slightly shifting the color. "That's with the IR enhanced."

Tam stepped up beside Torgussen's station and studied the ship. So many of the details had refined, right down to the line of shuttles berthed just below the lower cargo torus. The bulge of the reactor core was out of view, the image focused on the vessel's upper decks.

"Here's what I thought you would want to see." Torgussen highlighted an area along the hull.

"That means . . . ?" Tam tried to understand.

"That's the vessel registration. IS-C-27. IS means interstellar model. C stands for cargo. Vessel twenty-seven out of the shipyard."

"So it's ours?" Tam asked. "But I thought you said that nothing like that ship had ever been built."

"It hasn't. Advisor, we've only spaced three IS-type cargo ships. They're designed to deliver the basics for a small colony. And none of them is anything like that in size. She's huge."

Tam could see the confusion on Torgussen's face. "What does it mean?"

"Don't have a clue, sir. It would be nice to think that The Corporation was running another shipyard. Something covert. Hidden away out at the edge of Solar System. But it's absolutely impossible when you think about the resources, the personnel necessary, the logistics of building a monster like that. Even for The Corporation, it would be impossible to hide."

"And why would they need to?" Tam asked. "Trust me. Given my position, I'd have heard of it." Or Shayne would have. "Not even Chairman Radcek could conceal something of this magnitude."

"And the number twenty-seven is problematic. The Corporation is nothing if not methodical. They wouldn't just throw twenty-seven out as a random number. That means she's the twenty-seventh heavy hauler. We know of three, and a fourth was being built in the yards when we left. So where are the other twenty-two? When and where were they built?"

"You'd know better than I would, Captain. My talents lay

in another direction. A fact that allows me to state unequivocally that no secret Corporate shipyard exists. Nor is there any covert Corporate program to build such a fleet."

"You're positive?"

"Oh, yes." He actually smiled at that. He had even penetrated Radcek's security, and done it so thoroughly, he had been able to hand over the man's deepest business dealings to Shayne.

Torgussen took a deep breath, sighed wearily. "Then we're still stuck with the impossible."

"But we can rule out aliens?"

"What are the chances that aliens use Arabic numerals and script? No, this is human."

Ho was looking distinctly uncomfortable.

"Yes, Engineer?" Tam asked.

"It's a wild guess. Probably nothing."

"I'll take a wild guess." Tam crossed his arms.

"Multiverse theory was really kicked off by a guy named Everett back in the middle of the twentieth century. The hypothesis went through several modifications through the years, ending in what we now accept as established theory. Interstellar travel by symmetry inversion wouldn't work without it."

"Get to the point, please."

"What if that ship comes from another universe? One parallel to ours, but slightly different at the relativistic level? Maybe their universe has a minuscule difference in mass, making it run slightly faster than ours. What I'm trying to say is that if that ship didn't come from our universe, it had to come from somewhere, right? Maybe that ship came from a parallel that's running just slightly ahead of ours."

"When they reverted symmetry, why wouldn't they have returned to their own universe?" Torgussen looked skeptical.

"I have no idea, Captain." Ho rubbed the side of his head as if massaging a headache. "We have a tough enough time describing physics in our universe. It gets infinitely tougher in universes where we haven't a clue of the constants or dimensions, let alone the kind of mathematics necessary. I'm just offering an alternate hypothesis. Something we might be able to test for."

"Can't fault a man for that," Tam agreed.

"Got something else," Ho said. "I've done a count as that good old number twenty-seven rotates on its axis. It's missing two shuttles."

Tam turned, staring at the image. The shuttle bays were located just below what they assumed was the cargo torus. And yes, even as he looked he could see one of the bays was empty.

"Two missing?"

"Figure that she would have needed a crew of a hundred to one hundred and fifty to operate and maintain her," Torgussen said. "Figure fifty people per shuttle at full capacity. Means you'd have to take two if they were trying to get everyone off in a hurry. Beyond that, perhaps any additional personnel were already dirtside."

"Or there's still someone on board," Tam suggested.

"If so, the hyperlink and photonics aren't working. Nor did they opt to answer our radio hail."

"So, what about the planet? What does your sensor array indicate?"

"Perhaps the answer to all of our questions," Torgussen told him. "We've got two faint pinpoints of radio emissions on the planet. This far out, the signal's still pretty weak. We'll have a better idea in the next few days."

"Good." Tam continued to squint at the holo. "Remain on passive scan. I want to know as much about them as we possibly can before we initiate communications."

Torgussen hesitated, as if reluctant. "Something you want to tell me, Advisor? Something I should be aware of?"

"Knowledge is power, Captain. Chances are there will be some simple explanation for all of this, but it won't hurt to understand exactly what we'll be walking into when we arrive."

"Yes, sir."

Whatever awaited him, seizing it for his own would be no trouble for Shayne's deadly and talented scorpion.

18

Trish sat at the end of the bar in Inga Lock's Bloody Drink tavern. A mug of golden ale—one of Inga's latest brews—sat half empty by her elbow.

Beside her, Talina's chair remained symbolically empty.

The tavern was boisterous, this being the first night for one of the crews rotating in from Corporate Mine. Supervisor Aguila didn't allow alcohol down at the mine, so Inga's was the first place the crews hit. It was still the Corporate world down there. Regimented. Ordered. Everything by the book. And, fact was, most of Aguila's people—newcomers who'd arrived on *Turalon*—preferred it that way. It reminded them of the way things were back in Solar System.

Trish shot a glance over her shoulder. The Corporate folk stood out in their still-new coveralls, though some had managed to acquire Donovanian wear. Slowly but surely, they were beginning to blend in.

So many of the tensions that the *Turalon* transportees once had with the hardscrabble Donovanians had eased over the intervening months. They weren't soft meat anymore, nor were they quite Donovanian. Though some of the deserters who'd run for the bush—at least those few who were still alive—couldn't be told from locals.

Shig appeared on the steps leading down into Inga's. He was wearing his new fabric shirt under his water-slicked rain poncho. As he made his way down the central aisle, he called out in response to greetings.

Hofer's entire crew—having retired to the tavern after a hard day's work on the new school—lifted their glasses his direction.

A new school? Obviously some scheme by that walking piece of shit, Dan Wirth. Slimy quetzal in the grass that he was, the psychopath did nothing unless it ultimately benefited his interests. Just like when Trish had heard that

Wirth's goons had agitated for Talina's confinement in the interest of "public safety."

And now Tal was gone, escaped to the bush. Her aircar, rifle, and field pack missing in the middle of the night. And boy, was Raya pissed off.

Shig caught Trish's eye, raised a hand, and walked her way. He didn't hesitate, plopping himself in the high chair beside Trish.

"That's Talina's, you know."

"She's not here." Shig gave her one of his beaming smiles. "The fact that you save it for her says good things about your character."

"My character sucks toilet water."

Shig lifted one of his bushy eyebrows, curiosity in his dark and serene eyes. "How is Raya?"

"Mad enough to chew nails. Feeling humiliated that Tal not only tricked her, but left her strapped into one of her hospital beds so that she couldn't raise the alarm. By the time Step found her this morning, she was fit to commit murder."

"And like her, you're blaming yourself. Hence the character that sucks toilet water."

"I keep thinking back to the canyon that day." Trish picked up her beer and took a drink to wash down the pain. "If I'd not rushed that shot, if I'd dropped to a knee, aimed. If I'd center-punched that damn quetzal, it wouldn't have infected Talina."

"Humanity has spent most of its history torturing itself with the word *if*. Not even a hot poker in the hands of a sadistic inquisitor can elicit as much agony. Would you feel better if I asked Inga for that pair of pliers she keeps behind the bar? I could pull out some of your fingernails."

"Don't be silly."

"Advice, you yourself should take." He gestured to Inga as she looked his direction, and nodded. "Talina has to follow her path. And the way that can be named is not the true way."

"What?"

"I'm talking about the Tao. I gave that lecture when you were in school, remember?"

"I think I was sick that day."

"What I'm trying to say is that Talina, by nature of her karma, must be our warrior. From the day she shot Clemenceau, she has placed herself out in front. Our strength, our scout leading the way into the unknown. And, in many ways, our conscience."

"I'm not sure I buy that conscience bit."

Shig smiled as Inga set a half-full glass of wine on the battered chabacho wood bar. Shig tossed out an SDR.

"Think about it. Since when has Talina done anything but what was right by the people? She has taken it upon herself to rescue those in need, risked her life to break up fights, functioned as policeman and executioner, and stepped between the people and trouble. Sure, she threatens and dispenses violence, but when has she ever turned it upon the innocent?"

"Step says she thought she was shooting Sian Hmong the other day. Sian's like a pillar of the community."

"I'm not saying that Talina isn't compromised by the quetzal molecules, but when you think about it, her escape is totally in character. I'm willing to bet she won't be back until she knows she's no longer a threat."

"Tricky of her. Wejee was on the aircar field gate that night. He swears up and down he didn't see her." Trish drank again. "Where'd she go, Shig? You got any idea?"

"Rork Springs has good water. There's a cache of ammo and supplies at Two Falls Gap. She's always been tight with the Briggses. If she's leaving for good, she might have gone as far as the Andani holding or way out to Tyson Station. Wherever she went, we're not going to find her."

"She's not in her right mind, Shig. It's my fault. I should have known she'd do something like this."

"You have a failing. It is in you to protect others from themselves. It makes you a good security officer, but taken too far it becomes arrogance. The ultimate justification for denying freedom for others."

"I thought we had already established that Talina is having her brain jacked around by alien molecules? There's times, Shig, when a person needs to step in and act when someone's incapable of acting for themselves."

"Like with Cap Taggart?"

"I don't know what you're talking about."

"Ultimately I'm talking about love." Shig smiled at his wine. "Talina stepped in when your mother died. You were twelve. Talina has been the mass around which you orbit. A circumstance which is fine for a girl. You are now a woman. When are you going to dedicate yourself to your own Tao? Seek the wisdom that will establish your way?"

Trish fought her heart rate back to normal. "Maybe you haven't been paying attention. Tal and I haven't been the best of friends since she sided with that little quetzal."

"Yes. Difficult, isn't it, when your idol doesn't quite fulfill some of your deepest expectations? But would you have felt quite as stung had it been Step or Yvette who stood up for Rocket?" He smiled enigmatically. "Ah, I suspect not."

"A quetzal's a quetzal."

"You haven't heard a word I've said." Shig sighed, clapped hands to his thighs, and slipped down off Talina's chair. "Until you're ready to become the pathfinder and guide, to dare the unknown, you'll never step into her shoes."

With that, Shig turned and walked away, his glass untouched.

19

D ortmund hadn't slept for three days. At most he'd caught short naps, only to be driven from sleep by his racing mind. Beneath it all, he was powered by a conflicting hope and rage.

The culmination of his life's work lay down on that planet. Orbiting it was a ship. But whose?

Alien? Human?

Either way, his entire life's aspirations lay on the line. If it were aliens, then of course he was the man who would make contact.

If the ship were human, they were despoiling a sacred jewel for which he had prepared his entire life to save.

Obsessed, he had devoted every hour to two very different action protocols.

For the aliens, he had composed a fifty-page outline delineating each step he and *Vixen*'s crew would take to not only initiate contact, but to carefully develop the relationship so that there would be no misunderstandings; no communicable diseases passed—the quarantine protocol was twenty pages alone; how a mutually intelligible communications system could be devised using the periodic charts; information exchanges based on biology; even a first meeting scenario that would ensure that neither side might be slighted by posture, approach, or implications of lower status.

It would be a model—one studied for centuries by scholars of humanity's first contact.

His second paper, running to seventy-five pages, was based on the hypothesis that a group of human miscreants had commandeered a ship, traveled to Capella III, and were now in the process of looting the planet's resources.

First he laid out the legal ramifications of such an action vis-à-vis Corporate law. This was a criminal enterprise, after all. The Advisor would have full discretion, by law, to document, evaluate, and consider the extent of illegal actions taking place on the planet.

After that came a comprehensive list of methods necessary to document each and every infraction. How evidence should be recorded, who should record it, and how the chain of possession should be documented for later action back in Solar System.

He had gone through the *Vixen*'s crew manifest, detailing specific tasks for the two security personnel on board. Too bad that neither had more than the most basic training in law enforcement and criminal justice.

And then he had enumerated the possible scope of damage the interlopers could be doing to the planet, its wildlife, habitat, and ecosystems. Everything from the introduction of terrestrial organisms to the egregious exploitation of the native fauna. This he outlined down to the actual footprints of the looters as they tromped, heedless, upon the inoffensive native flora and fauna.

Blinking, haggard, he was putting in the final touches when the com announced, *"Meeting in the conference room in fifteen minutes. All scientific staff should be present."*

Dortmund wearily ran fingers through his oily hair. Glanced down at his wrinkled overalls. No. No time to change or shower.

Marking both of his papers as "Draft," he promptly mailed them to his colleagues. No matter what the determination, alien or human, he needed his team to have access to whichever report was pertinent to the new information. This way they could just call up the paragraph or section to which he referred in the meeting.

With a grimace, he also forwarded copies to the Advisor. As if the man could or would read them through.

Stepping out into the corridor, he realized he was famished. How long since he'd eaten? Some vague part of his brain recalled a tray of snacks. He couldn't remember if he'd gone for them, or if one of the others had delivered them.

He stepped into the conference room, his head muzzy, a weariness like lead in his bones. But with it was mixed a feeling of satisfaction. He had a plan for either contingency.

A part of him was crying, "Please, let it be aliens!"

If it turned out to be looters, then it would be with the realization that Capella III had been partly despoiled. Unable to direct the protection of the planet, he would at least be in a position to ameliorate the impact, and implement containment policies that might prevent any further damage.

Part of him hoped that the reason the ship hadn't answered was that some terrible contagious bacterium or parasite had infected the crew, killing them to the last person before more than a handful had set foot planetside. Fitting justice for daring to violate Corporate law.

"And the wages of greed turned out to be death." He smiled as he whispered the words. True poetic justice.

Sax and Jones were already seated. Shimodi walked in, followed by Benteen and the captain.

"Good day," the Advisor called, taking a seat at the head of the table.

Dortmund seated himself. Noticed that Shanteel sniffed, shot him a sidelong glance, and surreptitiously slid her chair to increase the space between them.

"What's the latest?" Dortmund couldn't help himself. "I assume we're close enough that optics have given us additional data? Perhaps something has come in on the ship's sensor array?"

"It has." Benteen studied him thoughtfully. "You look all-in, Dr. Weisbacher."

"I haven't had the leisure of waiting for additional information. I have put together two separate reports, one for the possibility that we're dealing with an alien—"

"It's human," Benteen cut him off. "Not just human, but Corporate."

Dortmund felt his guts sink. "Looters then. Very well, I have prepared a complete plan to deal with—"

"Apparently it's a bit more complicated and perplexing than that," Benteen told him, then shifted his gaze to the others. "Long-distance scan has determined that the ship is a Corporate interstellar cargo ship. A big one. Even more perplexing, we have no records of any such ship. If what we suspect is true, only three models of this series of ship have been built and a fourth is in the yards under construction. This one sports the registration number of twenty-seven."

"That doesn't make sense," Shimodi said.

"Okay, we're lost," Sax agreed. "You're saying this ship is from the future?"

"That's preposterous," Dortmund snapped. "Advisor,

this is a scam. The looters changed the registration, that's all. Pirates and raiders have always tried to hide the identity of their ships."

"Pretty dumb move on their part," Captain Torgussen said wryly. "If I were a criminal I'd pick an ID for an existing ship. If anything, this cries out, 'Hey look at me!' Like broadcasting, 'I'm also stupid.' No, Doctor, they're not trying to hide anything."

Dortmund blinked, trying to think through the fog in his brain. It seemed so hard to redirect his thoughts from an organized outline to data that didn't fit.

"What else have you got?" Shimodi asked, twirling her blond hair around a finger as she studied Benteen.

"Radio sources," Torgussen told them. "Two hot spots on the planet and occasional broadcasts from the surrounding areas." He made a face. "We're close enough now to monitor them."

Benteen took a deep breath. "The mystery deepens, people. This isn't some covert mining and looting party. Apparently it's a colony. And it's been on Capella III for years."

"Impossible!" Dortmund barked.

Benteen's lips bent with amusement. "Well, these protocol papers you've been slaving over might be worthless given the current turn of events, but we've still got the problem of who these people are, how long they've been here, and where they came from."

Dortmund struggled for words, couldn't find them. "You don't understand. There must be some mistake."

Benteen's oddly solicitous stare hinted that there wasn't.

20

When Tamarland stepped into the astrogation center, it was to find both Torgussen and Ho bent over the holo projection from the sensor array. Both men looked perplexed to the point that Ho was pulling on his ear.

On the main holo at the front of the room was a projection of the mystery ship. It now filled the forward screen, bathed in Capella's light. Just hanging there in space as it was, it looked somehow eerie. A peculiar shiver slipped down Tamarland's spine.

"Gentlemen, you asked to see me?"

"Advisor," Torgussen greeted warily. As quickly he returned his attention to the holo, adding to Ho, "Can you shift the frequency down ten hertz?"

"Been there, done that, Cap. Still nothing." Ho reached back and massaged his neck.

"What seems to be the problem?" Tam asked, irritated that they'd disturbed his reading.

"That damned ship." Torgussen tossed a hand toward the image. "We're a survey vessel, right? Got one of the best sensor arrays in Solar System, if not the best. We should be able to image every deck, bolt, washer, and seam in that bucket of air right down to the atomic composition of the sialon. Instead, we can get a reading on the hull, and after that, it's as if that thing's eating the beam."

"What do you mean, eating the beam?"

Ho looked up, frown lines marring his forehead. "Photonic sensing works on entanglement, right? We accept that the universe is filled with entangled particles. Even after all these years we still call it Einstein's 'spookiness at a distance.' You might know it as Einstein-Podolsky-Rosen effect. EPR effect is all about entangled particles. By observing an entangled particle here, we can understand the state of its twin aboard IS-C-27. By observing the relationships between a host of them, we can generate a partial image that we can fill in with fractal geometry."

He pointed at the screen. "We can read anything around the ship, but once we focus our sensors inside the ship, nothing. It might be perfect vacuum. But, particles appear in vacuum, right? That's part of the multiverse theory. Just not inside that bucket. According to the photonics we're seeing, that ship's like a black hole.

"We've tried focused microgravity. Bathed that thing in waves that should have given us a readable resonance. Nothing. It's like the hull is absorbing microgravitational waves. Which defies everything we know about materials physics."

"And then there's neutronic radiation," Torgussen added. "Neutrinos pass through everything, right?" He plastered an irritated smile on his lips. "Our detectors don't read anything on the other side. It's as if that ship out there is swallowing them."

"And here's the other peculiarity," Ho continued. "We know what that ship's albedo should be, given the emissions we're measuring from Capella. Somehow, some way, that ship is absorbing thirteen percent more solar energy than materials physics says it should."

"That's a lot of energy," Torgussen said bluntly. "And it's not being radiated back into space. The only conclusion, then, is that the hull is acting like a heat sink, which means that ship should be hotter than the hubs of Hell. Instead, the surface averages two hundred and ten kelvins. About normal for a starship's radiation given our levels of insulation and interior temperature."

"So where the hell is that energy going?" Ho raised frustrated hands. "The first and second laws of thermodynamics didn't just jump up, hold hands, and skip away."

"The thing's like a snot-sucking black hole," Torgussen repeated under his breath.

"Maybe that's why they didn't answer our photonic or hyperlink hails?"

"Then why is the radio beacon still broadcasting every thirty seconds. Granted, its antenna is well above the hull, but so is the photonic communications array."

"Maybe some kind of deadly radiation on board?"

"We wish. We have sensors for every form of radiation in the spectrum. If that ship was emitting so much as a crippled quark, we'd have it."

Tam spread his hands wide. "Gentlemen, I have nothing to tell you. According to my briefing we're supposed to find a virgin planet and conduct a detailed survey for the Board. Ghost ships aren't part of my experiential realm."

Torgussen arched a questioning eyebrow, but was bright enough not to pursue the question of what Tam's experience was.

"What about the planet? Is it as baffling?"

"No, sir." Torgussen straightened. "Well, let me clarify that. It poses its own problems. Especially in light of those mission parameters you just repeated to me. We're close enough we've got good resolution. Based on radio signals, we've plotted both of the source points. Give me a second and I'll bring up the visuals." A pause. "Dr. Weisbacher isn't going to like this a bit."

The ship on the main holo faded out to be replaced by an aerial shot of what was clearly a settlement. Oval shaped. Surrounded by what looked like a ditch and agricultural fields. A shuttle field, complete with a grounded shuttle and a small mountain of stacked shipping crates stuck out on one side. The buildings were basically gridded, mostly with various sizes of white domes, but had been filled in with rectangular structures of what had to be local manufacture.

A thin line ran north through the speckling of trees beyond the perimeter—obviously a road that led to an openpit mine. A big one. Tiny dots of equipment that had to be haulers and excavators could be seen.

A smaller lot on the west side of the perimeter ditch was cluttered with what had to be aircars.

"That's the northern and largest settlement."

Torgussen ordered up a second image. This one was in thick forest, an impenetrable carpet of treetops that mantled a tall line of ridge that trended to the west. In places on the heights, up-thrust peaks of bare stone could be seen. On the shoulder of the mountain, a flat had been created. Several domes—what had to be shops, a dormitory, another shuttle, and what was obviously a waste dump—

could be seen. Below the ridge lay a broad floodplain. Five kilometers to the north, on the shores of an oxbow-laced river, a smaller plot had been hacked out of the forest. The small square building, shuttle pad, and plot of agricultural land were connected to the mine by a tram line, though at this scale the details were hard to see.

"Another mine," Torgussen said. "Those are the two major settlements. We've picked up a scattering of what look like isolated camps. Most of them within a hundred kilometers of the northern settlement."

"Who *are* these people? This doesn't make sense. It's only been ten years since *Tempest* was here."

"Want me to let Dr. Shimodi look at this?"

"Sure. She's a geologist with a mining specialty. She'll make more out of it than you or I will."

"Yes, sir." Torgussen watched him warily. "Want us to signal them? Let them answer the questions for us?"

Tamarland chewed his lips, trying to think it through. Whatever this was, they were walking into a functioning colony world. It had been one thing to be in charge of a survey team on a virgin planet. But to find towns, mines, not to mention the giant cargo ship? That was something entirely different.

So where does the advantage lie?

He couldn't answer that question without additional data. If there was a government here, it would be rudimentary. Just like when he was plotting with Artollia, he needed to know who was in charge, how the colony's government was structured.

For the first time since leaving Solar System, a genuine thrill ran through him. He might be under a death sentence back in The Corporation, but they wouldn't have a clue here.

"Can you monitor their radio transmissions?"

"We have been for the last day. Not much to go on. Talk about medicines and machine parts mostly. Nothing really of substance. Some guy called Two Spot at Port Authority and some woman named Tallia O'Hanley at Corporate Mine." A pause. "Oh, and there was mention of a Supervisor. Some woman named Aguila."

"So they are from Solar System."

"Yes, sir. No doubt about it. Not that that makes any damn sense at all, assuming we're in the right place."

"Or the right time," Ho added darkly.

But the transition had been instantaneous. One minute they were off Neptune, the next they were in the Capella system.

Tam stopped short, wracking his brain. "A Supervisor? I knew them all, or had at least heard of them. None of the Supervisors were named Aguila. This doesn't make any sense."

"No, sir," Torgussen said. "None of it does. Not that ship, not that mine, and certainly not a Corporate colony on a supposedly empty world."

Once again, the question was begged: *Who the hell are they?*

21

"**T**a Li Na."

The words brought Talina wide awake. The first graying of Capella's dawn illuminated the shed's interior. Not that she needed it; her night vision was just fine these days, thank you.

She lay on a mattress she'd pulled out of the old dormitory and lugged to the storage shed where she'd parked her aircar. The faint odor of quetzal mixed with the stronger scents of dew, cherry and squash blossoms, and rich damp earth.

She sat up, senses clearing as she reached for her rifle.

The girl stood like a silhouette against the gray light, her blond hair hanging around her shoulders in tangles. She'd be turning eleven in a couple of months. Her frame remained rail-thin, the clothes she wore looking much the worse for wear and filthy. To Talina's dismay, the girl was barefoot, which seemed to be begging for attack from the closest slug.

"Kylee?" Talina asked, coughed to clear her throat, and swung her legs over the edge of the bed.

"You shouldn't be here."

"Neither should you. What happened to your shoes?"

"Didn't fit anymore." A pause. "They want to know why you are here. The experiment is over."

Talina stretched, stood, and slung her rifle. "Sorry, kid. It's anything but over."

"I'm not going back."

"I may not be either." Talina walked over to look down into Kylee's smudged face. "Had a visit from a quetzal the other day. We called him Whitey. Traded molecules, and I haven't been right since. I keep having visions. No, clarify that. I should say I'm possessed by the visions. Made me think I was shooting someone."

"Who?"

"A woman who once threatened Rocket."

"Deb Spiro?"

"She's dead."

Kylee cocked her head slightly. "When? Where?"

"About a year ago. I shot her in the middle of the street in Port Authority."

"Good."

"How's your hip and leg?"

"Aches now and then. What do you want here, Ta Li Na?"

"To find out what's screwing with my thoughts. It's like I've got five quetzals fighting inside me. All powered by a Maya spirit-possession glyph. Maybe you've got answers." Talina paused, staring out at the morning. Mist was rising from the ground, the first of the morning chime announcing a new day. "You need shoes. Surprised a slug hasn't gotten you."

"I try to stay on shallow soils and where it's rocky. And Flash helps. He lets me ride most places. Especially where it's boggy or dangerous. He thinks it's funny, a human riding around on his back."

"Who's Flash?"

"He's old. He gave birth to Diamond. Then Diamond gave birth to Leaper. Leaper gave birth to Rocket."

"Whole family, huh?"

"It's different with quetzals. No male copulating with a female to fertilize her. It takes three, exchanging molecules orally. The molecules are passed through tissues in the back of the mouth and into the reproductive tract. I'm not sure what happens next, but eventually a baby quetzal is popped out the anus."

Talina chuckled. "I forget that you're ten."

"People always said that. But only the ones that didn't know me."

"You really need shoes. I'm betting I can find something to cobble together a pair for you. Careful as you try to be, a slug's gonna get you."

"Doesn't matter."

"What do you mean, doesn't matter?"

The girl averted her eyes, shrugged in a guilty sort of way. Then, almost angrily, she said, "You can't stay here. I waited until Diamond and Leaper weren't looking. I came to warn you before it's too late."

Talina stepped out into the morning, stretching. "Yeah, well, that's just it. I don't have any place to go. In fact, I'm hoping that you can help me. You can talk to them, can't you?"

"Sort of. It's not like it was with Dya and . . . Well, the others. Quetzals and humans, we're different."

Talina carefully scented the morning breeze; the chime picked up volume. She could smell the farm, the scent of earthy vegetation mixed with the perfume of the forest. And yes, there was the taint of quetzal.

"They're close."

"They must have realized I got away. They'll be coming now. Probably upset with me."

"Well, first I'm going to find a place to pee, and then you and I are going to walk down and have a little heart-to-heart with your friend Flash."

"He's out hunting. It's Diamond and Leaper who are here. Which is too bad. Flash was the one that let you and Dya go last time. He still thinks there's a chance to learn something. Diamond and Leaper want you dead. Would have killed you yesterday when you were picking blueberries, but I asked them not to."

"Thought I felt quetzal yesterday. But tell me, was that really because you asked, or because I was picking blueberries with one hand and holding the rifle ready with the other?"

"Okay, maybe it was the rifle, but I asked, too."

Talina chuckled. "Yeah, you're all right, kid."

"You're really not here to steal me?"

"Nope. I'm here to figure this quetzal thing out. One way or another. And something tells me I'm going to need your help to do it."

"How?"

"Well, that remains to be . . ." Talina paused, gaze turned toward the forest. "Looks like your friends are here."

Two adult quetzals, collars expanded and pulsing in crimson and black, emerged from the tree line. At a fast clip, they came, heads down, tails out, looking anything but friendly.

Talina felt her quetzal squirming around behind her stomach. "Whoa, boys!" she cried, lifting her rifle. "That's far enough."

The quetzals stopped short as she covered them with the muzzle. They fully understood a loaded rifle.

The one on the right uttered a deep-throated chittering sound, its big triangular head lowered, a series of patterns running over the expanded ruff.

"No," Kylee told it, stepping forward. "She hasn't tried to take me. She wants your help."

Another pattern—pinks, yellows, browns, and indigo—formed, all shifting and merging. The three eyes remained pinned on Talina while the beast uttered some incomprehensible gargling sound.

Its mate, offspring, whatever, kept easing forward, gaze locked with Talina's.

"I said, far enough." Talina settled the butt of her rifle into her shoulder. "Which one is this, Kylee?"

"That's Leaper."

"Leaper, I'm not here to fight. The experiment is not over. You understand that? Not over?"

The quetzal froze, its patterns shifting to straight crimson.

"Oh, shit," Talina growled, her own quetzal hissing in preparation for an attack.

"No!" Kylee cried, stepping out in front of Leaper. "She'll kill you! She doesn't want a fight! She's a friend!"

The second quetzal—who had to be Diamond—uttered a clicking, its hide flashing a new pattern of complex colors.

Leaper seemed to relax, posture easing.

"Well, thank fucking God," Talina whispered, lowering her rifle to a less-threatening hip shot.

Even so, her heart was beating a staccato against her breast bone. Damn, quetzals were absofragginlutely scary.

"Thanks, kid. That was getting a bit hairy."

Kylee turned, looking back over Talina's shoulder, and said, "It's okay, Flash. She's not here to cause trouble."

Talina whirled. Found herself face-to-face with a giant

quetzal. Not a foot separated them. Frozen, muscles locked, she stood petrified as the beast used a claw to flip her rifle to the side and opened its scarred and serrated jaws.

The words *Oh, fuck* seemed to catch in Talina's mind as the creature lunged.

22

Acceleration pushed Kalico back into the commander's seat as her shuttle arrowed through high cirrus and into the stratosphere. Below her, Donovan dropped away; its now-familiar geography grew distant as her shuttle lanced into the heavens.

The first of the stars appeared in the darkening sky. She took a deep breath, her heart already starting to pound.

"You all right?" Fenn Bogarten, her industrial design fabricator, asked from the seat beside hers.

"You know how much I hate *Freelander*?"

"Yeah, me, too. I have nightmares for days afterward every time we set foot on that thing. Those glimpses from the corners of my eye?" He glanced away. "Saw myself once."

"You, too?"

"You mean, I'm not the only one?"

"Happened to me twice." Kalico reached up and curled a length of her black hair around a nervous finger. "Saw myself stepping out of the bone temple. I was dressed like I am today. Complete with the scars. Heard myself say, 'If you go back, you'll die.'"

"*Freelander*'s cursed, ma'am. But somehow, knowing that you're creep-freaked, too? Makes it easier."

"Glad to be of service, Engineer." A beat. "I think."

He studied her as the shuttle changed attitude. "You don't have to be there, you know. Just me and my team."

"I know." She chewed her lip for a moment. "Hard to ask my people to do what I won't."

"Because of that, anything you ever need, we're behind you, ma'am. Every Jack and Jill of us. Whether it's downhole or up in the sky. We ever make it back to Solar System? You want us to tear up the Board, we'll do it."

She laughed at the notion. "One thing at a time, Fenn. I'll be happy to get this last batch of carbon fiber spun. Having to do it on *Freelander* makes my teeth ache."

"To extrude cable with that tensile strength? Has to be done in freefall, ma'am. And in vacuum. Can't have the odd atom or molecule inserting itself in the matrix. Got to be a pure carbon lattice. *Freelander* is the only choice for the time being."

He arched a suggestive eyebrow. "But with the tram up, the smelter working, I don't see why we can't manufacture the materials we need. Design a station for freefall manufacturing. We've got the shuttles for lift, the raw material, including clay for sialon."

"All in good time, Engineer."

That was the thing about building a world. So much needed to be done, and it was accomplished so slowly. They'd just finished the tram. Powered it. And the first buckets of ore were being carried down from the mine to the smelter on the river.

Now she had to manufacture another batch of carbon fiber cable for Port Authority. She'd traded cable for the tram buckets and giant wheels and gears that had been sandcast in Mac Hanson's foundry. Sandcast? Eighteenth-century technology juxtaposed with carbon fiber from the twenty-first.

And traded? In the Corporate world, she could have just ordered the damn buckets and wheels. This business of free-market economy, of paying for everything, or trading for it, drove her half mad.

At the same time, she and her people had a whole new spirit. When they manufactured wealth out of nothing, it was theirs. To have and hold. It didn't just disappear, automatically surrendered to, and disseminated through, the Corporate system, bits allocated who knew where depending upon the algorithms.

Sure, her people were under Corporate contract. Upon their return to Solar System—assuming they ever made it back—they'd get a lump sum. Living quarters would be provided for the rest of their lives, and they'd receive additional rations as determined by the algorithms.

But here on Donovan—mostly because Port Authority ran on a market economy—she let her people keep the occasional nugget or gold bar. Paid them in PA-minted SDRs before sending them off to Port Authority for their R&R.

The fact that they could accumulate "plunder" had had the unanticipated effect of doubling their productivity.

Was it chaotic? Damn straight. Her old boss, Board-member Miko Taglioni, would have been apoplectic.

But then, Miko—arrogant and confident in his own god-like righteousness—would have ended in blood within his first hours on Donovan.

She smiled at that.

"Supervisor?"

"Just thinking, Engineer. Trying to understand who that woman was who stepped off the shuttle that day at Port Authority, come to take the planet back from the rebels."

He laughed, the sound of it slightly strained by the knowledge that *Freelander* lay just minutes away. "Wasn't like what we were expecting, was it, ma'am? Talk about a slap in the face."

No, she'd come a long way from the cold Corporate bitch who'd landed that day.

"Coming up on *Freelander,* ma'am," Ensign Juri Makarov, her pilot, called.

"Thank you, Ensign."

"I really hate this," Bogarten muttered between clenched teeth.

"You told me it would take ten hours."

"Aye, ma'am. That's after we get the raw carbon to feed and the machine starts extruding. Let's just hope that we don't run into any unforeseen problems."

Bogarten had his four helpers in the back. Still, Kalico said, "I don't know that I'd be of any use, but if you need a spare set of hands . . . ?"

He gave her a worried smile. "I appreciate that, Supervisor. Stryski's back there. He'll figure out any snag. You just relax, try and keep your sanity, and we'll have that cable spun out in no time."

"Coming up on dock," Makarov called. "Five, four, three, two, one." The shuttled bumped and lurched. Thumps could be heard. "Hard dock."

It had to be her imagination, the spooky reality of where they were, but a wavering shiver, like an undulation of water, seemed to flow through her body. The light shifted, as if slightly smeared.

"All right, people," she called, willing courage she didn't have into her voice. "Let's double check the hatch and lock. No mistakes now. Stay frosty."

A chorus of "Yes, ma'am" came from the back.

"Atmosphere checks green," Igor Stryski called from where he stood at the airlock. "We've got twenty-seven Celsius on the other side. Fourteen psi. Lock is sealed, ma'am."

"All right, people, let's go make cable."

She followed Stryski after he undogged the lock and stepped into the stuffy air. *Freelander* never smelled right. The dry air reeked of mold, of sweat, and the dust of long-dead human beings and their squalor. Sometimes she wondered if she was breathing the ghosts of the dead, sucking their wailing anguish into her lungs.

A single light panel, strung up and left by *Turalon* crewmen before they spaced, cast a hollow and yellow light on the lines of chairs in the waiting room and onto the scuffed sialon floor. Little motes, stirred by their presence, glowed in their handheld lights.

Kalico tugged her quetzal-hide jacket straight. She'd worn it instead of her suit because it was a tie to Donovan—a link to the sanity that existed on the other side of *Freelander*'s hull.

She checked her com. "Juri? Can you hear me?"

"Yes, ma'am. Loud and clear."

"Roger that. Keep the home fires burning in case we come running with the heebie-jeebies."

"'Firmative on that, ma'am. Watch yourself in there." A pause. *"Bateman has removed the crate with the carbon from the hold. He's floating it down to the manufacturing bay as we speak."*

Stryski and Bogarten led the way into the ship and down the corridor. No lights here but what they carried. The dingy walls seemed to close in as they moved inward toward the core. As angular acceleration decreased, they relied on handholds, and finally reached the freefall bay where Stryski and Bogarten had installed their precious carbon fiber extruding machine.

In the room's one dim light, Kalico anchored herself with a hand and watched through a grimy transparency as her people suited up in vacuum gear. One by one they cycled through the lock and floated out to help Bateman align the crate with the precious raw carbon. The container had to fit over the hopper just so. Then pins were removed and spring pressure squeezed the raw carbon into the machine's guts where it was heated, compressed, and spun into fibers.

Kalico gasped, swearing that something had just entered the room. She whirled, shining her light. Nothing. But she could feel the wrongness, like a viscous quality in the air.

Pus in a bucket, she hated *Freelander*.

"Supervisor?" Makarov's voice seemed to echo in her ear.

"Yes, Ensign?"

"You're not going to believe this, but I've got a shuttle on an inbound vector."

"The PA bird? What would they be doing—"

"Negative, ma'am. This one's reading a Corporate pipper. Definitely NOT Port Authority's bird. I'm sending a hail now. Haven't a clue as to who this is, but company is definitely coming."

23

Tamarland figured that he had a reasonable handle on the situation on Capella III from listening in on the planetary radio conversations over the last three days. Why they relied on old-fashioned radio when they could have been using photonics made no sense.

Whoever the people on Cap III were, they hadn't a clue that *Vixen* was in orbit. Impossible as it seemed, instead of a six-year exile, he'd stumbled upon a world ripe for the seizing. He could imagine Artollia smiling in anticipation. Maybe it wasn't like the Chairmanship, but it was better than nothing, and after the complicated gamesmanship he and Artollia had orchestrated back in Solar System, this would be like taking rations from a baby.

Tam had found his perfect opportunity to take the Supervisor by surprise when he heard the radio woman, O'Hanlan, announcing to Two Spot, *"The Supervisor is shuttling up to* Freelander *tomorrow with Bogarten and four of his crew to manufacture cable."*

Tam would be there, and the puzzle of Capella III's occupants would be solved on his terms. Backed by him and his two armed security officers.

Now he sat in the command chair as *Vixen*'s shuttle closed with the big mystery ship. He'd watched the Supervisor's shuttle dock through his own shuttle's telemetry.

In the seat beside him, First Officer Seesil Vacquillas looked pale and nervous. But then, there'd been more than enough frightened gazes and whispered conversations passing among the command crew.

When he'd asked Torgussen and Vacquillas point blank, they'd responded, "Nothing, sir."

Whatever they were afraid of, he'd let them keep it to themselves for the time being.

"Pilot, you can turn on the in-system navigational beacon. Let them know we're coming."

"Yes, sir." Mick Wilson told him, and a light on the instrument board illuminated.

It didn't take but thirty seconds before a voice asked, *"Inbound shuttle, please state your identification and purpose."*

"This is Corporate Advisor Tamarland Benteen, Corporate Survey Ship *Vixen*. IS-SE-17. We're inbound to dock at shuttle bay four. Please have personnel ready to receive us."

Silence.

He arched an eyebrow, glanced sidelong at Vacquillas. "Bet that took them by surprise."

"Lot of that going around, sir." If anything, she looked even more pale.

He glanced back of the command seat where his two security officers—armed and in uniform—were seated in the main cabin. Security Officer Huac Tu was in his twenties, a recent graduate from the academy. Jace Ali, in his thirties, was the veteran. Trained for hostile environment security, they wouldn't have been Tam's first choice for bracing the Supervisor, but they'd have to do.

Not that there was much chance of trouble. Corporate Supervisors were a separate and unique breed: They followed orders, implemented policy, and gave orders to inferiors. Their skill was organization and administration, not action.

She might outrank him, but in the end that would turn out to be a vulnerability on her part. He served Boardmember Shayne, second in power only to Radcek. Any action he decided to take, he could justify in Shayne's name, and as being by her instruction. With Solar System thirty light-years away, who'd know?

And if Supervisor Aguila were serving Radcek? First, she'd have no idea that Shayne had been toppled, and second, since Shayne and Radcek were locked in a battle to the death, any action Shayne's "scorpion" took to either defeat or destroy Aguila was all in the name of the game.

Poor woman, she's dead meat already and hasn't a clue.

The com announced, *"Corporate Shuttle, proceed to shuttle bay number four. You are authorized to dock. The Supervisor will meet you there as soon as she can return from the spindle. You are welcome to make yourself at home and await her arrival."*

A pause.

"Oh, and welcome to Freelander. *Good luck."*

"Make yourself at home?" Vacquillas asked. "Good luck? What's that all about?"

Tam savored the flavor of victory. "We've caught them completely off guard, First Officer. We've got them scrambling. Trust me, we'll gain a hell of a lot more by questioning them now than after they've had time to think it through."

"You make it sound like we're in some sort of competition."

"You tell me, First Officer. We arrive here to find an established mining colony. One that Dr. Shimodi says has to have been here for years given the size of that clay pit up north. And here's this ship, *Freelander.* Not a new vessel from the looks of her, and one that's not in the Corporate records. Someone knew about Cap III a long time ago. Has to be Radcek. Somehow he's run this entire operation without the Board finding out. We've stumbled upon the largest criminal conspiracy in human history."

"Jesus, I hope you're right."

"Want to explain that?"

"No. I mean . . . So you think *Tempest* was part of the cover-up?"

"Had to be. My bet is that when Boardmember Shayne ordered that I replace Maxim Grant at the last minute, the people running this operation were caught by complete surprise. If Grant were still in charge, *Vixen* would have probably become part of the cover-up."

"How? I mean, buy us all off? And the scientists, too?"

"Or they could have employed a more odious solution. Something involving deep-brain implants, excising areas of the memory and substituting their version of events. In the right physical psychiatric surgeon's hands, it would be as simple as skating on vacuum. Wouldn't be the first time, either."

"No shit?"

"You'd be surprised what kind of secrets are hidden in the deep archives."

"How do you know?"

"That was my job." He turned back to the security officers. "Do you both know who Boardmember Artollia Shayne is?"

They nodded. Of course they did; she was one of the most powerful human beings alive.

"This mission is operating under the Boardmember's single and unique authority. Do you understand? That means Board sanction at the highest levels."

Both of the security officers nodded, eyes wide.

"Given that I exercise that level of authority, when I give you an order, you are empowered, by the Board, to obey it without question."

"Yes, sir," they barked in unison.

"Any order," Tam stressed. "So, if I say arrest the Supervisor, you will do so. Immediately. Without question."

"Yes, sir."

Tam could feel Vacquillas' hard gaze boring into the side of his head, as he added, "Gentlemen, I just want to clarify my responsibilities vis-à-vis the mission. As you've overheard, we may well be in the middle of a huge criminal conspiracy. I will require your complete obedience."

"Yes, sir!" The enthusiasm was back.

To Vacquillas he said, "Now you know why Maxim Grant was recalled at the last instant, First Officer. But, to be honest, neither Boardmember Shayne nor the other members of the Board had any clue as to the scale or type of operation being run on Cap III. Otherwise, we'd have brought marines."

"Hope you're right, sir."

"That it's a criminal operation? Odd that you'd say that."

"Given the alternatives."

"Which are?"

"That we're not in the . . ." She shook her head. "Never mind. That's nuttier than some run-amok criminal conspiracy."

In the viewports the huge bulk of *Freelander* could be seen. Damn, that was a big ship. How had Radcek managed to construct such a thing without anyone knowing?

He watched as Pilot Wilson settled them down into a line of shuttle bays. Each was occupied by a delta-winged shuttle, all dark. No lights burning. The bays stygian and shadowed.

Then his view port dropped below the great ship's hull into darkness, the shuttle whining as it thrust to a stop.

With barely a tremor, Wilson settled the bird into the nest. Thumps and clangs sounded as the grapples engaged.

"Hard dock, people," Wilson announced. "Extending the lock." He watched his gauges. "We have a hard seal. Temperature is twenty-seven degrees Celsius on the other side. Normal atmosphere. Welcome aboard."

Tam unstrapped and stood, making his way to the main cabin. He'd dressed in natty black, and wore his full-length formal coat. Cut from the finest silk and tailored in Shanghai, it was his most treasured personal possession. He'd worn it at official Board functions, the gorgeous Shayne perched on his arm. And, even more to the point, it concealed his Talon 7 pistol with its smart rounds.

"First Officer?"

"Sir?"

"I need you to follow my lead. Speak only when spoken to."

"Yes, sir."

"This is odd," the pilot called. "It'll be a second. The other side's dead. We're having to use the shuttle's power to operate the lock." A pause. Finally lights flashed on the lock control. "You're good to go, Advisor."

"Oh brave new world." He pressed the hatch release. Heard a click. As the heavy hatch slid back, he strode forward.

Into . . . what?

He found himself in a waiting room. The place was lit by a single, dim, light panel. The others were dark. He blinked, waiting for his eyes to adjust, and was able to pick out trash scattered about and among the chairs. Smears marked the sialon floor.

And there was the odd odor: like the inside of a crypt, musty, somehow tainted. His instinct was to pull up the tail of his coat to breathe through.

"Screw me blind with a torque wrench," Vacquillas whispered.

Making a face, Tam stalked across the empty room, opened the hatch at the other end, and stepped into a black corridor beyond. He called, "Lights."

Nothing happened.

"Ship's AI. *Freelander*. Respond please."

Nothing.

Vacquillas was fingering along the wall. "Got the switch." A pause as she fiddled with it. "Give me a break. Still no lights."

"Hey! Fuck!" Security Officer Ali called, jumping and pulling his pistol. He whirled around, tense as a coiled spring.

"What?" Officer Tu demanded, clawing at his own pistol.

"It was . . . I mean, you saw that, right? Like it walked right through me." Ali was working his mouth, jaw muscles popping.

"What the hell are you talking about?" Tu was peering anxiously into the darkness.

"In Allah's name I swear it. Something like, passed . . . It was like it went right through me. No shit."

Tam fought a shiver himself. "Back to the waiting room, people. No sense in standing here in the dark. Ali, shake off your ghosts. There have to be hand lights on the shuttle. Go find us some."

"Yes, sir."

Ali moved with remarkable alacrity back through the room and disappeared into the hatch.

"What the hell happened here?" Vacquillas whispered the question hovering behind Tam's own lips.

Looking around at the dimly lit seats, the filth, Tam said, "This place looks like it's a mausoleum."

Vacquillas stepped over to the com panel. "AI, give me a ship's history."

She waited, staring at the dark holo. "Ship? *Freelander*, respond. This is First Officer Seesil Vacquillas. Respond, please."

The holo remained dark and silent.

"What the hell?" she growled under her breath.

"Advisor?" Tu asked. "What have we gotten ourselves into?"

Tam bit off a reply, his own anxiety rising. What was it about the room? Something just not sitting well. As if the very air was off, out of synch with reality.

Ho's words that day in astrogation came back to haunt him: *"It's like it's eating the beam."* Was that it? Like the very air was eating his bodily energy?

Ali emerged from the lock with five handheld torches. As he passed them around, he said, "Wilson's a little upset. Says he can't access any of the ship's systems through the umbilical."

"There may not be any ship's system to draw from," Vacquillas said. "I'm getting the spooky feeling that this thing's dead. How in thirteen levels of hell do you kill a ship like this?"

"In the case of *Freelander*," a voice called from the corridor, "it took one hundred and twenty-nine years. She didn't age well. Forget the ship's AI. Before they died, the crew chopped it out with an ax. You, however, Benteen, look as if not a day has passed since you disappeared."

Tam turned, staring at the apparition that emerged from the dark corridor beyond. The woman was tall, lithe, perfectly proportioned. Some kind of floppy-brimmed hat confined the thick raven hair that hung down over her shoulders. She wore an unusually cut leather jacket that shimmered in the dim light as if rainbow patterns flowed through it. Tight leather pants clung to long and toned legs. She had one hand propped on a military-grade pistol that was holstered on a heavy-duty utility belt with pouches. Tall boots crafted from the shining leather rose to her upper calves.

Only when she came close did he see the scars on her face and hands. Even more unsettling were the glacial-blue eyes she fixed on him. A clever smile bent her lips. "So, you're the famous scorpion. Welcome to Donovan."

"And just who, exactly, are you?" he asked, shocked at her use of the word *scorpion*. His hand slipped to the butt of his Talon 7.

"Kalico Aguila. Supervisor. I serve Boardmember Mika Taglioni. Currently I administer all Corporate assets on Donovan and run Corporate Mine."

"Never heard of Mika Taglioni."

"You wouldn't have. After your time. He wasn't born when you killed his grandfather. Clever bit of work, that. A tailored microRNA that caused the old man's immune system to literally devour his heart."

Impossible! Only Shayne knows!

A cold spear of disbelief chilled Tam to the core. "Who the hell are you? What kind of fucking game are you trying to play? Whatever it is, lady, you don't know the kind of hell you're messing with."

Vacquillas, despite orders, asked, "What's the date? Please. Tell me."

"Close as we can figure, relativity being what it is across thirty light-years, we're somewhere into late 2155."

Vacquillas actually staggered, as if struck.

"That's fucking space shit if I ever heard it!" Tam cried, stepping forward, his heart racing. "We just got here!"

"You've been missing for fifty years, Benteen. Just to clarify the historical record, did you kill Tayrell Torgussen and commandeer his ship? Historians have been debating that for half a century."

"What?" Vacquillas cried. "You killed Cap?"

"This is crazy! He's in astrogation aboard *Vixen*!"

He could feel himself losing control. She was playing him for an idiot, for a simple-minded fool. Wasn't anyone got away with shit like that. And this cold-eyed, pistol-packing slit wasn't any Supervisor.

"You're Radcek's soldier, aren't you?" The deadly smile fell into place. "Nice try."

The woman said, "Come on, I want to show you something. Maybe put the last fifty years into perspective."

And with that she turned, flipping on a handheld light and heading into the corridor's blackness.

"We're being played for idiots," he growled. "Ali, Tu, you be ready."

First there was the macabre waiting room that had to be a set of some kind. Then the ludicrous clothing and Supervisor act. Soon as he got an angle on the kind of game she was playing, he was going to shoot her himself.

24

The great quetzal pinned Talina between its front feet; the claws curved around her back. Talina was still stunned when the tongue shot into her mouth like a striking serpent.

The rope-like intrusion triggered her gag reflex, caused Talina to buck and dry heave. That implacable tongue followed every twist and jerk of her head, prodding, poking, filling her mouth. The intensity of the peppermint taste—concentrated to the point it brought tears—was almost beyond endurance. And the whole time the three black eyes atop the triangular head kept boring into Talina's.

It seemed an eternity.

And then she was free, cast loose to collapse on the ground, coughing, her mouth watering—eyes teared to the point she couldn't see. Her entire body shook, every muscle spasming and out of control.

When she finally could catch her breath, she shouted, "Fucking bullshit!" Mostly because no other words formed in her scattered mind.

Dragging a sleeve across her eyes, she cleared her vision and managed to collect her senses enough to stare up at the quetzal. Leaper and Diamond had stepped close behind, their triangular heads peering over her shoulders.

Leaper kept displaying fantastic threat patterns of iridescent crimson and midnight black. The beast's toothy mouth gaped, ready to strike. The clawed feet kept slashing suggestively at the air.

Kylee had shinnied out of the way and stood just beyond the circle of quetzals, peering in with wide blue eyes.

"Oh, damn," Talina managed between pants. "Next time, just kill me, all right? I haven't been that ill-used since I was dating Buck Berkholtz back in the academy."

She got her feet under her, staggered up, and rubbed her mouth before spitting to the side. She blinked, steadied herself, and faced the biggest one, Flash.

"That's the second time you've sneaked up behind me. Do it again, and I'll blow a hole through you."

The old quetzal expanded its collar; the colors and patterns could have been painted by a psychotic artist in his manic stage. But the creature's attention was on the other quetzals. Especially Leaper.

Then Diamond swiveled its head, uttered a sibilant whistle through its vents, and shot a series of pink, taupe, and turquoise patterns across its flared ruff. All the while its body was patterned in indigo and orange.

Leaper expelled irritation through the rear vents, and as quickly the crimson and black display vanished.

Talina ducked as the quetzals thrust their heads together, tongues lancing out and into each other's mouths to share molecules.

Talina took the moment to locate her rifle, not more than a pace to her right. She took a step, started to bend, only to have a menacing claw extended toward her abdomen. Looking up, she stared into Flash's lateral eye and read its warning.

Okay, so Flash thought that was a bad idea. Given the claw dimpling her coveralls, she could live with that. Besides, her pistol was still on her utility belt.

The quetzals were sharing the kind of colors and patterns that would have triggered a migraine in a marble bust.

Leaper let out an ear-splitting shriek that caused Talina to clap hands to her ears. The crimson and black were back. Then the quetzal wheeled, and like a blur, vanished into the tree line.

"Why do I guess he's not happy?"

Kylee said, "He was really looking forward to killing you. Figured he could share your molecules as easily when he digested you as when you were alive."

"Charming." Talina glanced back and forth between the other two, realizing she didn't have a clue about what the flipping beasts wanted or how to deal with them.

Kylee told her, "Leaper blames me for Rocket's death. He would have learned my body long ago if it wasn't for Flash and Diamond. And Diamond's not sure. Half the time he thinks Flash shouldn't have let me live either."

"Didn't know quetzals were so complicated. So, Flash is the leader?"

"He's fourth elder."

"Age matters, huh?"

"Among quetzals. Diamond and Leaper will kill him one of these days for his molecules."

"Damn, you'd think they were Romans."

Again Talina started to bend down for her rifle.

Again Flash flicked out a claw.

This time, she held his eyes, reached down, and pushed the deadly claw forcefully back. "The experiment isn't over. Understand?"

And with that, she picked up the rifle, saw Diamond tense to spring, but calmly hung the gun over her shoulder. Turning, she stared the younger quetzal in the eyes, her heart still hammering like it was about to burst from her chest. "So, there it is. Now, which one of you is going to tell me what the hell you figured out from those molecules I just brought you?"

Flash chittered in what she'd come to learn was quetzal laughter. The big quetzal flipped its head, as if indicating for her to precede him.

"What's up?" Talina asked Kylee.

"Breakfast," Kylee told her. "It's morning. Everyone's hungry."

"As long as it's not you or me on the menu, what have they got in mind?"

"They catch roos, I pick whatever from the garden."

Talina gave the old quetzal a grin. The demon quetzal in her belly, clearly upset, was bouncing around like a manic handball. Eat? She'd rather throw up. Then she forced herself to wink at Diamond as she struggled to find even a modicum of courage. "Well, I'm up for raspberries, how about you?"

Kylee, looking back and forth, said, "Leaper won't let this go, Talina. He's really upset."

"Yeah, well, we'll deal with that when we get to it."

She glanced at the tree line. Leaper was out there in the forest, carrying a grudge. The last time that had happened, people had died. And the only people here were her and Kylee.

25

Kalico followed the familiar way through the transportee section, her light cutting a cone through the blackness. The lights had failed again. *Turalon*'s technicians had cobbled together wiring for this section of the ship before they spaced for Solar System. Now it was blacker than the sewers of hell. And maybe just as fraught with horrors.

She could feel things in the air around her. Fart-sucking hell, she hated *Freelander*.

"Supervisor?" Bogarten asked through the com. *"You need us for anything? Backup? Whatever?"*

"Negative. Keep extruding cable. We don't want to be here for a second longer than it takes us to load up and beat feet out of here."

"A big roger on that!"

She stopped at the hatch to the crew's quarters. Glanced back at Benteen and the first officer who had introduced herself as Seesil Vacquillas. "This is where it gets a bit weird."

"Define weird," First Officer Vacquillas muttered from the side of her mouth. The two security guys looked as if they'd already shit themselves. A couple of times.

"The hypothesis is that *Freelander* dragged some of the universe she passed through into ours. Sort of like a bubble of unreality. Time's not right here. It kind of echoes, like waves. You can run into yourself, or at least an image of yourself from the past or the future."

"Maybe that's why our sensors couldn't get a reading." Vacquillas kept licking her lips as if she were nervous. Smart woman.

"Yeah, *Freelander* sucks energy. Drains it away into somewhere else."

Tamarland, however, had a crazy glitter in his dark eyes. The guy was scary. No wonder Artollia Shayne had called him her scorpion.

"What happened to the people?" Benteen asked.

"Dead." Kalico opened the hatch into the crew section. Thank the flipping lucky stars, the lights came on.

"What's this?" It was the ship-wise Vacquillas who immediately picked up on the anomaly.

The first officer was referring to the walls, covered with thousands of lines of script. Lines upon lines of it. Sometimes the flowing loops and letters were so overwritten they obscured the writing beneath. Vacquillas bent close to stare in disbelief.

Kalico told them, "Mostly they're odes to the dead. They'd write sayings over and over, like 'The exhalation of death is the breath of life. Draw it fully into your lungs.' Always makes me wish I was wearing a mask with a micron filter. Which brings me back to your question, Advisor Benteen."

Kalico hooked a thumb back over her shoulder toward the transportees' deck. "As soon as the crew figured out they were lost, they murdered the transportees. All five hundred of them. Suffocated them. Vacuum froze the bodies and added them to the hydroponics over the years as the chemistry broke down in the tanks."

"Jesus."

"You a Christian, First Officer?"

"No, my mother always said it when she was shocked."

"Christians, Jews, and Muslims don't do well in here. The Buddhists and Hindus don't creep out quite as much, but *Freelander* still gives them the soul-shakes."

Kalico led the way down the corridor with its endless writing. "Shig thinks they began worshipping the dead. They'd murdered them, right? And were living off the corpses. Dropping the bodies, one by one, into the hydroponics. Maybe it was the guilt, but they believed they became the dead."

"None of this makes sense," Benteen growled, his eyes like wary slits. "We're not even a month out of Solar System."

"How long was the transition?" Kalico asked, watching Vacquillas' expression. It was like the first officer already knew and just wanted to hear it confirmed.

"Instantaneous," Benteen told her. "We thought the inversion had failed. One minute we were talking to Neptune Control, the next we were in Capella's system."

"Sorry to piss in your milk, Advisor Benteen, but it really has been a half century since you made your escape from Solar System."

"You're sucking empty vacuum when you say that shit," Benteen declared. "Hey, Supervisor, or whoever the fuck you are, I was in astrogation. Sitting right there. It was like flipping a switch. One minute we're there, the next we're here. Torgussen is still chafing in his shorts. The guy's desperate to fill the tanks so he can invert back to Solar System and report."

He paused, a canny expression building. "But that's your game, isn't it? As soon as *Vixen* spaces back, your operation here will be blown. We'll report it all. Expose your whole covert organization."

Kalico had watched Vacquillas stop short, eyes wide. Yep, she'd definitely figured it out, that it really was 2155.

Kalico casually asked, "How much fuel did you burn? Maybe eighty percent?"

The first officer closed her eyes, seemed to sway. "You say it took this ship one hundred and twenty-nine years?"

"That was what they experienced in whatever universe or dimension the inversion pushed them into. Transition time in our universe? A little more than two and a half years. *Freelander* left Solar System six months ahead of *Turalon*. Got here a couple of weeks *after* we did. And the other thing you probably need to know: *Vixen* was the first of four exploration and survey ships lost on the transition to Donovan. And after the colony was established, another six of the big cargo ships like *Freelander* have vanished. After *Freelander* and now *Vixen*? Maybe they'll show up. But God alone knows where they will have gone, or what relative time they will have passed in whatever dimension or universe they went to."

She led the way into the crew mess and flicked on the lights.

An eerie shiver—one not of this existence—rolled through her like a wave. There it stood, looking just as it had that first time she'd seen it.

"Blessed Allah," the security officer called Ali said as he realized what he was seeing.

The structure was a dome, maybe two-and-one-half meters in diameter and four tall. The *Freelander* crew had built it in the middle of the large mess hall. In a way it reminded Kalico of the old American capitol dome, its top rounded like a half sphere. What might have been misconstrued for the vertical colonnade upon which the dome rested was actually a support crafted from a thousand and some human femora topped by a ring of human skulls that ran around the circumference. Then another colonnade of as many humeri, or arm bones. Then another ring of skulls upon which the dome itself rested. They'd constructed the dome of tibiae, radii, ulnae, and the flat bones of the pelvis and shoulders. Intricate decorations consisting of flowers composed of vertebrae, curlicues made of clavicles, and chevrons of finger bones covered the entire surface like some mad barococo ornamentation.

"What the hell?" Vacquillas asked.

"Their shrine to the dead." Kalico stepped to the side, watching the newcomers ease closer. "You can see the last skeleton. An old woman. The final survivor, she died right there in the doorway. Wasn't anyone left to clean her bones and wire them into the temple."

Benteen was shaking his head, his hand still on the pistol inside his coat.

"No need to pull that Talon, mister scorpion. I could give a damn who you were back in the day."

He pivoted on his heel, shaken, all the more deadly for it. "No one knows that she calls me her scorpion. Who the fuck are you?"

"It's in the history books, Benteen." She tapped the side of her head. "Implant. Pulled up all the data the moment Ensign Makarov reported that your shuttle came from *Vixen*. Anyone who plays the game of Corporate politics studies Radcek. Boardmember Shayne came within hours of overthrowing him. She was that close, making her move, when he had her arrested. Had his psychiatric techs cut every last scrap out of her brain. Dismembered her mind the way a butcher does a hog's carcass; they found out all about you."

"Boardmembers do not submit other Boardmembers to that kind of procedure. That's the unspoken rule, damn it."

"Until Radcek." She crossed her arms, fingers of her left hand tapping suggestively on the grip of her holstered pistol.

"Maybe, because it was a first, and maybe it was because she loved you with all of her heart, and maybe because of the number of prominent people the two of you murdered, compromised, and blackmailed. Whatever the reason people still remain preoccupied with your story."

"I don't have to listen to this. What if I just take the shuttle back to *Vixen*? As soon as Torgussen has enough fuel in the tanks, I can space. We've got the secret to instantaneous transition, now. Your whole covert operation here will be blown."

Vacquillas was looking at him like he'd lost his mind, but seemed to think better of saying anything.

Kalico walked up to the structure; her skin crawled like a thousand ants as she ran her fingers over the polished human bones. "Doesn't matter that it's been fifty years. You're still under a death sentence. The Taglionis would insist." She turned to face him. "If you go back, you'll die."

"Not to mention that it will be another fifty years," Vacquillas said in a hoarse whisper. "Everyone we knew. Well, most of them, anyway. They're dead, aren't they? Brothers and sisters grown to old age? Parents gone?"

"That's my guess."

Kalico gave the scowling Benteen a deadly smile. "So, Advisor, if you ship back in *Vixen,* it will be a whole century since you made your escape. Maybe by then you'll be such an historical oddity, they won't execute you. Maybe they'll just put you in a museum."

Benteen blinked, his hand finally leaving his pistol to hang limply. "You say Radcek had them dissect her brain?"

"The bastard was making a point. You and Boardmember Shayne came within a whisker of destroying him. He didn't want anyone else to try, no matter what kind of precedent mental dissection set."

"The tanks on *Freelander* have any fuel in them?"

"They do."

"So, if we fueled, inverted symmetry, I could get back in time. Maybe figure a way to save her."

"You don't *get* it!" Vacquillas thrust herself into his face. "She's been *dead* for *fifty* years. As dead as these bones. What seemed instantaneous? It wasn't. We're fucked, Advisor. We've lost everything."

Kalico watched the man's lips quiver, a glistening in his eyes. And as quickly they were replaced by a deadly calm. "But it wasn't even a second."

"It was *fifty years*." Vacquillas kept struggling to get the man to grasp the concept. "Look around. This is why Supervisor Aguila brought us here. This is the lesson. *Freelander* inverted symmetry and spent one hundred and twenty-nine years in a transition that only took two and a half years in our universe. *Vixen* just made a transition that seemed instantaneous to us. But it took fifty years in our universe. Something's wrong with the physics, Advisor."

He swallowed hard. "I don't fucking understand."

"Welcome to Donovan," Kalico told him, and wondered how long it was going to take before she had to murder the scorpion. Or if she should just draw her pistol and shoot him down right there on the spot.

26

The awl in Talina's hands needed sharpening as she punched it through the carbon-fiber cloth. If she had to be exiled anywhere on Donovan, Mundo Base was perfect. The abandoned research base was loaded with usable materials for survival, not to mention the farm.

She sat in the shade of the ramada that protected the cactus and continued to stitch the carbon cloth together. The material would make a serviceable pair of moccasins for Kylee. Ugly as sin, but no slug could chew its way through and into the girl's foot. Behind her the wreckage of Mundo's ruined dome added to the feeling of defeat.

Worse, images of the ancient Maya bowl she'd broken kept replaying. Especially that moment when it hit the tile floor and exploded. How the shattered fragments bounced and slid across the Saltillos. Felt that gut-numbing sense of horror. Even at six, Talina had known how valuable the bowl was. Had realized the magnitude of what she'd done.

And there was that damn glyph. It always landed face up and signified *Way*: the intermixed notion of the animal-possessed spirit dreamer, part human part animal. A Maya concept so fundamental to the notion of becoming more than just mere human.

Kylee, washed now, her hair shining, her face clean, fiddled with a ratchet, spinning it around and around by an extension and listening to it click.

Out in the direct sun, Flash slept, his hide a snowy white to reflect Capella's energy. His mouth gaped, the three vents at the root of the tail wide open and jetting air. Quetzals were incredibly efficient when it came to dissipating heat.

For once the quetzal in her gut was quiet, somehow pacified by the chaos in Talina's dreams and visions.

"You didn't sleep well," Kylee told her.

"Nothing but quetzal dreams." Talina blinked, the afterimages, even after all the hours she'd been awake, playing through her head. "Stuff I can't understand. Images, like memories. I swear, this is what dissociative disorder must be like. You know, seeing things, hearing voices? But none of them are human. And, like, they're all different. More and more it's Rocket and you when you were little."

"What does he say?"

"Say? Nothing. It's moments. Like the time you and he stole Rondo's prize squash. The one he was going to save for New Year's supper."

"Rondo never did figure out who did that," Kylee said with a grin.

"Here's what I don't get. Rondo was a big man, wasn't he? Thick black hair, wavy. And he had a little scar by the side of his left eye. The lower incisors were crooked. When he laughed, he always put his hands to his belly."

"Yeah. That's him. So?"

"So I never met Rondo. He was fourth ship. I came on seventh, and Rondo had been crosswise with Clemenceau before I set foot on Donovan. Rondo made it a point to be absent from the base the few times I was here with the Supervisor. And he never, ever, came to Port Authority while I was there." Talina gestured with the awl. "So how can I know what he looked like?"

"That's Rocket's memory."

"You're telling me that Rocket's TriNA is somehow putting an image of Rondo in my brain."

Kylee shrugged. "You once told me that the information only went one way. I told you then that you were wrong."

"Do you know how tough it is to get my head around this? I never learned all this RNA stuff. I'm a security officer, damn it. This is all voodoo."

"What's voodoo?"

"Magic. Spooky weird supernatural spirit stuff."

Kylee broke out in laughter, her teeth shining. Flash's eyes popped open, the one on the right swiveling to take in the scene, and then closing again.

"Talina, it's simple. Remember when you told me that quetzal TriNA is like our deoxyribonucleic acid? You said Dya told you, right? That the quetzal molecules were smart? They're using the imaging parts of your brain."

"How?"

"With transfer RNA. Duh!"

"How would you know? And what the hell's transfer RNA?"

Kylee gave her an exasperated look and whirled the ratchet around a couple of fast turns. "Oh, hey. I'm a microbiologist and psychologist like my mother. I understood metabolic pathways and gene expression when I was four. I was using CRISPR 12 to create organisms when I was six. In terrestrial life, cellular biology is everything. Donovanian life gets a little more complicated because the cells don't have a nucleus. And we see a lot more variability in the TriNA. Probably because everything's in threes instead of twos."

"I don't understand."

Kylee raised her eyebrows as if she were dealing with an idiot. "Two times two is what?"

"Four."

"Three times three is . . . ?"

"Nine."

"Which is the bigger number?"

"Nine."

"Right. Now, multiply that by sixteen, which is the number of possible combinations of adenine, thiamine, guanine, and cytosine."

"Um."

"One hundred and forty-four. Which is the power per base pair in TriNA. When you do the same math with potential combinations for the DNA from two parents, you only get sixty-four possible combinations per allele. Cubed is always more powerful than squared."

"So, what does the TriNA want?"

"To understand us. That's the purpose of evolution. To understand."

"Your mother and Cheng wonder if a quetzal is just a TriNA molecule's way of living forever. That the molecules just hop from quetzal to quetzal. It's complicated. I'm not sure I get it yet, either. So, help me here. If something happens to Flash, do you think Diamond's going to stand up for you? Or is he going to join Leaper in ripping you in two and making a meal out of you?"

Kylee's wistful smile matched her vacant gaze as she said, "Guess it's kind of a problem, huh?"

"Your mother's been torturing herself ever since she left you behind. You know that, don't you?"

"Yeah, she left me that radio."

"You've got an out any time you want to take it."

"Can't." The desolate look was back, the girl's gaze going to the dirt at her feet.

"Why?"

"'Cause death isn't the same with humans. Rebecca and Shantaya . . ." Kylee's face worked, guilt and pain glistening behind her eyes.

She'd watched Rebecca and Shantaya, people she'd loved and known all of her life, eaten before her eyes. How could she go back to her family, look them in the face, and not be feeling worthless as spit? Like it wasn't her fault?

Kylee, like any child, turned guilt into anger, declaring, "I can't go back to Port Authority. I won't do it. Those people would have killed Rocket. I want them all dead. Even more than Leaper wants me dead. I hate them, Talina. Really fucking hate them. And if they threw you out, they'd kill me faster than Leaper would."

The kid had a point. But damn, what was that like, to only be coming on eleven and realize how precarious your life was?

"Yeah, well, maybe we'll figure something out. Flash doesn't know it, but he's just picked up another backer. You like doing equations? How's this grab you? Flash plus Talina and an automatic rifle more than equals Diamond and Leaper."

The hallucination took her by surprise: Talina was terrified, her hide reflecting the vegetation, stone, and tumbled soil of the canyon wall. Her hearts were pumping, each intake of breath filtered through her mouth, venting fear along her tail.

In a moment, it would be morning. The eastern horizon was growing brighter by the moment.

She could hear the hunter. Feel the vibrations as gravel crunched under the hunter's feet, sense the nearing presence. Implacable, unreasoning. All of them, empty, devoid of thought. Impossible creatures. Their very existence defied experience.

She had made her gamble, that she could find a small one. Devour it, learn it, and understand.

For three days now, she'd run. No rest. Elude them, she might. But each time the flying things would eventually find her. How? And why did they serve the monsters? The things weren't even alive.

So they'd chased her here, to this last canyon. Beyond its head lay open ground, devoid of hiding places. Nor could she run. Her body had exhausted its reserves, had started to digest itself for sustenance.

And the hunter stepped even closer.

Talina could hear the rasping of the thing's clothing. Smell the peculiar odor of oils, salts, and fetid breath.

And then came the chime. Surely the monster, empty as it was, wouldn't understand the importance of the sound.

As the harmonic wave passed, she was the center of the dead spot. And yes, the human had stopped. Talina could almost hear the being's curious, thumping heart.

She opened her eyes, staring into death. The human had the tube up, was staring through the optic, right into Talina's soul.

She leapt, feeling the impact of the bullet as it tore through her flesh . . .

"Talina?" A hand grabbed her shoulder, shaking her.

"Fuck!" Talina fought her way through the vision, back to the ramada. She sucked a full breath. Aware that Flash had raised his head, the three eyes fixed on hers.

"Where where you?"

"Blood Mountains." Talina grunted out an uncertain laughter. "I was being hunted. By myself. Reliving it from the quetzal's perspective."

Kylee's gaze had intensified. "It was just like you were here and then gone."

"Yeah." Talina rubbed the back of her neck, feeling the roots of a blinding headache wind through her brain. "Wish that damned TriNA was out of my system. Wish I could just be me. How do you do it? You and Rocket were bonded for years. But you always stayed you."

Kylee pursed her lips, frowned. "I could help you."

"Oh? Got a way of washing all these quetzal molecules out of my tissues?"

"I can give you some of mine. The ones from Rocket."

"You mean . . . swap spit?"

The little girl nodded.

"I *don't* kiss little girls. Reeks of pedophilia." But she'd done it once in a desperate attempt to bring Kylee back from catatonia. It was different when the girl was awake and in her right mind.

Kylee's musical laughter rose on the hot air. "Yeah, but it's not, silly. I want your molecules. I've only got three quetzal molecules in me. You've got a whole bunch more."

"Why in the hell would you want them? They're not friendly."

"For the same reason you do. I want to understand."

And with that, Kylee leaned forward and pressed her lips against Talina's.

This isn't right.

But the rush of peppermint had already filled her mouth.

27

The notion was incredible. Beyond belief. Dortmund sat with his back rigid, arms crossed, as he glared across the conference table at Captain Torgussen and Advisor Benteen. The sober-eyed First Officer Vacquillas might have been carved of stone where she sat on the captain's right. Engineer Ho hunched at the table's head, looking like his guts had been kicked out.

The other members of the scientific team were situated around the table, expressions in various stages from outright disbelief to stunned.

Fifty years?

"I really do not understand this," Dortmund told them. "How could this happen?"

But nothing else explained *Freelander* or the colony.

Ho said glumly, "It's got to be an error in the math that got us here. Something in the predictive statistics programmed into the n-dimensional qubit matrix of the computers. Some deviation in the statistical package they uploaded from *Tempest*.

"Like *Freelander*, we went into a different universe. At least, that's the best guess we have. Some part of the multiverse where we didn't experience time. What passed as an instant in that universe was the equivalent of fifty years in ours."

"Why did time stop for us but not the computers? I mean, they should have experienced an instantaneous transition, right? They shouldn't have had time to work the math, flawed or not." Torgussen rubbed his temples, as if soothing a headache. "Some unexpected warping of time?"

"If time even exists," Vacquillas said wearily. "So much of modern physics is based on the hypothesis that what we perceive as time is an illusion. Nothing more than the changing relationships between particles in an eternal now."

"Hey, I'm not a physicist!" Torgussen barked.

Ho mumbled, "Whatever happened to us, it's a physics we can't even conceive of. When you force a bubble of our time-space into another dimension, you'd damn well better expect spooky shit to happen."

"It's spooky, all right." Vacquillas' eyes had gone dull.

"Let's get back to the problem," Benteen said bitterly. "I'm still not sure that this is everything that woman claiming to be a Supervisor says."

"You saw that ship, that temple of bones." Vacquillas shook her head. "You felt that same creepy sensation. Like Aguila said, it's dragged a bubble of wherever it was to here. That's where the energy is going. Leaking away into whatever universe that derelict came from."

Ho said shakily, "Symmetry inversion isn't working like the theoreticians said it would. Given what happened to us? *Freelander*? Those ships Aguila said were missing? Something's really wrong."

"Enough, already. These are things we can't answer for the time being," Dortmund insisted. "Let's deal with the immediate problem: What the hell has happened to my planet? This is a horrendous disaster. Humans are crawling all over down there. The entire biosphere is contaminated."

"Whatever happened, it occurred sometime in the last fifty years, Doctor," Torgussen said. "Maybe the records are in Port Authority."

"We need to get down there." Dortmund narrowed his eyes, glaring at Benteen. For once he was so enraged he didn't care that the man scared him.

"That's one vote." Benteen looked around. "What about the rest of you?"

Shimodi said, "You're saying that we've been gone from home for fifty years? My kid sister is seventy? Mom and Dad, they'd be in their hundreds?"

"And the chances are almost certain that if we refill the tanks, it'll be another fifty years back." Ho was fingering the tabletop as if it were a novel material. "That's a hundred years. No one we knew will be alive."

Vacquillas said, "The only upside—assuming everything happens the same way again—is that we arrive as young as we are now. Like Aguila said, we can be museum pieces. Even the scorpion here."

Dortmund perked up as Benteen faced the first officer. "If you ever call me that again, I will gut you and leave you to bleed."

Vacquillas turned a terrified shade of pale.

"Advisor Benteen, I've listened to my first officer's report. What's your explanation of this scorpion claim?" Torgussen asked.

"None of your damned business."

To Dortmund's surprise, the captain didn't back away. "Seesil, could you tell the others what the Supervisor said?"

Vacquillas bit her lip, looking away.

"That's an order, First Officer." Torgussen pointed at Benteen. "And I don't give a damn if you're the Advisor. This ship and her personnel come first. So, what's the story?"

It was Benteen who said, "I was appointed to *Vixen* by Boardmember Shayne at the last minute. Before her arrest by that shit-sucking Radcek. Let's say that my only concern is the ultimate success of my—"

Vacquillas blurted, "Supervisor Aguila says he's under a death sentence back in Solar System for murdering Boardmember Taglioni. That among other things, he's an assassin, extortion artist, and blackmailer. Aguila says Shayne called him her scorpion."

Dortmund leaned forward. "You're an assassin?"

Benteen's lips had pressed into a thin line. Then he said, "Politics at the Board level are played using much more sanguine rules than in your cutthroat university, Doctor. A fact that you might want to commit to that allegedly superior memory of yours."

"In addition," Torgussen said, "Supervisor Aguila was kind enough to provide me with some of her historical files on Shayne and the scorpion. After reviewing them, I have decided to take precautionary action."

Dortmund was as surprised as everyone else when Tu and Ali entered, side arms drawn and expressions cowed. How the hell had Torgussen orchestrated it so well?

They stepped up to either side of and behind Benteen and pressed the muzzles of their guns into the man's back, Torgussen said, "Officer Ali, you will place the Advisor in bonds and transport him to the holding cell until further notice."

Even as he spoke, Torgussen leaned across and slipped a sleek black pistol from a holster inside the Advisor's jacket.

Dortmund and his colleagues blinked. The man had a pistol? Here? On this ship? The sudden revelation sent a shiver down Dortmund's spine.

Tu clapped binders onto the Advisor's wrists as the man rose.

Dortmund thought Benteen's expression might have been likened to chiseled stone, but the rage burning behind the man's eyes was a reflection of the fires of Hell.

Only after the Advisor was marched out did Torgussen sigh and lay the pistol on the table. Dortmund stared at it the way he might have were it a black mamba.

Torgussen said, "I have to tell you, having that man aboard has kept me awake at night. Calling him the scorpion isn't the slightest bit of an understatement."

"What are you going to do with him?" Dortmund demanded.

"Kalico Aguila is a Supervisor. I'll leave his fate up to her."

Shimodi said, "So, the Advisor's a criminal? We're fifty years out of our time? There's a ghost ship in orbit around Cap III? And it could take us another fifty years to get home? How much more bizarre can this get?"

"It still doesn't solve our dilemma. What are we going to do?" Dortmund felt as brittle as cracked glass. This was a disaster—a complete and total mess.

Kobi Sax rubbed the back of her neck. "Fifty years? It's really 2155? I say we go ahead, adapt the mission to the new realities, and do science."

Shanteel Jones said woodenly. "How palatable is it to go back in *Vixen*? Arrive in Solar System in another fifty years? I mean, doesn't it make more sense to await the arrival of a ship that makes it in normal time, and when it does, take it back?"

"What's normal time?" Ho wondered.

Dortmund felt his heart hammering against his ribs. A hollow sensation filled his gut. His pristine planet was crawling with filthy humans. Someone did that. Some person during the last fifty years was ultimately responsible for ruining his world. Everything he'd planned . . . gone.

An entire life's work!

The anger and injustice was like a searing in his soul. The emotional impact akin to finding out that one's fragile and precious virgin daughter had been not only brutally raped, but was now pregnant and oozing syphilis and gonorrhea.

He snapped, "You all may do what you will. I am going down there. I am going to document everything. The extent of the contamination. How much humans have polluted the planet. Every single ecological crime that has been committed against that world and its organisms."

"It could be huge, Dortmund," Jones told him. "Might take you the rest of your life."

"What's my life worth?" He glared around the table. "Hmm? I had a chance. We all did. Whoever authorized the establishment of those colonies without proper study and guidelines has already taken my life. Destroyed everything I hoped for. Now I am going to accumulate the evidence of his or her crimes. And when I take it back to Solar System, I will use it to gut the Board."

"Brave words," Shimodi told him with an ironic smile. "If what they say is true, it's fifty years. What if your culprit is dead?"

"Then I will so damn him in history's opinion that his name is reviled for the rest of eternity."

Shimodi shot back, "But you're just the voice for one camp, Doctor. You're a preservationist. Don't the evolutionists have just as valid a point?"

"Figures that you, a geologist, would bring that up. Your only goal, Doctor Shimodi, is the mineral exploitation of the planet, and God help whatever poor life-forms happen to get in the way of the excavators and earthmovers."

"Come on," she goaded. "As you note, the damage is done. For all intent and purposes, the evolutionists have won. Aren't you the least bit curious as to how biological adaptation is reacting to the admixture of terrestrial life into an entirely new biosphere?"

"We've seen it." Dortmund rapped the table, surrendering to Shimodi's baiting. "All over Earth. And that was before the disaster of global warming. What was the culmination, Doctor? Hmm? Nothing but the most massive extinction event since the Permian Extinction two hundred and fifty-two million years ago."

"And you think we're going to see that here?" Sax asked.

"I think we're going to find a planet in the first stages of conflagration," Dortmund told her.

"So, you're going to make them pay?" Shimodi was smiling, as if in victory.

"Watch me, Doctor. Just watch me."

28

The clouds were rolling in from the east. Fluffy white masses of cumulus, they were as good as a promise that it would rain again that evening.

Kalico stared up at the patches of blue that retreated to the west. Donovan's sky had that deeper, more turquoise color than Earth's sky. Or at least Earth's sky as it currently existed.

She laced her fingers into the chain-link fence and clung to the wire as she searched the sky and listened for the sound of the shuttle.

Vixen had taken fifty years to make what seemed an instantaneous transition from Solar System to Donovan. *Freelander* had taken one hundred and twenty-nine years. Ships were still out there, lost. Or traveling through whatever permutation of time. Was *Turalon* halfway back to Solar System? Or had she lost herself in some unknowable universe?

What the hell did it mean in the grand sense of things? For Solar System? For humanity?

Beside her, Shig Mosadek and Yvette Dushane clung to the wire with equal tenacity. They, too, scanned the skies, as did the crowd of people who'd come for the unexpected excitement of not only new people, but the appearance of a ship thought lost for the last fifty years. That just wasn't an everyday occurrence in Port Authority.

Kalico's pilot had left her shuttle off to the side, closer to the five-high stacks of shipping containers.

"Would have preferred a cargo ship," Shig said thoughtfully. "Lot of wealth stacked up ready for shipment back to Solar System."

Kalico nodded, having set her sights on the exploration ship's rations. As a Corporate Supervisor, she'd already made her requisition for *Vixen*'s supplies. Torgussen had no idea of the bargaining power he'd already surrendered to Corporate Mine.

And yes, that included coffee!

Yvette said, "If *Vixen* can just drop out of the sky after fifty years, who knows? Maybe the rest will as well. You might have *Nemesis, Governor Han Xi, Tableau,* or any of the other missing ships pop in tomorrow."

"I just hope that *Turalon* is halfway home. Been counting down the time. If everything's running according to schedule, she should be a little less than a year away from popping back into orbit outside Neptune."

"We all have our hopes pinned on that happy fact." Shig paused. "Sometimes I wish I was a pagan. That I might sacrifice a crest or chamois at midnight under a full moon in the belief that such an offering of blood and life would affect the quantum nature of reality."

"Hey, I'm not holding you back," Yvette told him.

"What are you going to do with Benteen?" Kalico asked.

"He will have to take his chances here," Shig said wistfully.

"I've told you what kind of man he is."

"Yeah, we know." Yvette didn't sound happy. "It'd be nice to think that he'll step off that shuttle, say, 'Welcome to a new life,' and find a nice quiet occupation as a farmer, prospector, or history teacher."

"It's something of a moral quandary for us," Shig said. "We're not Corporate here. He's welcome as long as he does nothing to infringe on the rights of others. Nor do we care that he's under a death sentence back in Solar System." He smiled. "Wasn't that long ago, that Yvette, me, and Talina were going to be shot for high crimes if I recall."

Kalico cast him a knowing glance. "Sometimes I'm still tempted."

"Oh, silly you," Shig replied humbly. "With whom would you drink wine and share the burdens of command? Talina's vanished. Yvette doesn't drink but once in a blue moon. And, I'm told, Donovan's months don't line out the way they do back on Earth, so we really don't have a blue moon."

Kalico replied with a knowing grin, feeling the scars in her cheeks pull. "Good point. No firing squad for Shig.

But, I'm serious. You might find that Tamarland Benteen is a different kind of fish. Talina would call him a quetzal. Or she would have, back in the day."

Kalico looked around at the crowd. "Actually, if she were here, I could just tell her, 'Tal, put a bullet in Benteen the moment he sets foot on dirt. If you think Deb Spiro was bad, that woman couldn't lick the spit off Benteen's boots.'"

"We already have one psychopath to deal with." Yvette made a face. "Cunning bastard that he is. Half the parents in town are singing his praises, if warily so."

Kalico told them, "Benteen's an interesting study. Absolutely ruthless and driven. He had several opportunities to betray Artollia Shayne in order to gain even greater reward, but didn't. They made a remarkable team; Benteen loved her. Wanted to see her take the Chairmanship. And once there, he was apparently happy to lurk in her shadow and continue eliminating any opposition that might have arisen."

"Assuming he wasn't playing her." Yvette leaned against the wire, shifting her fingers.

"You should have seen him on *Freelander*."

"No thanks."

"The guy was cool as an ice block right up to the point when I mentioned that Radcek dissected Shayne's brain. Like flipping a switch. He knew she was arrested, right? That's why he made his escape in the first place. Like he'd come to terms that she'd lost. But when he learned that she'd been tortured and abused by Radcek's psychiatric team, he was all set to grab *Vixen* and space back to save her."

At that moment, Dan Wirth appeared out of the crowd, stepping up in all of his dapper glory. The man wore a tailored shirt made of the local fabric, a quetzal-hide vest bedecked with rhodium chains that shone in the light, and form-fitting chamois pants that tucked into knee-high quetzal boots. He was bareheaded, his wavy light-brown hair perfectly coiffed. That devil-may-care lady-charmer smile—dimples and all—lay on his lips; and the twinkle glinted from his brown eyes. She knew that face, the one he used to allay suspicions about his true nature.

"Why, I do declare," Wirth cried. "Supervisor Aguila,

come down from the mountain. What an honor you do us on this glorious day. And what a monumental occasion. A ship, lo and behold, once thought lost to the ages, has returned to us. Come to see the new prospects, have you?"

Kalico narrowed an eye. "Given that you're here, I'm not the only one. Got to tell you, Dan, it's a survey ship. Small crew, mostly scientists and technicians. Not much you can skin them out of. Not to mention they're a bit traumatized to find out that while they were away the universe has aged another fifty years." No need to tell him she'd already beaten everyone to the *Vixen*'s best resources.

"Skin them out of? Where, possibly, could you have developed such a low opinion of me? But then, one never knows where one will find talent, Supervisor." He arched a provocative brow. "Made any bomb threats lately?"

"Haven't had to. Your spy has been conspicuously quiet. No mysterious agents in the night have been threatening my peace and health." She thinned her lips. "Though you might be warned. Tamarland Benteen's on that ship. I doubt you'd know who Artollia Shayne was, but Benteen was her master of dirty tricks, assassination, and extortion. He's under death sentence back home. Before you cozy up to him, understand that there's a reason they call him the scorpion."

She saw that cunning flicker of the eyes as Wirth began considering the implications.

"I'm serious, Dan. He's not the kind of trouble even you can handle."

Wirth bowed low, arm extended. "I consider myself warned, Supervisor. My gratitude for your kind concern runs deep. Drop by sometime. I'll stand you to a fine whiskey. Even the good stuff if you promise not to pour it on the floor."

He glanced at Shig and Yvette, touched a mock, two-fingered salute to his brow. "Shig. Yvette. Good day to you both."

"Whiskey?" Shig asked as he watched Wirth make his way into the crowd.

"We were negotiating an armistice. Sometimes blunt statements have to be made."

The familiar roar built in the west, the sound of a shuttle hitting atmosphere at supersonic speeds.

Tension ran through the crowd, people calling, "Here she comes!"

Kalico chewed her lip, turned her head, and caught the first faint gleam of silver in the afternoon sky.

"Glad you flew over for this," Yvette added. "Kind of nice to be able to put up a unified front for the new folks."

Shig pushed himself back and forth on the wire. "Dya said that Dortmund Weisbacher was one of the leading planetologists and ecologists in his time. Was up to his neck in a fight with the evolutionary biologists."

"He was the force behind many of the re-wilding areas back on Earth." Kalico said thoughtfully. "What a disaster that was."

"Wonder how he's going to take to Donovan?" Shig mused. "I hate really famous people. Especially professors of great renown. Takes too long to educate them about the realities of life in the real world."

The shuttle banked wide, dropped down under the clouds off to the east and lifted its nose as it cupped air in its deceleration glide.

"Good pilot," Yvette noted as the sleek craft slowed, dropped, and settled on its landing skids. The blast of hot air barely curled dust from the baked clay. It tossed Kalico's hair, and batted at her clothing.

The crowd behind the fence broke into applause, clapping and hooting.

"Let's go be a delegation," Shig said amiably. He let loose of the fence and stepped to the "man gate" where Stepan Allenovich stood with a rifle, his quetzal-hide hat perched at a jaunty angle.

Allenovich threw the gate open and Shig led the way, Kalico and Yvette a step behind. She smiled at that. Not so long ago she'd have considered it an imperative to have been at the head of the procession. Somehow the drive for status and position didn't mean as much on Donovan.

She marveled at how much she'd changed since setting foot on Donovan.

The A-6 model shuttle had *Vixen-1* and the stylized

drawing of a fox head on the side. The ramp dropped. A man in a captain's uniform, followed by First Officer Vacquillas, strode down at the head of a contingent of people.

"Welcome to Donovan," Yvette called. "I'm Yvette Dushane. With me is Shig Mosadek. We are also honored to have Supervisor Kalico Aguila with us today from Corporate Mine. Behind me are the people of Port Authority. We are delighted to welcome you into our town and open our gates to you."

The crowd cheered.

The captain pulled himself up, a grim smile on his face. He stood maybe five-eight, blond with brown eyes, early fifties. "I'm Captain Tayrell Torgussen, commander of the *Vixen*. Given the disturbing revelations of our arrival, your welcome is heartily accepted."

He gestured to Vacquillas. "May I introduce my first officer, Seesil Vacquillas?"

Behind Vacquillas, a tall gray-haired man who might have been in his sixties, pushed forward in obvious annoyance. He wore a long-out-of-style black suit; the charcoal-gray dress coat hung nearly to his knees. Though his face had lines commensurate to his years and looked drawn, fiery dark eyes glared out from under bushy brows. Kalico thought his chin and jaw might have been modeled from a block of wood.

"I'm Doctor Dortmund Weisbacher," he announced, "Chair of the department of planetology, Tubingen University at Transluna and scientific director for this expedition. *Vixen* was dispatched to Capella III in order that my team and I could conduct a thorough survey of the planet in order to implement a sane management policy that protected not only human interests but those of the planet and its biosphere as well."

He paused, glancing around. "Apparently, given recent disturbing revelations, we are going to have to amend that mission statement. However, I look forward to working with all of you as we document the changes on Donovan. And, perhaps, ultimately, we can offer ways to decrease your conflicts with the local environment and at the same time ameliorate your impact upon it."

Okay, no ego here, Kalico told herself.

"What did he just say?" Pamlico Jones asked from where he stood behind Kalico.

Weisbacher's expression went suddenly quizzical and he tilted his head, shaking it faintly. "Where is the net? Why can't my implants access data?"

"We have no net here," Shig said politely. "Just a com system for anyone who wishes to monitor local communications."

"Oh." The man looked perplexed. "I hadn't thought of that. How absolutely disarming to find oneself in constant silence. How do people manage?"

A thin-faced blond woman, thirtysomething, with a slender build, shot Weisbacher a sidelong and amused glance as she stepped forward. "I'm Doctor Lea Shimodi. I'm a Corporate survey geologist, Resources Division. I was tasked with conducting an in-depth survey of Capella III's mineral assets. I hear I'm a bit late for that, but, while that initial survey has no doubt been completed by others, something tells me that Donovan's geological secrets have barely been tapped. Hopefully I can make a contribution to your continued success and profit."

Weisbacher looked dyspeptic as Shimodi was talking.

You bet, Dr. Shimodi. And you are mine. Kalico hid a smile. The woman was Corporate. A trained geologist. She was probably under contract for life, but, if after fifty years she wasn't, no one could make a better offer for her services than Kalico.

Kalico waited through the introductions of the botanist—a woman in her twenties named Sax—and the xenobiologist, Shanteel Jones. Both seemed to realize that they were fifty years behind the curve when it came to understanding Donovanian life-forms.

Still, with their training, no doubt Cheng and Dya Simonov would find useful places for them. If there was one thing Donovan was short of, it was talented researchers.

Shig stepped forward, hands raised. "Come. We have domes set aside for you. But first, if you would accompany us to the cafeteria, we'd like to give you an orientation." He turned to Torgussen. "Captain? Are you still planning on spending the night with us?"

"If that's not a problem."

"Not at all, but you'll need to button up your shuttle. No one is allowed past the gate after dark. It's just not safe."

"What do you mean?" Weisbacher asked indignantly.

Kalico stepped forward, aware that the professor was fixing on her facial scars. "We wouldn't want you eaten on the first night, Doctor. It sets a bad, if sobering, precedent for the rest of your team."

"Excuse me, but remind me. Who are you?"

"Corporate Supervisor Aguila. Tubingen on Transluna was part of my district before I moved to Boardmember Taglioni's personal staff. Tell me, as a full professor, were you under section 6 of Contract for Life at the university?"

"Of course. I was the department chair, holder of—"

"Then you will refer to me as Supervisor when you address me. Ma'am will be sufficient in less formal situations. During your stay on Donovan, you will be under my direct authority."

The professor's mouth opened, closed, and his expression hardened, but good Corporate citizen that he was, he said nothing as he fumed and ground his teeth.

She glanced at the others. "Dr. Shimodi, I assume that you, also, were contracted for life?"

"Yes, ma'am." Shimodi was watching her with cautious brown eyes.

"Relax, Doctor. I think you're going to find your new working environment a great deal more liberating and stimulating than anything you've known back in Solar System. Consider your future to be wide open here."

Sax immediately said, "I was under ten-year contract, Supervisor."

"Me, too," Jones chimed in.

Which meant that neither had achieved full professor status.

"Then your contracts would have expired forty years ago. Consider yourselves free agents, but I suggest you visit with Raya Turnienko. She's in a position to offer you immediate employment. Market economy, you see." Kalico gestured to Shig and Yvette. "Welcome to the libertarian paradise of Port Authority."

"What do you want us to do with Benteen?" Torgussen

asked warily. "He's in restraints on the ship. You want him, ma'am?"

"Hauling him off to Corporate Mine and putting a bullet in his brain might be in the colony's best long-term interest."

Shig quickly added, "But we're not on Corporate territory here. Nor is he the first soul to land on Donovan with a warrant in his name back in Solar System. I will be most happy to take him off your hands."

Shig glanced at Kalico, a weary smile of acceptance on his lips as he said, "As much as I may regret it later, some of us are bound just as tightly by the strictures of philosophical belief as others are by Corporate contract and law."

"Hope you know what you're doing," Kalico whispered from the corner of her mouth.

Shig laced his fingers together over his belly. "Me, too."

29

The first time Talina had seen Kylee riding on Flash's back had left her speechless. That a petite blond girl would be perched on the back of one of Donovan's biggest and most feared predators just did not compute. It seemed to violate all the laws of nature.

But then, so did kissing a little girl. Talina had been fretting over that. Half wondering if she should shoot herself for impropriety.

"Wasn't any sexual stuff, right?" Kylee had reminded her with a cocked eyebrow. "And you've been sleeping better, right?"

Talina had. Somewhere in her cocked-up brain, she'd realized she could shift the pieces of the broken Mayan pot, and a different image would come up, faint, fuzzy, unrecognizable.

But though her sleep was less disturbed, her subconscious had become a chaos of images and flashes of memory. Odd fragments of visions and thoughts that were not hers. Instantly she'd be on edge, reaching for her pistol. A moment later, she'd be possessed by a calm serenity for reasons she couldn't understand.

Half the time the quetzal in her gut seemed to purr with contentment. At others it was verging on violence. Especially when the visions were of Rocket or Kylee. As if the thing hated the competition.

"Wish you'd just go away and leave me alone," she muttered to it.

Becoming.

"Becoming what?"

Impotent.

Whatever that meant. She hadn't felt any weakening of the thing's presence.

She had noticed something new, however: she'd just had a dream of Rocket. The difference, this time, was that she'd been in Kylee's head. Hearing her thoughts. Feeling her emotions as she and the little quetzal tormented Damien by playing "lost" in the forest.

Talina had lived Kylee's rising glee as she watched from behind a stone outcrop as Damien's panic rose, heard his shouts of "Kylee! Please! Where are you?"

All that just because the boy had been tasked to take care of her. She could see his rising terror as he realized that if anything had happened to her, it would have been his fault.

And then the image had ended as quickly as it began, though it had taken Talina's emotional high a bit longer to fade.

And with it had come a deeper appreciation for Kylee's guilt. Damien had been her best friend, and his sister, Shantaya, was Kylee's age. They'd grown up in a polygamous household. All brothers and sisters. Kylee had watched both Damien's mother, Rebecca, and their sister, Shantaya, torn apart and eaten before her eyes. That, coupled with grief over Rocket's murder, had torn a huge black and terrible hole in the girl's soul.

How did a child ever cope? Repair herself? No wonder she didn't care if Leaper ate her. It would be an end to the pain.

Flash strode up, Kylee riding on his back as if he were some monstrous horse. The quetzal fixed his three-eyed gaze on Talina where she chopped up carrots in front of the shed. Her aircar was up to sixty-percent charge. Still not enough to head for home, but she could make Corporate Mine if she needed to bug out.

"Have a nice hunt?" Talina asked, glancing across the yard toward the forest. Neither she nor Kylee had seen hide nor hair of Diamond or Leaper since the first day.

Kylee slipped down Flash's back, landing lightly on her newly shod feet. "Flash caught a roo just the other side of the tree line." The kid had a grin that nearly split her face in two. "I just *love* going fast!"

"You're lucky you didn't fall off and break your silly neck."

"You sound like my mother."

"Yeah, maybe I do."

Flash yawned in a very earthlike manner, then clapped his toothy jaws shut with loud snap. Happy quetzal. Nothing gave the beasts a sense of well-being like a full belly did. That flush of . . .

Talina stopped short, staring thoughtfully at the knife where it half transected a carrot.

"What?" Kylee asked.

"Trying to put it all in perspective. I was just in your head. You and Rocket were hiding from Damien. Out in the forest. You were hidden in a rock outcrop. Rocket was camouflaged. Damien was terrified that something had happened to you. He was calling out, panicked."

"I remember that." Kylee grinned. She mimicked Damien's voice: "Kylee, so help me . . ."

". . . You ever do that again, I'll flush your underwear," Talina finished.

"He almost hit me. Might have except Rocket would have bit him, and he knew it."

Talina laid the knife to one side, seating herself beside Kylee as Flash curled himself into a ball and turned blue and pink. He was studying Talina through intelligent eyes.

"This is something new," Talina told the girl. "That's *your* memory. Out of *your* head. Not Rocket's. I saw through your eyes. Heard your thoughts."

"Told you it went both ways." Kylee seemed nonplussed. "Who's Mitch?"

"He was my husband. What do you know about Mitch?"

"You buried him. Stepped down in the grave with him. He was covered in some kind of cloth. You and somebody called Step. The way you laid his head on the bottom of the grave, down between your feet. You thought, 'Is that all there is? The end of love, the end of life?' Then you shoveled the dirt in."

Cold fingers wrapped fearfully around Talina's gut and seemed to tighten. "You can't know that."

"Just like I can't know how you feel a quetzal living behind your stomach?"

"Screw me with a skewer, do you know how crazy this is?"

"Seems pretty normal to me."

Talina stared incredulously into the little girl's innocent

blue eyes. "Well, it's not. Not for the rest of us. We live alone. Our thoughts are ours. Inviolate. Private. I mean, how far does this go? How intimate?"

"Your demon quetzal was amused by the way you had sex with Cap."

"Oh, for God's sake!" Talina cried, her heart beginning to hammer. "That's . . . That's . . ."

Kylee shrugged. "I always wondered what it was like. Sex, I mean. I tried to imagine it between me and Damien. That was like, yuck." Her expression turned thoughtful, as she added, "I really like orgasm."

"But . . . You . . ."

Talina felt her world reel and slip, as it if had just come loose from its underpinnings. She sucked a deep breath. "Listen, I don't want to do this. I can't. I . . . This isn't happening."

"Like, big wow. You're starting to understand."

"Understand *what*?" she cried in panic. "You're in my head. Do you know what it's like? Suddenly knowing that someone is reading your most private thoughts? Knowing all the things I've done that I . . ." The words seemed to have fled. How did a person get her mind around the immensity of it?

That damned little girl could see right into all the terrible lies that Talina Perez told the world, know her for the shameful things she'd done. The petty, ruthless mistakes she'd made over the years. The times she'd cheated and used people. The things she regretted more than life itself.

Images, shameful, of all the . . .

"Stop it!" Kylee was in her face. "It's not like that."

"The hell you say, you know who I am." Talina felt tears, hot on her face, the anger flashing inside. Her quetzal was hissing and churning in her gut. "This is like psychiatric dissection."

"What's that?"

"They cut the top of your skull off to expose the brain. Then they insert probes, trigger memories that are read by algorithms that recognize neurological patterns in the nerve cells. It's a form of torture and interrogation."

Kylee's frown had grown deeper. "What did I have for supper on my ninth birthday?"

"Who gives a—"

"What did I have? It's one of the most important days of my life. What did Dya make me?"

Talina struggled to clear her thoughts, searching, who knew where, for the answer. "I haven't a clue."

"Ask me a question I wouldn't know the answer to. Something about when you were a girl."

"Who was Paco Mendoza?"

Kylee seemed to think, then shook her head, no guile behind her eyes. "Who was he?"

"Tried to have my mother murdered after she arrested him for tomb robbing. I'll never forget the way globs of spit came out of his mouth as he shouted at Mama and swore he'd kill her in the end."

Kylee had been concentrating. "It's not in my head, Talina." The girl's eyes cleared. "I don't have you inside. Just pieces. Do you have all of me?"

Talina struggled to form an image, but kept coming up with her own memories. Seeing the little girl for the first time on the operating table as Dya and Rocket cowered in the corner. Then a memory: "Got one. You changing Shine's diapers. How the smell made you want to throw up."

"I did throw up. Wasn't Shine's shit that made me sick. Turned out it was staph."

Talina was starting to breathe again. It wasn't as bad as she'd first thought. The panic began to recede. "Kid, something tells me that you and I . . ." She couldn't finish the sentence.

"I can guess how you're feeling. Got some fragments."

"No shit. No one's ever been in my head before."

"It won't be the same. I mean as it was between me and Rocket." She glanced off where Flash was watching, listening. And who knew how much the quetzal was understanding. "I still have a hole inside from Rocket. You get it? Half of me is missing. And I watched as Rebecca and Shantaya were killed. I didn't understand. So, if Leaper kills me, who cares?"

Talina shot a look at Flash. "She right? Is Leaper going to kill her in the end?"

The old quetzal uttered a deep-throated clicking. His

collar expanded in a fluorescent orange sheet that patterned and fluctuated. Not just yes, but a big yes.

As if anything could make this day more upsetting, it
was a real toilet-sucker to know she was reading quetzal
perfectly.

30

What kind of shithole is this? The question kept repeating in Tam's brain as he walked in purple twilight down the central avenue in Port Authority. The main thoroughfare—and it was gravel. *Gravel!* Not even paved. Everywhere he looked was squalor. People dipped water out of rain barrels? Seriously? Half the equipment was sitting up on blocks and looking butchered for parts? This truly was the end of the universe.

He had his duffel—all of his worldly possessions—over his shoulder. His Talon once again rode in its holster under his jacket, though he'd chosen black overalls instead of his suit.

The domes were ordinary enough. Just like a person would see on Earth, Moon, or Mars. But the locally built structures reminded him of something out of the Middle Ages. Stone and timber edifices, the walls of dressed ashlars. Gabled roofs shingled with shakes.

And the people? They reminded him of some sort of circus freaks, dressed as they were in homespun, fitted leather, and the most incredible shimmering hide. The old term "psychedelic" seemed the most descriptive of the rainbow patterns of light that rippled across the leather.

Nevertheless they were tough looking; each Donovanian carried either a pistol, rifle, or large knife. Despite coming off like old-time pirates, all offered him the friendliest of salutations. One woman—three children at her side—even greeted him by calling, "Hello, Mr. Scorpion. Welcome to Donovan. Let me know if you need anything."

And she said it without even a hint of irony.

In his ambitious and adventurous life, he'd dealt often enough with adversity. Setbacks, failures, and defeats had come with frequency. That he'd survived, prospered, could be attributed to his dogged perseverance. His cunning and ability to quickly adapt to new situations, not to mention that he and Artollia had come within a whisker of seizing The Corporation.

What had crashed down on him over the last day and a half, however, had left him staggered. They'd cut her brain apart. The woman he loved more than life itself. And she was fifty years dead.

Fifty years! How did a man get his mind around that?

He'd been all right with the knowledge that Radcek would have executed her. Shayne, herself, had made no bones about her fate if she failed. She had accepted the risk. But the price of failure in Board politics had always been an honorable, quick, and painless death. Not the rape of one's brain and most intimate thoughts.

That the woman he'd loved had suffered such an indignity left him enraged. No, not just enraged, but feeling impotent. The news had hit like a punch to the gut when he had finally heard it: Radcek had been laid out in his family tomb for more than twenty years now. Out of reach of Tam's justice by two decades and thirty light-years.

But to him, it had been barely a month since he'd seen her. Shared that last night with her. Remembered the gleam of excitement in her eyes as she kissed him and said, "Two days, Tam. That's all we have left. Little more than forty-eight hours, and we'll have that bastard on his knees. The courts will do the rest. The information you've obtained will see to it. And you will be there when I am seated in the Chairman's seat."

She'd kissed him that last time, her body pressed to his. Vibrant. Alive. "See you in two days."

He'd been on his way to the Boardroom, prepared to witness their triumph, when he was picked up just outside the ornate doors. Escorted by Artollia's armed guards to the shuttle.

Fifty years?

Unfuckingreal. In the blink of an eye, he'd gone from Corporate Advisor to a criminal. At least as far as *Vixen* was concerned. And he wasn't sure what he wanted to do about Supervisor Aguila. Part of him hated her for her knowledge of his and Shayne's private and most intimate moments. Another part of him recognized her for what she was: a most formidable woman.

Maybe as formidable as Shayne. The difference was that Aguila, with her scars and pistol, had dirt, and probably blood, under her fingernails. The sort of woman who fought her battles firsthand and looked a man in the eyes when she shot him dead.

He'd done well as Shayne's foil. Was there a chance . . . ?

No. He'd seen it in Aguila's eyes when they met aboard *Freelander.* Kalico Aguila was definitely not his future on Donovan.

He reached the patchwork fence at the end of the avenue. The thing had to be fifty feet tall, and the huge gate was closed. Not only that, but an armed sentry stood there, looking out into the gloom of evening where a road disappeared into the scrubby trees beyond.

Guess they weren't kidding about not leaving the compound at night.

He turned, staring at the warehouses to either side, the ugly pieces of mining equipment parked here and there. A curious melody rose in the air. Some kind of wildlife out beyond the fence.

"So this is exile?" he asked himself. "This sucking collection of huts and barbarians?"

He forcefully reminded himself that it beat the hell out of having his brain cut apart, stimulated, and his innermost thoughts shared with an audience of thousands.

That fence represented the absolute end of the line. As far as he could go. Beyond it lay nothing but alien wilderness and death.

"I've lost everything. Shayne. Even my world."

Think, Tam.

This was it, his last chance.

Aguila had told him that if he ever set foot on Corporate Mine, she'd execute him. But then, she served a Taglioni. Fair enough.

He started his steps south again, headed back into the main part of the village. Hard to call the damn collection of ramshackle buildings and junk anything but. And the locals called it a town? Port Authority wouldn't even qualify for the term if it had been built in the desert wastes of Sudan.

That soft and mushy Hindu, Shig, had told him that he was free.

"We are not Corporate. Our creed is that every man can achieve his personal goals, provided his actions do not harm others. If we find you intimidating, exploiting, or abusing another human being against their will, we will put a bullet in your head. Government here is by mutual contract. If you enter into a contract with another, we will uphold the letter of that contract, whatever is written. My advice is that you think carefully about the ramifications before you sign anything. Don't be afraid to ask questions, especially of Yvette, if you need contract advice before signing."

Shig had given him the most enigmatic smile. "In short, you are free to ruin your life in any way you see fit as long as you don't interfere with the lives of others. My last advice? Don't mess with the people; they're not Corporate in either belief or behavior."

Then Shig had given him coins minted of gold and silver. "There are fifty SDRs. We have a cash-or-trade economy. If spent frugally, fifty should last you a couple of weeks. After that, you're going to have to be producing your own wealth. Oh, but understand, theft here is punishable by exile into the bush or a bullet."

Lunatics, all of them.

"If I am to be king, I must become the king of lunatics and squalor."

He stopped short at the sound of music issuing from a corner doorway in a large stone-and-timber building. The imposing sign on the building's front proclaimed it The Jewel.

He could hear the cry, "Ladies and gentlemen, place your bets!"

Well, what the hell?

If this was to be his world, he'd damned well better begin learning its ways and how he was going to conquer it.

And he would conquer here. When it came to leadership, a blind fish could do a better job than that fool Shig Mosadek.

31

Dortmund walked to the fence and stared out at the lights that glowed on the agricultural fields. The feeling in his gut was akin to that sick, tingly sensation of freefall, where everything inside rose up against the diaphragm and made him want to throw up.

From the sky, a gentle rain fell. Alien rain. On a planet thirty light-years and half a century away from Solar System.

Dortmund tried to get what was supposed to be his "formidable" intellect around that.

He kept trying to access data as he had for his entire life. The silence in his head was unsettling. Like a room gone black and still. How did these people function without constant net interaction? It filled him with a half panic. A sudden and eerie deprivation. It was akin to having part of his brain amputated.

Looking out beyond the wall of interlocked wire he saw nothing but abomination. Terrestrial plants. Corn, beans, squash, rows of garlic, wheat, rye, barley, cactuses, and who knew what. All domesticates from Earth growing unchallenged in Capella III's dirt. And beyond them, nothing. Not so much as a fence before the fields abutted Donovan's native savannah.

All of this should have been contained in a dome! Isolated from the rest of the planet. With complex locks for ingress and egress and sophisticated bio-quarantine protocols.

Whatever fault had sent *Vixen* fifty years into the future had damned an entire planet to terrestrial pollution.

"Sir?" a voice asked from behind.

Dortmund turned, water dripping off the hood of his jacket. The woman was indistinct, water shining where it beaded on her hat and trickled down a rain slicker. Like all Donovanians, the outline of a rifle could be seen under the slicker. Given the angle of the floodlights, her face was shadowed.

"Yes? Can I help you?"

"I'm Trish Monagan. Just wondered what you were up to. Since you're soft meat we want to make sure you don't get into trouble."

"Trouble's already here," he told her, waving out toward the fields. "They've ruined it."

"Ruined what?"

"Capella III."

"We call it Donovan. For the guy who got ate here first. We consider it a rare honor."

"What did you say your name was?"

"Trish. Port Authority security. And you are?"

"You may address me as Dr. Weisbacher."

She chuckled at that. "Raya's finally going to be able to get a full night's sleep. You might want to go check with her. She's got a pretty severe case of heavy metal poisoning. I had to fly out to Milt's claim and get him. Milt's a Wild One. Started having the bloody shits, lost feeling in his arms. Not that Milt ever had a lot going for him to begin with, but he was getting stupider and stupider. Raya's got him on a chelation protocol for cadmium and selenium for mercury."

"What are you talking about?"

"You said you were a doctor."

"A professor. Planetary conservation ecology, young woman." He paused, then carefully said, "Dr. Weisbacher. Department head and chair of planetology, Tubingen—"

"Now that's going to prove about the most useful thing on Donovan since beef cows." The woman's tone was snide, insulting.

"They imported cattle? Here? What were they thinking?"

"Free lunch for quetzals?"

"And what, pray tell, is a quetzal?"

She seemed stunned. "Doctor . . . ?"

"Weisbacher. I'm the director for the scientific team; we're here to document the mismanagement of the human presence on Capella III. That means the different ways in which human beings have adversely affected the biosphere, both botanical and zoological."

"Raya has antipsychotic medications, too."

"I don't understand."

"Yeah, well, most people have to be here for a couple of months before they go crazy."

"Are you mocking me?"

"Something tells me that would be a waste of effort. Listen, Doctor . . . ?"

"Weisbacher."

"Dr. Weisbacher, maybe you'd better come along with me before you get yourself in trouble. Wet night like this, in those thin shoes of yours, you're just as likely to pick up a slug, and Raya's too busy with Milt to take the time to cut it out."

"I don't have the slightest idea what you're—"

"No, Skull, you don't. So shut the fuck up and follow me over to the hospital. My job is keeping people safe. I'm getting the feeling that the only way I can do that with you is by sitting you down with Cheng, Iji, and Dya, so they can tell you what the hell Donovan is all about."

"You talk to me like that? I'm the department chair at Tubingen Transluna! I hold the—"

"Fuck this!" She stepped closer, staring up into his face. Now that the light was shining on it, he could see a dusting of freckles on her nose and hard green eyes shining in the light. "Mister, you want to come along peaceably, or do you want me to put you in a fucking headlock and haul your ass?"

Dortmund struggled for words as he stared into those implacable eyes. "I . . ."

"Coming? Or do I humiliate the hell out of you as I drag your squealing carcass across town?"

"This is a nightmare."

"No, they live a bit farther to the south."

Dortmund lifted his arms, letting them fall. "Go ahead, officer. Lead forth. But so help me, you will rue the day you raised your voice to me."

"Yeah, yeah, I'm trembling in my boots."

Dortmund took a deep breath, shot one last look at the abomination of crops where they grew in Capella III's now-polluted soil.

Someone is going to pay for this, I swear.

32

What in hell are we? The Three Musketeers? The question rolled around Talina's head as they traveled through the dim recesses of the forest.

She was a lot happier with the notion that they were musketeers than the darker possibility that they were *Wayob.* The spirit-possessed Maya witches, or *brujas,* as her great-aunt supposedly had been.

That mocking *Way* potsherd continued to haunt her imagination.

Given the shallow soils atop the basalt, the trees around Mundo Base were neither as thick nor as tall as they were in the lowlands immediately to the south.

In the dappled shadows, Talina walked carefully, picking her steps across the roots; her soft boots barely irritated the thick root mat.

Didn't matter that Flash was walking beside her; every bit of her quetzal sense was alert. This was still virgin forest. She'd already spotted sidewinders, a skewer, a couple of bems, and she knew for a fact that at least one nightmare lurked in the area.

Oddly, the way was familiar. Had to be Rocket's molecules inserting memories, because she was looking at specific trees, outcrops, and patterns of roots. When she did, she experienced splintered memories of different times, of happy thoughts and bad. Saw ghostly and partial images.

And just up ahead was where a sidewinder had almost got Kylee. Only to have Rocket leap on it at the last second and snap it in two.

The little girl rode on Flash's back. A crest lay draped limply across the big quetzal's neck just ahead of the girl. It had fallen to a single shot from Talina's pistol.

"Dimly, dully, I begin to see," Talina said.

Flash shot her a sidelong glance from his right eye.

"I see fine." Kylee mocked a scout's action, raising her

hand flat to her forehead and peering around. "Thought you had quetzal vision, too."

"I do. It's just that I'm seeing other things. Other times through Rocket's eyes."

To Flash, Talina said, "You're right, old pal. The experiment isn't over. I get the bits and pieces. I think it's a hint of knowing what it's like to be a quetzal."

Taupe and umber, patterned with yellow, green, and pink, effectively asked, "How so?"

"It's about the acquisition of memory. For humans, memory starts when we're born. Some notions and behaviors are determined by our genes, but not physical memories. We might intuitively know that snakes are dangerous and to beware of heights. But we don't inherit images from our parents' memories that form in our heads."

The eye was still taking her measure when she said, "But for you, tasting, learning, as you call it. You absorb the molecules that contain memory, and then they express themselves inside you. When you ate your elder way back when, you absorbed his memories and experiences, too, didn't you?"

Orange ran in waves down the beast's hide, and faded to forest tones.

"The first quetzal who infected me did so in order that its mate could eventually find me and kill me. What we call revenge. Is that common among quetzals?"

Again the orange.

"You wanted to know what humans were. So much so that you risked Rocket's life in an attempt to bond him to Kylee. But before that, how many humans had you killed and tasted without results?"

Three spots of black darkened on Flash's hide and faded. Then came a pattern of colors and shapes beyond Talina's recognition.

"Didn't get that last part, but you killed and ate three people." She gave him a wicked smile. "Not to mention Rebecca and Shantaya. Good thing I'm not into vendetta, huh? But getting back to the point, all quetzals are different, right? Like the fact that if anything happens to you, Leaper will kill Kylee because he blames her for Rocket's death."

The patterns of orange flashed again.

"Killing Kylee? Flawed logic since it wasn't Kylee's fault."

Talina couldn't read the patterns and colors that followed.

"Can't you just share molecules instead of having to eat each other for a fuller understanding of motivation?"

A kaleidoscope of colors flickered across the quetzal's hide. Way too much information there.

"So, my next question: Are you in contact with other quetzals up north? Maybe with Whitey? The one whose molecules you got when you tasted me?"

Brown. That meant no.

"Then every lineage of quetzals has its own agenda? Makes its own decisions?"

Orange again.

She stepped around a jutting outcrop of angular basalt, seeing the words ALL THINGS END.

"What's that mean?"

"Mark left his armor there," Kylee said from her high perch. "He thought he was going to die. Almost did. He was fighting with the old nightmare when Rocket and I smelled him."

"Smelled?"

"Like old rotten socks. Anything that noxious had to be a pedophile."

"Noxious? Even knowing your mother and the things she would have insisted that you learn, you still amaze me sometimes."

"Just a kid full of hate."

"How's that?"

"I'm like the quetzals. I have Rocket inside me. And I don't. There was him and me. And then there's just me. Alone. Like the emptiness is swallowing me . . . like with each day there's less and less of me. So I hate. I think about what I'm going to do to those shits in Port Authority, and what's left of me doesn't drain away as fast."

"That heals over time, kid."

"It's not like with you and Mitch, or you and Cap. I know how you feel. But take that hurt and emptiness and cube it. Maybe you'll come close to where I'm at."

Trouble was, the kid was right. Not a damn thing Talina could say. She'd felt the edges of Kylee's grief. Not just for Rocket, but guilt for Rebecca and Shantaya. Like a stygian void that would consume Talina's soul if she so much as let the least bit of it slip past her defenses.

Made her wonder how the little girl hung on day by day.

So, out here, with only Flash for a friend, what the hell did Kylee have to look forward to? Especially when the kid was right; she'd never fit in back in Port Authority.

The quetzal in Talina's gut gave off one of its hissing chitters of amusement.

"Yeah? You're a piece of shit."

"What'd I do?" Kylee cried.

"Not you, the quetzal in my gut. He thinks this is funny." She glanced at Flash. "Why don't your molecules eat his molecules? You're a decent kind of guy, even if you did eat a bunch of people."

White and iridescent-red patterns ran across Flash's hide as the old quetzal uttered a clicking of laughter.

None of which hinted at a solution to the problem: What the hell kind of future did Kylee have to look forward to?

33

The song "Shake Me, Suzie" had always brought a smile to Dan's lips. The band Neutron EERHT had released it back in the late thirties, and it had become a classic. Dan had first heard it when he was on the streets as a teen. Used to listen to it when he was fucking a woman. Something about matching the lyrics and beat to the timing of each thrust. He'd save his orgasm until that last crashing crescendo.

He'd hired the local band for this evening, knowing it would bring in extra traffic. People bet more when they were in a good mood, and *Vixen* had brought a real high. Maybe the other ships weren't as "lost" as people wanted to believe.

As he sat at his elevated table in the rear, he watched Allison. She was delivering drinks for Vik Schemenski, who was busy pouring behind the bar. God, she was a beauty. He could look at her for the rest of his life.

Thinking of sex, he allowed himself a crooked smile as he watched Allison undulate her way across the room. She wore form-fitting silver tonight, and Dan flexed his hands, imagining them as they cupped her full, round ass.

They hadn't screwed for almost a week. Just too damn busy. But tonight, as things began to wind down, it was time. Take her back to the office, lock the door, and do it on his desk. Maybe before the band quit. He'd tell them to play "Shake Me, Suzie" every other song. He'd never fucked to live music before.

With the arrival of the shuttle from *Vixen*, The Jewel was doing a solid night's business. People crowded around the tables. Shin Wong ran the roulette while Angelina captivated her audience at the craps table. She was wearing a loose, low-cut one-piece belted at her waist. Each time a mark shook the bones and made a toss, she'd bend low, letting the shooter get a glimpse of her endowment.

For the moment, the shooter was Dube Dushku. Dan supposed that the last thing the guy's wife, Friga, needed to know was that her husband—good family sort that he was—was drooling and dropping the family's SDRs so he could ogle Angelina's tits.

Dan had worked too hard to win the acceptance, if not the love, of Port Authority's doting mothers to allow Dube to fuck it all up should word get out that he was desirous of fondling Angelina's globes.

How many schools could a man build?

The "upstanding folk" had to be treated with such delicacy. Wasn't like the bachelor clay miners and prospectors. If they got randy, all it took was a whack to the head, then dump them in the alley.

Piss off the "decent" folk, and it could get you killed.

He made a face. If it weren't for the shit-sucking intricacies of politics a man's life would be so much easier.

Dan pulled a toothpick from his pocket and gestured to Art Maniken. Gave a flick of his fingers and glanced toward Dube.

Art nodded, stepped over, and asked, "What do you need, boss?"

"Get his cherry ass back to his house. And if his wife is there, be fucking polite, respectful, and tell her I didn't want her hubby to misbehave."

"Right, boss."

"And remember the polite part."

"Hey, I was civilized once."

"Yeah, in a quetzal's ass."

Art sidled up to Dube and said, "How much of your plunder's left?"

Dube blinked, obviously more than a little drunk. "Hey, I'm gonna win any throw now."

"Sorry, pal. You just hit the jackpot. C'mon. Boss says you're headed back to the missus."

Dube wasn't too drunk to know when to cut his losses. Not when it came to Art Maniken.

At that moment a man in black stepped in the door. Definitely a newcomer. He made way, thoughtfully observing as Art manhandled the protesting Dube out the door and into the evening drizzle.

Soft meat. Had to be from *Vixen*, though Dan didn't remember seeing him earlier. Then he really got a good look at the guy. Their eyes met from across the room.

He might be a Skull, but this one was anything but soft meat.

Dan pasted his good-guy smile on his face, inclining his head.

At that moment, Allison crossed between them, having delivered a round of drinks to the pinochle table.

The newcomer fixed on her like radar on a missile. The look in the guy's eyes turned downright predatory. A faint smile bent those thin and bloodless lips as he ran his gaze up Allison's legs, past the sleek hips and thin waist to the full breasts. Put a whole new meaning to the words "eye fuck."

"Oh my," Dan whispered to himself. "Why do I think you want to put fingerprints all over the merchandise?"

Dan stepped around the table, and the new guy shifted his gaze back. The smile vanished like mist in the desert.

"Why, I do declare," Dan said, and stuck his hand out. "A new face, and what a change from the usual ugly mugs I have to endure. I'm Dan Wirth, at your service. Welcome to The Jewel."

"Tamarland Benteen," the man in black said, his flat gaze seeming to bore right through Dan's happy mask. "But then I'd imagine if you're the kind of man you appear to be, you'd have heard of me by now."

Dan gave him a knowing smile. "The Supervisor, cunning slit that she is, already warned me. Said that you were more trouble than I could handle. So I asked around. One of my people talked to one of the *Vixen* people. Said you had a death penalty awaiting you back in Solar System. That tells me, at least in my book, you might just be all right."

Dan gestured to his table in the rear. "Light and set. I'll stand you to a drink." Over his shoulder he called, "Vik! Two glasses. The good stuff."

"They ship the liquor in?" Benteen asked, his alert eyes taking in the room. Something about the way the man seated himself in a fluid motion, the fact that he missed nothing, seemed to monitor everything in his peripheral vision, had Dan's internal claxon wailing.

"Donovan is an acquired taste, but not without its rewards.

Inga Lock—the woman who runs the tavern—distills, brews, and wines, whatever they call that. The grains and fruits are locally grown. As long as you like vegetables, life's good. The local meat sucks compared to a good cut of beef or pork."

"And you run this place?"

"Among other businesses."

Allison came striding over from the bar, an amused curl on her full lips. And, damn her, she was playing it for everything, hips swaying, the silver fabric clinging to her loins shimmering with every step. She gave Benteen a radiant smile and lifted a golden eyebrow as she said, "And who might you be?"

Benteen stood, interest in his eyes like a glistening question. "Tamarland Benteen, lovely lady. Champion of the poor, trampler of tyrants, and humbled by your charm."

Dan experienced that slow burn as Benteen took his drink; as he did the man's fingers stroked the length of the back of Allison's hand. She seemed to start. And damn if Dan didn't see that familiar widening of her pupils, that slight blush on her pale flesh. Then came that cunning look, the new one she'd been giving people since she stopped taking the drugs.

"Thank you, angel of mine," Dan told her bluffly, but his heart had slowed to a deadly beat. A coldness in his chest. He took the drink she handed him, and added, "Vik's got the bar. I think you can finally get back to the office and those pesky ledgers. Oh, and don't forget the cage accounts on your way."

That wry curl of the lips was back as Benteen watched her walk in her saucy way back to the cage, grab the accounts, and disappear into the rear.

"An exquisite creature," Benteen said softly, then flicked his knowing gaze at Dan. "Here's to Capella III and new horizons."

Dan clicked his glass to Benteen's. "We call it Donovan. As to the horizons, that depends on the quality of your eyesight. Nearsighted, or far. And it helps to know what's what so that you don't mistakenly step in a trap that will get your ass killed."

"I try to be nimble on my feet." Benteen tasted the whiskey. "I'm impressed."

"Inga will blush. But now that you're here, and I understand you're not about to leave, what are your plans? Anything I can help with?"

The steely eyes didn't waver. "What's with Aguila's scars? And the dressed-like-a-barbarian circus clothes?"

Dan hadn't seen that one coming. "Don't underestimate the Supervisor. If you go up against her, you'd better be prepared to take on the whole of Corporate Mine. She got the scars putting her ass on the line, fighting mobbers. Um, flying predators. The colorful and vicious little fuckers come in flocks that, trust me, you really don't want to mess with. She dresses like she does because she could give a shit about the old Corporation, and her people know it."

"She got a man?"

"Nope."

"Pity. That's nice packaging around a very competent woman." He smiled. "Could be most interesting. I have a fondness for beautiful women who can handle themselves."

Dan raised his glass. "If you're going to make a play for Aguila, I salute you! But be warned, she shoots people who disappoint her."

"You ever tangled with her?"

Dan gave the man a heartless grin. "We have what's called *détente*. She keeps to her world, and I keep to mine. Her people come here to relax, which they need, and I make money, which I enjoy. It's mutually beneficial. Beyond that, we're both very careful not to upset the balance."

"What about these contracts?"

"That's how Donovan works. A relic of the Corporation. The contract is absolute law. Just be damn sure you know what you're getting into."

"And this Shig Mosadek?"

"From your tone, I gather you don't think much of him."

Benteen shrugged, his eyes on the guys at the pinochle table as one shouted over a lost hand.

"Another one you don't want to fuck with. Sure, the guy comes across as a roly-poly absent-minded dreamer with his head in the clouds. He's sharper than he looks. A third of the triumvirate. What's important for you to know is that the people here love him."

"What's the triumvirate?"

"Shig Mosadek, Yvette Dushane, and Talina Perez. Shig's the ideas guy and anointed holy priest, Yvette does the down-to-details management, and Perez is the enforcer. Or was. Hard bitch all the way through. Got herself infected with a quetzal and crossed some of the 'decent folk.' She's run off to the bush somewhere. Status uncertain. In the meantime, security is handled by Trish Monagan. Young, idealistic, but you can cow her when it comes to a bluff."

Benteen stared thoughtfully at Angelina as she was calling for a new shooter. "And how do you fit into the mix?"

"Me? I'm just a humble businessman." Dan leaned forward, pointing a finger. "Here's the thing: Donovan ain't the fucking Corporation. You remember the old fairy tale of the goose and the golden egg? You can become richer than Croesus, but don't piss off the goose. You've got to let these hardheaded local bastards do it their way."

"And what's their way?" Benteen's emotionless stare was like a challenge.

"They don't take orders worth a shit here. And you don't fuck around with the townsfolk. I mean it. Unlike back in Solar System, these people solve their own problems in their own way. Hard world, hard people."

"And the blonde?"

"Allison. A rare vintage." Dan smiled thinly. "Let's call her the boss's special reserve."

Benteen nodded pleasantly.

And if you don't get what I'm saying, Art's going to have a moment of glee when he slits your throat and drops you on the other side of the fence.

34

Talina and Kylee had taken shelter under a stretched tarp.
The usual afternoon rain was falling from beneath black
and oily clouds. Occasional lightning burst and sent its
thunder rolling across the forest.

Under the awning, Talina had a fire going. A pot filled
with chia, teff, sunflower seeds, walnuts, chunks of squash,
and the ever-present staple of garlic bubbled over the flames.

The day had been a hard one for Talina. Half the time
she couldn't think. When she did get hold of a thought
something else would steal it away, leaving a totally unre-
lated image, emotion, or inclination in her head.

And she kept having flashbacks of the broken potsherds
on the tile floor, how they'd scattered, but now it was different, with some shards concentrated here, other shards
over there, all backed by Mother's shriek of disbelief and
horror coming from the kitchen door.

Too many damned people in her head. Or, in this case,
a little girl and six or seven quetzals.

It should have been getting better. Instead, Talina's
brain seemed to be fragmenting, thinking in a lot of different directions all at once, and she could only catch a glimpse
of herself among the various threads. Just like those damn
potsherds.

Sometimes she'd just find herself sitting, dully staring
at the ground. Nothing. Everything. A limestone temple in
the forests of Chiapas. A fight with another quetzal. A lecture at the academy from Officer Ryan. Her mother's
homemade tortillas. Clemenceau's thin-lipped smile as his
eyes narrowed. The feel of a bullet as she leaped at another
version of Talina in the canyon. The scratchy rug against
her bare back when she had her first sex with Pablo Ruiz.
The fulfilling sensation as she snapped a chamois' neck in

two between her jaws. Rondo locking her away in her room for knocking Taung down that time when he took her tablet and deleted her homework.

Endlessly they spun out of her mind, broken and unconnected.

"Talina?" Kylee asked as she stirred the stew.

A starscape just off the crescent horizon of Mars . . .

"Fuck you! Wake up!" Kylee was shaking her.

Talina dropped her head between her knees. "It's like I'm falling apart, kid. Thought I was getting a handle on it, and now it's all mush inside. You think that's what Whitey wanted? He gave me a molecule that was like a computer virus? Something that scrambled the server? Nothing's coherent anymore."

"It's probably brain remodeling."

"What?"

"I think you're like a newborn. You have to grow new brain tissues."

"Is there anything you don't know?"

"Torrey was a historian as well as an agronomist. When he died, that was pretty much it for history. All I know is that Earth was full of history."

Talina blinked, chuckled. "How about getting quetzal molecules out of my system? You got anything for that?"

"No. Who was Buck Berkholtz?"

"Why'd you dredge him up? Crap. Don't tell me you got a memory with good ol' Bucky in it."

"You mentioned him that first day. Said you hadn't been used like that since you were dating Buck Berkholtz."

"Yeah. Right. Bucky. In the academy. He was pretty hot stuff. Smart, fast, and deadly handsome. Not so much on grades, but he aced the operational training, you know?"

She could feel Kylee's gaze on her.

"I thought I was pretty hot shit, too. Seemed natural that we'd team up. Thing was, he liked everything rough. Hell, I was young, thought I was tough. Every time we . . ."

"What?"

"Why am I telling you this? You're ten."

Kylee gave her that toothy kid smile. "Come on, Talina. As if I'm ever leaving here." She glanced away as the guilt rose. "You're my only human friend. The rest, they'd kill my ass, right?"

"Damien and your family wouldn't."

Her face contorted, pain reflected in the pinch of her mouth, the scrunching of her nose as if she were fighting tears. Fists knotted, she turned away. Fought for control, and asked, "You said the other day that Damien had a girl-friend?"

"Yep. Sally Montoya. She's helping him with his geom-etry."

"He always wanted to meet new people." Kylee stamped a foot. "How'd this get so fucked up?"

Talina could see the tear that streaked the little girl's cheek. Kylee dropped to the ground, eyes on the distant forest.

"Where's all this profanity coming from? Girl your age ought to mind her mouth."

"Who gives a damn? Huh? It's not like Dya's gonna come back and send me to my room for bad behavior."

"Hey, I got some of your molecules, remember? I know how much you miss your mother and Su and your brothers and sisters."

"You know I can't go back!" she shrilled. "I was *there*. I saw! And I didn't *care*! I didn't understand. Death's differ-ent for humans than it is for quetzals." The little girl ran her fingers through the dirt just back of the drip line where the rain was pattering. "It's like . . . forever. They're just gone."

"Yeah, well, that's a problem all right."

"If I die it won't hurt anymore. I can just be gone, too."

The way she said it was like a skewer to Talina's heart. She forced a memory of climbing high in the forest canopy out of her head. Fought to focus on Kylee. Okay, no wonder the kid's language was going to hell.

"If I could get my head together, I'd go out in the forest and hunt Diamond and Leaper down."

"Why?"

"Be one less thing to worry about, wouldn't it?"

Kylee said nothing, just made a fist in the dirt.

Talina struggled through a memory of her first time in

Transluna, getting lost in the terminal. The feeling of panic that she was going to miss her flight to . . .

She was in Rocket's head, bouncing as Kylee threw a triple-knotted rag in the air. He raced out, two eyes on the flying rag, one to keep track of where he was going. Leaped, grabbed the rag out of the air. She felt Rocket's claws rip into the damp soil as he whirled, tail slashing the air. Mouthing the soft rag, he turned and started . . .

"Give me a *damn* break!" Talina scrunched her eyes closed, wondering where she'd lost the trail of thought. "What were we talking about?"

"How quetzals transfer knowledge. Leaper and Diamond think Flash made a mistake. That humans are bad. And they're right. Look around. Rocket's dead. Mundo Base is a failure and falling to pieces. It's all for nothing."

"Maybe their TriNA isn't as smart as it thinks it is. They don't understand humans."

"We're just as goofy. DNA? Just mixing and matching? Got a lethal mutation? If DNA was smart, it'd weed itself of the genetic load."

"The . . . what?" Talina was trying to concentrate despite half of her mind chasing through the bush after fastbreak.

"Don't you know anything about biology?"

"Not since I was in high school. And that was a long time ago."

"Guess it's a good thing I'm not going to survive then. I like being ten and smart instead of thirty and dumb."

Even as the Kylee said it, Talina watched her face redden.

"Then you go and mouth off like that, and it reminds me you're still ten. And a kid."

Kylee bit her lip, looking off to the south.

"So what did Dya do when you mouthed off like that?"

"I got extra duty. Had to clean the toilets or some such."

"Good thing I'm not your mom, huh?"

Talina could see the drop in the girl's face. Watched her bite off a comment. Probably something like, "Wish you were." Words Kylee blamed herself too much to say.

"There's Flash. Finally."

Talina shook off a memory of Trish and how guilty she'd looked the time she'd been fourteen—and first come home drunk.

She fixed her eyes on the causeway that bisected the fields. Just past the tree line came Flash, his hide a mottled pattern of browns, greens, and teal.

Kylee stood, stepping out in the rain, waving.

As the quetzal fixed its three eyes on the girl, two shapes burst from the trees, moving so fast they were blurs.

Flash must have heard them, for he barely turned his eyes back when they hit him. Even across the distance, the meaty thump of the hard bodies came loud and painful.

Flash shuddered under the impact, stumbled, hit hard on his breast in the mud.

Over the distance, Talina couldn't tell which of the younger animals had him by the back of the neck, but the second had fastened its jaws over the head of the tail where Flash's lungs vented.

Holy shit, they're strangling him!

Flash bucked, whipped his muscular frame back and forth. Sodden dirt flew; plants were ripped from the ground.

Across the distance, a whistling howl, like an unloosed fury, carried through the rain. Shrill squealing, an odd, bagpipe-like harmonic, and grunts of pain and rage sent Talina's quetzal into a frenzy that knotted her stomach and caused her to gasp.

She stumbled to her feet, reached for her rifle, and shouldered it. Through the optic, she tried to pick a target. In the thrashing of the beasts, she couldn't be sure of a shot. Not without hitting Flash.

Taking a chance, she fired a round a couple of feet above the battling titans. She could have spit for all the effect it had.

Or did it?

Through the optic, Talina could see that Leaper and Diamond had changed their tactics and were dragging Flash back toward the safety of the trees. In the process, they used the older animal's body as a shield.

Flash's struggle was waning. The slapping of his tail had

weakened; each pitch of his body had less energy than the last.

"No!" Kylee was screaming, tears and rain running down her face. "He's my friend! *My only friend!*"

Talina dropped to her knee, stabilizing the rifle with as much bone as she could. Found the sight picture, tried to slow her hammering heart, and pressed the trigger.

Her rifle boomed. She lost the shot in the recoil, but when the gun dropped and she got her sight, the quetzals were just disappearing into the trees.

Kylee was running, already twenty yards away, and sprinting flat out.

"Kylee, no!"

Tossing the rifle to the side, Talina was hot on the girl's heels.

The kid might have been ten, but it took Talina nearly a hundred yards to catch her. Together they tumbled into the mud, Talina shouting, "They'll kill you!"

"Let me go! Let me go, damn you!"

Then Kylee cried out, "Flash! Please. *Don't hurt Flash.*"

Coughing, panting, the little girl struggled in Talina's arms, sobbing, "He's my *only* friend. I *want* my friend!"

Stroking the child's soaked hair, Talina pulled the kid to her feet. "Come on. Nothing we can do down there."

"No! I gotta help Flash."

Talina shot another quick glance at the tree line, her imagination conjuring images of what was happening to Flash's body. "He's dead, Kylee. And you don't want to see what happens next."

The little girl's struggles ceased only to be replaced by wild sobs.

"Hey, there. Come on. We need to get back to the fire. There's nothing you can do."

"Everyone I love *dies*!"

"No, they don't. Your mom, Su, Damien, they're still just fine and missing you."

The rain intensified, leaving Talina crouched in the mud, drops like pellets hammering on her head as she hugged the devastated child.

She kept her squinted vision fixed on the distant trees. Blinking as water streaked down her face. One thing was sure: Leaper, and probably Diamond as well, would be coming for Kylee. Maybe not tonight—given they had full guts—but soon.

They wouldn't come headlong, or in a manner that would allow Talina the chance to shoot them. It would be from the side, tricky, and lightning-like in surprise.

And what the hell are you going to do about it, Talina?

35

The ache in Dortmund's back brought him awake. Slanting morning light poured through an uncommonly dirty
window. He stared up at a low ceiling molded of plain
white duraplast. The kind commonly used in utility structures. Two square light fixtures were fixed to the ceiling, of
which, he remembered, only one worked.

He sat up, a flimsy blanket falling away. Blinking, he
realized he was in a hospital bed, and all the events from
the night before came crashing back like a really bad
dream. First was that incorrigible young Trish who'd disre-
spected not only his position, but his person as well as she
practically marched him to the hospital.

After that indignity, he'd spent a couple of hours sitting
at a table in what was supposed to be a lab. Half the equipment had been stored along one wall, wrapped in plastic
sheeting, mothballed because it didn't work for lack of either parts or anyone skilled enough to repair it.

The table had been scarred, the only beverage being
cups of mint tea. Nothing with caffeine. Damn it, what
kind of madness was that? Didn't they understand that caffeine powered all true scholarship?

The woman, Dya Simonov, had tried to explain. "We've
got immature coffee trees from *Turalon* growing in the
greenhouse. But it will take years. Either caffeine-producing
plants were never included in the original farm manifest for
the settlement, or for whatever reason, they didn't survive
here. Which would be odd. Plants usually do well. It's the
livestock that failed miserably."

"Livestock? They just let domesticated animals loose in
a pristine environment?" he'd murmured. "Didn't they
take any precautions?"

"Sure," Cheng had told him. "But Donovanian life was
a lot smarter. Quetzals, it turned out, just loved beef and
hogs. And chickens? They jumped on invertebrates, most

of which didn't digest but chewed their way out through the chickens' bodies."

Dortmund had blinked. The cretin actually thought he was talking about protecting the livestock?

"Once the survey was finally completed," the round-faced Cheng continued, "the initial colonization was planned by Bill Tabor. He was the architect—"

"Of all the imbecilic fanatics!" Dortmund had cried. "That naïve young idiot isn't smart enough to know his nose from his anus! He and his deluded followers are nothing more than evolutionist puppets, played by Corporate policy wonks."

"Hey," Cheng had almost barked. "The guy was appointed head of Corporate planetology after you were presumed lost. Chairman Radcek wanted somebody young, bright, and—"

"Controlled by the Corporate teat," Dortmund had thundered in response.

And with that knowledge, everything made sense. Even when Cheng had told him wryly that, for a while, Capella III was even officially known as Radcek's Planet back in Solar System. It wasn't until after the Chairman's demise that the name had been officially changed, though no one on Donovan had ever called it anything but Donovan.

The night had gone downhill after that.

So, here he was in the hospital. He glanced around the Spartan room: the cubicle small, white, with its single window that looked out at a chain-link fence and the shuttle field.

Dortmund swung his lanky legs off the bed and stood. He'd folded his good suit and coat over the back of the chair. Rather than brave the rain, let alone discover what sort of atrocious dwelling the environmentalist barbarians might have assigned him, he'd chosen to accept Dr. Turnienko's offer of a bed here.

He'd dressed and just finished using the toilet when a soft knock preceded Dya Simonov's call of, "Doctor? You awake?"

"Yes." He opened the door to find the woman looking wary, something reluctant in her eyes.

"Did you sleep well?"

"Perfectly, thank you," he lied.

She made a beckoning gesture. "Come on. Inga's is opening for her first breakfast. It'll be packed and slow, but the whole town is going to be there. Millie even shut down the cafeteria so she could be there, too."

Breakfast in a tavern. Oh, what joy. Dortmund took a deep breath, slung his formal coat around his shoulders, and followed the woman as she asked, "So, has your head stopped spinning yet?"

"No. It's like waking up to a nightmare. The idea that the evolutionists won, that they've ruined this entire world . . ." He winced. "I call it downright dyspeptic."

"I realize that Donovan is coming as a shock, Doctor. But keep an open mind. It may not be as bad as you think. Granted, it's only been thirty years since the colony was established, but our work out at Mundo indicates that for the most part, terrestrial and Donovanian organisms don't mix well. At least on the macroscopic level."

"Macroscopic? That's a curious qualifier."

"Nothing curious about it. Terrestrial biology—be it plant, animal, or microbes—doesn't seem to find much compatibility with Donovanian life. While we can digest most animal products, albeit not as efficiently, the plant life has a polymer cellular structure that doesn't break down in our stomach acids. On the other hand, Donovanian molecules, especially TriNA, are finding their way into our bodies."

He remembered the holographic displays Cheng and Simonov had shown him the night before. He had likened their crash course on Donovanian biology as an experience rather similar to trying to catch a drink at the bottom of a waterfall.

The thought kept repeating: *What's happening here is criminal.*

This was Bill Tabor's work. The young firebrand had been little more than an acolyte in the evolutionary movement. Loud, brash, and foolish, but it appeared that he'd won in the end.

As they stepped out into the damp morning, Dortmund asked, "Doesn't it bother you? There's no telling what sort of mayhem has been let loose here. When I left Solar System, there were laws protecting environments."

"In the decade after you disappeared, most of those

laws were changed. Especially with the collapse of the re-wilding areas. They were such failures."

"I beg your pardon," Dortmund snapped. "It's the only way we can reclaim the planet. Turn those vast tracts over to the native flora and fauna. Extirpate any invasive species, be it a grass, mold, or bacteria. We have to return the planet to its pristine pre-human condition." He could hear himself getting heated.

She shot him a hard look as they approached the large dome. A faded sign over the door read The Bloody Drink. Surely that had to be an attempt at ill humor.

"It cost too much to manage, Doctor. What everyone forgot in the flurry to recreate a 'living museum of the past'—that was the term, wasn't it?—was that humans had been managing supposedly 'wild' environments for tens of thousands of years. Even a couple of million when it came to Africa and East Asia. You thought you could take humans out of the equation. You were wrong."

Dortmund stopped short, his anger rising. "Humans were responsible for one extinction after another. All the way back to the end of the Pleistocene."

"Further than that actually," she told him dryly, refusing to rise to the bait. "Why do you think there's only one species of hominin? Some we killed off as competitors, the others we absorbed into the main line of human evolution. Call it the numbers game of genetic swamping."

He struggled to slow his heart. "You're nothing but an evolutionist yourself."

"Well, Doctor, there was a reason that Pak and I were chosen for Donovan. We accepted that evolution was an ongoing process and one of the fundamental laws that governed life in the universe."

"Then you're another one of these selfish 'humans first' types. If humanity can't find a use for a species, let it die." He didn't care that the vitriol came through.

She held the door open. "Actually, my philosophy is a bit more complicated and nuanced. Further, my adherence to the principles I believe in have cost me a couple of husbands and a daughter who may be alive or dead out there somewhere. I could give a pile of quetzal shit what you think."

He fought to control his temper, some final thread of sanity holding him back.

She arched a challenging eyebrow, adding, "You, however, have a decision to make. Through Radcek's patronage, Tabor won. That's history. So what are you going to do? Stomp off and live like a hermit while you condemn the rest of us as heretics and enemies of the true faith?"

Dortmund's heart had started to hammer. He lifted his hands. "I can't be a party to this. Go on. I'll find my own breakfast, thank you."

And with that he turned on his heel, striding off toward . . . Where?

He stopped in the middle of the avenue. Tried to access the net. There was no net. Looked owlishly around. The morning light shone on the domes, glinted off the parked equipment. A group of children came racing past, calling hellos and good mornings.

He watched them laughing and bouncing as only children could, before they flung the tavern door wide and went charging inside.

"The cafeteria's closed," he whispered miserably to himself. The empty knot in his stomach reminded him that it had been nearly twelve hours since he'd eaten.

So, what to do? Head back to the shuttle? Take it up to the ship? Live there until either a decision was made to return to Solar System or another ship arrived? Hopefully one that didn't have the flawed mathematics that had cost him fifty years in an instant's time?

He turned back, took a couple of steps toward the tavern.

No!

He knotted his bony hands at his sides. The last thing he could do was walk in, let Dya Simonov see his defeat.

Evolutionists! They were all stinking, vile evolutionists. Worse, they'd unleashed chaos on Capella III. He wouldn't deign to call it Donovan, which, in its way, was a monument to an evolutionist catastrophe when they left the man's body to contaminate alien soil.

This was like being dropped into the pits of hell.

And where in the name of Hob had Sax and Jones disappeared to? He needed them. More than ever. Somehow he had to cobble together a solid front in order to counter the disaster that was Donovan.

But how did one man ever seek to repair the damage? Could it even be done? Or was he—as so many conservationists over the decades—bound to simply record the unfolding disaster? Mark the collapsing ecosystems as yet another proof of the unlearned lessons of humanity?

"Those who know history are condemned to bear witness as those who do not make the same mistakes over and over." The words rolled acerbically from his lips.

"Professor?"

Dortmund turned, seeing a twentysomething fellow in a marine uniform. The man stood in the middle of the avenue, hair close-cropped, a utility belt at his waist. "Yes? May I help you?"

"I'm Private Kalen Tompzen, sir. The Supervisor would like you to join her for breakfast. If you'd follow me."

Very well, a small victory. At least he'd spend the rest of the day being disgruntled with a full belly.

He followed the marine back to the double doors that led into the tavern. To his surprise, a set of wooden stairs led down into a spacious subterranean room. The place was crowded, packed with the gun-toting and horrendously garbed locals in their shiny leather and coarsely woven cloth.

Private Tompzen led him through the roar of conversation, clinking plates, and clatter, to a table at the front of the room. Given the nature of the local clientele, it came as no surprise to see a young man pouring drinks behind the bar. The waitstaff couldn't be told apart from the rest of the riffraff as they hustled plates back and forth.

To his relief, he didn't see Dya Simonov in the press.

Supervisor Aguila, dressed in a fitted black one-piece suit this morning, was seated at one of the long benches with Shimodi and the tall woman, Yvette Dushane.

The marine indicated that he should take the seat next to Shimodi and across from the Supervisor and Dushane.

"Doctor," Aguila said, a faint smile on her lips. "Thank you for joining us."

Dortmund seated himself. "Thank you for the kind invitation to join you." He glanced around. "I just hope the company proves better than my recent experiences."

"How's that, Doctor?" Dushane asked as she fixed him with reserved green eyes.

He ordered his thoughts, seeking to come to grips with the reality of the situation. "It's been disheartening. First, to lose fifty years? That's mind-numbing. But the greatest shock has been to discover the extent of the evolutionist disaster here on Capella III."

"I don't get what you mean," Dushane responded.

Aguila said, "It's an academic disagreement between people in the biological sciences. Started in the early twenty-first century. Scientists and lawyers began crusading for large tracts of land to be set aside as what they called wild zones. Then they used the developing technology to recreate extinct species to put on those lands. Results were mixed, mostly because of the changing climate, and then the wars and famines that intensified in the 2020s. The movement declined until just after the turn of the century when scholars like Dr. Weisbacher here managed to convince the Board that re-wilding was the only way to restore Earth to any kind of stable climate."

"Had some spectacular failures, too," Shimodi noted through a mouthful of whatever she was eating. It looked like boiled greens and beans. Whatever it was, it sure smelled delicious. Dortmund's belly growled its anticipation.

He gave her a sidelong glare and clarified: "We had to learn from our mistakes."

"Yeah," Shimodi said. "Like all those dead bison."

"How's that?" Dushane asked.

Dortmund cut Shimodi off, quickly saying, "They turned huge tracts of the North American plains into bison ranges in an attempt to reestablish the northern plains grasslands. Millions of acres were confiscated from beef ranchers, fences were torn down, and the bison turned free to roam."

Shimodi couldn't resist. "Yeah, no management. Went swimmingly until something called *Micoplasma bovis* infected the herd, followed by a new strain of anthrax, and then somehow hoof and mouth got introduced from Europe. Being a 'wild' population, they had no way to gather the animals or vaccinate them. Fifty thousand bison. Dead. Just like that."

"It's not quite that simple, and we learned important lessons. As a result we were able to implement improvements in my programs," Dortmund replied, eyes narrowed.

Supervisor Aguila said, "These things are never simple. But then the conservationists have always wanted to take humans out of the equation. The problem is, once humans are no longer managing the system, it usually ends in disaster."

"How then, Supervisor, did life manage for all those billions of years before we came along?" Dortmund asked mildly. "Or Capella III for that matter? And now, here we are. Loose and spilling our vile pollution across the face of a new world. I can't wait to see what evolutionists make of this."

Dushane shot a wary glance at Aguila. "So, I get conservationists, what's an evolutionist?"

Aguila fingered the long scar along her jaw. "The underlying principle is that environments are always changing, that life was made to constantly evolve and adapt to new circumstances, diseases, and changes. So, yes, you're going to have extinctions that—"

"A criminal excuse to avoid human responsibility," Dortmund interrupted. "That way any egregious action that results in the extinction of another species is laid to Darwinian law rather than human greed."

Aguila's gaze turned cold. "Doctor, if you ever interrupt me in that manner or tone again, I will have you shot. Do you understand?"

Dortmund knotted his hands before him. "Supervisor, forgive me, but I'm unaware of your academic expertise in the disciplines of planetology, biology, or resource management. I'm the department chair, the author of more than two hundred articles—"

"You are a Corporate employee. Under my authority. Upon the conclusion of my business here, you will accompany me to Corporate Mine where I will seek to find some suitable employment for you."

The Supervisor glanced up at the marine who'd been standing at parade rest to one side. "Please escort Dr. Weisbacher to the shuttle."

"Yes, ma'am."

While Dortmund tried not to stumble over his words of

protest, a young man appeared, asking, "What can I get you for breakfast?"

"The doctor was just leaving," Aguila told him.

"But I—"

"Come, Doctor," the marine said. "On your feet."

As Dortmund stood, the hunger knot in his stomach tightened.

What the hell was wrong with these people?

36

It really pissed Talina off. Mundo was the agricultural breadbasket. The fields were filled with terrestrial foods, grains, fruits, vegetables, nuts, and berries. Enough to feed every human on the planet, and when it came to staying here, she didn't have a chance in hell.

She chewed on that knowledge as Capella's morning light filtered through the forest off to the east. The purple dawn was greeted by the invertebrates with a new chime. Mist rose from the fields, hanging low, limiting visibility at ground level to less than a hundred yards.

From her vantage point at the shed, Talina sniffed the still air, searched for any movement in the mist. She rearranged her stiff back where she'd positioned herself in an old duralon chair. Her rifle lay across her knees, its action damp with dew.

She glanced down at Kylee. The girl slept just back from the shed door, her thin body curled in a blanket. For most of the night, the kid had moaned, made whimpering noises.

One of Talina's quetzal hallucinations tried to steal her brain. Some image of blending with stones and sucking shrub while a crest ambled slowly up a game trail and into range.

"Stop it, Tal," she whispered to herself, half wondering if she wouldn't eventually imagine herself being eaten by a quetzal. Only to awaken with the realization that it wasn't an hallucination, but that the jaws around her body belonged to Leaper.

Her stomach had been turning for hours now, adding to the sense of premonition. The demon quetzal huddling behind her liver was telling her that a fight was coming. She even thought she heard Rocket whispering in her mind.

"Damn it, I really am spirit-possessed," she whispered to herself, and she imagined the potsherds on her mother's kitchen floor rearranging themselves, as if by a magical hand.

She stood, wincing at the stiffness in her back and butt. Stepping over to the aircar, it was to find the charge at seventy-one percent. Barely enough to make it to Port Authority, but Corporate Mine was well within range.

After making another survey to ensure that a quetzal wasn't racing down on top of her, she glanced again at the sleeping girl.

"Can't stay here, Kylee."

Careful not to disturb the girl, Talina pushed her aircar out into the morning and loaded the solar panel and charger into the back. Between constantly scanning for quetzals and fighting to keep her attention focused as images were triggered in her head, she managed to load a small crate with produce they'd gathered, and then poured the last of the stew into a bucket.

"What are you doing?" Kylee was sitting up, rubbing sleep-heavy eyes with a grimy hand.

"Making ready to pull our stakes and save our butts, kid."

"I'm not going."

Talina sighed, slapped a hand on the aircar's side, and asked, "Dedicated to becoming a meal for Leaper, are you?"

"This is my home. Rocket's buried here. So's my dad." She pulled stringy blond hair out of her face, looking north. "What's up there? Just mean people."

"What's here? Just a quick death. As soon as they digest and absorb Flash, you know they're coming for you."

"What if they learn what Flash did?"

"What if they do? You willing to bet your life that good old Leaper's going to trot up here, kneel down, and say, 'Hey, girl. Let's go for a ride?'"

Kylee gave a surly shrug. "What do I care? I don't want to hurt anymore. I don't want to be scared and lonely. All I do is feel sad. It really fucking stinks."

"Don't cuss."

"Why not?"

"The rulebook says you have to be at least nineteen and in a profession."

"What rulebook?"

"*The* rulebook. The big one. They keep it in Transluna

in a glass case in the Hall of Justice. Corporate Board-members walk by it each morning, touching the glass with white-gloved fingers. Sometimes the Chairman breathes on the glass, polishing it with his sleeve."

"I don't believe you."

"That's 'cause you're a smart girl. And like it or not, we're beating feet out of here."

Kylee stood, wadded up her blanket, and tossed it onto Talina's chair. "I'm not going to Port Authority. I've sworn to make those people pay for what they did to Rocket."

"That was Deb Spiro."

"They made us leave." Kylee crossed her arms defiantly. "They made *you* leave. 'Cause you've got quetzal molecules. They hate anything quetzal."

"Yeah, well, I don't want to belabor a point, but Leaper and Diamond aren't all warm and fuzzy."

"Quetzals are warm-blooded, Talina. And you know they don't have hair. Sometimes you don't make sense."

"It's an old saying, kid. Warm and fuzzy. Means they're not cuddly and nice. Not the sort of happy carnivores you want to snuggle up with." She paused. "So, you're telling me your plan is to have Leaper and Diamond eat you?"

A sadness welled in Kylee's eyes. "Being dead would be better. That's all."

"Then, I guess you've got nothing to lose, huh?"

Kylee shrugged her thin shoulders, eyes on the ground.

"Yeah, well, I . . ." Talina saw the movement, the characteristic rising and curling column that appeared above the trees to the south.

"Get in the car!" Talina reached for her pack, tossing it in. "*Now!*"

She slapped her rifle into the rack.

"I'm not . . ." Kylee didn't have a chance to finish as Talina grabbed the girl around the waist and heaved her into the car. Kylee landed with a hollow thump, tumbling across the deck.

Talina vaulted the rail immediately after, powering up the fans. A stream of the four-winged fliers were lining out, attracted by her movement.

"What are you *doing*!" Kylee shrieked. "You're not my mother! You can't make me—"

"Shut up, kid." Talina gave the car full throttle, scooting north, weaving between the abandoned sheds, keeping low. She skirted the curved ruin of the Mundo Base dome and shot a look over her shoulder. Kylee clambered high on the back seat, as if ready to leap.

Worse, the damn mobbers were flapping right behind. Reds, yellows, blacks, and violet shades of color—probably their colors for pursuit—were egging on the hindmost.

"Get your ass in the seat and buckle in," Talina cried over her shoulder. "Got mobbers back there!"

"What?" Kylee was looking scared. Probably wanting to jump, but worried given the speed at which they were traveling.

"Death fliers! That's what you call them."

Kylee glanced back, froze as she finally realized the peril.

"If you just hold still, they won't bother you," Kylee shouted.

"You've got a lot more faith than I do, kid." Talina arrowed the car back toward the south, building speed. The column of mobbers was still flowing out of the trees. Now they turned in her direction.

She shot a glance back over her shoulder. The mobbers behind were no longer gaining.

"Look!" Kylee pointed. "There's a bunch hovering over the place where Flash's body was dragged. Be fitting justice, don't you think? Leaper and Diamond kill Flash, and then while they're digesting, the mobbers got them?"

"Yeah." Quetzals froze, right? Camouflaged themselves. She steered straight for the middle of the mob. If nothing else, she'd splash their rainbow-colored guts all over the front of the aircar. She was up to eighty kph now, grinning with the thrill of combat. The quetzal in her gut was literally vibrating with terror.

Kylee called, "Here they come."

As Talina shot into the middle of the column she braced for the impact of their bodies. Nothing. To her amazement, the beasts ducked, dodged, flitted to the side, scrambling in all directions. She heard their scimitar-sharp claws striking the aircar's hull—a hail-like rattling sound—but she didn't hit a one.

"If that isn't the damnedest thing. Talk about agility on the wing."

Talina pulled up on the wheel, turned tightly, and shot a glance over her shoulder. The whole line was strung out behind her.

She aimed the aircar down into the gap between the defensive line of pines and the Donovanian forest. There, in the dead zone between, lay Flash's torn remains. Most of the polymer skeleton remained intact enough to give the carcass an identity.

Talina dove, picking up speed. Behind her came the pursuing horde, the entire sky behind the racing aircar like a winding ribbon of flashing colors.

A sinking feeling deadened Talina's gut. How damn fast could the creep-freaking mobbers fly?

She pulled out, skimmed across the top of Flash's bones, and caught the barest glimpse as the panicked Leaper and Diamond dropped their camouflage. One instant the ground next to Flash's corpse appeared empty, the next it turned yellow and black, signs of quetzal fear. Knowing they were discovered, the two quetzals broke for the pines. The stream of mobbers split, some chasing the racing quetzals, others flapping for all they were worth in pursuit of the aircar.

"Come on," Talina growled to herself. "There's got to be a limit on how fast those bastards can fly."

She turned north, the throttle all the way forward.

Leaper and Diamond were racing down the causeway, literal streaks as they lined out, mouths like Os and tail vents wide, legs a blur. Their bodies blazed a startling white as they sought to dump the incredible heat their muscles were producing.

A running quetzal could hit up to one hundred and sixty kph for a limited time. Diamond and Leaper were outdistancing the pursuit.

Talina couldn't help but watch with awe as the two quetzals rounded one of the sheds and dove into a hole torn in the ruins of the Mundo dome. She was whizzing past when the first of the pursuing mobbers rounded the shed, split into smaller groups, and began searching for their vanished prey.

Over her shoulder, Talina could see her own mobbers hot on the aircar's tail.

To her amazement, the mobbers, too, had turned blaze-white for better thermoregulation.

And worse, pegged to the dash like the throttle was, she was pulling everything the battery had. Not that there had been a lot of it to start with.

Looking behind, the mobbers were slowly closing the distance.

37

Living with Dan Wirth had provided Allison Chomko with a hard education, especially when it came to men. She considered that as Tamarland Benteen sauntered across the main room on his way to the cage where she sat.

It had been Dan's chance remark: "There's two kinds of people. Those who are played for cunts, and the few who play them."

She and Dan had been lying in bed one morning after an unusually vigorous bout of sex. That had been a couple of months ago. And she'd realized, sharply and instantly, that she was one of the former. Since that day, Allison had carefully, cautiously, begun laying the groundwork necessary to ultimately change her situation. She was, after all, the daughter of two remarkably intelligent parents, both brilliant in their fields. Somehow, after their deaths, she'd devoted herself to Rick, made him the center of her life. After his crushing death, her battered emotions had fixed on little Jessie. Only to lose her to a quetzal through negligence. Somehow, in the wake of that tragedy, she'd allowed Dan Wirth to turn her into a drugged-out, high-cost prostitute and bookkeeper.

Not exactly the vision of her future that Allison had dreamed as a girl.

As she'd cut back on the drugs, it hit her: She couldn't go back. Couldn't undo what she'd become. What she did have was a choice. She could continue to be played until she despised herself enough to end it all, or she could take steps to use her intellect to become a player herself. Surely she had to have some of her parents' smarts, that innate intelligence.

Allison fully understood that she was in bed with a stone-cold killer and psychopath. Challenging Dan Wirth would be the most dangerous game on the planet.

Now, here came Tamarland Benteen.

"So your name is Allison," Benteen noted as he leaned an elbow against the cashier's cage and glanced thoughtfully out at The Jewel's gaming room. Given that it was midday, only a few of the tables were occupied. Shafts of light angled through the high windows to illuminate the place.

"And you are the scorpion." Allison gave him a wary, half-lidded look. "Quite a reputation. We've never had such a celebrity. Heard they have a death warrant out for you back in Solar System."

"Does that worry you?"

"Look around. Take Art over there, watching you like he is. Anywhere but Donovan, he'd have a death warrant out in his name. It's a tough world filled with tough men." She gave him the slightest trace of a smile. "So, you've killed people. If I lifted a hand, Art would take you out this quick." She snapped her fingers.

"I'm harmless."

Sure. She knew a dangerous man when one was leaning on her counter.

Something made him chuckle. "Let me guess, you like dangerous men."

"Dan's as dangerous as they get on Donovan." *Careful, Allison. Don't underestimate this guy.*

"He's made quite the empire here. He's got a casino, a whorehouse, interest in a half-dozen mines, and controls a lot of property. He sits on the Port Authority city council, if you can call it that. So, given all the above, what's wrong with him?"

Her gaze narrowed. "What do you mean, what's wrong with him?"

"Why isn't he the big boss, the Chairman, whatever you want to call it?"

She gave him a "you're not serious" look.

"Hard to believe that a woman of your beauty would be stuck in a hole like this, cashing chips, and turning the occasional trick. Back in Solar System you'd be a Boardmember's escort in the finest establishments in Transluna."

"Forget the flattery. I'm the richest woman on Donovan after the Supervisor. Back in Solar System, I could buy you."

He met her challenging gaze with his own. "I could care a fig for your wealth. I'm interested in power."

"How is that working out for you? Or, wait, aren't you throwing out your bedroll in Talina's wrecked dome? Wandering around in the middle of the day, leaning on my cage? A bit ambitious of you, isn't it? To be talking about power?" She paused. "Given that I could have your throat cut, and your body left outside the fence, who's the more powerful here?"

"Cut my throat?" He kept his voice casual. "No one on this ball of rock has the requisite talent."

She thought he was boasting, tried to keep the skepticism out of her eyes.

"What do you charge for a night?"

"More than that initial fifty Shig advanced you, that's for sure. And even then, just because you come in with the plunder, chances are you'll be turned down. Most are."

"Why?"

"Because I choose." She lifted a teasing eyebrow. "I'm a businesswoman. If I'm going to take a man into my bed, I'm coming out of it with a nice profit as well as a nice time."

"Do you gamble?"

"Um, look around."

"I'm a gambler myself. I think you and I can do business. Along with your wealth, how would you like to be the law in Port Authority? Think dictator. Queen. Whatever authoritarian term you might want to apply to single-party rule."

She tried to figure his angle. Granted, things were different back in Solar System, but this was Port Authority. Even Dan had come to an understanding of where the limits of his power lay. "Are you out of your mind?"

"Not at all. I've taken Shig and Yvette's measure. And that's the best Port Authority can offer? Then there's your man Dan. Clever, but bumbling in his bid to win favor. A school? Just to curry favor with the local families?"

Time to bait him, but not too far. "What would you do?"

"Delegate, provide the funds, and let them know that they can build their own damn school. My suspicion is that those who complained about my governance would simply disappear."

"And you call that a policy?" His self-assurance intrigued her. She wasn't sure he understood what he was dealing with in PA, but something in his smooth delivery smacked of confidence and competency.

"Humans are susceptible creatures. Each has a weakness, a fault that can be exploited. Among the most useful is fear. The best way to feed fear is through uncertainty. And when critics begin to mysteriously vanish in the night?" He shrugged. "How much more uncertain can you get than that?"

"You talk a good fight."

He studied her thoughtfully, softly asked, "Do you really want to play the game? Become not just the second richest woman, but the richest? And most powerful?"

She experienced that tingling moment of excitement. He'd just dangled the bait. Time to raise the ante. "That means you would have to eliminate the Supervisor."

"I guess it would, wouldn't it? But everything in its time. For the moment, I'd rather wager with you."

"Wager what?" Here it came.

"You. In my bed. Willingly, and for free."

"That will be the day." Shit, this wasn't teasing, he meant it.

"You're a dreamer at heart. I can see it in your eyes. You long for greater things. Dan Wirth is content with his slice of Port Authority. The casino, his money-making interests, but he's willing to let the others run things. Thinks it's beneath his dignity."

"You don't know Dan very well."

"Better than you, my love. People like him? I've spent my life bringing them down and turning them into my willing servants."

"Hot air." But something about him had her warning bells ringing. A year working in The Jewel had sharpened her wits, as if she could detect danger through some sixth sense.

"You want to take my bet? If I win, take control of all of this"—he lifted his upraised palms to indicate The Jewel—"you come to my bed. Join me. Work at my side as my partner."

Suppose he could eliminate Dan? What then? Where would she be? A line girl like Angelina? She sure as hell wasn't going to be welcomed back in the community with open arms. "Why me?"

"You lived all your life here. You know Donovan in ways I don't. I need a second, and you're the most ravishing thing I've seen here. Maybe the smartest, too. Let me guess, since *Turalon*'s arrival, you've gone from nothing to all of this. In another year, why wouldn't you want the whole show?"

She had half started to believe him, and then broke into laughter. "Yeah, sure. You take all of this over? I'll bed you. It'd take a miracle." She pointed. "And you'd have to deal with the likes of Art long before you ever got to Dan. And believe me, you wouldn't like his kind of trouble. The kind that will find your body out at the edge of the fields, swarmed by invertebrates as they devour your corpse."

But under the bravado, Allison had a shiver run down her spine. It was something about Tam Benteen, that creeping sensation that she was in the presence of the most dangerous man she'd ever met. That something irrevocable had once again changed in her life, and if she didn't play it just right, she'd come out of it either dead or forever broken.

38

In the drift wall copper gleamed at the outside, edging imperceptibly into green and then to a metallic gray almost mindful of lead. In the white glare of the arc lights, the remarkable streak of metal was absolutely beautiful. Worth a fortune. And a real pain in the ass. It ran down one side of the tunnel wall and filled the entire face where it continued into the rock.

"Hard to believe, isn't it?" Lea Shimodi asked through her suit com. "I would have said it was impossible. But here it is, more wealth than I would have believed could be concentrated in one place."

Kalico stepped closer, careful of her footing as she crossed the muck, or piled ore, and peered at the vein. "Deadly stuff, eh?" She fought the urge to poke the gray metal.

"You really don't want to breathe it," Aurobindo Ghosh told her. "And, Supervisor, you're looking at a bloody damn fortune right there. That's pure beryllium surrounded by copper. Like some giant glob of it was blasted out of a star, compacted here as part of the planetary accretion process when Donovan was formed."

"Ituri said that the beryllium fraction was increasing with depth."

"Yeah, well, we're at four hundred and eighty feet. Problem is, we've only got four hazard suits. We can't let anyone down here to stope this out unless they're suited. That's why I've got this tunnel sealed off with that plastic sheeting."

"How big do you think this deposit is?" Kalico again resisted the urge to finger the ghostly gray. An alkaline earth metal, beryllium had remarkable properties when mixed with copper, iron, or nickel. And here it was: pure.

And no way to know how many metric tons might be waiting to be freed from its rocky confinement.

"No telling, Supervisor. The farther it goes, the more fantastic it is." Shimodi's voice communicated the woman's awe. But then, she'd been starstruck from the moment she stepped off the shuttle at Corporate Mine. Called it a wonderland.

"Wish we had more suits," Ghosh was muttering.

"We'll work with what we've got, my friend." Kalico mollified herself by patting the gleaming copper at the outside of the deposit where it surrendered to greenish rock.

"Supervisor?" O'Hanley's voice asked through her com.

"Here."

"We've got an aircar coming from the south. Weak signal. Talina Perez is asking for permission to land. Says that she's about out of battery."

"Roger that. Put her over by the fence. I'll be up in about ten minutes."

"Yes, ma'am."

"You heard?" she asked Ghosh.

"Yes. Go."

"Yeah, let me guess. You're just happy to have me out of the suit and somebody productive back in it."

Ghosh was grinning at her through his face mask. "The thought never crossed my mind. But do remember the protocol. Follow Desch's instructions while they decontaminate you."

She raised a gloved hand and saluted, seeing a flash of Ghosh's teeth in return.

Making her way back up the tunnel, it surprised her that she no longer reacted to the gleaming threads of gold that ran through the rock. In one day her smelter turned out more than the combined mines on Earth, Luna, Mars, and in the asteroids. And they were doing it out of two holes, with a makeshift aerial tram, and a smelter that only ran part time because she had a cobbled-together reactor.

At the plastic, she passed through into an ad hoc washroom where her suit was sprayed down, the water collected, and a blower finished the job of drying and removing droplets.

Next she stepped out into a lantern-lit dressing room. Yes, lantern-lit. The light came from an old-fashioned lantern made in PA that burned kerosene distilled from crude oil that came from west of the Wind Mountains. She didn't have enough electric lights to illuminate the entire mine.

"Did you see it?" Desch Ituri asked as she removed the hood. "What did you think?"

"I was thinking we could buy Transluna if we had that whole deposit back in Solar System. How'd you like that? Your own high-rise overlooking the business district?"

Ituri's dark face lit with a smile. "What are we gonna do with all those pesky Boardmembers? They might not sell."

"Maybe sic some Wild Ones on them. That'd send fear through their soft bones, wouldn't it?"

Ituri helped her out of the suit, handed it to Talovich.

"What do you think it's going to take to stope that out?" she asked.

Ituri glanced at Talovich, who was wasting no time putting the suit on. "We're working on that. The trick is to get it out without breaking it up too much. Every surface we create exposes more of it to oxidation. And we can't be contaminating the rest of the mine with beryllium dust in the process."

"We might want to ferry the pure stuff up to orbit," Talovich said. "Storing it in vacuum would solve a lot of problems."

"Just got to fabricate the containers," Ituri agreed. "We've got credit for that carbon-fiber cable we made for PA, right? Maybe I can get with Lawson to make us custom containers. We could peel the beryllium right out of the rock, box it, and ship it."

"Whatever you need," she told them as she took her pistol and utility belt down from a peg driven into the rock.

"Yes, ma'am." Talovich gave a smile and a salute before slipping through the plastic.

"How's ventilation?" she asked.

"Got a hose running up to the surface." Ituri rubbed the back of his head. "Not the best of solutions since it's venting out on the other side of the fence, but as long as people stay away, it's going to oxidize relatively quickly."

"There might be something we haven't inventoried in the *Freelander* cargo that would help. I'll see."

She turned, rode the skip back to the main shaft, and took the lift to the surface.

When she stepped out from under the head frame, it was to see Talina Perez, her butt braced against the side of her battered old aircar. The woman grinned, ran fingers through windblown black hair, and propped her hand on her pistol.

Beside her, a skinny ragamuffin of a blond girl had her arms crossed, tangles of hair falling over her shoulders and down her back. The kid was in rags. Almost to the point of indecency given the location of the rents and holes. Kalico had seen more prosperous-looking urchins in the streets of Mumbai.

"Talina, what brings you to my little corner of Donovan?"

"Had to flee Mundo this morning." She indicated the little girl. "You remember Kylee Simonov?"

Kalico allowed herself a surprised smile. "Hello, Kylee."

If chaos and death could be concentrated, it was in the girl's hard glare. She seemed to be smoldering.

"We're about out of charge in the aircar," Talina said. "We had to make a hasty exit from Mundo this morning. Not only did the quetzal situation fall apart, but a huge flock of mobbers appeared this morning. Look at the gouges those little bastards cut into the sialon on my air crate."

"That close, huh?"

Talina grinned. "Yeah. Had to do a bit of dicey flying. But, for the record, mobbers top out a hundred and ten, and can only maintain it for about four minutes before they start to flag."

Kalico couldn't help it; she absently fingered one of the scars running along her cheek, her eyes turning to the south. "Any way they could have followed you?"

"I don't think so. We ran north at one hundred and thirty, and they turned back toward Mundo a couple of kilometers this side of the base. Better pickings. They had two quetzals to hunt and the better part of a corpse to scavenge."

Kalico really got a close look at Kylee. The kid looked like she hadn't had a real bath in forever. Hostility and frustration glittered behind those peculiar eyes. Something about them wasn't quite . . . human?

To her com, Kalico said, "Have Stryski wheel Security Officer Perez's aircar over and give it a charge and a check over."

"Roger that," O'Hanley replied.

To Talina she said, "You eaten?"

"We shared a couple of cups of stew on the way up."

Kalico fixed on Kylee. "You got a change of clothes?"

The girl's jaws bunched, eyes narrowing.

"She talk?" Kalico asked Talina.

"Yeah. But give her a break. She's taken a couple of hard hits. One after another. And I'm not doing so well, either."

"How's that?"

"Too many damn quetzals in my head. Hard to concentrate. Half the time I'm on the verge of tears, the other half I'm wanting to shoot something."

"I heard that you were responsible for the negligent discharge of a firearm up in PA."

"Thought I was shooting a hole in Sian Hmong."

"Schoolteacher, isn't she?"

"You have to be careful about schoolteachers; they're more dangerous than you'd think. And you never know what they're pouring into the heads of these impressionable young kids." Talina winced. "What's Raya saying about me?"

"I wouldn't go asking her for an emergency appendectomy for a while. And Trish is on a holy tear."

Talina avoided her eyes. "Yeah, I'm figuring Kylee and I better stick to the bush for a while."

"Where are you going to go?"

"Haven't a clue. Mundo's out of the question. Maybe Rork Springs. Two Falls Gap is another possibility. Someplace where I can't hurt anyone if I go nuts again. I'd consider dropping Kylee with her mom at PA, but trust me, that would be a recipe for disaster."

"I could put you up here. Dya's due tomorrow for her

rotation in the clinic. Hard to picture Corporate Mine as a halfway house, but we could think up something."

Kalico caught the panicked flash as Kylee shot a horrified look at Talina.

"Thanks, Kalico. I appreciate that. But really, Kylee and I need a little more time out and away from people. We're both what you'd call brittle around the edges."

"You heard about the ship?"

"What ship?"

"*Vixen* showed up out of the blue. You know, the one that was lost over fifty years ago. Survey ship sent here after *Tempest*. Crew hasn't aged. They claim it was an instantaneous transition from Solar System to here. Well, but for the small problem that we perceive it as fifty years. Puts a whole new wrinkle on symmetry inversions. I'm still trying to get my head around what it means for us."

"No shit? Just popped in and thought it was like, yesterday."

"That's about the size of it." Kalico arched an eyebrow. "You have any inclination to shoot me?"

"No."

"Well, I haven't eaten. Want chicken-fried steak? Maybe a falafel? A Shanghai stir fry? Maybe finish it all off with a cup of coffee?"

"You shitting me?"

"Nope. Requisitioned *Vixen*'s rations. Torgussen's Corporate. He didn't even protest, just shipped it all down. In return I told him he was getting fresh vegetables."

"Yes, feed me. I'll give you my soul in return."

"And you think that will entice me? Talk about the bottom of the barrel."

Kalico glanced at the girl. "And I'm betting we can find some decent clothes for Kylee, too."

The little girl looked daggers at Kalico.

"What did I do?"

"Deb Spiro worked for you," Talina said softly.

Kalico bent down, eyes level with the little girl's. Unflinching. "I liked Rocket. I thought he was remarkable. Spiro disobeyed my orders when she shot Rocket. After she did, she knew enough to never return here. If she had, I would have shot her myself. We clear on that?"

The little girl's gaze softened. Not much. But a little, and she gave Kalico a faint nod of acceptance.

So, Talina and the kid were headed back out into the bush? That was about as crazy as things went on Donovan. But, Talina wasn't one of hers. With that, Kalico turned and headed for the dome, Talina pressing close behind. Must have been the offer of coffee.

39

It's just a toilet-sucking school! Dan Wirth stomped his way down the avenue in time with the grinding of his teeth. Beside him, the normally taciturn Hofer kept pace. The builder had an odd expression on his face, like he was choking on something amusing.

"Interesting morning, huh?" Hofer finally said.

Dan gave him an expansive gesture. "What's so damn hard about it? Build the fricking building, put the little rat chasers inside, and stuff it with a couple of teachers to educate the screaming imps on how to generate wealth from Donovan's vast resources. What am I missing?"

Which, of course, was the long-term plan. The more wealth Donovan generated, the more successful the colony, the more Dan could rake out for his own gain. It wasn't exactly like computing inverse symmetry probability. Hardly a mentally challenging feat of comprehension.

"But no!" he cried out, gesturing with knotted fists. "Way too fucking early this morning, who gets a call? I do. Amal Oshanti and Friga Dushku. 'Mr. Wirth, we need to see you at the school.'

"And what do I do? I drag my chapped butt out of a nice comfy bed, where I'm snuggled up around Allison's soft warm ass. I miss my morning tea and go confront those two sorry slits. And what do I hear? 'We need a science lab. Not enough common space. Gotta change this. Gotta change that.'

"Can I tell them to go screw themselves with broomsticks? No. They're the 'good people.' *Solid* members of the community." He almost bellowed the words, "Looked up to!"

Dan shook his head. "As if, by virtue of being successful breeders, teachers, and home builders, that makes them pillars of the community? So what if they're the only benighted souls in PA who've got the patience to work with the yelling little vermin?"

"It's just a few changes, Dan," Hofer said easily.

"A few changes? We're moving two fucking walls!" Again he mimicked their voices, 'Oh, no, Mr. Wirth, this just won't do. We need a larger community area. But, Mr. Wirth, the visual projection and VR space won't accommodate the number of students we anticipate in the future.'"

"I'll give a call to O'Hanley. See if Corporate can't shuttle up another load of logs on its next trip north. Lee Halston can run them through his mill, won't take but another week."

"Who the fuck knows what Aguila's going to charge me? And then you've got to get the damn stone. It's another five hundred square feet. And I've got to pay to have Vanveer's shed and dome moved."

"So, what? Aguila's people are going to be having kids soon. I heard four of the women down there are pregnant. They gotta go to school somewhere. I got kids, I know."

"You got kids? Yeah. Thirty light-years away where some other asshole is educating them." Dan shot the grumpy builder a sidelong look. "So, what was it? Back in the beginning, you were one of the loudest bastards, hollering to be shipped back to Solar System and your wife and family."

Hofer's brows lowered, gaze distant. "*Freelander*. Spooked the shit out of me. Now with *Vixen*? I'm even gladder I stayed. Maybe I don't miss Agnes so much. Fact is the woman's a pain in my ass. But I wonder about the kids. Pete and Mary. They're mostly grown now." He grinned. "Since I'm out of system, and way beyond contract, their benefits are outstanding. Me being on this miserable rock is probably the best thing I ever could have done for them."

As they came even with The Jewel, Wirth said, "All right, do it. Make the fucking school however those witches want it. Just get it done and get them the fuck out of my life."

Hofer, failing to hide his amusement, said, "Well, it's not like you can't raise the take on the tables for a couple of weeks to cover the expense."

"Hey, married man, maybe I'll just raise the cost of tail over at Betty Able's. Charge an extra fifty SDRs for a fuck. For everybody except you. I hear you're dropping in about three times a week to bang Flossey. For you it could be an extra hundred just on account of."

Hofer shrugged, nonplussed. "Yeah, that's fine. I think, however, I see an unforeseen increase in expenses on the school coming, Dan. About an extra three hundred a week."

"Ya gotta love a free-market economy. I begin to see the lure of inflation and why those Corporate bastards back in Solar System outlawed it."

Giving Hofer a salute with flicked fingers, Dan stepped into The Jewel to find Shin Wong, his best faro dealer, wiping down the tables. Allison was at a back table, leaning forward on her elbows, laughing at something Tamarland Benteen was saying.

Stepping over to the bar, Dan asked, "Art, how long's the soft meat been in?"

"Since just after opening, boss." Maniken shot a disapproving glance toward Benteen. "Seems like every time you're out, he's hitting on Ali. The guy's a slug. Buys a beer, nurses it until some of the locals come in. Then he gets to telling stories about shit he's done with that Boardmember, and they buy him another drink that he nurses. He sits in, but doesn't gamble much, tells more stories. Slows the games. House take is down about fifteen percent when he's at a table."

"Pour me two whiskeys."

Art took down the house bottle and poured a finger into each tumbler before handing them over.

Taking the glasses, Dan ambled over to Allison's table, smiled, and said, "Ali, my love, I'd call you an angel if you'd wander over to the cafeteria and bring me a plate of breakfast. The charming Mr. Benteen and I are going to toast the morning and have a little chat."

"Anything special you want?" Allison asked as she rose, the faintest trace of worry behind her blue eyes.

"Whatever Millie's serving up. Good to give her a little business given what Inga has carved out of her traffic."

He watched her walk away, admiring the curves and

swing of her hips. As he dropped into the chair, he said, "Ah, the wonder of that woman. Still leaves me breathless."

Dan slid the whiskey in Benteen's direction. "On the house."

Benteen took it, a sliver of smile on his lips. The man lifted the glass, inhaled through his mouth—as only real whiskey drinkers did—and savored the aroma. "Must be difficult to make a palatable whiskey without oak to age it in. Still, there's something about it, a sweet almost spice rather than fruitiness. Like no whiskey I've ever tasted, and believe me, I've had opportunity to taste the best. Ship this back as a limited batch reserve and you could sell it for a fortune in the finer establishments."

"Inga makes do. That chickenshit sawyer, Lee Halston, cuts the staves, makes her barrels from aquajade, then chars them. That's the unusual aroma and taste. Here's to balls, buttocks, and bitches."

Dan raised his glass in toast and took a sip as Benteen did the same.

"My thanks for the morning libation." Benteen leaned back in his chair, wary eyes on Dan's. "I've come to develop an appreciation for what you've built here. My compliments."

"You should try building a school."

"That's for menials."

Dan felt that cold calming of his heart and the slowing of his pulse. His vision took on that old familiar clarity of focus as he studied Benteen. The man seemed oddly oblivious, totally at ease. Either the fool didn't get it, or he was so damned confident of himself he knew just what he was doing.

"I've come to consider The Jewel as refuge," Benteen continued.

"Yeah, well, that seems to be something of a problem. I don't run a refuge. Might not be a bad idea, Donovan being what it is, but I don't see any money in it. And that's a key word. Money. SDRs, sidders, coin, plunder, whatever you want to call it. You're not adding significantly to the take. It seems that the few drinks you cadge along the side don't make up for what your loquacious proclivities detract from real drinking and gambling. Tell me if I'm outpacing your comprehension here."

Benteen's smile had thinned, his eyes sharpening.

When he said nothing, Dan told him, "In summary, given the above, I'd suggest that after you finish that whiskey, you move on. Find a refuge in the cafeteria or Inga's."

This time, Dan plastered a fake smile on his lips, all the while his heart and blood pumping in an expectation of action.

Benteen took a sip of his whiskey, swished it around his mouth, and carefully returned the glass to the table. He hadn't changed posture, still leaned back, looking relaxed. Finally, he said, "After due consideration, I think I'll decline your kind suggestion."

"Perhaps you didn't follow my drift, as the miners hereabouts would say. It wasn't a suggestion, and this is not a negotiable topic. Finish your whiskey, and after you leave, don't come back."

Benteen's sudden smile went all the way to his eyes. "Good play, Wirth. I'll bet it even works with these penny-ante miners, hunters, and assorted locals. As to what's negotiable? That's everything under the sun, my friend. Including where I go, who I spend my time with, and which chair I choose to sit in. For the time being, I like this one."

"Art?" Dan called, "Could you come over here for a second?"

Maniken stepped out from behind the bar, a leather-wrapped stonewood bat held suggestively in his gnarled right hand. As he stepped up to the table, he asked, "Yeah, boss?"

"Mr. Benteen here was just leaving. I was wondering if you would be so kind as to escort him out the back way. I'd hate to think what might happen if he were not incredibly polite and courteous during his rapid removal from the premises."

"On your feet," Art ordered with all the sensitivity of a corrections officer.

"This is the way it has to be?" Benteen asked Dan.

"'Fraid so."

"Very well." The man sighed, straightened, and rose.

Art stepped up behind him, smacking the leather-wrapped bat into his meaty left palm with a hollow pop.

Benteen seemed to blur, spin. Dan caught the faintest image of the man's hand flashing under the coat, then out and up. Even as Benteen lunged, the meaty smack of metal on bone could be heard.

Maniken's head jerked to the side. The man's eyes started wide. A spindle of saliva slung from his mouth at the impact.

The big man was falling as Benteen danced to one side, caught Art's weight, and supported his sagging bulk. A black pistol was pressed to the side of Maniken's head, the bouncer's expression slack, lips loose and eyes unfocused.

"Tiresome," Benteen said, mildly. "Three pounds of pressure on the trigger and I blow what few brains this lunkard has all over your nicely polished table. Shin Wong was so careful with his wiping this morning. Be a shame to muck it all up with gore."

Dan hadn't had time to react. Now his heart, uncharacteristically, was hammering. "You really shouldn't have done that."

Art tried to straighten, only to have his eyes roll back as he flopped limply.

Benteen let him slip to the floor, reholstered the pistol, and resumed his seat across from Dan. Without so much as a tremor in the fingers, he picked up his whiskey and took another sip.

Dan was aware that everyone in the room was frozen, watching. Shin, Vik, Angelina, and Dalia might have been rabbits in a spotlight.

Benteen smiled. "You had to try. You wouldn't have been worth spit if you hadn't. To your credit, I thought it would take you another day. That it didn't shows a well-developed sense for trouble and what to do about it. The 'Art, come over here' was a bit ham-handed, but maybe that's how you have to communicate with these miners and the like."

"You know this isn't going to end well."

"Your decision to make." Benteen raised his voice. "Vik? If you can break yourself loose from imitating a tree trunk, could you bring Dan and me a refill, please? The good bottle this time."

Vik started forward, stopped short, looking back and forth from Dan to Benteen.

"Hate to have to get up and show poor Vik his place, too." Benteen glanced sidelong at Dan, an eyebrow arched. "Or is this the moment you decide to rear up on your hind legs and push the point? Granted, it will be heroic, but with a bullet through your heart, I don't think Vik, Shin, and the rest will debate my authority afterward."

Dan considered Benteen's hand, resting so innocently on the table. Considered his own pistol, back in the office. Not that it would have done him much good. Even if it were in the wire basket under the table, he doubted he could so much as get fingers on the grip before Benteen shot him.

"Vik," Dan barked. "Bring the bottle."

Fractured glass wasn't as brittle as the atmosphere when Vik refilled both glasses and backed away to the bar.

"Now, that's better," Benteen told him after inhaling over the whiskey. "Aquajade you say? It really is marvelous."

"Enjoy it while you can."

"Relax. I'm not interested in seeing you dead, let alone have any interest in taking over your operations. Hell, I don't even want a cut of the action. Let's just forget that this morning even happened."

Dan lifted his whiskey, every bit of him focused on Benteen. "Then what, pray tell, are you after?"

"One thing at a time, Dan. First, I notice that Allison does what you tell her."

"For the most part. That what this play was about? Allison?"

"Only tangentially. Here're the new rules: I come and go. You run The Jewel and Betty Able's and all of your other businesses. Your next move, of course, will be to bide your time. Shoot me in the back. Maybe a rifle shot from ambush. Don't. It's been tried by some of the smartest professionals in Solar System. They're dead. I'm not. I've got a sense for these things. Anyone attempts it, you'll be a corpse within the hour, and I get all this by default."

"Then, what's your play?"

Benteen chuckled. "I'm not your enemy, Dan. Just the opposite. Help me achieve my goals, and your life is going to be a whole lot easier." Benteen paused. "What is libertarianism, anyway? Seems like a real waste."

"There might be resistance against what you're planning. Remember that first night we talked?"

"My take, Dan, is that you really hate fucking around building things like schools."

40

The scream—by virtue of the sheer terror that filled it—sent shivers up Talina's back. She crouched in the forest trail, pistol gripped before her. Eyes trying to see everything around her. Sweat was dripping from her skin in the damp equatorial heat. Her heart tried to hammer its way out of her chest. She'd warned him. Hoped for just this, actually. Call it the coward's way out. But the horror of what she saw left her weak and trembling.

Again, he screamed. And his eyes fixed on hers as he dangled three, maybe four meters off the ground. Another of the tentacles wrapped slowly around his upper thigh, the tip finding its way into the coverall's front pocket, piercing the thin inner pocket material. Then the tip wormed its way into the tender skin beside the testicles.

"For God's sake, Talina!" he cried. "Shoot me!"

Talina's mouth had gone dry. She lifted the pistol, discovered that her hands were shaking.

Up among the mundo leaves, Clemenceau drew another breath, filling his lungs for another plea. As he did, the tentacle that had grabbed his shoulder ate its way deeper into the hollow between the clavicle and pectoral. The scream grated across Talina's nerves.

She fought the urge to back away. Turn, wind her way to the trail she'd led Clemenceau down not an hour before.

Wasn't anything more than the bastard deserved after the things he'd done. The problem with petty tyrants was that they used their power for the most unsavory things. The latest—just the day before—he'd pointed to a tarp, ordering, "Take that out over the Gulf. At least ten minutes offshore before you dump it."

Turned out that Clemenceau had finally had his way with Sheila Monagan. The man had been making a pest of himself, stalking the woman. Sheila had been terrified, a widow with a precocious daughter, and no one to stand up for her. Then Clemenceau had threatened to molest Sheila's twelve-year-old daughter, Trish, and Sheila had given in, willing to endure the inevitable in an attempt to save her child. Not that it had turned out all that well for her.

On that flight out to the gulf, Talina had checked. Unzipped the tarp to stare into Sheila's dead eyes. Had cataloged the signs of sexual abuse. Nothing that the woman Talina had known would have consented to.

Why the hell did I dump her? I could have taken her back, laid her body in the main street, and exposed Clemenceau for everything he was.

She hadn't because Clemenceau was the Supervisor. Heads of security followed orders.

Just like the day Talina had shot down Pak and Paolo in the street.

People raised in The Corporation didn't question. It was unthinkable.

"I will not countenance open rebellion!" Clemenceau's voice thundered in her ear. *"Security Officer, shoot them. Shoot them now!"*

Talina struggled to swallow as she stared into Clemenceau's eyes. She raised the pistol. The same pistol she'd shot Pak and Paolo with. Stared into his face over the pistol sights.

"Please?" he whimpered.

She didn't will it. The pistol just seemed to buck in her hand. The round caught Clemenceau in the left cheek next to the nose. The way his head was hanging, the bullet blew out the spinal cord and base of the skull. After the jerk at impact, he hung, limp in the tentacles, left eye bulged out of its socket, blood dribbling from his mouth and nostrils as the head drained.

Talina was panting; it seemed impossible to draw a breath from the muggy and stifling air.

"Talina? Hey!"

Something poked her hard in the side.

Talina blinked, the forest vanishing like a mirage.

She was in a locker room. Showers. Toilet stalls and sinks. The place smelled wet and soapy. Her butt was astraddle a bench, a comb was grasped by one end in her hand.

"For Sheila's funeral, we buried a bunch of packing inside a rolled blanket so that Trish would never know," she said absently. "I couldn't have that kid knowing what that shit-fucker had done to her mother."

"What are you talking about?" Kylee asked.

Talina's quetzal was gnawing at the back of her spine. She imagined Rocket's three eyes staring sympathetically out of her memory.

Kylee was twisted around, inspecting her with worried blue eyes, her freshly washed hair wet and half combed. "You come back here. To this place. We're at that fucking mine."

Talina's scrambled thoughts tried to tumble into some kind of order. Potsherds rearranging into yet another pattern. "Corporate Mine?"

"Duh?"

"If your mother ever hears you cursing like that . . ."

"Where were you just now? I know it was Clemenceau. And who's Sheila?"

"A woman he raped and murdered. That was a long time ago."

"You whimpered something about 'not Trish.' She her daughter?"

"Yes." Talina started. Shit. She wasn't thinking. "Forget it. It was a long time ago. He was a bad man."

Kylee was watching her with those knowing eyes. "Did you kill him because of Sheila?"

"Among other reasons."

"Like my father and Paolo?"

"You know too much for your own good."

The girl took the comb from Talina's hand and tried to work it through her tangles. Talina took it back. "Here, let me."

"We really going to Rork Springs?"

"Probably. It's a hideout that I've kept stocked for emergencies. Same with Two Falls Gap. There's shelter, good water. Not much chance of poisoning. It's bush country. Not as dangerous as deep forest."

"It's scary when you go away like that."

"You ought to try it from my perspective. What if I'm flying? Or in the middle of a fight with a bunch of mobbers and my brain goes whacko?"

"What's whacko?"

"Old term. Before your time. Means abnormal. Off track."

Kylee's shoulders tensed. "You really believe that? What the scarred woman said? That Spiro disobeyed orders?"

"I do."

"Why?"

"Because Kalico Aguila is many things, but never a liar. That's one of the qualities I like about her. She tells you how it is straight out."

"She made Mark and Dya miserable in the hospital before we left. She would have taken Mundo."

"That's right. But don't be too hard on her. She was doing everything she could to keep her mine and her people alive. If you were in her place, you damn well might have done the same. Sometimes, like shooting Clemenceau, it all comes down to survival. Like you, standing there, watching Flash and Diamond eating Rebecca and Shantaya. I know for a fact you'd take that back in a second."

Kylee was silent for a long moment, then finally jerked her head in a miserable nod.

"People back in Solar System wouldn't understand, kid. If I could go back, I'd have shot Clemenceau the first time I realized what a sick and twisted piece of shit he was." She gestured with the comb. "And believe me, I've had to ride herd on my impulse to shoot first and question later ever since."

"So you really should have shot Sian Hmong?"

Talina made a face. "No. Well, not when I'm in my right mind. Sian's a good mother and a great teacher. Her husband and her three kids love her, and she loves them. She didn't understand Rocket. None of us did. Not at first. But because she didn't understand, is that a reason to murder her? Leave her husband and those three little kids grieving, feeling like their guts are torn out?"

Talina stood, heart beginning to hammer. "I'd be just like Deb Spiro."

"You're not."

"You weren't there that day in Port Authority. I mean, just like now with Clemenceau, I was locked away in the hallucination. It was so real. I just sort of woke up with my gun in my hand and a fresh bullet hole in a shipping crate. If Sian had been standing there . . . ?"

Talina walked over to the folded clothing O'Hanley had brought while Kylee showered. "Try these on. I think they're a little big, but they're smaller than anyone here can wear."

She watched as Kylee dressed, looking baggy in the bright yellow overalls. With the cuffs rolled up, however, the kid no longer looked like a refugee out of one of those pictures in a twentieth-century history book.

Talina led the way to the dormitory door, stepped out into the sun, and squinted as she started across the fired clay on the landing field. She could see her aircar, plugged in to the large solar panel array.

She grabbed Kylee's hand, stopping the girl as one of the big haulers went grinding and roaring past. The thing rocked and lurched on its oversized tires. A spear of pride warmed Talina's breast. Those were Cheng's tires. Molded out of vulcanized mundo-leaf rubber.

She followed along in the monster's dusty wake.

"What are those?" Kylee asked, pointing with her other hand.

"Cannons," Talina told her. "For shooting down your death fliers. Could have used a couple of those when we were jumped down at Mundo. Kalico's destroyed a whole flock with those guns."

"Wonder if Leaper and Diamond got away?"

"I saw them dive into a hole torn in the side of the Mundo dome. Maybe. I couldn't tell if the death fliers saw where they hid." Talina glanced down. "Do you want them dead?"

Kylee pursed her lips as she stared at the looming head-stock over the Number 1 mine shaft. The great wheel on top was turning as the cage was being winched up with another load of ore.

"That a yes or no?" Talina prodded.

Kylee glanced up, eyes fierce. "I want them *dead*, okay?"

"Kid, you're going to have to figure out that if everybody dies who hurts you, you're going to depopulate half the planet."

Kylee didn't seem to buy it. "Here's the deal. Let's go have our meal with the scarred lady. I'll be good. Promise not to make a scene. Then just get me the hell out of here and back to the bush, okay?"

"You're really going to have to stop cussing."

"Why? It's coming out of your mouth all the time."

"That's different."

"Why? 'Cause you're an adult? 'Cause you've earned the right? That's what Rebecca always said. That she'd been hard-used by life, so it was okay. Well I've been hard-used, too. Harder than Rebecca ever was, so I'm cussing. And you can't make me stop."

"Don't bet on that."

"Oh yeah? What could you do to me that hasn't already been done worse? Break my other hip? Kill someone I love?"

Talina felt her resistance crumble. "You got a point there. So, I'll take your deal. Be nice while we eat. Don't antagonize Kalico, and I'll have you back out in the bush before you know it."

"Good. Just so we're long gone before Dya shows up."

"She's your mother."

"I don't have family. Makes it easier to hate people."

Talina glanced down, an uneasy feeling in her gut. How did a child get that broken? And was there any way to fix it?

41

The night was remarkably quiet. So much so that it brought Tamarland awake. As he'd been trained, he took the moment to listen, heard the soft breathing of the woman beside him. Aware of the round pressure of her naked hip against his.

A board creaked somewhere beyond the door. The building settling? Or the weight of a stealthy foot?

All in all, it had been a good day. He and Wirth had come to an agreement. There would be no trouble, as Tam had predicted. Wirth was a known quantity. A true psychopath, as his emotional control indicated, along with his careful surrender. The guy really believed, down deep, that he was going to come out ahead in the end. Psychopaths had that trait hardwired into their personalities.

Tam could work with that. No reason Wirth shouldn't emerge with his empire untouched. Unthreatened in the end, he'd be a perfect lieutenant when it came to maintaining control of Port Authority.

Shig Mosadek and Yvette Dushane, on the other hand, would be harder nuts to crack. Political ideologues always were. Any kind of true believer, especially the ones with an emotional investment, were always trouble. No sense of compromise. He'd probably have to eliminate them. That was going to be touchy on two fronts. First, people genuinely liked Shig. Even Wirth, who didn't really like anyone except himself. Second, Yvette was the savvy operations officer. She understood the files, the management, oversaw the way that Port Authority actually worked.

Wonder if I could find some lever, a flaw in her personality?

Just off the cuff, that didn't seem likely. What the hell could she have to hide? In libertarian Port Authority, no one seemed to give much of a damn about licentious behavior. She was single, so there was no lover to compromise a marriage. All the records were wide open to anyone's inspection, and money was cash, kept in people's homes or on their persons. Worse, everyone knew everyone else, so graft and corruption, abuse of office, were like an open book. There were no rations to cheat on or skim. No special access to buy. When it came to exploiting good old corruption in the name of political manipulation, Port Authority sucked toilet water.

So, if Dushane couldn't be compromised by means of flaws in her character, it would have to be through intimidation. Threat of pain or death.

He eased his legs over the side of the bed and sat up, the room dim in the nightlight's glow.

Allison lay on her back, head pillowed on a slender white arm, her hair in a white-blond tangle on the pillow. The woman's rounded left breast with its pink nipple lay exposed where the sheet was wadded.

To his surprise, she hadn't immediately turned down his advance, but had looked to Wirth, who'd given her a slight nod. Still, Tam would remember that smoky look of irritation in the man's eyes. Not jealousy so much as surrendering, without due compensation, what he thought was his. That he'd acquiesced at all was a mark in Wirth's favor. The man fundamentally understood when his best interests were at stake.

As had Allison Chomko. He had read the tension in her. The woman had no illusions about the role she now found herself in, a pawn between him and Wirth. Better yet, she'd proved herself to be a player. Not like sex with Shayne—given her implants and trained body—and certainly not like the professional courtesans who served the moneyed and powerful that gravitated around the Board. Instead, the fact that Allison had honestly committed herself to good and fulfilling sex rather than a professional performance served to make it a most memorable night.

He stood, stretched, and cocked his head to listen. At the door, he unlocked it, let it swing silently open, and waited. The Jewel was quiet in the few hours between closing and when Shin Wong would show up to begin cleaning prior to opening.

Barefoot, Tam made his way down to the staff toilet, let himself in, and emptied his bladder.

For a moment, he stood, listening.

There, the faintest rasping of clothing. He could almost sense the person's breath, a soft inhaling, then a careful exhalation.

If there was any surprise, it was that it had come so quickly. As in all high-stakes games, making a point early and unambiguously generally paid dividends in the end.

Tam flushed, letting the sound of the water cover his movement as he opened the door. His augmented night vision gave him a good identification of his attacker. Let him easily duck the blow that would have crushed his skull. Instead the club cracked loudly into the door jamb.

"Sorry, Art. Missed."

Again the man swung. Tam bent to one side. The long club crashed into the opposite wall.

Tam ducked and bobbed, backing away.

"You sucking snot!" Maniken bellowed. "Whack me in the head? I'll show you."

Art Maniken charged forward. Tam sidestepped, tripped him, and watched Maniken hit the floor. The big man seemed to be all elbows and knees as he scrambled to get up.

The hall lights went on, the effect blinding. From long training, Tam slitted his eyes. He skipped back as Maniken made another wild swing with his club.

"Dan send you?" Tam asked pleasantly.

"I'm here 'cause nobody does what you did. Wanna bet Dan gives me a bonus when he comes in tomorrow and finds your dead body?"

"Dead men don't collect bonuses."

Tam kept track when each of the doors opened. Angelina's, Dalia's, and of course Allison's as she peered out with wide blue eyes, a sheet pulled loosely over her shoulders.

"You're dead, snot bucket!" Maniken sorted himself out. Got his feet under him.

He was rising when Tam skipped, lashed out with his right foot, and snap-kicked Maniken in the Adam's apple. The blow was devastating enough that it whipped the man's head back and forth.

Tam landed lightly on his left foot, recovered his balance, and watched Art Maniken sink to the duraplast floor. The big man's eyes were bugged, his tongue out, lungs heaving against the crushed trachea. Hands to his throat, Maniken collapsed onto his back.

Tam kicked the club out of the way, stepped over, and dropped the point of his right knee on Maniken's crushed throat.

Game to the end, Maniken grasped futilely at Tam's dangling genitals, but the weakening and flailing hands were easy to bat away. As Maniken's heart and pulsing lungs faded, Tam looked up at the wide-eyed audience, including a miner who'd bought Angelina for the night. "Said he'd kill me. You all heard. Went after me with a club. Seems to me, as I understand it, this falls under what's called fair fight."

"Yeah," the miner said as he hitched up his underwear. "We all heard."

Maniken's hands fell away, the arms thumping limply on the duraplast. Tam gave him just a little longer, then reached down and touched an eyeball, got no response. Only then did he rise.

"So, what's protocol?" Tam smacked his hands together as if to clap any dust away.

"Call the wagon in the morning," Angelina said as she ran fingers through her long hair. She wore a robe belted at the waist. "Boss is gonna be in a piss and fit when he finds out. He put a lot of store in Art."

"Always thought he was a mean fucker," Dalia said sullenly as she pulled her own robe tighter. "Won't miss him crawling drunk into my bed anytime soon."

"Wrap him in a sheet and put him out back," Allison said. "No sense in advertising."

"You all do what you want." The miner turned back into Angelina's room. "I'm outta here. Don't want Dan thinking I got anything to do with this."

Once they had Maniken wrapped up, Tam helped the women drag his corpse to the back door and out into the alley.

"Fart-sucking hell," Allison whispered as she closed the door behind her. "This will put Dan into a bitch of a mood."

Tam took her hand, aware of the women watching as he led her back to her room. "That's for tomorrow."

"Good, 'cause I'm sure not sleeping for the rest of the night."

Tam chuckled, slapping her on the ass as he trolled her through the door. "Suits me. Sleep's about the last thing on my mind."

"You want to fuck?" she asked, shutting the door. "With Art's body still warm?"

He peeled the sheet away from her body and toppled her back onto the bed with a playful shove. She fixed on his erection, slowly shaking her head in disbelief.

"Amazing how fast a man can get a hard-on after a good fight, isn't it?"

"You're a maniac," she whispered as he lowered himself between her smooth white thighs.

42

This was insane. Dortmund stepped from the dormitory and into the early morning. His gaze traveled out past the Corporate Mine fence. He could hear the chime, wondered at the rich harmonics as the invertebrates greeted the morning.

Invertebrates. Different from the Earthly concept, he had learned, but like so many things in a new environment, humans needed to call them something. Problem was, no one had taken the time as yet to study them in depth.

That, he'd discovered, was the trouble with so much of Donovan. Chairman Radcek, in his greed and arrogance, had placed the study of Donovanian life way down the list when it came to priorities.

Radcek. The guilty party totally unmasked. Driven by hubris and ambition, the Chairman had considered Donovan to be his legacy. A planet of incredible wealth that he had ordered his minions to refer to as Radcek's Planet, it was to have solidified his reputation in the history books. Proved him to be a sort of Augustus Caesar, the first true autocrat and Corporate emperor.

Dortmund leaned up against the fence and locked his fingers in the wire as he stared out at the dawn that was now bathing the tops of trees. Huge, alien-looking forest giants, the likes of which he could never have imagined. He sucked the perfumed air into his lungs.

Alas, poor Radcek. The first hint of justice came from the knowledge that no one even remembered that Capella III had once borne the man's name. The second, and larger, blow was that Capella III had turned into a disaster. A colony on the verge of failure, doomed by the unexpected revelation that symmetry inversion as a means of interstellar travel was turning out to be fraught with dangers and difficulties.

"So here is the wealth," he announced to the chime-filled morning. "And no way to get it back to Solar System."

Fact was, he needed to get out there. To see for himself. Here, at Corporate Mine, he was locked away at the Supervisor's will and pleasure. Heartless Corporate spider that she was, she was going to assign him to some menial data compilation, or perhaps an equally silly graduate-level research project down at her farm. Which, fascinating as that might have been, was still a hideous waste of his potential.

The woman was impossible. He should have been outlining an overall study of human impact on the planet, tasking Jones and Sax with survey strategies and developing methodology. Yes, it was a disaster, but also the biggest living laboratory ever when it came to proving conservationist values.

He sighed, rubbed his eyes, and shook his head. The last thing he wanted to do was draw the Supervisor's ire, but the bunk he'd been assigned to in the dormitory was an unmitigated affront. Like he was a common laborer. A menial to be given a bunk three up from the floor in a room filled with men. As a full professor he merited no less than private quarters, even if they did turn out to be Spartan. One expected at least a little privation in the field.

But to be treated as a sort of employee? Worse, Aguila was going to *assign* him a project? Some bit of make-work? After his illustrious career?

This is untenable.

He turned as the first of the miners began trickling out of the large central dome. The worker bees had finished their breakfast and now spread out across the compound, some heading for equipment, others for the headstock and mine.

Dortmund looked back through the chain-link.

"I will not be Kalico Aguila's slave." No, he had to get back to *Vixen*. There, at least, he would be free to write up his notes, have access to the ship's AI and computers. He'd be tied into the net again instead of this insidious silence in his head.

"Another ship will come." He closed his eyes, imagining that day. He'd just have to wait it out up in orbit, but then he'd planned on four years in *Vixen* just in transit out and back to the Solar System. The time would be well spent as he wrote his blistering polemic that would damn Radcek, Aguila, and the rest of the looters who'd condemned Capella III to an ecological nightmare.

But how are you going to get away? Aguila has you locked up like a common prisoner.

Which is when he noticed the aircar. That woman and the little girl. They'd arrived yesterday. He'd heard the woman was a security officer in Port Authority. They'd be leaving this morning.

A thought wedged itself in his head. No. Impossible. He was a full professor, not a silly youth. And what would they say if his professional colleagues ever heard?

"Dortmund, what you are considering is totally beneath your dignity."

Then he looked back at the tall fence, the dome, and the dormitory. This was indeed prison. And he was desperate.

43

"**Y**ou've got your radio," Kalico said as she led the way across the baked clay of the landing field to Talina's aircar. "I haven't a clue about where Rork Springs is, but as long as you can transmit, we can follow the signal to you."

Talina, a sack of supplies over her shoulder, glanced sidelong at Kalico. Beside her, Kylee strode along in her yellow overalls, her hair in a single braid down the back. The girl might have been cataloging targets for later destruction given the wolfish look in her eyes.

"I'd think you were really worried, but that would lead me to embrace notions too unsettling even for me." Talina gave the woman a wry smile, her memory having dredged up the time she'd contemplated shooting Aguila in the head. Shig had talked her out of it.

Kalico grinned back, the scars on her face not diminishing the warmth expressed. "It's all selfishness on my part. I really want you back in Port Authority by the next time I'm up there. I need someone to drink with at Inga's. If I have to endure another night of Shig and his damn philosophy, I'll slit my wrists."

"Why do you think I ran for the bush? It was that or give up drinking."

As they reached the aircar, Talina glanced around and took final stock. Corporate Mine was humming to work; the chime rolling in from the surrounding forest contrasted with the sound of machines. Overhead thin strands of high cirrus made patterns on the morning sky.

"Thanks for taking care of us. The food was a special treat. Not to mention two whole cups of coffee. I won't forget it."

"Neither will I. I've had Ituri list it as a charge on your account. I just hope it isn't a bad debt."

Kylee said, "We ready to go?" as she climbed over the side and into the aircar. A large crate had been laid in.

Must have been in addition to the other supplies Kalico had given them.

Kalico crossed her arms, studied the kid. "You sure you don't want to wait for your mother? She'll be here in another couple of hours."

Kylee shook her head with a ten-year-old's virulence. Behind her stricken eyes lay a deep-seated terror, and she appeared on the verge of tears. A desperate panic was building inside the kid. To make her point, Kylee clicked herself into the safety restraints, and stared fixedly forward through the windshield.

"Trust me on this," Tal told Kalico.

"You've never struck me as the motherly type," Kalico told Talina. "You sure you know what you're doing, flying out into the bush like this? And taking Dya's daughter with you?"

"She's my quetzal guide. I've got to get through this. Figure out what's going on in my head. As for Kylee, she's got her own demons to slay. Hell, maybe we can save each other."

Talina tossed her war bag onto the back seat and climbed in.

"You be careful out there." Kalico was watching her through concerned eyes.

"Me? You're the one with a mine, a farm, and an unstable reactor. All I have to worry about is quetzals, skewers, bems, and the occasional flock of mobbers."

Talina checked the charge, delighted that it read ninety-six percent. Old as the battery was, it was a miracle it still took ninety.

"Tell Dya that Kylee and I are making our way through a rough patch. Sort of propping each other up."

"Done." Kalico's gaze narrowed. "What if you have an episode? Get carried away by your hallucinations while you're flying?"

Talina jabbed a thumb at the kid. "Kylee's got the drill down. I start to whiz out, she jabs me in the ribs. But I think I'm beginning to get a handle on the flashbacks and visions. Comes from my Maya heritage. My people are used to being possessed by spirits."

"Fly safely."

"And thanks for the supplies. With what's in the garden out at Rork, it'll keep us fed for a time. By then maybe we'll have whipped our demons."

"Yeah, if you don't end up as quetzal shit," Kalico called back as Talina stepped to the wheel and throttled up the fans.

She gave a final wave and dialed in the lift, turning the car toward the northwest as they rose.

Damn. What the hell had Kalico given them? The crate took up half the deck. And with the dried vegetables and packet of coffee the Supervisor had had the kitchen provision her with, it was like a bonanza.

"So, kid, you survived a night at Corporate Mine. Didn't even have to kill anyone."

Kylee had placed herself next to Talina, peering through the windshield as they rose over the high peaks that were now known as the Corporate Range. Part of the uplift from the ancient impact crater, exposed rock strata gleamed where Capella's light reflected from threads of gold, silver, copper, and platinum.

Then they were across the divide, the sloping ground dropping away into an endless forest. It lay like some rumpled, mounded, and irregular carpet of greens, turquoise, teal, and blue. A trackless expanse of mundo, chabacho, stonewood, broadvine, and giant aquajade. There were other species, too. Whole varieties of trees that no one had cataloged, still unnamed and unseen by human eyes. Sometimes the vastness of Donovan left her feeling humbled and awed.

"How far is Rork Springs?" Kylee asked, her hands braced on the dash, intent gaze on the far horizon.

"Five, maybe six hours. It's on the west side of the Wind Mountains. One of the original research bases was established there. It's been abandoned for more than a decade now. Last time I was there, the dome was still intact. There was a small garden plot down in the drainage, but who knows what kind of shape it's in? The important thing is that it has good water. The spring comes out of sandstone. Not much heavy metal. It's a good place to hole up."

"Quetzals?"

"Hey, kid. It's Donovan. The good news is that no one

ever reported mobbers there. Doesn't mean they're not around. Cap and I had our first encounter with mobbers about fifty kilometers west of Rork Springs."

"Kalico got her scars fighting death fliers?"

"She did."

"You like her."

"That's the thing about Donovan. You've heard the old saying?"

"What saying?"

"That people come to Donovan to find themselves, to die, or to leave. Kalico's changed since the day she landed here. I think she's starting to find herself."

"What about you?"

"Yeah, well that's a problem. Just about the time I thought I'd found myself, I got infected by quetzals. Since I don't have a friggin' clue if I'm coming or going, I'm either about to die or find myself as something new."

"Don't die."

"It's not in the operational handbook, but the way I keep making people mad? Never can tell. Half of Port Authority wants to chew on a chunk of my butt these days."

Kylee glanced up with knowing blue eyes. "You killed my father, remember? And that's supposed to make people love you?"

"Shut up and watch the scenery, kid."

And then there she was, on the central avenue, Clemenceau's voice thundering the order. And Pak and Paolo, armed, staring at her with angry, hate-filled, and scared eyes as her pistol raised. That momentary realization in their eyes, the disbelief that they were about to . . .

The jab in her ribs caused the image to vanish, the tree-thick horizon seeming to rise in front of the aircar.

"Wake up, Talina," Kylee said sharply. "We're going down. I don't want to crash."

Talina jerked the wheel back, putting them into a climb. She felt her heart skip. Fought to clear the images from her brain, but the damn things clung like cobwebs, flickering in and out of her vision.

The image of the *Way* glyph seemed to lurk in the back of her mind.

"Where were you just now?" Kylee asked.

"In the street. Moments before I shot your father and Paolo. It was so real." She shook her head. "I justified it by believing it was for the common good. That's the lie. The Corporation thrives because of it. The greatest good for the greatest number. The algorithms have made us into little walking automatons. Ants and bees. Milling about our hives, serving the Corporate queen, and ignorant of everything that once made us human."

Kylee gave her a sidelong "you're just raving" glance.

"Guess you wouldn't know." Talina smiled. "And I guess we're talking. When I talk, I don't fall into the visions and crash us into the forest."

So they talked. Kylee told of her adventures with Rocket. What it was like growing up and thinking the whole world was Mundo Base. Talina talked about Chiapas, about the Maya, and her mother, and what it meant to escape to Corporate Security.

She managed to finish the flight, following the curve of the Wind Mountains, around until they intersected the headwaters of Rork River. Next Talina located the long anticline, used it to find the tiny valley where a tributary fault had cracked the sandstone.

She throttled back as the aircar descended toward the canted layer of slickrock. Here a ripple in the formation's strike had created a sheltered hollow. To Talina's relief, the dome still stood, perched as it was on bare sandstone. Below it, the springs had been reclaimed by vegetation, trees and brush having retaken any patch of soil. She'd seen Donovanian plants cross slickrock, but they never lingered in the process.

Dropping down, she could see that the door was still closed on the dome; the utility sheds and dormitory out back appeared to be intact as well. The big solar panels atop poles sunk into bedrock appeared to be tracking Capella for maximum energy gain, so the servos must still be working. Hopefully the batteries weren't fried due to a lack of maintenance.

"Forgot how pretty it is here," Talina added as she settled the aircar onto the worn sandstone before the dome.

Kylee climbed up on the gunwale, staring around with

the kind of curiosity only a child can muster. "Nobody lives here?"

"Not now. This is one of the oldest base camps. A sort of jumping off place for further exploration to the west."

"Why'd they leave?"

"Ran out of people." Talina climbed over the side and set foot on the solid stone. "Too many got eaten out in the bush. No ships came with replacements. The last three people here packed up and moved back to PA."

"Why'd they build on rocks?" Kylee had hopped down next to Talina and was stomping her ad hoc shoe on the stone. "It's really hard."

"No slugs, no bems, no skewers, and you can see the quetzals coming. Doesn't get dangerous until you're down in the canyon bottom in the brush."

"You said there's a garden?"

"Down below the spring. We'll have to see what's still alive, or if it has all been crowded out by Donovanian plants."

Talina reached in, unclipped her rifle from the rack, and was just about to head up to the dome when the big supply crate shifted. Then, before she could react, the lid raised and a gray-matted head popped up.

The face that went with it was long, lined, and possessed of a thick jaw, bushy eyebrows, and startled brown eyes to either side of a patrician nose.

"What the fuck?" Talina asked. "Who the hell are you?"

"I think I'm crippled for life." The brown eyes fixed first on Talina, and then Kylee where she peered over the aircar's side. "I really need your help. My legs are so stiff I don't think I can climb out of this miserable coffin. I may never walk again."

"I said: Who the hell are you?"

"I'm Doctor Dortmund Weisbacher, Chair of the Department of Planetology, Tubingen University, Transluna." He shook his head. "And I can't believe that I was so desperate that I stowed away in a miserable crate to get the hell out of Corporate Mine. So, please, take me to Inga's so I can drink the memory away before booking passage back up to *Vixen*."

44

Inga's was loud, voices rising and falling. Utensils clattered and plates scraped on the hardwood tables. People were crowded around Flight Officer Seesil Vacquillas. Like all the *Vixen* crew who came down on rotation, she was the center of attention for the locals.

Somehow, for once, word hadn't gotten out about Maniken. Maybe Wye Vanveer figured he was in enough trouble with Dan. Not that the clay miner could have done anything to stop it.

Dan shook his head, made a face. He slowly turned the cup he held, trying to think his way through this latest calamity. Beside him, Allison stared dully in the direction of the new kitchen where people were dishing up potatoes, chunky crest gravy, and broccoli. Pancakes were the other item on the menu.

"Surprised he let you out this morning," Dan told her.

"I told him I had to get ready for work. That I had to go home and get dressed. Thought you'd want to have all the details before you walked into the place. But, I don't know . . ."

"How's that?"

"The way Benteen looked at me, like he knew exactly why I wanted to get out of there. And like, well, I was doing just what he wanted me to."

"Canny guy." He slammed the cup down. "Art's really dead?"

"I felt Tam get up. He moves like a ghost. Wary like. Knew he went down the hall. Figured he had to pee. Then there's this loud bang and Art screaming."

"Art was as good as they get. And you say Benteen was buck-assed naked?"

"The way Benteen moved, it was like a dance. Art swinging that club, Benteen . . ." She shook her head. "I mean I saw. Like they'd rehearsed it all. The way Art's club whished past Benteen's head. The way the guy avoided getting whacked was like magic."

Art's dead?

The thought was stunning. Who on this gilded ball of rock could take his place? No one. All it had taken was a look from Art, maybe a whispered word, and the chuckleheads were right back in line. Talent like that didn't just grow on every fart-sucking thorncactus.

"Okay, let's think." Dan rubbed his temples. "Who the hell is Benteen, anyway?"

"The scorpion. I can believe it."

"How'd he fuck? Hard? Possessive? Anything painful or kinky?"

She shook her head. "He said no mash, no eros. So I figured it would be hard and fast the first time. Wasn't. Takes his time like it's an art form. Knows his way around a woman's body. He calls it a poetry of pleasure."

Her lips quirked. "He was into getting me off as many times as he could. Seemed to make it better for him when he finally came. Hard to believe, but he's as good as you."

"Okay, so nothing there we can use." Dan paused. "Did he say anything? Give anything away?"

She shook her head absently. "Wanted to know about boring stuff. How Port Authority works. Did Shig have any lovers, anyone he cared about. Same about Yvette. Who was the man in her life."

"Looking for vulnerabilities," Dan mused. "That's got to frustrate the hell out of him."

She turned her worried eyes his way. "What are we going to do, Dan? I mean, it's going to get out. Mean, deadly old Art went after him in the middle of the night with a club. Naked as a newborn, Benteen took him down. I tell you, the man acted as if he hadn't a care in the world. Killing Art came across almost like boring routine."

"How'd he act afterward?"

She laughed dismissively. "My ass barely bounced on the bed before he was hard as a rock and doing me." She paused. "I mean, he'd just been in a fight for his life. All those chemicals in the limbic system should have made him desperate, right? Survival of life and all."

"Sex and death do dance hand in hand."

"Well it wasn't. It was all slow and sensual. I can't figure him."

"I hear that tone in your voice. What's he offered?"

"To be his queen. Co-ruler. Whatever. I wrote it off. Just talk to get in my bed, you know? Now? Screw me with a skewer but I think he means it."

"What are you going to do?"

He knew that slight pursing of her lips. She turned her puzzled eyes on his. "I don't know. You and me, we're partners. What do you think?"

"What if I asked you to drop some brown cap sap in his whiskey some night? Or maybe cut this throat?"

He watched the interplay of her thoughts, reflected so clearly behind her eyes. "I don't know."

"Do you love me?"

She gave him a "you're not serious" look. "I did once. Back when you first got here. Took me a couple of months to figure out who and what you are. No hard feelings, but you're as heartless as it turns out I am. I learned a lot from you."

Who the hell was this new Allison? What the hell had changed her? And more to the point, how had he missed it? The new woman she was turning into upset him almost as much as Art's death had. What else had he missed while he fucked around building schools?

"So?"

"So here's what I know about him: He's using me just the way you used me in the beginning. But you let me work into the business. I keep the books, do the finances, and I get my share. He says he's going to take Donovan for himself, and I can sit at his side."

Dan felt his blood run cold. "Pretty tempting offer."

"Here's where you and he are different: He's in it for the power. You're in it for the money. He doesn't care what he does to Port Authority or Donovan as long as everyone serves him. He's meaner, tougher, deadly, and competent. But in the end, I think you're smarter. You're in it for the long haul."

"When did you get so fucking good at reading people?"

"When I finally figured out I wanted to be more than an ornament in your bed. So I started cutting down the drugs, watching you. Really paying attention. You learn a lot about people in a casino."

"How'd I miss this?"

"Because you weren't paying attention."

"Guess I just had a wakeup call."

"Dan. You need to understand that Benteen will kill you without a second thought."

"He's figuring I'm going to shoot him in the back. Whatever I do, it's going to have to be something a bit more devious."

"Then you better be more damned clever than you've ever been. He's the most dangerous man on this planet."

"Yeah, where's Deb Spiro when I need her, huh?"

"She's laying in a grave up on cemetery hill. Where you'll be if you aren't really careful with this guy."

He blinked. Shook his head. It was like a bad holo-vid. Once again, some Corporate muckety-muck had shown up to fix the game and take everything he had. Fucking high-bred Corporate bastard.

And then there was Allison. When had she turned into this hard-eyed, no-bullshit woman? Sure, he let her do the books, and sure, she got a piece of the take, but when push came to shove, which side was she going to come down on? His or Benteen's?

Art is dead?

Winning this thing, taking back what was his, was going to be one of the hardest and trickiest things he'd ever had to do.

45

The pain in Dortmund's legs had finally subsided to the point that he thought he could walk again. He had propped himself against the side of the aircar, legs like sticks, knees locked, as he took in this latest calamity to befall him.

To call it a rude awakening was an understatement.

He had expected to climb out of his box at Port Authority. Just a short walk across town from the shuttle port and a ride up to *Vixen*. Instead he found himself in an erosional niche on a sandstone slope, the strike of the formation running roughly north-south, with a dip of about fifteen degrees. A kilometer to the west, the shallow valley was filled with curious green-blue vegetation before another jutting wall of stratified sandstone—this one more yellow in color—indicated yet another anticline that dipped off to the west.

A dome, and behind it a rectangular structure with windows, solar panels, and utility sheds, had all been anchored to solid rock. The slickrock continued to rise to the eastern horizon. It appeared rounded and cracked against the Cap III sky.

To his right, what he took to be the south, the sandstone dropped down three or four meters to a vegetation-choked drainage maybe fifteen meters across. Beyond that, the tan slickrock resumed, running off to the south until it curved out of view.

"I don't think I have ever endured anything as excruciating as this last day," he admitted. "It really makes a person respect such a simple action as just being able to breathe."

"I'll bet." The woman called Talina, in her thirties, regarded him through obsidian-hard eyes. Her face reminded him of a disapproving warrior's. She wore a leather hat that did little to confine a wealth of thick black hair that spilled down her back. Her dress consisted of a worn black uniform of some sort. From the cut of it, it might once have been security issue. Now, however, it looked more like a hobo's patchwork. Tough quetzal-hide boots clad her feet. She carried the rifle like it was part of her, and the holstered pistol, large knife, and pouch-packed utility belt reminded him of the archetypal pirate's gear.

And then there was the little girl. Kylee. Blond, in over-sized yellow overalls, but with a feral look to her oddly inhuman blue eyes, as if she was deciding on whether to slit his throat, or just stick something sharp into his guts.

Now the woman's fingers tapped on the pistol's grip as she said, "You still haven't told me why you're here. That makes me patently suspicious, let alone the fact that you stowed away in a crate."

"In addition to my university responsibilities, I chair the Corporate Science and Planetology Advisory Committee and report directly to the Board. I was appointed to head the first scientific survey of Capella III, reporting directly to Boardmember Shayne, and am director of—"

"You came on *Vixen*. That's why I've never seen you."

"That's right, I—"

"I've got a deal with the Supervisor. I return all of her runaways. The ones she can still use, she just punishes. The ones that don't serve a useful purpose, she shoots. Person-ally. Why do I think you fall into that latter category?"

Dortmund blinked. "I beg your pardon? I told you, I'm Dr. Dort—"

"Hey, you don't need my pardon." She rapped a staccato on the pistol butt. "Or maybe you do. I'm not only stuck with your sorry ass, but it's going to be a day of my time to run you back to Corporate Mine. And then Kalico's just going to shoot you in the head and toss your corpse over the fence for the invertebrates, like she does."

"Maybe you should just shoot him now," the little girl said, her feral blue gaze fixed on Dortmund's. "Save every-one the effort."

"There's that," the dark-haired woman agreed, and started pulling the pistol.

"Wait! By all that's right, wait!" Dortmund jerked onto his feet, hands out. Every ache and pain was forgotten. "I'll do anything you say!"

The woman's hand retreated from the pistol grip. What might have been a mocking smile flickered at her lips.

Dortmund swallowed hard, realized he really needed to pee. Somehow, that had been forgotten, though it had become increasingly urgent during the last hour in the crate. Now it threatened to bend him double, let alone cause him even more humiliation.

Dortmund took a deep breath, wondering how this could get any worse. "Could we continue this discussion after I visit the facilities?" He winced at the pain in his bladder as he tried to straighten. "Even better. Just go ahead and shoot me."

God, did he really just say that?

The woman chuckled, waved. "Yeah, go take a leak. I'd use the off-side of the aircar. No telling what might be lurking around the toilet, and since you're soft meat, I'd rather that Kylee and I check out the dome before we figure out that a sidewinder might have found its way into the loo."

"The off-side of the aircar?"

"What? You've never urinated in the great outdoors before?" the woman asked over her shoulder as she strode off toward the dome. "Oh, and Doc, don't wander off. No sense in getting eaten by something before we can figure out whether or not to shoot you."

Dortmund stumbled around to the other side of the aircar. Of all the silly questions. Of course he'd never relieved himself outside. What did that stupid woman think? That it was still the twenty-first century? Even when he went into the field at the re-wilding tracts, they always had portable facilities to keep from impacting the local ecologies.

He stopped short, sure to keep the bulk of the aircar between himself and the females, looked over his shoulder just to be sure they weren't watching. Reassured, he saw them enter the dome, and breathed a sigh of relief.

He pointed himself downhill and froze, eyes on the vegetation-filled drainage. And beyond that, infinity. Anyone could be out there. Perhaps with glasses, watching him.

His first instinct was to waddle back up to the dome, ask them to check the toilet.

Oh, sure. Imagine their expressions.

What the hell has happened to me?

Dortmund bit his lip, closed his eyes, and let the relief course through his lower body.

It's all right. It's just sandstone. You're not creating an environmental impact. Nothing is going to suffer for this.

Was this the culmination of millions of years of primate evolution? A man who felt traumatized by the simple act of urinating in the outdoors?

Shaking his head, he refastened and turned his steps up the slope toward the dome. "Oh, how the mighty have fallen."

Here he was, not back in Port Authority, but carried even deeper into the wilderness. Looking around, he could tell the place was abandoned. No other aircars, no sign of recent habitation.

He stepped carefully into the dome, glancing around at a bare-bones, faintly dusty, room. It boasted a single utilitarian table, chairs, couch, two windows, a small kitchen with counter and cabinets, a couple of desks, and crates stacked along the back wall. Beside the front door, next to what had to be a rifle rack, were scrawled the words: *quetzal*, *bem*, *skewer*, *sidewinder*. Below *quetzal* were seven hash marks, *bem* had five, *skewer* three, and *sidewinder* six.

Body count? Even the thought made him queasy.

He made his way through the doorway in the rear and into a hallway. On the left was an obvious laboratory, a few pieces of plastic-wrapped equipment on the back work counter. To his right he discovered a conference room with maps on the wall and a long central table with chairs. Next on the right he found a lavatory with toilets, shower, sinks, and lockers. Equipment room with mostly bare shelves opposite, and finally living quarters in the rear. Two beds, wardrobes, night tables, mirror on the wall.

Talina had just checked a chest of drawers and turned, stating, "Glad to see nothing ate you."

The little girl was peering into a closet as she flipped through the few pairs of hanging overalls. She turned to regard him with those weirdly dismissive eyes.

"What are we doing here?" Dortmund asked. "I really need to get to Port Authority."

"Why?"

"This is all a disaster. The journey on *Vixen,* our arrival here to discover that this is a conservationist's nightmare. I just want to gain passage back to *Vixen*. I'm willing to live the rest of my life there, write my report, and wait for either another vessel, or for *Vixen* to space back."

"A conservationist's nightmare? I haven't heard that term in ages." Talina snapped her fingers. "Wait. The re-wilding zones. Conservationists. You're that Weisbacher?"

"Who's he?" Kylee asked. "And what's a conservationist?"

"Big academic and political kerfuffle that dominated most of the twenty-first century," Talina told the child. "Conservationists wanted to set aside huge tracts of land for wildlife. Hands off. No human intervention whatsoever. Re-establish an extirpated ecology, and let nature take its course."

"What's extirpated?" the little girl asked before Dortmund could interrupt.

"Means a species that's been eliminated from its original range. As the conservationists became more powerful, they used fossil DNA to recreate extinct species. They turned those once-extinct creatures loose in the re-wilded areas in an effort to make the Earth primitive again."

"It's the only way to save the planet," Dortmund protested.

"Didn't work out so well as I understand." Talina shrugged, pulling back the bedding and staring curiously at it. "No telling how long it's been since the bedding was washed. Might want to stake this out in the creek for a day or two before we sleep in it."

"About getting me back to Port Authority." Dortmund crossed his arms.

"Listen"—Talina let the bedding drop—"for the time being, Kylee and I would rather stay away from PA. We didn't ask you to come here. Didn't want you here. Maybe you'd better wise up to some things."

"Like what?"

"Like the fact that we've got to recharge the power pack in the aircar before we go anywhere. Like the fact that I meant it: I take Kalico's runaways back to her. Just knowing that you'd stow away in a crate in an unknown aircar? That you'd do anything to escape Corporate Mine? Means whatever you did, it must be pretty serious. Which, for soft meat, makes you either really stupid or particularly incompetent."

"Maybe he's a pedophile," Kylee chimed in, her eyes going wide.

Dortmund choked off his response to Talina's charge so he could stare wide-eyed at the girl. "A . . . A what am I?"

"Pedophile." Kylee regarded him through her not-quite-right eyes. "The kind of man who sexually violates young girls like me. Pedophiles are known to inhabit Solar System, which is, like, where you're from, right?"

"But I never . . ."

"Do you have a daughter?" the girl demanded.

"No! I never got around to procreating. My career—"

"My mother told me that most pedophiles don't have children," Kylee insisted. Then she shot a questioning look at Talina. "Should we shoot him now?"

"Not here, kid. We'd have to clean up the blood and brains. Let's wait and do it when he's outside, maybe down-hill where the rains can wash the mess away."

"Are you both mad? Don't you know who I am? What I . . ."

But the woman had burst into laughter, managing to say, "Pus in a bucket, Doc. You ought to see the expression on your face. Oh, damn." And she burst into even louder peals of laughter.

46

Trish Monagan was in the mood to bust heads. She'd been awakened that morning by a chime on her com, only to have it followed by Two Spot informing her, *"Sorry to wake you, Trish. But Art Maniken was killed at The Jewel last night. They claim it was a fair fight."*

She'd acknowledged, rolled over, and tossed the covers back. For a moment she'd stared at the left side of her bed. Empty, as it always was. One of her favorite fantasies was that she would someday find exactly the right guy to awaken with. So far that had been a real no go.

With Talina vanished who knew where, and perhaps for good—Donovan being what it was—she felt even more achingly alone.

Not that things were exactly perfect between her and Talina now. Blame the frigging quetzals for that. But damn it, the woman had taken Trish in, given her a direction when all she wanted to do was drown in grief and loneliness after her mother's death.

She'd worshipped Talina, which made it all the worse to watch her friend and mentor descend into madness as alien molecules turned the toughest woman on Donovan into a crate-shooting lunatic.

A fact that just added another layer to Trish's hatred for quetzals. Not to mention even more guilt. She should have shot straighter that day in the canyon. Had she, Talina wouldn't be infected and on the run.

Trish cradled her head in her hands and hated herself. After all the things Tal had done for her, she should have been more supportive. If she could go back, she wouldn't have stood against Talina that night when Hmong and the rest wanted Rocket dead.

"I'll make it up to her," Trish whispered, straightening, forcing herself onto her feet.

That is, if she could. If Talina ever came back. People who disappeared into the bush, as often as not, were never seen again.

"Damn, I'm a real piece of work, aren't I?"

She pulled on her clothes, stared at her reflection in the mirror, and managed to make herself look presentable enough to deal with Dan Wirth and the bipedal flotsam he kept at The Jewel.

Somebody killed Art Maniken? Call that a community service. She was tempted to nominate whomever had done the deed as citizen of the year. Too bad it was just Maniken and not Wirth.

Thinking that, she strapped on her pistol and headed out the door. Who knew? Maybe there'd be a way to finally pin something on Wirth. Bring the smug bastard down. Or at least put some kind of crimp on his style.

Morning light slanted in through The Jewel's high windows as she strode through the front door. The usual crew, looking oddly somber, were tackling their morning chores, stocking the bar, mopping the floors. Neither Wirth nor Allison were in evidence.

A dapper-looking man, dressed in fancy black, sat at a table in the rear. Someone she'd never seen before. Soft meat. Had to be from the *Vixen*.

Tamarland Benteen. From the description she'd been given, it had to be.

A cup of tea sat beside his hand as he slouched in the chair, one foot braced on another. An amused smile curved his lips, almost mocking. His eyes, however—flat and deadly—had fixed on her like lasers.

"So Art's dead, huh?" Trish announced as she stopped by the craps table. "Where's Wirth?"

"Not here, Trish," Vik told her where he washed glasses behind the bar. "He went to see Art buried. But you want to talk to this fella. I'll go back and get Angelina. She saw the whole thing."

Trish walked over, taking the man's measure. His complete lack of concern set her off. Like he didn't know who he was talking to, nor care in the least. "Let me guess, you're Tamarland Benteen."

Tam smiled up. "And you are?"

Angelina, still in her robe, stepped out of the back. Stopped short, looking frightened at sight of Benteen.

"Trish Monagan. Security second. The story's started to make the rounds. Word is that you and Art had words yesterday, then, last night, he jumped you in the back hall."

"That's pretty much it."

"Go on."

"Not much more to it. He tried to kill me. I didn't let him. End of story."

What was it about the guy? Just being close to him made her skin crawl. Trish shot a look at Angelina. "That true?"

"Yeah. Art had a club. Kept trying to brain Benteen. Cussing and swinging the whole time. I was staring out the door by the time Benteen tripped Art and he went down. Then Benteen kicked Art in the throat. Hard. Crushed his windpipe. Killed him dead."

Tam cocked his head inquisitively as Trish turned his way. Art had been known as one of the toughest men in town. Though she couldn't prove it, she knew he'd killed at least five or six men who'd crossed Wirth, and beaten a score more bloody before dropping them in the alley behind The Jewel.

Finally she said, "You're a brave man, Benteen. Dastardly Dan relied on Art to do his less-savory dirty work. Not that Dan isn't above the occasional strangling and backstabbing himself. He's not the kind of guy to let something like this go. Not a bygones-be-bygones sort. Yet here you sit drinking tea."

And that was a real puzzle. Sure, she'd heard the stories. The guy was called the scorpion. But Solar System tough and Donovan tough were two different things. Still, the way he was watching her, like she was meaningless, some sort of insect? It sent tingles of unease down her spine.

"Dan and I have established an understanding."

"What kind of understanding?"

"That, Officer Monagan, need not concern you." He lowered a warning eyebrow. "Now, be on your way."

"And what were you doing before the attack?"

"Enjoying the best fuck a man can have within thirty light-years of Solar System, not that it's any of your business." He stood, slamming the chair back.

Something cold danced up Trish's spine as she stared into those flat and deadly eyes; a primeval warning tickled in her gut.

"Remarkable place, this Port Authority," Benteen told her in a toneless voice. "A fellow named Fred Han Chow and two of his sons brought a cart, picked up Art Maniken's body from the alley, and trundled it away to the cemetery."

The way he spoke, toneless, without pity, ate its way into Trish's soul.

"How absolutely and amazingly simple. No muss, no fuss. In Solar System it would have taken a small staff and months to process the forms, write the reports, coordinate the handling of the corpse, official letters from Shayne's staff to ensure the proper law enforcement agencies were mollified, and even then it still might have gone to a hearing before a security ombudsperson.

"Lot to be said for Port Authority." A beat. "Shithole that it is."

A tightness squeezed her lungs, as if she couldn't breathe. Satan would have those eyes. He reeked of evil—pure and undiluted. Like the man was filled with a black malignancy.

As if he could read her growing distress, Benteen added, "Four hundred and some people. A crappy collection of domes, hovels, and crude buildings, atop all the gold, jewels, and metallic wealth in the universe.

"Shayne, if you only knew."

Trish's heart was beginning to pound, her mouth gone dry. "Maybe you better be minding that mouth of yours. This shithole, as you call it, is all that you've got left. People here—"

"Now, Art attacked me." He leaned close, those flat and deadly eyes burning into hers.

In that crystalline moment, she understood the hunger in Benteen's heartless soul. That in an instant she'd die. Crushed. Instantly forgotten in the black void of his being.

"So, are you finished here, or did you come specifically to get into my shit? If that's your plan, try me."

His movement was like a flash; she rocked as he snatched the pistol from her holster, pressed it into her stomach.

"Bang."

Trish stood paralyzed. He'd snuff her like a candle flame—a meaningless gesture with as little thought. Frozen, she could only stare into those terrible eyes, feel them drain her of hope.

"I'm . . ."

"You're shit, little girl. Now get out."

Swallowing past the knot, she battled to glance helplessly at Angelina. "Fair fight?"

Angelina, lips pursed and looking unhappy, nodded.

"Then that's all I needed to know," Trish barely whispered, and hated herself for it.

His face a mask of disdain, he tossed her pistol back to her, a mocking grin twisting his lips.

Trish spun on her heel and stalked out, back stiff, struggling to keep her legs from buckling.

Outside, she took a deep breath, staggered to the side, and braced her back against the building's wall while she fought for control. Her hands were shaking where they clutched her pistol, her stomach hard and aching.

"That's odd," she heard Benteen call from inside the building.

"What is?" Angelina's voice.

"Do you think she wears a diaper?"

"I don't understand."

"I know she pissed herself, but there's not so much as a drop on the floor. Maybe that's why she wears those tall boots?"

Trish sucked air, sweat breaking out on her skin. Ashamed, she stared down at herself. Fought to stop the shaking, and failed.

All those times she'd faced death, the dangerous men she'd taken down, the times in the bush when her life had hung by a thread, and this one man had gutted her?

It didn't make sense. Like he was evil, inhuman, some creature of empty hate. She'd never known such humiliation, that she was not only meaningless, but detestably weak.

How the hell did he do that to me?

47

A light rain fell from the cloud-blackened sky. Talina filled her lungs, smelling the night air. The scent of wet rock, the anise and cardamom of the vegetation, together they filtered like perfume through her nose. Her quetzal-enhanced vision assured her that the wet slickrock was devoid of threats. Quetzals needed some kind of topography or vegetation to hide in; here, even camouflaged, they'd look like a lump where the bare rock had been flat only hours before. The same with a bem or skewer.

She checked the aircar one last time where she'd hooked it up to the solar chargers. Turned out that the Rork Springs power packs still had almost eighty percent of their original efficiency. She could be charged by morning.

But did she really want to waste the day taking Weisbacher back to Kalico?

Pus in a bucket, but I'm tired of feeling fragmented.

If she could only put herself together again. She reached under the dash in the aircar and retrieved her bottle. It felt like that kind of a night.

Turning, she made her way to the dome and stepped inside, taking a moment for her eyes to adjust after the darkness.

At the table, Weisbacher sat, head in his hands. The guy looked like all the stuffing had been kicked out of him. Talina locked the door, racked her rifle, and shrugged out of her poncho.

Padding back, she checked to see that Kylee was asleep. They'd rolled out their bedrolls on the stripped beds. Weisbacher was relegated to the dormitory out back. They'd found clean bedding and assigned him to a bunk before Talina made a supper of dried peppers, beans, and cabbage. Hardly epicurean, but better than empty bellies.

Kylee had done the dishes.

Taking down a glass and pulling out a chair, Talina settled herself across from Weisbacher. "You drink?"

He looked up, brown eyes dull. They sharpened at sight of the bottle. "Where'd you find that?"

"My special stock. One of Inga's better barrels. Get your own glass."

Weisbacher moved with unusual alacrity to retrieve a tumbler, watched her pour. "Am I going to regret this?" He lifted the amber liquid, holding it up to stare skeptically at it in the overhead light.

"Probably. But that's the way with most things in life." She clinked his glass and took a swig. "Shit on a shoe, I needed that."

Weisbacher carefully sipped, worked his mouth, and said, "Not at all like I expected."

"Are you always so pessimistic?" Talina leaned back in her chair, pulled up her leg, and propped her foot on a second chair.

The man's lips pursed, gaze seeing into a distance beyond the battered table and his glass of whiskey. "I just keep reeling. Wondering what the next blow is going to be. How this could have happened to me, of all people?"

"Ah, there it is: You, of all people? It's always refreshing to know that the universe reserves special treatment for an elite few like yourself. Too bad the rest of us didn't make the grade."

"I meant as a conservationist and a professor."

"Right. Silly of me to have missed that. So, tell me. I'm a little hazy on this whole conservationist, evolutionist thing. That was settled before my time. But as I recall, each of the re-wilded areas, they were supposed to be like living museums, right? Areas kept pristine like they were before humanity showed up on the scene and screwed it all up."

"It was the best way to save the planet. The climate just kept deteriorating. Sure, atmospheric carbon scrubbing was showing ever greater promise, and solar shielding was lowering the amount of energy trapped by the greenhouse gasses, but we had to heal the biosphere. Reestablished biomes had a better chance of rebuilding soils, generating

O_2. And there was the wealth of animal life, the remarkable variability. Tell me that wasn't worth fighting for."

"If memory serves, it didn't take more than a decade after *Vixen* vanished before they were declared failures. Either they required too many resources and too much labor—to the point that everything was being managed down to the soil organisms—or there just wasn't any way to keep the systems going. Life just kept adapting, hybridizing. In the end, even most of the conservationists threw up their hands."

"Really? Or is that just official propaganda? Radcek's? A justification for the rape and exploitation of those areas?"

"I haven't a clue. Not my battleground. The consensus when I went to school, and what I saw of the re-wilded areas in Central America, was that adaptation was taking its own path. Mom took me to Georgia and Tennessee once. We were there to see the parrots and macaws that were living in the Appalachians. Just so we could know what they were like a millennia ago when the Maya kept them for their feathers. Extinct in Chiapas, thriving in eastern Tennessee."

"But not everything made it?"

"No. It was the diseases more than anything. I remember that rinderpest and hoof-and-mouth really hit the North American Great Plains reserves. All the public herds of sacred 'genetically pure' bison, elk, and deer, along with the cloned mammoths, sloths, and camels, were wiped out. They spent billions of SDRs trying to figure out how to vaccinate all those bison. Couldn't do it fast enough. Skeletons everywhere. So the grass and invasive weeds grew, and then it all caught fire and burned. It's back to commercial property now."

"That makes no sense."

"I was taught that as the number of species in an unmanaged area increases, then the management protocol and possibility for unintended consequences rises exponentially." She sipped again. "Something about life always looks for a new way to express itself. Just like our constant battle against diseases. They are constantly adapting in ways you either didn't expect, or didn't want them to."

"Evolutionists were relying on that tired argument even when I was crushing them under my feet with real data."

"No ego there, huh, Doc?"

"You're what? A security officer? An official head-breaker and enforcer?"

"Don't pull that appeal-to-authority shit. Not here. Not with me. 'Cause here's how I read it: You shipped off to Donovan, all set to make a conservationist haven. But, damn, you got here fifty years too late. Now, here you are, adrift in the Donovanian bush, and you blush when you have to pee outside."

"Don't take that condescending tone with me. I had my first PhD by the time I was twenty."

She snapped her fingers, causing him to start. "Wake up. That's right. Listen, soft meat. Hear what I have to say, and hammer it into that crap-filled head of yours. The evolutionists were right. It's about survival, and you're up to your ass in the real world. We're not winning here. Donovan is."

"Winning how?"

"Kylee and me? We're out here because we're full of quetzal TriNA. The reason this base is abandoned? It's because too many people out here in the bush were eaten. Donovan isn't the victim you think it is in your morality play about humanity, Doc. It's fighting back, so maybe you'd better get an updated playlist and figure out that your PhDs and conservationist crusade aren't worth shit out here."

His stare grew more distant, and he licked his lips. "Just don't want to see us ruin another world."

"Maybe we didn't ruin Earth. Maybe the evolutionists are right, and humans were generated by and remain part of the ecology even as they change it. It's just another phase of evolution. But here's the thing: We need to figure out what it means to have Donovanian TriNA in our systems, what it's doing to our brains."

He smiled for the first time, took another sip of his whiskey. "If that's true, Donovan might make my argument for me. Keep away. Get too close, and you're infected."

"Too late."

"What do you mean, too late?"

"*Turalon* spaced back with no less than thirty people testing positive for Donovanian molecules in their blood and tissues, and there's no telling how many were infected that returned to Solar System long before that."

She gave him a deadly smile. "So, Doc. The milk is spilt, the bullet is fired, and the eggs are broken. And that tells me that the evolutionists were right all along: it's all about organisms adapting to new environments and the devil take the hindmost."

He studied her thoughtfully. "You have no idea how much I'd like to have you back in Transluna. I'd lock you and that little urchin into a quarantine facility and take you apart molecule by molecule as proof of Radcek's crimes against humanity and nature."

48

Dan Wirth made a face as he stepped through Inga's double doors and stopped at the top of the landing. Fact was he would just as soon never set foot in this place. It had been the site of too many of his most ignominious moments. Like the time the three *Turalon* deserters had humiliated him over the Damitiri scandal, only to have that slit Aguila very publicly swipe them from under his nose.

Shit like that caused men like him to have to build schools to keep the locals at least slightly on his side.

Today Inga's was moderately full, people trickling in as their work day was coming to a close. Most of the "decent folk," of course, were headed home to cook their suppers and share family time. Others were headed for Millie's cafeteria, though a substantial part of her business was now flocking to Inga's for more adventurous fare and the chance to drink something alcoholic with their meal.

All in all, maybe fifty or sixty people were clustered around the tables or placing orders at the bar or kitchen.

And yes, there he was. Sitting at the right end of the bar, back to Dan. There was no mistaking the stature, let alone the wild mop of unruly black hair, the sides tinged with gray.

Dan descended the stairs, adopting the old arrogant swing of his feet, thumbs tucked in the side of his belt with his pistol stuck through in a jaunty angle near the buckle. He kept his expression hard, eyes narrowed, jaw out. After all, presentation was everything. Besides, he was still raging over burying Art.

He ignored the looks he got along with the occasional greeting called by one of his regulars and made his way straight to the spot beside Shig Mosadek.

Two Spot Smith—on a rare break from the radio room—perched on the stool next to Shig and raised startled brows as Dan tapped him on the shoulder. "Hope you don't mind.

Got business with Shig. Have a nice day and don't let the door hit you in the ass on the way out."

Two Spot nodded, Adam's apple lurching up and down in his skinny throat as he piled off the chair and beat a hasty retreat.

Dan clambered up, stared down the bar at Inga, and flicked his fingers at the whiskey keg. She nodded, something smoldering behind her hard blue eyes.

"You do amaze me sometimes," Shig told him mildly, fingers wrapped around his half glass of wine. "That gentle diplomatic approach you have toward other human beings forever impresses me as a model of eloquence."

"I'm not in the mood for eloquence. This is more of a hit-them-in-the-head-with-a-keen-bitted-ax kind of day. Which means I'm coming right to the point: Benteen's got you and Yvette in his sights. He thinks he just put me in my place—not that he has by a damn sight—and he's figuring to take out you two next."

"I see."

"Good. You're warned." Dan tossed a ten-SDR coin onto the bar and made a "keep the change" gesture with his fingers. Inga was another person he had to have on his side. She was the only source of good alcohol on the planet. Lots of the locals made their own hooch in tubs, buckets, and jugs, but Inga's was quality.

"I was sorry to hear about Art." Shig gave a lift of his shoulders. "Not that he was necessarily one of the community's shining assets, but because of the implications. Which leads me to ask: What is Benteen's intent toward your businesses?"

"He says he's not interested, that I can keep doing what I'm doing. Knowing the slimy Corporate kind of creature that he is, that tells me he figures that after he takes over, I work for him. I think he refers to me as a menial."

"I see." Shig toyed with his wineglass, eyes distant.

"You don't seem to be getting what I'm telling you."

"Of course I do. And it's a mark of your concern that you came to warn me. Not concern for my person, but rather for the nature of the threat Mr. Benteen presents to Port Authority. I'm not used to seeing you rattled in this manner."

"You didn't see him with Art yesterday. Never seen anyone move like that. Well, maybe Perez the day she shot Deb Spiro. One second Art's standing, ready to show the guy the door. The next Benteen's cold-cocked Art with a pistol. And Art's out of it. Quicker than I can snap my fingers."

"Implants. Must be."

"That would explain last night. Listen, Art had a beef. Benteen made him look small. So Art hangs out in The Jewel, catches Benteen coming out of the john. Allison and the girls say it was like Benteen was playacting. Ducks every swing. Doesn't even seem to be trying. And then Benteen kills Art. Neat, quick, no muss or fuss."

"Implants," Shig repeated. "He was, after all, a Corporate assassin in cahoots with one of the most bloodthirsty Boardmembers in history. The only reason Artollia Shayne was defeated was because Radcek was even more ruthless."

"Hello! Shig? You in there? You hearing what you're saying? Bloodthirsty? Ruthless? Right here in Port Authority? And didn't I mention something about you and Yvette being next?"

The guy seemed to miss the guts of the message, noting instead, "I thought you wanted to take over eventually as the big dog. Step into the spotlight as the central figure. Assume the mantle of leadership."

"You and Yvette do fine."

Shig turned a curious glance Dan's way and arched a questioning eyebrow.

Dan laughed. "Whoever said a psychopath couldn't be smart? Yeah, I'm building a fucking school for the carpet crawlers. Do you think I like doing that shit? How about sweating the small details of contracts like Yvette spends her days doing? Filing papers? Dealing with the likes of Friga Dushku on a daily basis? Filling orders for Corporate Mine?"

Dan shook his head. "Fuck that. Here's the thing: I'm where I want to be. Nothing happens here that I'm not part of. Got a nice operation. Nicer than that shithead Benteen could guess. I've got the refinery, an interest in half the local mining claims, and I'm carrying loans for a bunch of people. Do I want to muck that all up by having to go to work herding a bunch of the local folk?"

"Once again, Dan, you leave me speechless, if not a little amused."

"Yeah, well, happy to be entertaining, but Benteen's for real. Heard he terrified Trish today."

Shig lifted his wine. Dan wasn't certain if he took a tiny sip or just let it touch his lips.

Shig replaced the glass on the bar and asked, "I thought you didn't approve of Officer Monagan."

"Damn straight. She's a fricking pain." Dan used his index finger to emphasize the point. "Here's the thing: In her eyes, I'm not shit on her shoe. We're locked in a game, her and me. She just knows she's gonna bust my ass for something. I know I'm smart enough that the kid doesn't stand a chance. A fact that entertains me to no end. That doesn't mean that Benteen can go around treating her like he did."

Shig chuckled under his breath, a twinkle of disbelief in his brown eyes.

"What?" Dan demanded.

"Understanding is such a rare gift."

"Yeah, and I wish you'd get some. Calling Benteen the scorpion isn't a joke. It's a statement of fucking fact. He paid for that moniker with other people's pain and sorrow. So how about you and Yvette and me putting our heads together, we can come up with something."

"What would you suggest?"

"Ambush. Trish is supposed to be the best shot on the planet. Maybe post her on top of one of the buildings along the avenue. Then you send a message to The Jewel. Something about 'We give up. PA's yours. Come at noon and we'll hand it over.' Then as he walks past, Bam!"

"That would indeed be pragmatic."

"Tell me you're not thinking of something more complicated. You gotta trust me on this. He's not the kind you can try and out-game. I get the feeling he's two jumps ahead before you've even thought it."

"Most likely." Shig rocked his glass thoughtfully on its base, eyes on the wine coating the inside of the glass. "He didn't rise to become Shayne's lover and partner without having the necessary skill set that made him competitive in one of the most Byzantine political arenas ever."

"I don't believe this. You're discussing this guy like he's a history lesson. Maybe you ought to accompany me down to my place and sit face-to-face with the fucker for a while. Have a chance to really scare the shit out of yourself."

"I did actually. When he stepped off the shuttle. I told him everything he needed to know to survive."

Dan blinked, rubbed his eyes. "Why do I think I could get better results by beating myself in the head with a brick? Shig, we don't need the guy to *survive*. We need him dead."

"I suspect he didn't hear a word I said that day," Shig said easily. "Too bad. He was warned."

"And people think I have a psychiatric disorder? Did you just hear yourself? You, me, and Yvette, we don't always see eye-to-eye. I need you to help me take him out. If you guys go down, we lose everything. He takes over, and you watch. It's going to be all about him."

"Actually, that's what I'm hoping." This time actually Shig took a drink of the wine.

"You've got a reputation for not making any sense with all your Eastern philosophy crap. You know that, don't you?"

"What you fail to understand is that underlying this entire discussion is faith."

"Oh, fuck." Dan winced, raised his whiskey, and took a bracing gulp. "That's it. I'm screwed."

"If you are, then everything we built here was for nothing," Shig said absently. "It's a matter of principle, you see. Most aren't willing to test it."

"How about Talina?" Dan straightened. "I mean, she went nuts, right? Thought she was shooting Sian Hmong in the middle of the street?" He paused thoughtfully. "Not that I blame her. You ever actually had to *work* with that slit? Half my problems building that fucking school would have been solved if Perez really had shot that woman. All my problems if she'd taken Oshanti and Dushku down with Hmong."

"According to Kalico, Tal is out at Rork Springs." Shig fingered his chin. "Actually, that might not be a bad choice."

"Now you're talking!" Dan grinned, took another sip of the whiskey. "I wanted the good security officer dead after she shot Spiro. God, I miss Spiro. Now there was a vicious bitch I could control. I mean, that was the thing about Spiro. I could point her. Say, 'Deb, blow a hole in his brains,' and bam! End of problem."

Dan nodded to himself. "Deb was fast. Talina Perez was even faster. Right there in the street. Talina's the solution. Plead with her to return. Shig, she'll come for you. Let's wander down to the radio room and solve this whole fucking mess. Hell, I'll even build her a new house. Big as mine."

Shig lifted his wine, slowly drank it. Not that it was that big a glass to start with. Finished, he set it carefully on the bar. Turning to Dan, he smiled, expression benign. "No sense in bothering Talina. Like I said, I told Benteen everything he needed to know. If he didn't listen, that's not my fault."

And with that, Shig slipped off the stool and strolled his way through the crowd. His hands were clasped behind him as he climbed the steps and disappeared outside.

49

Breakfast consisted of the unexpected delight of purple sweet potatoes. Dortmund hadn't expected the treat, especially after the utilitarian food at Corporate Mine, or the greens from supper the night before. He promised himself that the moment he got back to Transluna, he was eating an entire plate of bacon and eggs.

The spooky little girl was doing the dishes while Talina fiddled with the radio she'd discovered in one of the cabinets.

Dortmund sat at the table, his head slightly fuzzy from last night's whiskey, and tried to put everything Talina had told him into context. It was so damned hard to accept her version of history when it was his inconceivable future.

"Last night you told me that all the re-wilded bison are dead in the Great Plains preserve. They are an iconic keystone species. The notion that they could all just die? Unacceptable." He'd spent half the night fretting about it.

Talina plugged in the power, lights on the radio glowing to life. "Yep. I remember that rinderpest was the final knockout."

"Rinderpest? In North America? Impossible. It's only in South Africa."

"Hey, climate was changing, right? Maybe conditions in the Great Plains got similar enough that the disease was viable. Some tourist from Johannesburg stepped out of a tube and opened his suitcase. Out came a tsetse fly. I don't know how it happened, it just did."

He played with his cup, having drunk all of the tea. "Was it only the genetically pure Yellowstone animals that died? What about the commercial bison?"

"Most of them made it. The ranchers had corrals, could vaccinate. A lot of them used gene therapy to introduce rinderpest resistance from Cape buffalo to their animals." Talina turned a knob and a scratchy voice talking about some mine could be heard through what looked like a homemade speaker.

"What about the other preserves? The Arctic one? The Siberian steppe? The reintroduced mammoths, polar bears, and Irish elk?"

"Pretty much the same story," Talina told him. "I do remember that when the evolutionists stepped in, they saved the mammoths by injecting them with elephant genes. Something about the immune system."

"They turned them into *hybrids*!" he thundered. "Polluted the genetic purity of those animals?"

Talina shot him a sidelong look. "You make it sound like sacrilege."

"More like an abomination," he growled, aware that Kylee was studying him through those wide blue eyes that gave him the chills. They seemed too large, the oversized pupils too black. Like they should be in some alien's face.

Talina turned the radio off. "If there's an emergency, just flip the switch and call Port Authority."

Then she walked over, bent down to stare into Dortmund's eyes. Something violent was stirring in those abnormally dark pupils as Talina said, "Here's the thing, Doc: You're looking right at a hybrid. Me. I'm chock full of quetzal TriNA. So, I guess in your book, I'm an abomination. Makes me really sensitive after that comment last night about locking me into a lab."

He blinked, an unaccustomed shiver of fear fingering its way through his guts.

She chuckled then, reading his unease. Backing away, she said, "Come on. Time to check what's left of the garden."

Dortmund exhaled his tension and fingered his empty teacup. He wondered what disturbed him the most, that his precious genetically pure animals were dead? That the only way to save other species had been to pollute them by the addition of tailored genes? Or that he was stuck in the wilderness with a heartless bitch like Talina or her weird child?

"Doc? You coming?" Talina called from the door where she had grabbed up her rifle. "This is your chance to get a feel for the bush. See what damage the evolutionists have done to Donovan."

"Wouldn't miss it," he murmured dully and climbed to his feet.

He followed them out into the morning, Capella's bright light warm and reassuring on his skin as he accompanied the woman and girl down a faint path in the stone. Again the perfume of the morning air filled his nostrils. The musical hum of the invertebrates rose from the vegetation-filled drainage toward which the trail descended.

On the way they passed the trash dump. Humans were such pigs. Among the old containers he could see cans, packaging, and, much to his surprise, even the angular fragments of a Delftware bowl. The blue-and-white pattern looked so out of place on this distant world. What bizarre circumstances had brought the Delft bowl across the stars, clear out to Rork Springs Base, only to have it end up dropped and shattered?

"Doc," Talina called over her shoulder, "you stay close. Just about everything out here will kill you. We're in the transition zone between the bush and true forest, so watch out for the roots."

"The roots?"

"Yeah, most of the plants move. If the roots grab you, it can be really tough to pull loose. Listen to Kylee. If she gives you an order, follow it. Immediately."

"That little girl?"

"She's survived alone in the forest for a year, Doc."

"I'm not a child!" Weisbacher objected indignantly.

"As good as," the little girl mumbled. "Even Tuska knew when to shut up and learn."

"Who's Tuska?" Dortmund asked as he paid attention to the steep footing. Then they encountered steps cut into the stone.

"Her little brother," Talina answered.

Dortmund rolled his eyes, figuring there was no sense in provoking more abuse.

He got his first good look at the trees growing up out of the drainage. Dendritically patterned, similar to terrestrial trees, but different in that the branches were triangular in cross section. Then it hit him that they had a much more uniform morphology, not as random as earthly specimens. And the leaves were different, broader, curiously blue in tint. He stopped short, aware that the branches were moving, shifting the leaves to better reap Capella's energy.

"Amazing! Do you see the movement?"

"It gets even better, Doc," Talina called from below. "Unlike Earth, the whole plant moves, travels. Plant a tree in your yard, you could come home a week later and it's halfway down the block."

"Are they sentient?" He scrambled to catch up.

"We don't know. Not enough research done. And Iji tells me that he's not sure where the division is between what's a plant and what's an animal. Unlike Earth, the kingdoms might just blur together in the middle. You'll find what we call 'live vines' in the trees. They look just like a plant, but they move like an animal. Seem to hunt as well as photosynthesize."

At the bottom of the stone steps, Talina had stopped. She was sniffing the air, as was the little girl. The sight made Dortmund think of hunting dogs at the edge of a woods.

He looked around the blue-green paradise, tried to take in the unusual forms of plants, the slightly off coloration, as if a color-blind child had painted them. The chime was louder here, almost enough to be uncomfortable.

"What are you smelling?" he asked, sniffing on his own.

"Checking for quetzal or one of the other predators," Talina told him. "Each has its own odor."

He sniffed again. "Like what?"

"Forget it, Doc. You're not an abomination like Kylee and me. Best you'll get is the slight tang of vinegar. If you do, stop. Back away the way you came. It means a bem or skewer are way too close."

"Vinegar."

"Yeah, that's about the only warning you'll get. But if you look close at the rocks, you'll finally figure out which is the real predator. When you pick out the two rocks that look the same, one is real and the other is ready to kill you."

Step by step he followed them into a world of blue green. Thumb-sized creatures flitted from branch to branch, hanging vines graced with peculiarly shaped leaves shifted as he passed, and he was surprised when the plants he brushed either recoiled or turned their leaves toward him, as if to discern the nature of his intrusion upon their world.

I shouldn't be out here without a protective suit.

As soon as he thought it, the notion struck him as ludicrous. Humans had been wandering around here for almost thirty years now. Any damage had been done. And Talina had told him that quetzal contamination had to be up close and personal. He recoiled at the thought of sharing saliva with any creature, let alone an alien.

Hard to think of Talina and the girl as hybrids, their bodies polluted by alien genetic material. The conservationists had steered clear of discussions about humans and purity, arguing that the intermixture of African, Neandertal, Denisovan, Heidlbergensis, and Java genes were just variations accumulated from isolated loops of the human gene pool that finally returned to the main trunk of human evolution.

Now, who knew what was going on in Talina and Kylee's genes? This was more than inserting Cape buffalo genes into a bison to provide the animal with resistance to rinderpest, as horrifying as that was. This was the making of something beyond the worst conservationist's nightmare.

And Donovanian TriNA has already been carried back to Solar System?

The true impact finally began to settle in.

God, I'm a fool. I was so worried about our impact on Donovan when it might be that humanity itself is already doomed.

He *had* to get back to Solar System. Raise the alarm. It would require screening, registration, and removal of all suspect humans. The best course would be to concentrate them into special stations, separate them from the general population, and maintain a strict quarantine. Implement rigid protocols that . . .

He lost the thought, distracted by a flight of the most remarkable flying animals cavorting through the high branches; their colors were an almost iridescent red.

"What are those?" He pointed.

"Scarlet fliers. One of the most common avian species. Mostly they feed on invertebrates. But you see any fliers with four wings, two front, two rear? You freeze immedi-

ately. They're mobbers, death fliers, the same creatures
that almost killed Supervisor Aguila."

"She was out here?"

"They got her in the mine yard, maybe ten meters from
where you hid in my aircar." Talina jabbed a finger his way,
her eyes gimlet hard. "You see them, you freeze. Like
stone. And you don't fucking move until they've flown
away. It's your only chance. You panic and strike at them,
try and bat them away? You'll be sliced thinner than sand-
wich meat. After five minutes, only your bloody skeleton
will be left."

"Aren't you being a bit melodramatic?"

She turned away, saying, "Might as well let Donovan
kill you right off. Sooner or later stupid is always a death
sentence."

Dortmund felt the flare of anger, knotted his fists. He
was on the verge of storming off into the underbrush when
the little girl reached out and grabbed his pants, saying,
"You don't want to go that way."

He stopped short, glanced down in irritation. "Why
not?"

She pointed at a delicate lacing of vine with what looked
like crimson and orange fruits. "That's called you're
screwed vine."

Dortmund squinted at it, unnerved enough to actually
trust the child rather than accede to his initial impression
that she was having fun at his expense. Somehow the alien-
eyed child didn't strike him as the usual juvenile prankster.

"You're screwed vine? That's really its name?"

The little girl nodded. "It drops around you like a net
and draws tight. Then those orange globes start digesting
you."

Dortmund couldn't help it, he burst out laughing. "Is
everything here deadly?"

"Pretty much," the girl told him solemnly. "You follow
me. Put your feet where I put mine. And don't blow Talina
off. She means it about being stupid."

Dortmund took a deep breath, a curious tension around
his heart. Taking a glance back at the you're screwed vine,
he shook his head but did as the little girl told him.

The spring could have been locked away in a sylvan hollow somewhere on Earth but for the slightly too-blue vegetation. The water leaked out of the sandstone, maybe ten gallons per minute. A sialon collector led to a small solar electric pump, which sent water uphill to the dome through a flexible pipeline.

"That's the water supply," Talina told him. Then she gave him a ghoulish grin. "It's always nice to check the source, don't you think? Make sure there's not a dead chamois decomposing just up from the intake."

He made a face, hand to his stomach. "I could have gone all day and not heard that."

"Sorry, Doc. But you tend to set yourself up for that kind of abuse."

He didn't find it funny. "Where's this garden supposed to be?"

"Just downstream." Talina eased around him, careful not to disturb a low plant with four-inch thorns. "That's thorncactus. Trust me, you don't want to be stuck."

For once he could agree without skepticism. Again he surrendered himself to following the little girl, mimicking her steps and actions.

He could almost believe the child had indeed survived on her own in the bush. Everything these people told him defied credulity, but he was slowly coming to the conclusion that it was all a staggering truth.

They hadn't gone more than twenty meters before the narrow sandstone walls opened. Here the larger trees were missing. In their place he could see decomposing stumps. Among them, looking remarkably alien, but reassuringly familiar, were sprinkled terrestrial plants. Each growing in an open patch of soil.

"Who tends this?" he asked. "Looks like someone weeded it."

"Doc, no one's lived here for over a decade now." Talina bent down, snapped a green bean from one of the plants, and popped it into her mouth. After chewing, she said, "That's why there's no corn. It's so much of a domesticate it can't broadcast its kernels past the husks. Hey, look! Poblanos!"

Dortmund watched her pick a large green pepper from a waist-high plant.

"Not as good as Mundo," Kylee said. "But it will do. 'Specially if there's hunting here."

"Should be crest and fastbreak," Talina answered. To Dortmund she said, "We can digest the animal proteins. As to the native plants? Forget it. If they don't poison you outright, you shit it out exactly as it went in."

"What a charming mental image you've just conjured," he muttered to himself, taking an inventory of the garden. Peas, beans, peppers, what looked like potatoes, several grains that grew in different clumps, grapes, and an apple tree. One of the genetically augmented varieties that bloomed and produced fruit year round.

He walked over, was about to reach for one of the low-hanging fruit when Kylee shouted, "No!"

Dortmund froze, more out of start than understanding.

"Look up the branch a ways," Kylee told him. "See the blue-green plant?"

"I do."

"That's gotcha vine. It won't kill you, but pulling the little hooks out of your skin really hurts and takes hours."

Talina stepped up and studied the length of plant. "Unusual to see one in a terrestrial tree." She wandered around, followed the long body of the vine down, then across the ground almost three meters to where the roots appeared to have a tenuous hold on the soil.

"I don't get it? Why's it rooted way out here?" Dortmund looked around. "In fact there's nothing growing under the tree. Or around any of the garden plants. What gives?"

"Chemistry," Kylee told him, her voice filled with little-girl pride. "Earth plants have roots that produce chemicals. It's how they compete for space. Donovan's plants don't use chemicals in the roots. Instead they move, try and strangle the other plants' roots."

"She's right," Talina added as she plucked a small red tomato from a vine. "You get into deep forest and you'll see giant trees uprooting each other."

"So, how long has this garden been here?"

"Maybe twenty-five, twenty-six years."

"Has it spread? Traveled down the drainage? Is it crowding out Donovanian plants?"

"Don't know. Let's go look."

Again Talina led the way, Kylee following. Twice she stopped, made them back away, and circle around. Once it was for something called a sidewinder, the second time for inoffensive-looking stalks that stood about knee high. She called them brown caps.

All in all, they traveled half a kilometer down the drainage and found only two terrestrial plants: a grape vine and a large prickly pear cactus.

Climbing out onto the slickrock, Dortmund seated himself and looked back up the barren stone incline toward the Rork Springs dome. "The question is begged: Why aren't the terrestrial plants expanding if their root chemistry keeps Donovanian plants at bay?"

"Rebecca monitored the same thing at Mundo," Kylee told him.

"That's out of my league, Doc"—Talina seated herself and laid her rifle across her lap—"but I think they're two mutually exclusive biological systems. Two different evolutions. Even if some of the critters look sort of earthly. Take quetzals for example. Some people have called them dragons. Other people say they look like dinosaurs, but there's nothing about their bones or organs that's remotely earthlike."

"Parallel evolution," Dortmund suggested. "There are only so many ways animals can move: legs, wings, paddles, constriction or expansion, cilia, or a screw. Maybe some sort of jet in a high-density atmosphere or a liquid environment. And when you look at legs, essentially they're just springs. How many ways can you make a spring? Especially when simple is always the best?"

"Donovanian life is different way down at the bottom," Kylee said, her gaze fixed on the distant sandstone ridge.

"What do you mean, child?"

"It starts at the molecular level. With the TriNA. Dya thinks the nucleotides are the same because that's the easiest way to build an information molecule. Like you said: Simple is best. And that's what's simple in our universe."

"Do you know what you're saying?"

"Duh. It's basic organic chemistry. Carbon, hydrogen, oxygen chemistry. It's about shapes: triangles, squares, pentagons, hexagons, and heptagons. When I was eight,

Dya made me try and program information into amino acids. Didn't matter how many times I tried. Didn't work. But making even the simplest RNA? Like, I could do that in the lab when I was seven. It's fundamental chemistry."

Dortmund blinked. What the hell? "Who taught you this?"

"My mother."

"Dya Simonov?"

"That's her." Those eerie blue eyes were fixed on his. "She's just an evolutionist."

"How much farther can you fall, Doc?" Talina asked. "Here you are, locked away on a world where survival of the fittest is put to the test every day, and dependent upon two infected and exiled hybrids for your very survival. Hell, you're as much a pariah as we are."

"Me?"

"From the way you tell it, your charming personality alienated Dya, Cheng, and the rest. Then you made such a nuisance of yourself that Kalico hauled you off to Corporate Mine in an attempt to figure out what to do with you. A fate you found so reprehensible, you stowed away in my aircar. And here you are, a human being so detestable, you're stuck with us."

"Do you know who I really am?"

"Yeah, blow it out your ass, Doc." Talina chuckled softly under her breath, the breeze playfully flipping her raven hair over her shoulder.

Kylee giggled.

"But, I . . ." The words faded into a sense of desperation.

Talina stiffened, tightened her grip on her rifle. "On your feet. Company's coming."

Kylee had picked out the threat and was scrambling to rise even as Talina brought her rifle up.

Dortmund took two tries before he could get his feet under him on the slippery rock.

"What is it?" He followed their gazes, trying to place the two beasts scampering up the stone slope toward them. Indeed, they might have been some sort of dinosaurs, maybe allosaurus, or one of the species of raptors. Bipedal things, but with larger front legs tucked up under their chests.

"My God," Dortmund wondered. "They're sky blue? What kind of predator wants to stand out like that?"

"Means they're wary," Kylee told him. "When they turn blood red and the expandable collars are extended? That's your last warning before they eat you."

Dortmund put a hand to his suddenly queasy stomach. It was dawning on him as they drew closer: They were huge. Maybe two meters tall and another five or six in length.

"Shoot them," Dortmund whispered, looking around for any direction to run. The only way that seemed even remotely feasible was back into the vegetation in the drainage. Maybe he could hide down in the biteya bush, side-winders, and you're screwed. Anywhere out on the open rock there was nowhere that he wouldn't stand out like a signpost.

"Shoot them?" Talina asked through a wry laugh. "Why, Doc, whatever happened to your conservation ethic?"

Dortmund swallowed hard, wondering the same thing.

"What do we do?"

"See what they want, silly," Kylee told him. "And if they're starved, we've always got you."

"Me?"

"Yeah, like, you know, an offering while we make our escape."

50

A s the quetzals charged closer, Talina shot a sidelong glance at Weisbacher. The guy was whiter than bleached flour. Absently, she wondered if the panicked professor was going to piss himself. Hell, the quetzals hadn't even dropped their light blue color yet, let alone turned the faintest shade of red.

Her own quetzal was actively tying her guts into a knot. She could taste the first hint of peppermint. Damn it, life was easier back in the old days. All it would have taken was two shots. No muss, no threat. Then skin the carcasses for the leather and cut some of the steaks from along what passed for a backbone.

She could feel Rocket's disapproval.

Yeah, well, little buddy, if we get eaten today, you share my disappointment with these two when they digest your molecules.

Talina let them get within thirty meters before calling, "Far enough!" As she did she shouldered the rifle, muzzle slightly lowered, but ready for a snap shot.

The quetzals stopped, tails lashing, colors shifting to patterns of yellow, green, and pink. Questioning. So far, so good.

"What do you think they know?" Kylee asked.

"Hard to say," Talina answered. "But we're west of Port Authority. My quetzals come from this country. This is the direction Whitey was headed. Who knows? They could very well have shared molecules, or maybe they've never seen a human before."

Talina lowered the rifle to her hip, the quetzals apparently understanding the gesture.

"Kylee, check out what's behind us. Be just like them to send a third one in from the rear."

"Yeah, looks empty," the kid told her after scanning the bare rock.

"Keep your eyes peeled on the creek bottom, too. One could make a run at us from the vegetation."

"What are you going to do?" Dortmund demanded.

"Shut up, Doc. I'm going to try and keep anyone from being killed." And with that she stepped forward, her mouth beginning to salivate out of control. The taste of peppermint ran bitter over her tongue.

At the halfway point, she stopped. Spit into her hand, and offered it.

The larger of the quetzals turned the white, mauve, and orange interplaying with yellow, green, and pink: curious and questioning. Hissing, it vented an explosive exhale rearward through its vents. The three eyes were watching her with a burning intensity.

Again Talina spit into her hand, offering it. Her heart had begun to pound. The demon quetzal in her gut had gone apeshit crazy.

This close, her rifle dangling by one hand, her left extended, there was no way she could raise the weapon and fire before the quetzal was on her.

"Come on, damn it. I'm trying to communicate here."

The second quetzal stepped warily forward, head lowered like the first, the three-eyed gaze so intense the air seemed to burn.

Once more she spit into her palm, extended it, saying, "This isn't like computing inverted symmetry mathematics, guys. Taste the spit. Give me a break."

The first quetzal cocked its head in what would have been a quizzical gesture for a terrestrial species. Could have meant anything on Donovan. Or nothing.

"All right, I'm calling this a bust," Talina said. "Weisbacher, Kylee, I'm going to back away. Be sure that nothing's sneaking up on us from another direction."

And so saying, Talina took a step back.

As she did, the first quetzal opened its mouth, made a clicking and twittering sound down in its throat, then literally blew a harmonic organ-like tone out its rear vents.

"Never heard that before," Talina muttered. "Kylee?"

"Don't know."

She took another step back, and started to raise . . .

A flash of brilliant crimson. A blur of speed. And then

the impact. A claw tore her rifle from her grip. She felt herself knocked backward. Hit the rock hard on her butt. A clawed foot slammed her down.

She had a vision of the Mayan bowl hitting the floor. Its hollow *pop* matched the hard impact as her head hit the implacable sandstone. Fragments of pottery flew through her head; strobing light blasted in her vision. A sensation of breathlessness, the distant sound of clattering potsherds, and then darkness drowned any other sense . . .

51

In all of his life Dortmund had never known total and abject terror. The son of two professors, he'd grown up in a privileged household in a university environment. He had been a brilliant student and then an ambitious and acclaimed professor. The worst fright he'd ever endured was that he might embarrass himself in a professional setting. Might have a paper dismissed, or be academically humiliated.

The quetzals terrified him down to the roots of his soul. Paralyzed him with a consuming fear. Like mythical monsters come to life. Not to mention that they ate people. And there was nothing between them and him except Talina Perez.

But when they flashed red and leaped on the woman, hammered her against the hard stone, Dortmund seized up tight.

The image seared into his brain: horrifying beasts, iridescent colors flashing, crouched atop Talina's limp body. Their wedge-shaped heads where bumping as their tongues lashed out, distorting Talina's mouth, protruding her cheeks, knocking her jaw about as her head jerked under the impact. The woman's long black hair gleamed bluish in the sunlight as it was splashed this way and that with each jarring insult.

Dortmund couldn't breathe, heard a broken whimpering from deep in his throat. Something warm rushed down the inside of his thighs.

Time stopped. A crystal quality to his vision. The beasts before him rendered in such precise detail. The glint of light on their eyes, the armored, scale-covered muzzles. Each serration of the jaws. How the tongues looked bruised-purple in the harsh glare. The incredible vivid red—almost painfully crimson—radiating from the flared collar membranes.

A ringing heterodyne blared in his ears, as though they refused to recognize the chittering and growling, or the hollow thumping of Talina's head against the stone.

He'd never quite know how long he was lithic. How time had compressed, or the horror made manifest.

It shattered when Kylee uttered a shrieking and shrill wailing. Like something torn by its roots from pure pain.

It startled Dortmund to the point that he jerked his head around. Fixed on the little girl's face, now turned demonic red, mouth twisted into a savage visage that showed her teeth.

She was moving. Charging forward, small hands like claws as she rushed the stunned quetzals. Like whips, the tongues slapped back into the gaping mouths, the eyes fixing on the girl.

"No." It came as a whisper choked from Dortmund's throat.

But Kylee was upon them, and again the eerily tortured shriek broke from her throat.

Just as Dortmund thought the girl would leap onto the beasts, only to be torn asunder, she stopped, bent forward, craning her neck and head in a lowered and extended manner. Again she screamed, then thrust her arms out to the side, almost like a dancer's bow.

Dortmund tried to swallow, choked as it caught in his dry throat.

The quetzals forgot Talina's body, seemed to swivel on their hips, heads lowered eyeball to eyeball with the little girl.

Oh, dear God. They're going to kill her before my eyes.

Instead—and nearly as awful—the girl opened her mouth. Like striking serpents, the tongues lashed out. Kylee's head was batted this way and that with the impact. Somehow she kept her feet.

A moment later the two quetzals sucked their tongues back, retreated a couple of steps. Stared at each other, a thousand patterns of color flickering on their hides.

Dortmund had recovered his ability to breathe. Now he sucked one desperate breath after another. His heart was trying to explode in his chest. A nervous sweat broke out on his face, neck, and chest.

It surprised him that he was parked on his butt, legs akimbo, braced by his shaking arms. When had he collapsed?

The quetzals flashed white and pink followed by a day-glow orange. Almost quicker than the eye could see they turned, trotting off in that bipedal lope that reminded Dortmund of a racing ostrich.

Kylee braced her hands on her knees, head down, gasping for air. Then she stiffened, her body convulsing as she threw up.

Dortmund took two tries to get to his feet. Only then did he feel the cool wetness, horrified to look down at the urine stain darkening his pants. A cry of disbelief stuck in his throat.

He turned, considered how far it was to the Rork Springs dome. He could go now. Before anyone could see his shame. Change clothes. Maybe one of the pairs of overalls in the closet would fit. Then come back.

Torn, he glanced back at where Kylee now knelt beside Talina, struggled to hold the woman's head up.

Whatever possessed me to come to this appalling planet?

"Help me!" Kylee called.

The little girl was glaring at him. He clamped his eyes shut—damned in his humiliation—and wearily turned his steps to where Talina and the girl waited.

He could smell himself. Was gratified that the little girl barely gave his soaked pants a glance, then turned back to where she cradled Talina's head in her lap. "She's still breathing."

Dortmund sniffed. Over the smell of urine, he could identify the most unusual and spicy odor coming from the unconscious woman's mouth.

"What just happened here? Was she out of her mind? Just walking up to them? And you? Were you trying to get killed?"

Kylee said emotionlessly, "They may be back once they think it through. We've got to get Talina to the dome. You get her rifle."

Dortmund shot a worried glance at the weapon—more malignant in its own way than even the quetzals. "I don't touch guns. I don't believe in them. You take the gun. I'll get Talina."

And so saying, he reached down, only to discover that he hadn't the strength to lift the limp woman. Every time he got a hold, she'd slip through his fumbling grasp.

"Are you a complete waste of skin?" Kylee asked skeptically.

"What do you mean, waste of skin?"

"Can't you do anything?"

"I'll have you know—"

"Sure, you're a fucking professor. What can you do in the real world? So, like, squat down behind her, slip your arms under her armpits, and lift with your legs. I'll hold her head up, until she's braced, and you can drag her."

Dortmund—despite the fact that he was still shaking and nauseated—managed as the little girl suggested. It wasn't far to the dome. Not more than a few hundred meters.

Turned out to be a distance that seemed beyond forever. By the time he dragged Talina into the dome's protection, it was a couple of hours, way too many rests, and more effort than he'd ever spent at anything. The urine had long dried. He considered it a miracle that his heart hadn't burst, and it felt like every muscle in his body had been pulled from its anchoring.

Levering Talina into one of the beds at last, he collapsed onto the floor. Unable to help himself, he lowered his head into his hands and wept.

52

Talina Perez wasn't sleeping easily. She thrashed periodically, and twice Dortmund caught the woman just before she flipped herself off onto the floor. In the end, he tied her onto the bed, feeling curiously vulgar as he wound the strap around her body.

"You do that like you don't want to touch her." Kylee was watching from the room door.

"It feels like a violation." Dortmund pulled the strap tight, double checking to make sure Talina couldn't accidentally strangle herself.

Dortmund straightened, every muscle in his body on fire. Talina had a slight swelling on the back of her head. The scalp was barely lacerated. He checked the woman one last time, wondering what he was going to do if she had brain damage.

As if he'd recognize the signs.

The only thing he'd known to do was check her pupils; he found her irises fluctuating in unison when he pulled her lids up. What the hell was happening to the woman's eyes? He couldn't quite place what the difference was.

With a sigh he turned, flicked off the lights, and followed Kylee back to the main room. He'd washed and dried his pants, still thunderstruck. He'd just survived the worst day of his life.

"I should use the radio to call Port Authority," he stated as he walked up to the door and peered out through the duraplast window at the yard. The familiar stone out front gleamed in the white yard light's glow. No quetzal was peering back in at him. Only a swirling cloud of flying bug-like things were moving as they swarmed the overhead light.

Sometimes the similarities with Earth amazed him. But then Simons in his 2098 paper had demonstrated mathematically that there were only so many ways organisms could evolve morphologically within given environments. Legs were limited to certain structural limits to bear weight and move mass by the universal laws of physics. It didn't matter if it was on Earth or Donovan; when it came to limb dimensions, phi—the golden ratio—ultimately remained the best solution to minimize the amount of energy expended to move a creature over a given distance with the greatest efficiency. A wing, no matter what its composition, was limited in shape by the laws of aerodynamics in a gaseous environment. Biomechanics was an exact science based on physics. Period.

"See anything?" Kylee asked.

"No." Dortmund double checked the lock on the door and retreated to the table. He seated himself, stared at Talina's bottle, and surrendered to temptation, pouring a finger into his glass. As far as he was concerned, it was the best-tasting whiskey he'd ever laid lips to.

Kylee gave a halfhearted shrug. "You know how to fly an aircar?"

"What? You mean it's not automatic? You don't just tell it where you want to go and it takes you?"

"Duh. You're on Donovan now."

He wondered how many things in life he'd never learned, and what the value of all his education really turned out to be. Somehow the imperative to create administrative policies within the halls of academia seemed to fly in the face of reality when a person was nose to nose with quetzals.

"Not like you thought, huh? Being here, I mean."

"No." He braced his elbows and rubbed his cheeks with his palms. "What happened out there today? I don't understand any of it. Why did Talina just walk out there? Why didn't she shoot them? That rifle of hers, it can kill a quetzal, right? But she just walked out and spit in her hand? It makes no sense."

"That's how quetzals communicate. Talina thought she could talk instead of kill." Kylee shrugged, looking away absently.

"And then you made that sound? Ran out there. What was that all about?"

"They would have tasted her. Tried to learn her."

"They what?"

"Quetzals learn by eating. Ingesting molecules. I had to stop them. I did it like a young quetzal would. I let myself be Rocket. They didn't expect that. Or what Talina did, either. I'm starting to get hints about them. I think more than anything, they're puzzled."

"And you know this . . . how?"

"By what they said to each other. The patterns and colors they display. It's how they talk. And then there's what the molecules are telling me."

Dortmund ground his teeth. "These are the quetzal molecules you and Talina say you have inside of yourselves? I just have trouble visualizing how that works."

"We're infected. What's to visualize?" The girl looked toward the back bedroom. "It's harder for Talina. Her brain was all adult. I got to grow up with Rocket. Dya told me my brain is structurally different. That I can think in quetzal. That makes me more integrated. By morning I'll probably know what they want. Sometimes it comes clear in dreams."

"That's your subconscious. Not true communication."

She gave him the sort of look she'd give an idiot. "It worked with Rocket."

"Such are the wages of Radcek's megalomania. You're paying the price for his evolutionist idiocy. How many more innocents are going to suffer in the name of his vanity and greed?"

"What would you have done?"

"Developed quarantined colonies. Large sealed domes that would have allowed subsurface mineral extraction while keeping the Capella III and human environments totally and completely separate."

The look she gave him would have frozen liquid oxygen. "Then Rocket and me could never have been friends."

"You could have been a normal little girl. Played with other children, shared all the joys of childhood and friends."

"Fuck that."

Dortmund started at the virulence behind her foul mouth. "And maybe you could have grown up as a proper young lady instead of like a . . . a . . ."

The child stuck her tongue out at him. "Monster? Hybrid? Didn't I hear you say I was polluted the other day?" She crossed her arms. "I should have let the quetzals eat you."

Dortmund started to give her his usual response. Realized how absolutely asinine it sounded here, in this tiny dome, who knew where in the vastness of the Donovanian bush?

Dortmund, you're turning out to be a real fool.

All those years playing the university game, scrapping with the evolutionists, dismantling their arguments through his acumen. He'd wielded data like a sword, sometimes bowling his opposition over just through the force of his personality.

I almost died today.

He studied Kylee again, forcing himself to remember how she'd rushed out to face the monsters. Bent nearly double at the waist? Hell, he thought she'd been offering herself as a sacrifice. Turned out she was appealing to the quetzals.

How did that happen? And, more to the point, what did it mean? Not just for him and Talina at that moment, but what did it imply about humanity? Its chances for the future?

Donovanian TriNA was already back in Solar System. But how much? How large was the infection? What would be the etiology of the disease? How would it manifest? And worse, *Turalon* was halfway there with another source of infection. Would it just be the returnees? Or did the molecules spread, communicated by touch, or aerosol? Would the entire ship's complement spread the infection through Solar System?

They should be quarantined. Every last one of them.

If only he could get word back to Solar System. Warn them of the impending threat.

"I feel as if everything I ever believed has been looted away. That the man that I was has lost everything."

"Not even close, bucko."

"Bucko?"

She got to her feet, saying, "You don't even talk like a real person." She paused, expression thoughtful. "What rhymes with Dortmund? Cortfund? Snort kund? No, wait, I got it! Short Mind. Dortmind Short Mind. Dortmind Short Mind." She began repeating it in a singsongy mantra.

I really hate children. Disgusting little beasts.

He wanted to jam his fingers in his ears.

"I think the thing to do is call Port Authority. Have them come and pick us up. Take us back. I'll be hauled off to Corporate Mine again, but at least there are no wild beasts to devour me."

He nodded, seeing it all fall into place. "Dr. Turnienko will know what to do about Talina. She can check for a subdural hematoma. Can monitor her recovery. And you can be placed once again under your mother's authority. God help the poor woman."

So saying, he got to his feet, stepped over to the cabinet and opened the doors. He stared thoughtfully at the radio. Turned the knob as he had seen Talina do.

Nothing.

Dortmund squinted. Surely he could figure out a technology as primitive as radio. He turned the other knob, hearing a gratifying click. Rotated it all the way, and went back to turning the first knob.

Nothing.

He checked to make sure the power was connected. Yes.

Again he tried the knobs, moving them in combination, turning left and right.

"You might as well go back to your whiskey," Kylee told him, arms crossed defiantly as she gave him her "you're an idiot" stare.

"Why doesn't this work?"

"Because I knew you'd want to call Port Authority. They killed Rocket."

"Well, fix the radio! That's an order."

"No."

He stepped toward her, knotting a fist in a threatening motion. "Whatever you did, undo it."

"Can't make me."

"I could thrash you within an inch of your life."

"Pedophile."

Dortmund stopped short. Winced.

He made a calming motion with his hands. "Sorry. Lost my temper. Will you *please* fix the radio?"

"My mother always told me, 'Go to bed. You'll see it clearer in the morning.' G'night."

She left him standing there—went skipping her way down the hall toward the back bedroom.

Dortmund took a step after her. Stopped. The little shit had called his bluff. What was he going to do?

He stepped back to the radio, stared thoughtfully at it. Checked the casing, but couldn't see anything missing. No plugs or holes that might have held a part.

"If there is a dark side to the universe, I'm in it," he murmured as he closed the cabinet. Two PhDs and he couldn't even fix a radio?

53

The bowl was broken. That fact could not be undone. Could not be taken back.

Guilt and horror remained, painful in its intensity. Would always remain. Talina hadn't meant to. She'd just wanted to touch it, turn it so she could see the colorful images painted on the side. They were like cartoons, those images of feathered men in profile. Those were the heroes. And the others—monstrous, with sagging bellies and spots on their skin—were the Lords of Death who ruled in Xibalba, the Maya Underworld.

To reach the bowl up on the old wooden table, she had to stretch, standing on tiptoes. She could barely touch it, feel it. With a bit more effort she got her fingers around it.

And then, extended as she was, she slipped on the Saltillo tile floor.

The sight of the bowl, teetering on the edge of the table, tipping so slowly, then falling . . .

Her panic would never be forgotten. The sound of the beautiful and ancient bowl as it shattered on the tiles echoed. Jarring. An ache resonating in her bones.

"It will be all right," Mother had told her when she finally settled down and stopped crying. "Not as good as it was, but it's not a total loss, *chica mia*. For some it would be a tragedy. What was once worth a fortune is now worth less. But we are not like the looters. As archaeologists, our values are different."

Talina, tears still streaking down her cheeks, had stared anxiously up at her mother. She'd cried and cried. Wishing she could take it back, that she'd never gotten out of bed that day. Wished Mother's team had never opened the dead Mayan king's tomb and found the burial pot.

Despite Mother's words, Talina had known; she'd seen the dismay, the heartbreak Mother hid so well behind her large dark eyes.

That night they sat side-by-side at the kitchen table, the smell of cooking tamales drifting from the stove. On the scarred old wooden table, Mother had placed a large plastic bowl, its insides filled with sand. In a plate next to it were the broken potsherds.

"You see, *hija mia*, because we are archaeologists, nothing has been lost."

"But I broke it!" Once again the tears began to silver her vision.

"So the pot broke? To those *cholo pendejo* antiquities thieves, that would be a tragedy. What was worth a fortune to them on the black market in Transluna is now almost worthless. But for us, we have only lost a little time."

"But, Mama? It's all apart. It won't be right again."

"That's not the pot's true value."

"I don't understand."

Mother studied Talina thoughtfully where she was seated beside her; Mother's long fingers rested on the edge of the sand-filled bowl. "Why did you want to touch the pot?"

"To see the colors and pictures."

Mother nodded, a faint smile bending her lips. "Do you know why the pot was buried next to the head of the king? It was to serve him in the next world. To catch his blood when he made sacrifices, hold his spirit plants, and to burn his offerings. That's why it had such pretty paintings. They told a story."

"What story?"

"The story of the death and rebirth of One-Hunahpu. Along with his little twin brother, Seven-Hunahpu, he was killed by the Lords of Xibalba after the brothers lost a ball game in the Underworld. Not just any ball game, but *pitz:* the ball game played by the gods just after the second Creation. In the game you can't touch the ball with your hands or feet. You have to hit it with your hips, head, or elbows. Each time the brothers hit the ball, or it bounced, it made a *ta-thump* sound. When the brothers smacked it back and forth, or it bounced on the alley or sloping walls of the ballcourt, it kept going *ta-thump*. The twins made so much noise they woke the Lords of Xibalba who lived under the ballcourt's floor."

This story Talina knew: "And so the Lords of Xibalba

summoned the brothers to Xibalba to play ball with the Lords of Death. They went and played ball and lost, so the Lords of Xibalba killed them. They cut off One-Hunahpu's head and buried the brothers' bodies under the ballcourt."

"That's right. The Lords of Death hung One-Hunahpu's head in a calabash tree overlooking the ballcourt. It hung there until it was only a skull. One of the Lords of Death, who was named Blood Gatherer, had a daughter called Blood Moon. She heard about the skull in the tree, and though it was forbidden, went to see.

"There she saw One-Hunahpu's skull. And it spoke to her, and told her not to be afraid. Then it asked her to hold out her hand, and the skull spit into it. And you know what happened?"

"She got pregnant with the skull's twin sons."

"That's right. And when the Lords of Death found out, they told four of the messenger owls to sacrifice Blood Moon and bring back her heart. But the owls took pity and led Blood Moon to the surface of the earth and took back a fake heart to fool the Lords of Death."

"And Blood Moon went up and had twin sons."

"She did. The first born was named Hun Ajaw and the second Xbalanque. Years later they found their father and uncle's ball-playing equipment. And went back and played the Lords of Death in a ball game in Xibalba. And won, and brought their father back to life. That was the story told by the paintings on the pot. It illustrated the moment that Hun Ajaw and Xbalanque brought their father back to life. It's the Mayan resurrection story. Now, will you help me?"

"Do what?"

"Make the pot whole again."

Talina, standing on her chair, watched as her mother began sorting through the broken potsherds that they had carefully picked up from the floor.

"Let's begin," her mother told her. She took two of the broken shards and placed them together to make sure they fit. Then she took them apart again, carefully glued the edges, and fit them back together. These she stuck in the loose sand in the bowl; the sand kept them positioned perfectly.

"It will take a long time, *hija*. It must be done carefully, piece by piece. And thoughtfully so that no pieces are glued together out of order."

"And what then?"

"Then it will tell the story again. It will teach us about who we are and where we came from. It even tells us the name of the king in whose tomb the pot was buried."

Mama picked up the potsherd with the tri-part glyph. "His name was Laju'n Way. A very powerful name because it had several meanings. *Laju'n* is the number ten in Mayan. The word *Way* in Mayan meant transformation, and had several meanings, including 'dreamer,' 'animal companion spirit,' 'spirit possessed,' and 'to sleep.'"

"Those are funny names."

"Not to the Maya. Laju'n Way must have been a very powerful and spooky man. I'll bet he had animal spirits in his head that gave him visions. No wonder his people treated him with such respect."

"Oh." Talina tried to understand what it would be like to have animals in her head.

"So you see, *chica mia,* breaking the pot wasn't such a tragedy. Each of the fragments carries bits of information. Even if they are cracked and glued together, the pictures will once again tell the story of the twins bringing their father back to life. We can still analyze what the Maya used for paint. Scrapings from the inside of the pot will tell us what it once held. If offerings were burned inside it. Or, if we get a spot of the king's blood from when he made sacrifice, we'll learn his blood type and get his DNA. Even pinpoint where the clay for the pot originally came from through its chemistry. A thousand things."

Talina remembered staring at the two glued fragments where they were stuck in the sand, wondering at all the secrets they still held.

When the pieces are all back together . . .

The pot hasn't been destroyed. It still has value.

All the pieces carry bits of information.

The king was a dreamer who had animal spirits in his head.

The image shifted, and the tripartite glyph of Laju'n Way's name faded, started to grow fuzzy, as though it were sinking down into a layer of fog. Shifting. Moving. Stirring the currents as its shape morphed, turned triangular. When it did the three parts of the glyph began to glow, lining up at the top of a multicolored and wedge-shaped head.

The familiar quetzal's head opened its mouth, the three eyes shining with piercing intensity.

Terror speared through Talina's heart, lancelike, sharp and fierce.

As she wavered in the dream, she called out, *"Mother! How do I fix myself? Where is my bowl of sand?"*

But try as Talina might, when she reached for a piece of her shattered soul it seemed to slip through her fingers like mist. Each time she could hear the soft chittering of quetzals.

54

Tamarland could almost pity Allison and Wirth. First came Wirth. A petty criminal, the guy was completely outclassed. He'd never had to play on the same level of sophistication and intrigue that Tam had. And then there was Allison: small-town girl, young, and totally naïve when it came to the complexity of true gamesmanship.

Each was floundering along in his or her clumsy way, and each would remain useful in Tam's long-term plans. That was the thing about subordinates. They always had their uses—though Port Authority and Corporate Mine offered nothing like the daunting complexities of Solar System.

Tam chuckled to himself as he donned his suit and slipped his coat around his shoulders. Then he checked his reflection in Allison's mirror where it hung on the back of her door. Living in her room at The Jewel wasn't the worst of accommodations, but he didn't want to evict Wirth out of his supposed mansion. Yet.

Assuming anyone could call that three-story monstrosity of stone and timber a mansion. It might have been the most imposing dwelling in Port Authority, but the place was more reminiscent of a fourteenth-century feudal pile in the north of Germany than anything an enlightened twenty-second-century aristocrat would call home.

He savored his reflection, how the coat hung over his suit. He almost cut too good a figure. One that came across as foppish given the realities of Port Authority. But it would have to do. With a wry glance at the bed, he enjoyed a moment's replay from his morning's frolic with Allison.

Clever girl, she'd given him full measure. To his surprise, she'd managed to play her role beyond his expectations. But for his years of experience, he might actually have believed that she'd taken his side against Wirth. Back in Solar System, with a little training, she might have made a fairly effective agent. She had more than enough native intelligence, and she certainly had the looks.

"And that, my beauty, makes you valuable." He winked at his reflection.

Opening the door, he strode out, hearing the midday chatter that indicated an average afternoon in The Jewel. Ten men and one woman occupied the tables, some peering at cards, others drinking as they watched one of the Wild One prospectors cry out in anguish at the craps table. A ruby the size of a robin's egg seemed to be the stakes for that particular throw.

The casual treatment of what the locals referred to as "plunder" still amazed him. Call it the measure of Donovan's wealth that itinerant prospectors living out in the bush in practical squalor showed up in their homemade hide clothing, dropped a sack full of precious stones, ingots of gold, or chunks of palladium, on food, drink, sex, and gambling, and then retired back to the bush. The kind of psychology that made that existence in any way appealing completely eluded him.

"What a waste of productivity," he muttered under his breath as he stepped out into the midmorning. Capella burned down through a partly cloudy sky, the faint sound of the chime coming from here and there.

It would be a hot one today, muggy. Not the sort of weather he wanted to be out in for long, dressed as he was.

Best to get on with the day's business. He strode rapidly down the avenue, taking in the electronics shop, the tannery, the glassblower's, the gunsmith's, and the assay office. Then passed Inga's tavern. Hard to believe these places were the beating economic heart of his new world. From the foundry came the clang of a hammer on iron.

Really? Had he just stepped back into the early nineteenth century?

Only to have the illusion shattered as one of the big haulers came whining and roaring down the main avenue, headed for the shuttle port with a load of clay. The behemoth forced Tam to step to the side. As the big wheels churned past, they coated his immaculate black coat with a fine layer of dust.

In the wake of the big machine, he brushed himself off

and grimaced. As soon as he had control of the place, one of his first orders of business was going to be the construction of a new haul road outside the fence. It might be a longer way around since it would have to skirt the greenhouses and some of the cornfields, but at least he could walk the streets in peace.

At the double doors leading into the admin building he resettled his Talon and ensured it rested easily in its holster. Not that he expected trouble, but one could never be too sure.

Then he stepped inside. Of course, the first person he encountered was Trish Monagan. The young woman started, eyes widening in both surprise and distaste.

"I'm here to see Shig Mosadek and Yvette Dushane. I hear there's a conference room. Bring them to me. Now."

"But they're—"

"Is there something about the word *now* that you don't understand? Get them, or I'll take that pistol off your hip and use it to hammer a little respect into that ignorant head of yours."

He watched her swallow hard, chin trembling. Saw the tensing of her right arm and shoulder. Said, "Go ahead. Reach for that pistol. Then, when I kill you, it's self-defense, right?"

He saw it in her eyes, that moment of defeat.

Then she nodded and left at a run.

Good. Hopefully the young woman would transmit her dismay to the others.

He wondered how many of them he'd have to kill today.

55

What the hell was it about that man? Trish ground her teeth, on the verge of tears. After all the promises she'd made her herself, he'd done it to her again!

It was that cold promise behind his flat and emotionless eyes. Trish would never have believed that a human being could radiate such an intense malignancy and threat. Problem was, she'd known she was outclassed. If she'd tried to draw, Benteen meant every bit of what he said. No bluster. No bluff. He'd have beaten her with her own gun at best, killed her at worst.

When Trish looked into his eyes, she wasn't even a person—just a thing to either obey his orders or be disposed of.

If only Stepan Allenovich would have been there, Step would have . . .

She winced. *No, don't even think it.* Step would have got his back up, got that old familiar squint in his eyes. That "boy, I'm gonna hammer you" smile would have crossed Step's lips. And as soon as he started to make something of it, Benteen would have killed him.

"What the hell have we gotten ourselves into?" she asked, sick to her stomach with worry and humiliation as she hurried down the hall and thrust her head into Shig's office.

He sat at his desk wearing a simple fabric shirt and chamois pants. Yvette was bent over his shoulder, one arm propped on the desktop as she studied something on Shig's holo screen. Yvette's fading blond hair was up, and she wore a casual smock that accented her tall body.

"We got trouble," Trish announced, her heart like a frantic machine in her breast. "Benteen's here. Wants to see the two of you in the conference room. My advice is to bug out Shig's back door. Maybe call a public meeting in Inga's where you can unify the community."

Shig ducked his head to peer at Trish from under Yvette's arm, his eyes thoughtful. "Conference room you say?"

"Yes."

Yvette sighed as she straightened and turned thoughtful. "Any idea what he wants to talk about?"

"He just said he wanted you to meet him in the conference room."

"It may be nothing." Shig pushed his chair back. "Let us see what the man wants."

"And if it's trouble?" Yvette asked.

"We take the second option."

Second option? What the hell was that?

Yvette pulled her dress straight, a resigned smile on her thin lips. "Shig, you sure you want to do it this way?"

"Beliefs need to be tested, their validity periodically refreshed. If we're not living what we profess, it would behoove us to find out."

Trish, one hand on her pistol, asked, "What are you talking about?"

"Choices, Trish." Shig stood and eased past Yvette to face her. The man's round face bore a weary smile, a knowing sadness behind his eyes. "Whatever happens in there, I want you to say nothing. Even more importantly, I want you to do nothing. No silly heroics. Nothing that will get you injured. Just sit there and listen. Can you promise me that?"

"I don't know. He just threatened to whip me with my own pistol."

"Yvette and I have been giving this a lot of thought, and we're going to ask you to trust us. Can you promise me that you have enough faith in us to follow whatever decision we think is best?"

"Well, sure, but you better know that he's—"

"Capable of killing us all?" Yvette interrupted with an arched eyebrow. "We know. He might even be looking for an opportunity to do just that. Use one of us as an example to keep the others in line. And we don't need you to make a martyr of yourself. Just promise us that you'll let us handle it, and that you'll back our decisions."

The floor under Trish's feet had turned to shifting sand.

"Okay. Yeah. Sure. I promise."

But it felt like she had just signed away her life. That something terrible was about to explode; and it would do so in a way that would never be put back right again.

Grimly she followed Shig and Yvette into the conference room where Tamarland Benteen had already seated himself at the far end of the table, his back to the wall. The way Benteen sat with his hands spread wide on the table, his black suit coat hanging down from his shoulders like devil's wings, left no doubt as to his lethality. And, while Donovan had no scorpions, Trish had seen enough predators to recognize one when she saw it.

Shig, however, seemed oblivious as he strolled in and seated himself in one of the mismatched chairs. Trish could see the tension in Yvette. It lay in the hard corners of the woman's mouth, in her spring-tight body as she took a chair one down from Shig's.

Shig said amiably, "I've heard that you've managed to settle in without much issue. Seems as if you've made a place for yourself at The Jewel. Must be a nice improvement after bunking in Talina's old ruined dome."

"I do hope the incident with Art Maniken didn't cast the community in a bad light," Yvette added in a voice that belied her attempt at a smile.

"Fair fight, we hear," Shig agreed.

Benteen cocked his head slightly, fingers flexing on the tabletop. "Yes. Too bad. Remarkably boorish. Attacking an unarmed man in a hallway as he's leaving the lavatory? Smacks of the actions of a coward, don't you think?"

Trish felt herself go cold on the inside and bit her lip. She shot a sidelong glance at Shig and Yvette to see how they were taking it. Not that Art had ever been any favorite of hers. A thug was a thug. If anyone were to shed tears over his departure, it would be that weasel, Dan Wirth.

Shig's reply was accompanied by a shrug. "No government has ever been able to legislate morality. Ultimately freedom rests upon the shoulders of the free. Art was free to try what he would. Egregious as it was, it would appear that justice was served."

Benteen arched a mocking eyebrow. "Justice is a concern of yours?"

"It preoccupies us," Yvette said. "Justice and freedom, two

very interlocked concepts that often seem at odds. Ultimately, neither can exist without the other, though governments often seek to redefine them for their own purposes."

"Sometimes they need to be redefined for the common good," Benteen said pointedly. "It is the responsibility of those in power to care for the governed . . . and sometimes that requires certain changes be made in order that the people may prosper."

"For the common good?" Yvette chuckled softly. "Since when is good ever common? But we'll drop that for now, as it's an esoteric question that cannot be answered with any satisfaction. Especially since that's another term for which governments have a sliding definition. Suffice it to say that for the foreseeable future, 'the common good' is whatever the people of Port Authority think it is."

"That's ominous," Benteen murmured, his hard gaze fixed on Shig and Yvette. "Government for the rabble and by the rabble? That's the core of your beliefs, the heart of your libertarianism? If so it would appear that you've staked your future and prosperity on a foundation of chaos and the transient whim of popularity."

Shig pointed in the direction of the entrance. "Out there, beyond those doors, everyone in Port Authority is following his or her own path, master of his or her destiny. The goals of the individual interacting with those of the society as a whole. When a need develops, people pitch in to accommodate it."

"It helps that we're still small," Yvette added. "Port Authority has considerably more flexibility in that regard. The extent of a problem is easily discernible, and the appropriate people apply themselves to fixing it. After all, there are only about four hundred of us, including the Wild Ones, within a couple of days' travel."

"You have a problem and just hope that someone will fix it?" Benteen leaned his head back and laughed.

Trish's gut hardened in rage, her hand on her pistol. Benteen hadn't so much as glanced her way, but somehow she knew he was aware of every move she made.

Benteen then asked, "Who put you in charge? How do you manage it? Elections?"

Shig's smile hinted at wistful benevolence. "No one put

us in charge. No elections. As a result of circumstances we more or less inherited the job. Part of the reason we do it is because no one else really wants it."

"I suppose," Yvette added, "that there's a bit of respect involved. At least, we haven't received any complaints."

"Who pays you?"

"No one," Shig said. "Yvette sells her crocheting, and people have developed the habit of leaving a couple of SDRs in return for her filing. Me, I sell vegetables from my garden, and Lawson saves me out a couple of the SDRs each time we run a new stamping of coins."

"Let me get this straight. You're dipping out of the coinage? Taking a percentage?"

"Just fifty siddars this last time," Shig said easily. He pointed proudly at his shirt. "Pietre Strazinsky made this for me. He only asked thirty for it, but given his recent loss, I wanted to pay him fifty."

"He's barely fifteen," Yvette broke in. "Orphaned. A good kid. Raising his brothers and sisters. The whole community has adopted them."

"Unbelievable." Benteen leaned forward, a gleam in his eyes. "Who would have imagined?"

"Imagined what?" Shig asked.

"No wonder this place looks like a misbegotten mishmash of medieval and modern. Are there any restrictions? Any rules?"

Shig replied, "You know the rules. I told you everything you needed to know to succeed here and make your way."

"Charming. But I think I'll choose another way."

"At your peril," Yvette said. "Unlike Supervisor Aguila down at Corporate Mine, we have no mandate to keep you out. Port Authority is an open city. Anyone can come or go. There are no restrictions except during alerts and after dark when the gates are locked. Relationships are governed by contract and free market."

"I hope it doesn't come as too much of a surprise, but as of today I'm going to change the rules, and you are going to help me."

Trish stiffened in shock, only to have Benteen's warning glare flick her way. He gave the slightest shake of the head, the warning implicit enough to send a bolt of fear through her.

Shig, attentive as usual, barely lifted his fingers in a restraining gesture. Trish took a breath.

"From here on out, we're going to do things differently," Benteen explained in a precise voice. "Improve efficiency, reorganize the village into a more productive structure. Establish regular work hours, mandate production, and centralize authority."

Trish clenched her fists to keep from vibrating with anger.

"Try what you like," Yvette said. "We'll have no part of it."

"Of course you will." Benteen propped his elbows and leaned forward. "To use a historical perspective, this is a coup. A takeover of the government. A coup operates under a simple rule: You can take my orders and do your best to see that they are implemented, or you can be eliminated."

Trish caught herself before the gasp escaped her throat. She expected some outburst. A demonstration of outrage.

Instead Shig and Yvette looked at each other, shrugged, and it was Shig who said, "Okay. It's yours."

Benteen looked as if he'd expected anything but this.

Trish started to rise, saw Shig's calming fingers flick her direction. *You've got to trust us.*

Right. They just handed Port Authority over to creep-freaking Benteen? The guy was a monster. She forced herself to settle back into the seat.

Shig and Yvette were no one's fools. They had to have seen this coming. Had to have some sort of plan.

They're going to take him from behind. Shoot him from ambush. Poison. Something he won't be expecting.

Benteen now smiled. "I imagine you're thinking that the next step is to quietly assassinate me. An attack from the shadows when I least expect it. That's the smart move. However, I think you might want to reconsider. First, for the coming weeks, I don't intend to be caught in a situation where I might be taken out by a sniper. Second, we'll take our meals together here, in the admin dome. All of us, sharing everything lest something unhealthy be added to the food. I assume it will be no problem to have Millie deliver. I've heard that she's done so in the past."

"She has," Shig said amiably.

"As to your duties, nothing changes. You still hold your positions and authority. The only difference is that you take orders from me. Think of it as the same old administration, just new leadership at the top."

"And what are your first orders?" Yvette asked.

Benteen fixed on her, eyes glittering with excitement. "I need instant obedience. You will carry out my commands quickly, efficiently, and without fail. Any deviance, any sabotage, will result in immediate and painful punishment. My inclination is to make an example of Trish here."

Trish's mouth had gone dry.

"That won't be necessary," Yvette told him. "Your history is sufficiently full of examples of your skill when it comes to torture."

"It is?" Trish asked.

Shig turned eyes her way. "Benteen, here, was a master at torture, extortion, murder, and blackmail. His talents stand out, even for the age in which he thrived. His implants gave him a thorough knowledge of neuro anatomy and of the history and various methodologies of torture, not to mention the innovations spurred by his own creativity."

"Cruel is an understatement," Yvette added.

"Then you do understand me." Benteen glanced back and forth between them.

"Of course," Shig answered. "You were half of Board-member Shayne's success, she in the forefront, you in the shadows: ruthless, cunning, remarkably clever, and diabolical at your chosen profession."

"You sound as if you are leaving something out." Benteen's eyes narrowed.

Yvette told him: "Our question is whether you can govern without her acting as the public façade."

"Which is why I rely on you. I expect your counsel, even the wheedling you will employ to get me to act against my best interests. But ultimately, any decision made is mine. I would sincerely suggest that you do not, shall we say, innovate in the implementation. To do so will have the most unfortunate consequences."

"Where do you see Port Authority heading in the next year?" Yvette asked.

"I intend on making Port Authority into a finely tuned machine. Instead of this hodgepodge of chaos you call an economy we need to direct people into maximizing production. I've heard individuals wondering if the colony will survive. Complaining that birth rates are low. That a ship may never come back from Solar System."

"And you will change that?"

"All females of breeding age will be pregnant. All people with skills necessary for the survival of this colony will be placed in jobs that maximize overall survivability. These Wild Ones? The ones out mining and living in the bush? They will be rounded up as they come in, confined, and put to work on construction projects for the good of the colony."

"What about freedom?" Trish blurted.

Benteen turned his icy eyes on hers. "The concept is the ultimate lie. Humans have never been free. Not even when they were roaming hunters stalking the ancient forests on Earth. They were bound by the tyranny of their stomachs, the constant need to feed themselves. To find shelter and craft clothing and tools and to dig roots. The only thing that has changed is the rise of the state, which is most efficient when, like the Corporation, it places every individual in a position that best serves the whole."

"And how do we address you?" Yvette asked. "Call you Tamarland? Mr. Benteen?"

"Director shall suffice."

"Very well, Director," Shig told him. "I think we understand the situation perfectly. Further, we'll put your mind at rest by telling you that neither Yvette, Trish, nor I will seek to hinder you in your bid to make Port Authority into this finely functioning machine. In fact, if you will repair to the Supervisor's office, Yvette will bring you the personnel files so that you can begin making your changes."

"Shig?" Trish couldn't help but ask.

He gave her one of his benevolent smiles. "Just follow

orders, Trish. No need for any of us to get hurt. We are no longer in charge; the Director is."

"Turns out you're a lot smarter man than I thought you were," Benteen told him. "I thought you'd stand on some silly principle, and I'd have to knock some heads to bring you to your senses."

"Knocking heads, as you say, would serve no purpose since in the end you would win. Sometimes principles must be tested. Other times they stand on their own. Now, if I could make a suggestion, it might behoove you to make an announcement tonight at Inga's. Explain the new government, how you see it functioning, and the new direction you envision for Port Authority. I can have Two Spot make the announcement."

"There will be no announcements. No grand proclamations. Better that I work behind the scenes for a while. No need to shock the system."

"As you wish," Shig said, standing. "Now, come. Let's get you situated in your new office."

Trish gaped. *What the hell are Shig and Yvette doing? Just giving up?*

She fought to swallow down her tight throat. They weren't even putting up a fight.

"Why is it that I don't trust you?" Benteen asked suddenly.

"It's not a matter of trust," Yvette told him. "With your skills you could disable the three of us before Trish could pull her pistol. After that you could torture us until we'd beg for death. So, fine, the government's yours. I'll repeat this yet again: It's not like we wanted the job in the first place."

"And," Shig added, "you are right. The economy is chaotic. It could indeed be organized to be much more efficient. When you ask, we promise to give you the best advice we can. You have our word. Nor will we raise a hand against you. In the end it will be what it will be."

Trish fought to keep from gagging, thinking, *Shig, there're times when asking me to trust you is like asking me to cut off my leg.*

Benteen, still skeptical, stood. "All right, let's get to

work. The first necessity of social control is a census and registration that identifies every individual. That will be followed by a comprehensive list of property and possessions. As soon as everyone has a number, and we know their locations, we can begin assessing how best to manage their lives."

Yvette led the man out the door, headed toward the Supervisor's office.

As she did, Trish made a face at Shig to communicate her dismay.

In return all she got was a knowing wink, and a whispered, "Go home. Pack your bags."

56

Ta-thunk, ta-thunk, ta-thunk.

Talina was conscious of the sound as she hung weightless in a deep, thick blackness so intense and concentrated it was almost solid.

Ek'way. The ancient Maya words formed out of nothingness. The Black Transformer-Dreamer, an almost starless place of total darkness Talina's ancestors had observed at the zenith of the night sky when the Milky Way lay flat on the southern horizon.

She floated there in free fall, locked in the dream, on the flimsy horizon between death and life, only to drift into deeper darkness as her soul was devoured by blackness and sucked down into Xibalba.

Ta-thunk, ta-thunk, ta-thunk. As she was swallowed, the rhythmic monotony reassured her—and with it came the awareness that she was hearing the beat of her heart. She clung to each beat with desperation. A final link to identity.

As her eyes trained on the sucking black, she saw the first slight glow, yellowish, barely more than a mirage in the ink black. The smudge of yellow morphed, shifted, almost as though seen through a watery surface.

Clinging to her heartbeat she watched it. Confused. Intrigued. Slightly fearful.

The yellow blob began to match the rhythm, pulsing slightly with each beat. As it did, the sunflower-bright yellow dulled into a smoky orange, four-sided with rounded corners. It continued to pulse with the beat of her heart.

The dirty smudge shifted, clarified, turned into lines and images. It separated into a tri-part design. An oval with a central dot formed at the bottom, the top two thirds separated by a wavering line. On the right Talina could make out eight dots. One dot was centrally located in the field in the left.

She knew it: the *Way* glyph, pronounced "wh-eye" in Maya. The hieroglyph that communicated transformation. Spirit possession. Animal companionship. All happening in a dream state.

The act of becoming something different.

The glyph that had named the Maya king. The glyph that had landed right-side up and unbroken the day she'd shattered the pot.

Recognition triggered a sense of unease.

Around her, the darkness began to waver. Each *ta-thunk* of her heart sent out ripples to roll through the blackness in waves that rebounded like corrupt echoes from the eternal night.

A chill stole into her flesh. Faint stirrings of something in the consuming dark tickled lightly across her skin.

Talina could sense the malevolence that permeated the endless black as the glyph glowed orange and wavered in time to the beat of her heart.

She tried to flee, struck out, kicked her legs. To no effect. She continued to hang in the viscous black, floating in free fall as fear and terror formed in the emptiness around her.

Ta-thunk, ta-thunk, ta-thunk-thunk.

The beat had changed, slightly irregular.

Was it her eyes, or did she perceive a graying, a flicker of image spawned out of the darkness?

She could see a floor now. Hard stone and flat. Low walls bounded it on either side to the height of her waist. From that point the sides sloped up at a forty-five-degree angle only to end in vertical walls at the top. Above them stood a temple that overlooked the ballcourt.

Yes, that was what it was. A Mesoamerican ballcourt. The place where the ancient game of *pitz* was played.

As it solidified into stone before her, Talina knew this place. Had stood on this very spot as a child with her mother: the great ballcourt at Copan.

Ta-thunk, ta-thunk. A pause. *Ta-thunk, ta-thunk.*

Amorphous and colorful shadows batted the *Way* glyph each time her heart beat. Blurred shadows, they moved and seemed to bleed color. As if being brought into focus, the fuzzy images sharpened into athletic young men wearing remarkable wooden yokes around their waists and exotic headgear. Streaks of yellow, red, orange, and blue became feathers bedecking the headdresses and breech-cloths. Talina recognized scarlet macaw, the brilliant iridescent feathers from a Latin American quetzal, the striking yellow from parrots, all flowing behind as the players leaped and lunged.

The glyph had changed, too, and was now a large rubber ball that the players batted between them. Each player darted, contorted, smacked the ball with his hips, only to have it bounce, *ta*. And be batted back, *thunk*, by an opponent's sudden leap as he threw his body in front of the flying orb.

Ta-thunk, ta-thunk, ta-thunk-thunk. The sounds of the ball bouncing from the stone, hitting hips, rebounding, grew louder and louder.

Talina could feel it now. Each *ta-thunk* reverberated on the sounding drum of the very stone—echoed through the heart of the earth, thundering and melting into the heartbeat of Creation.

. . . She feels the moment it happens.

They have awakened the Lords of Xibalba.

Talina senses the Lords of Death stirring, coming by twos as they emerge from the ebbing darkness. First come the high rulers of Xibalba: Lord One Death and Lord Seven Death. Behind them appear the lesser gods: Blood Gatherer; Scab Stripper; the demon of Pus; the demon of Jaundice; then she sees Bone Scepter and Skull Scepter whose powers emaciate and waste human beings. The demons of Filth and Woe arrive, followed by Wing and then Packstrap, who murder travelers on lonely roads.

In order of rank, the gods of Xibalba ascend to take their places in the high temple overlooking the ballcourt.

The Lords of Xibalba assemble so for one reason: At the end of the game someone will be sacrificed. The Lords will feed on that person's blood, drink the sacred *itz*, the sap of life. They will roast the person's heart. Strip the bloody flesh from arms and legs, suck the brain from the skull. And in the end they will hang the bones as trophies of the sacrifice.

They are watching Talina now, postures indicating a building anticipation.

I am the sacrifice!

Talina tries to turn, to run, but she discovers that she has become rooted in place.

The ballcourt play accelerates as her heart beats frantically, the ball a flying blur. The impacts, like a staccato, become furious as the brightly colored ball players move faster and faster.

Remarkably, they gyrate, slide, and contort their bodies as they slam their hips into the flying ball.

She sees it happen: A player—bedecked in quetzal feathers who plays for the Lords of Death—leaps into the air, twists his hip to the right, and hammers the ball with his yoke.

Talina's heart stops. Silence fills the ballcourt as the ball sails high. Then a *thunk* as it bounces on the slanted side of the court. It hits the vertical wall above with another *thunk*. And neatly flies through the center of the scoring ring that protrudes like a sideways basketball hoop from the high wall.

Time freezes.

Talina stares in disbelief.

A moment passes and she hears sounds of delight rise from the Lords of Death.

Talina tries to cry out, finds her lungs as paralyzed as the rest of her. Tears well and leak from her eyes, sobs are stillborn in her throat.

The players are turning now, their colors shifting as they lean forward at the waist, and the feathered headdresses flair out into expanding collars around their necks.

The ball has rolled down the incline; it bounces from the ballcourt floor and is once again the *Way* glyph. It glows in meaning: transformation, animal possession, and the dreamer who experiences both.

A scream finally breaks through Talina's fear.

She looks up from the glyph to see the final morphing of the players. They are now quetzals, their feathers turned into patterns of color that stream down their sides. They are racing toward her with fully flared collars. Their eyes are gleaming, dark, and lustrous. They are the eyes of the Lords of Death.

She recognizes them now. The closest has a bullet

wound in his head. Her quetzal, the demon who lives in her gut. And there is the mate, with its crushed neck: The quetzal who tried to kill her in her house. And Whitey, Flash, Leaper, and Diamond. All are rushing toward her.

Her body suffers a brutal impact. She is lifted, shaken. Demon has his teeth in her right shoulder. Her right leg is grabbed by Leaper, her left by Diamond. More jaws fasten on her torso.

She experiences the pain—the sheer terror and disbelief of popping bones, her skin pierced by a hundred teeth. The crushing and tearing of her muscles.

The last sound is the *ta-thunk, ta-thunk* of her heart.

And then silence.

57

For two days now Talina Perez had lain in a stupor. Or maybe it was a coma. Dortmund hadn't the first clue about how to tell the difference. For all he knew, the woman might have been dying.

From the moment aboard *Vixen* when he'd been told that his carefully constructed quarantine plans for the exploration of Capella III were suddenly obsolete, to his landfall at Port Authority, his subsequent extradition to Corporate Mine, and final escape to this desolate and remote speck, Dortmund had felt he was spiraling down into a whirlwind. No sooner had he recognized one insanity, than his feet had been knocked out from beneath him, and he was precipitated into an even more incomprehensible situation.

He'd been tossed like a blown leaf, twisted this way and that, to finally settle here, on this patch of bare rock. Adrift in wilderness on an alien world. And now that he finally had time to catch his breath, it was to face the gloomy knowledge that he had no clue about what to do next.

That reality hit home again as he stared at Talina Perez's slack features, watched her uneven breathing as she lay under the sheet that he and Kylee had just placed over her body.

All those years of study, his degrees and learned papers, the hypotheses offered and models built and tested, theories established, and exalted positions and accolades achieved, and he hadn't a clue as to how to deal with his situation at Rork Springs.

He and Kylee had taken turns caring for Talina. They'd spooned water into the woman's mouth to keep her hydrated. Fed her soup. And while she would swallow the liquids they placed on her tongue, she hadn't come back to consciousness.

Instead, as now, her eyes twitched under the closed lids,

the pace of her breathing would change, and tortured sounds would remain partially muted in her throat.

Then had come his horror that morning when he walked in and Kylee was bent over Talina, her lips locked with the woman's in what appeared to be a passionate kiss. The tongue-in-mouth kind.

"What are you doing?"

Kylee pulled back, shot a look across the room at Dortmund. "We're helping."

"That wasn't the kind of kiss a little girl should give to an older woman. And what do you mean, we?"

"Rocket, Flash, and me. We're helping her. She needs more of what we know if she's going to fight off Whitey."

"You sound crazy. As if, what? You're going to awaken her? Who do you think you are, some sort of prince and she's Sleeping Beauty?"

"Who's Sleeping Beauty?"

"Didn't your mother ever tell you fairy tales?"

"She told me organic chemistry."

Impossible child. Just another layer to the madness in which he now found himself. Walking over to the bed, he sniffed, pulled the sheet down. Winced. The woman had fouled herself.

"You going to help me, or what?" Kylee demanded as she struggled to undo Talina's belt.

"I'm not a nurse."

"See anybody else around here who can do it?"

"Can you fix the radio?"

"Yes."

"Then we can call Port Authority and have them come get her and treat her."

"I think I'll let a chokeya bush kill you when we go down to the garden in a little bit. Can't you, like, help me with anything around here? Are all men back in Solar System as worthless as you?"

Chastened, he managed. Driven to it by the girl's scorn. He simply shut off his mind. Tried not to think about what he was doing. Ignored the warm wetness on his fingers and denied the odor of urine and feces as he tugged her coveralls down. He tried to avert his eyes from the somnolent woman's nudity.

He let Kylee do the intimate sponging.

But in the end, they had the woman cleaned, her soiled pants in the wash, and she was resting quietly under a blanket.

Only after they were through did he manage to ask, "How did you know to make a diaper with that towel?"

Kylee's disbelieving alien-blue eyes fixed on his. "I had little brothers and sisters. Babies need changing. Didn't you ever have to change a baby?"

"Never was around one," he told her as they walked out through the main room and into the day. "Not that that was ever an option."

"Why not?"

Standing outside the dome, sniffing the curiously scented air, he leaned his head back and tried to forget the smell of human excrement. Let Capella's rays warm and symbolically cleanse his face.

Then he glanced down at the girl. "I married once. He was a colleague. We authored papers together. Not that I didn't have romances when I was young. I just never . . ." His voice trailed off as he remembered back through the years. How the hell had everything ended in acrimony?

"Never what?"

"Well, they never lasted. The relationships, I mean. My partners always demanded too much. Wanted too much of my time. That or they didn't understand the value of my work. Why it was so important that I finish that next paper, complete that next project. They didn't understand the stakes, that it was a battle to save the planet. Conserve something of the past when human inevitability stands poised to destroy it."

The girl was giving him a skeptical look. "I don't get it. You like to call yourself a fighter. How come you're so squeamish? You almost threw up handling Talina's soiled pants."

"That's a job for nurses, medical technicians, other menials."

"And moms and dads and sisters and brothers."

"Well, professors don't do those things. We hire it to be done."

"Sounds like we're back to that waste of skin thing."

He laughed at the insanity of it. "What could you know

of the better things in life?" He looked around at the bare stone—reddish tan in the morning sun—at the distant ridges and bluish-green forested bottoms.

"You understand Darwin, right? The whole notion of adaptation to changed environments?"

He shot a worried look at the child. "To quote you in your most eloquent of phrases: Duh."

"So when are you going to start adapting?"

"Oh, go to hell. I've been a scholar all of my life. Always a master of my discipline and a force to be reckoned with." A beat. "It's just that none of this makes sense. It's Radcek's fault. All of it."

Kylee handed him the basket and started down the scuffed trail in the sandstone. "You'd think a professor would at least know something worthwhile. I can't even let you go to the garden without being there to make sure you don't get eaten."

"Do you have any idea how humiliating it is to know that my life depends on an unwashed urchin such as yourself?"

"Yeah, lucky me."

He made a face. He hadn't been able to tell the difference between a rock and the bem they'd run into. Not even after she pointed out the patterns that exactly mimicked the bedrock the beast was leaned against. She'd had to hit it with a thrown stone, startle it enough that it changed color before he'd finally been able to admit the loathsome creature was actually there.

"It's just so much to learn," he muttered under his breath. "And besides, if you find me so meritless, why do you keep me alive? You could have told me to walk right up to that bem. I wouldn't have known any difference."

She threw a taunting smile over her shoulder. "You can do some stuff. Like wash the dishes. Carry some stuff I can't. So, if Talina dies? How do I get her body out of that bed and down to where I don't have to smell it when it rots?"

"That's a callous way to talk about your friend, isn't it?"

Kylee stopped short, head down, features hidden by her blond curls. When she looked up, it was with haunted eyes. "You ever see anyone die?"

"Die? Of course not."

"And you're *old*. How do people die in Solar System?"

"They die in hospice. When their systems fail and they can't afford the medical to keep their organs functioning. Or sometimes, rarely, in accidents."

"Nobody eaten? Nobody murdered?" She shook her head and continued down the trail. "Must be a weird way to live."

He followed her down the steps cut in stone, watching, as he always did, when she stopped at the bottom to sniff the breeze that blew up from the canyon bottom.

"Smell anything?" he asked.

"I think that bem moved on. I'm not getting that vinegar smell like last time. Maybe he didn't want to be whacked by another rock."

"You do amaze me sometimes."

As she led the way to the path, he tried to look for the common threats. He was still new enough to Donovan to be surprised that the trail had changed from the day before. Some of the plants had moved. He stepped wide around the thorncactus, but had to duck back before he encountered the gotcha vine. The damned thorncactus would have the trail blocked by tomorrow, which meant they'd have to figure another way to the garden. Or maybe Kylee could just whack it with a rock?

Somehow he didn't think the thorn-thick plant would get the hint.

When they reached the garden, he let Kylee go first, hoping she'd see anything dangerous that might have crawled in around the stems or hidden in the leaves.

"I really think the smartest move is to fix the radio," he told her. "Seriously, even if you don't want to go back to Port Authority, Talina needs medical aid. I wouldn't make you go. I give you my word."

She ignored him until she finished her inspection of the garden. "Don't get close to that mating cluster of invertebrates. Those red ones with the black spots? When they're in a ball like that, they'll attack you. Not only do they take a chunk out of your skin, but it burns like fire."

Dortmund bent, studying the roiling ball of active creatures. Each was about the size of his thumb, all shell and milling legs as they climbed over each other.

"I won't."

Ten minutes later, their basket was full. Kylee gave him a skeptical look. "Do you think you can take the basket home, start the beans and sugar peas to cooking?"

"Where are you going?"

"Remember that snare I set down at the canyon mouth on that chamois trail?"

"I do. Are you sure that it's a good idea for you to go down there by yourself?"

She brushed unruly hair back, that now-familiar disapproving scowl on her face. "If there's something in the snare, it's cruel to leave it hanging. Worse, what if I wait until tomorrow and go down there to find it half rotten? Then we killed something for no reason. Finally, if there is something hanging there, better we get it before a wandering quetzal, skewer, or that blue nasty vine sends a tendril up to start eating it."

"What if you run into something dangerous?"

She arched a thin "are-you-kidding" eyebrow.

"Sarcasm ill suits you. I should go with you."

"Yeah? Like the day we set the snare? Took us two hours just to get down there because I had to make sure you didn't step in anything, get stung, bitten, skewered, or grabbed. You can't even smell a bem when it's five paces in front of you."

He winced at the tone in her voice, allowing his petulance free rein. "Well, go on then. Just don't be late for supper."

He watched her grin, shake her head, and like a wraith, disappear silently into the foliage.

Turning, he sighed, shouldered the basket, and carefully made his way back up the trail. *Yes, concentrate. Look. Think about where you're putting your feet.*

He veered wide of the gotcha vine, skirted the thorncactus, and safely made his way to the steps. Not that the load was heavy—what did the vegetables weigh? A couple of pounds—but he was panting by the time he'd climbed up to the flat.

Feeling secure out in the open, he trudged his way up to the dome. Not for the first time did he stare longingly at Talina's aircar. Why the hell had he never learned to fly one of the things?

Because people who spend their lives in the vested halls of higher education use automated transportation. Even in the re-wilded areas, vehicles drive themselves. State a location and an aircar carries you there.

But here he was, smack in a world where global navigation wasn't even a dream. Talk about primitive. It was like stepping back in time to the twentieth century.

Dortmund slapped a hand to the aircar's side and puffed out a weary breath. He'd go in, check on Talina Perez, and then take another look at the radio. As if he were any more knowledgeable about radios than the last time he'd looked.

"Go ahead," Kylee had told him. "Try and fix it. If you really screw it up, or worse, electrocute yourself, that's one less thing that I need to worry about."

"Asshole kid," he muttered, and turned away from the car.

Right face-to-face with a quetzal.

The thing was huge. So much so that its body seemed to blot out the world.

As close as he was, Dortmund had to stare from eye to eye to eye atop the big wedge of a head. He could have reached out without fully extending his arm and touched that fearsome jaw. That it could come so close, and do it soundlessly, left him in momentary disbelief. He could smell the beast—a curiously spicy scent that hinted of cardamom, mint, and saffron.

Terror locked him up. Paralyzed him as his heart began to pound, and fear ran liquid through his body.

Time ceased. Every feature of the creature's muzzle, the wide jaw, the tooth-like serrations, had a crystalline clarity. Scars crisscrossed the leathery gums, bits of what might have been tissue could be seen stuck at the roots of the teeth.

And the color nearly overwhelmed him—so bright with that laser-like radiance. The creature's hide simmered through intricate patterns of violet, mauve, and orange that might have had an infrared element given the heat projected onto Dortmund's face.

The ruff-like collar membrane spread like a giant sail and puffed air against Dortmund's skin as blazing patterns of color intensified. Dazzled. They caused him to blink in an attempt to clear the afterimages from behind his eyes.

Dortmund sucked a panicked breath. Whispered, "Oh, God." And tried unsuccessfully to swallow.

It's going to kill me.

He couldn't move. Like some great hand squeezed him, his heart and guts felt crushed inside him. The muscles in his legs shivered and shook.

He whimpered as the jaws parted, expected to see them open wide as the beast lunged and bit.

Instead the tongue flicked out; snakelike, it traced around his face, the touch light, and then it slipped along his lips like an alien finger.

Dortmund threw himself backward, would have toppled over the aircar's railing, but the two forelegs flashed out and trapped him—the curve of the claws hard against the small of his back.

Dortmund tried to jerk his head away from that horrible questing tongue, only to have the monster shake him. As he opened his mouth to scream, the tongue darted past his lips. Hit the back of his mouth.

The gag reflex made him heave.

Through it all, his brain remained terror-shocked, his body disconnected. He slumped, ragdoll-flaccid in the beast's grip.

Then the tongue was gone. The grip receded. Dortmund collapsed like a pile of boneless meat on the sandstone, his back partially braced by the aircar. A bitter and wretchedly astringent taste filled his mouth.

The quetzal loomed over him, blanking the sky, the great expanded collar shooting psychotic patterns of white, pink, yellow, violet, and orange.

Dortmund could hear a melodic, flute-and-oboe-pitched sound as the terrible beast vented.

"What . . . what do you . . . ?" He gasped for breath, felt oddly hot, his skin beginning to perspire.

Again the quetzal drew air and vented it in a musical tremolo that sounded of tubes and flutes.

"I don't understand!" Dortmund cried. Every urge was to huddle into a ball. Accept the inevitable. What the hell was the thing waiting for? Get it over with already.

But the jaws didn't reach down to crush and maim his body. Instead the beast reached out, opened its right front hand, and spilled a collection of blue-and-white ceramic shards to clatter musically onto the sandstone.

Dortmund gaped in disbelief, seeing the Delft bowl fragments. As out of place as they might have been in the trash pile outback, to see them spilled upon the sandstone by an alien predator was mind-boggling.

Dortmund stared up at the three gleaming black eyes. More of the insane patterns were flowing across the beast's hide. Then it gestured with the forelegs, the claws flashing.

Alien the monster might be, but the intent of the gesture couldn't be misread: it wanted him to do something with the fragments of broken bowl. But what?

Dortmund blinked, his lungs now heaving in desperate breaths.

Again the gesture—accented this time with an irritated harmonic blown out of the posterior vents.

Somehow Dortmund managed to get his feet under him. Trembling, damp with fear-sweat, he took three tries to stand. Mouth salivating, he kept having to swallow the odd mixture of bile and the new hint of bitter peppermint.

Bracing himself against the aircar, on the verge of tears, he demanded, "What do you *want* from me?"

The quetzal's head lowered and extended; jaws parted, it made a gargling sound. The patterns of color went insane again, flickering in violet, orange, snowy white, taupe, and umber madness. The thing pointed down with its long claws. As it did, its sides beamed in yellow, green, and pink.

"I don't understand!"

The quetzal paused. Then, deliberately, it reached down with a claw and rearranged the bowl shards. Dortmund flinched as it tapped the long claws on the sandstone. His guts clenched with each loud click.

The gargling sounded again from deep in the beast's throat. Then, with the other clawed foreleg, the quetzal made a circular motion. The head cocked in a most terrestrial manner. suggestive of an interrogative.

"Yes, it was once round," Dortmund told it, understanding flooding through him. "A bowl." With trembling hands, he pointed at the shards and then made a cup of his hands as if mimicking a bowl.

This time the patterns flashed in blaze-orange. The quetzal made a gurgling half chitter. The claw pointed at him. Then the shards.

"No. I can't fix it. It's broken. You don't have all the pieces." How the hell did he communicate with the thing? Outside of a cocked head and pointing, what did they share in common?

Dortmund tapped himself on the chest, ground his teeth in frustration, and clapped both hands to the sides of his head in despair.

To his surprise the quetzal mimicked the gestures.

"No, no." Dortmund took a steadying breath and pointed at himself. "Me." He pointed at the quetzal. "You." Then he repeated the gestures, saying "Me" and "You."

The quetzal snapped its jaws closed with a painfully loud clap that caused Dortmund to jump half out of his skin.

Orange patterns flashed across the beast's hide as it pointed at itself and made a sound like water draining down sewer pipes. When it pointed at Dortmund it made a sound like elephant belching.

Dortmund turned toward the dome. Pointed at it. "Other bowls," he said. "I could get you a complete one. This one is broken."

Brown, yellow, and green flashed across the quetzal's hide.

Again it tilted its head down, flicked the claws to re-arrange the shards, then made the "you" sound, indicating Dortmund.

"You want me to fix the bowl? What could have possibly possessed you to pick the Delft shards in the first place. Why come to me?"

That was when the quetzal stiffened, glanced off to the west, and uttered a clicking.

Dortmund turned, seeing Kylee as she climbed the long sandstone slope from where the snare had been placed. She carried a limp creature over her shoulder.

"She caught something," Dortmund told the quetzal.

Again the clicking sound from deep inside the beast. It

watched Kylee with two eyes, the third still fixed on Dortmund.

"She's the one you really ought to talk to. She was bonded with a quetzal. She . . ."

In a swift move, the quetzal trapped Dortmund's arm between two of its three fore claws. As Dortmund cried out, the other foreleg flashed, one of the claws driving deep into the meat of his forearm just below the elbow.

To Dortmund's horror the beast pierced its own foreleg and pressed it against the oozing wound in Dortmund's arm.

"What the hell are you doing?" he wailed in shock. The stinging pain built as images of terrible infection flashed in his head.

He threw himself against the restraining hold. The grip held him like the jaws of a vise. For maybe a minute the quetzal kept him pinned, the two wounds bleeding against each other.

As if a final insult, the creature pulled Dortmund's arm out straight, shot its tongue into the puncture. Dortmund screamed as he felt the thick knot of tongue probe the inside of the wound.

And then he was free, the action so quick Dortmund tumbled down onto the hard stone. "Why'd you do that?" he demanded, clutching his traumatized arm to his chest and gripping the wound to staunch the flow of blood.

The quetzal bent its head down low to peer at Dortmund. Whites and iridescent reds flowed across the hide, intermixed with yellow, green, and pink patterns. Then came combinations of colors Dortmund could barely see, so fast did they flash across the beast's scaly skin.

Climbing to his feet again, Dortmund shot a glance in Kylee's direction. The kid was coming at a trot, her body swaying under the weight of some colorful scaled creature that was slung over her shoulder. Even as he watched, she dropped it and came on at a run.

"It's all right," he shouted.

"What the hell? I leave you alone for five minutes and you're in trouble!" Kylee cried between panted breaths as she closed the distance. "Don't piss him off!"

"Too late," Dortmund said through a grimace. His arm was really starting to hurt now.

The quetzal backed away, all the while sounding a clucking, clicking gurgle. Then it vented another musical harmony.

Kylee puffed her way to a stop on the other side of the aircar. The quetzal flashed a series of white, pink, orange, and red of various patterns and hues.

"Okay," Kylee said, the tension easing from her voice. Then she flapped her arms at the thing, saying, "Go on! Get."

The quetzal turned a combination of snowy white and glorious red as it made a chittering sound, backed another couple of steps, and took off down the hill at a lope. It never even hesitated as it scooped up the rainbow-scaled creature Kylee had left on the bedrock. Tilting its head back, it gulped the creature down in one swallow.

"That's mine, you piece of shit!" Kylee called after it. Then she turned, asking, "What the hell happened here? What's with the bits of broken bowl?"

Dortmund, despite the agony in his arm, laughed in a sudden sense of exhilaration. "It wanted me to put the bowl back together. Do you know what that means?"

"Nope."

"And then it speared me!"

She was staring at the blood leaking between his fingers where he held his arm. "Yeah. We'd better get that sterilized or you're going to know a whole new world of hurt."

58

The air is warm and heavy with humidity. Talina can feel the branch sway as the breeze rises and falls. The calabash tree in which her head hangs pulses with life, somehow fed by her death. She can sense the *itz,* the life-bearing sap that rises in the trunk; it flows through the branches and is both nourished and replenished by the leaves.

Though she has no eyes, from her vantage point in the calabash tree she can see the ballcourt a few tens of meters away, and before it the stone paving where she was devoured and died.

She has known since that day when she shot Clemenceau that there is no more horrible fate than being eaten alive. Nothing equals the pain of having one's vibrant body torn apart, ground between jaws, and swallowed. Knowing that the living cells are being digested, that the blood is still leaking from sundered bits of muscle, liver, kidney, and lungs. And to what fate?

The breeze shifts, gently playing with the branch on which Talina's skull rests.

She has an unimpeded view of the temple above the ballcourt. Remembers the Lords of Death screaming in delight as they danced in celebration of her death. Odd memory, that. Talina can see each of their movements, the gyrating of their bodies, the placement of their feet and graceful undulation of their arms.

Among the ancient Maya, dance was prayer.

So many memories now fill the hollow of her skull, as if without the brain to take up space, there is more than enough room for them all. She has her own recollections, of course. Living with Mother, the sights and sounds of Chiapas, the smells of forest and cooking corn. The taste of *recado rojo* in the bean-and-beef enchiladas on Saturdays.

There are other memories as well. Quetzal memories.

She savors the long past, experiencing the lives of quetzals eons dead. To her amazement she can call up knowledge of the time of fire, when drought turned the bush into a tinderbox. How the quetzals who survived overcame their fear and waded out into the rivers. Trembling in their terror, they kept their mouths above water, every effort spent to constantly force air down through their lungs to vent in noisy bubbles.

And now, for the first time, she can understand the quetzals' fear of water. Their three lungs are just tubes after all, and they don't have nostrils they can close. Water can run in from both ends.

Talina's memories go back to Chiapas, thirty years ago. Quetzals remember differently. They live the past as an eternal now. Their sense of existence stretches into hundreds of years—not as an abstract, but as a tangible reality.

What they lose, however, is the sense of individuality. The identity of the quetzal who mimicked a rotten log to avoid a flock of mobbers is gone; only the memory of what he did remains without a linear chronology or timeline. And there are other memories of terrors she cannot understand. Visions of terrible beasts beyond imagination.

Talina can't tell from which quetzal a given memory came. She can only place Rocket's memories as his because they include Kylee or Mundo Base. Or her demon's memory of eating Allison's baby because she was there. Some event that she can use to tag a place in her own timeline.

Beyond that, visions of lightning, group hunts, or the murder and devouring of other, long-dead quetzals remains just that: events out of time. Valuable for the information they might impart, but without reference to its place in time.

Quetzals would write history in a very different manner than humans.

Had quetzals a Rome, what would have been important was not that it burned in 410 C.E., or that Alaric's sacking of the city was the end of the empire in the west. To a quetzal, all that mattered was which strategies were useful in getting out of the city and saving oneself.

All of which put Talina's demon in perspective. The intensity of the repetitive dream of eating Allison's baby now acquired new meaning. What mattered was how to gain entry to Port Authority, which steps to take to ensure success, and most of all, how to escape with the knowledge and hopefully pass it on to future generations of quetzals.

To Talina's way of thinking, her quetzal's actions might not have been right in the grand scheme of things, but at least they could be placed within a context of understanding.

So, too, could the bitter battles between aging quetzals and their successors. Knowledge was status. Not to be surrendered lightly. Elders age knowing that as they gain status and wisdom, they are increasing the odds for their own murder.

And that put a whole new spin on Rocket's death at the hands of Deb Spiro: All that information garnered from his interactions with humans was gone, only a fragment of it saved through Talina and Kylee.

The only universal was that random chance plays as much a role in quetzal planning as it does for humans.

Talina—now hanging as a skull in a calabash tree—can't even smile in ironic amusement.

A calabash tree? Why there? In an ancestral story from a people who conceived of time as turning wheels. Perhaps that is the quetzals' influence. That appreciation for the long-ago past as yesterday. What can be more ancient in Talina's psyche than the Maya Creation story? These are her deep roots, the iconic stories of her ancestors: One Hunahpu being reborn as the Maize God after his death in Xibalba, emerging from a cracked turtle shell to raise the World Tree that would hold up the sky.

She wonders what the quetzals think of ancient Maya beliefs? Of gods, games, and buildings?

In Talina's version of the story, she has been devoured by the Lords of Death: the quetzals. The same quetzals that lived within her body. The Creation stories of the Maya? The molecular memories of the quetzals? They are all about resurrection.

Call it a fundamental truth: One can't be resurrected into something new until after he or she dies. In Mayan mythology it took Hun Ajaw and Xbalanque to teach that lesson to the Xibalbans.

The warm breeze continues to bathe Talina's skull, whispers along zygomatic arches, caresses the cavities of her eye sockets, and slips through the hollows of her empty nose.

Talina first glimpses the young woman as she appears at the far end of the ballcourt. She is a slender thing, wearing a wraparound skirt woven in bands of bright yellow, scarlet, deepest indigo, and royal blue. The luminescent fabric glows of its own light. Black hair hangs down in a flowing wealth behind her, and she wears oversized shell ear ornaments of pearlescent white. Her round breasts are bared, with large aureoles and prominent nipples.

Talina watches the young woman cross the empty ballcourt, her hips swinging with each step. Curiosity burns behind the woman's eyes as she reaches the spot where Talina was devoured. The young woman hesitates for a moment, looks down at the stained stones where Talina's blood had pooled.

Then she walks up to the tree.

She might be in her late teens, her youthful skin flush with life. When Talina stares into the woman's face, it is to see herself as she was half a lifetime ago: vital with the bloom of youth.

"I'm looking for the fruit this tree is said to bear."

"I'm only a skull. What would you want with old bones?"

"I want to know what you know."

"Such knowledge comes with a terrible price."

"I would still know it."

"Then open your hand and extend it to me."

Talina watches her younger self extend her slim brown arm without hesitation and open her hand. Those familiar dark eyes glisten with excitement. Fearless. Driven by the same spirit that goaded young Talina Perez to cross thirty light-years to an alien planet.

As in the ancient Mayan stories, it doesn't matter that she is only a skull. Talina spits into the young woman's palm. As she does, images, like echoes, play through her empty braincase. Time after time, each instance is recalled when she spit in her hand: for Rocket; for Whitey; for Flash, Diamond, and Leaper. For the Rork Springs quetzals.

The bitter and overpowering taste of peppermint floods her senses, almost leaves her reeling with its intensity.

"There is no end and no beginning," Talina tells her younger self as the woman inspects the saliva in her hand. "You have what you need to fix the pot. Keep the words of the ancestors. You are my legacy."

Talina watches her younger self raise her hand to her nose, sniff, and then look in disbelief as she realizes the spittle has vanished.

Yes, it is absorbed. You have become one with that knowledge.

Young Talina nods, a faint smile on her full lips. Then she turns, her skirt flashing with light as she walks away with a saucy swing of the hips.

"What do you think?" Rocket asks where he appears near the trunk of the calabash tree.

"I think I have been reborn," Talina tells him.

In the vision of her sightless eyes she can see the *Way* glyph: the transformer, the symbol of spiritual co-essence, animal spirit possession, and the spirit dreamer. So many meanings, all packed into that one remarkable ancient symbol.

59

Hard to believe that it had been this easy. But then, if the Supervisor's office was any indication of his new status, Tamarland was now lord of a dung heap. The room was maybe thirty-five square meters in size, the back wall cramped as it was part of the dome's curving radius. He had a one-by-two-meter window behind the scarred desk. From the green stain on the wall below the sill, it leaked.

His first official action had been to move the desk so that his back wasn't to the window. Apparently he wasn't the first to fear a shot through the glass. The scars on the floor showed that some previous occupant had placed the desk so that his back was safely to the wall.

The only view was of the chain-link fence that surrounded the shuttle field. A series of shelves stood along one wall, and were filled with various odds and ends. An empty weapons rack was bolted next to the door.

He had five chairs of various makes and colors, including the auto-adjusting office chair behind the desk. He'd immediately discovered that the auto-adjust didn't work. The only piece of functioning equipment seemed to be the holo-projector.

It now displayed the colony records. Yvette had sent him the files on various Port Authority personnel. To call the information lacking was an understatement. Also sobering were the number of names listed as "deceased." That led to the looming problem of registration and organization. How the hell was he going to govern Port Authority when he hadn't a clue as to who had which skills? Just ask them during the registration process? And more to the point, he needed enforcers, hard people who wouldn't mind breaking a few heads to get the masses under some semblance of control.

He'd looked up Dan Wirth first thing. All the records

stated was: Transportee: Wirth, Dan. Arrived: *Turalon*.
Occupation: Livestock Technician II.

Or take the man named Rude Marsdome. Arrived:
Phantom. Occupation: Cordwainer.

What the hell was a cordwainer? Tam had had to look it
up: cobbler. Which he'd also had to look up. Turns out the
guy made footwear. Where did they come up with these
terms anyway?

He sighed, pushed back in his broken chair, and stared
out the window. *Vixen*'s shuttle was sitting in the middle of
the field, its ramp down. Someone was unloading crates of
something from one of the loaders. Probably food. Next
to it, the Corporate Mine shuttle was unloading spools
of cable after having disgorged its passengers for their
rotational R&R.

And what was he going to do about that? Aguila considered him a criminal, so did he want her people wandering
around PA? Or should he shut down the whole thing? Teach
Aguila a lesson about what it cost to cross him?

No, best to leave it as it was for now. The time was going
to come when he'd have to move against her. And to do
that would take preparation. He'd have to remake Port Authority first, solidify his position. Only then could he assassinate her and move his people into place down at the
mine.

And that brought his thoughts back to Port Authority,
pathetic as it was.

Hard to believe that my life has come to this.

Memories of Transluna played in the back of his mind: fine
meals, the melodic sound of Shayne's laughter, shared inti-
macy as she stared into his eyes, a smile on her full lips. The
exotic luxury of the Solar Elan Hotel with its transparent
room walls high over the city. He had always loved the penthouse, adorned as it was with water sculptures, free-floating
orchids, and sensational staff.

"Shayne, if you only knew." He pictured her smile, could
imagine her amusement at the knowledge that instead of
ruling Solar System, he'd only managed to conquer a failing
colony. In that moment, he ached with grief. Wished with all
of his might that she might be here, that he might once again
look into her eyes, hold her body against his. But all he had

was a dingy office in a leaky dome on a faraway world thirty light-years from anything.

"Not quite what we planned, is it my love?"

I could walk out to the shuttle field, have Wilson fly me up to Vixen. *Once aboard, if I put a gun to his head, Torgussen would space us back to Solar System.*

"It would be another fifty years in the future," he told himself. "Into a changed universe."

The rules might be completely different. A whole new political structure. And would The Corporation enforce a century-old death penalty? Or could he have the charges dropped in exchange for an offer of service to whomever was currently in power?

That was the choice. A wager on that future against the dubious honor of serving as high potentate of this crummy shithole with its four hundred people.

What value was a pile of rubies, emeralds, diamonds, gold, and platinum when all it would buy him was a chamois steak and a bottle of Inga Lock's wine?

He actually, if momentarily, wondered whether Shayne had done him any favors by sending him to *Vixen.*

"Don't be an idiot. Had Artollia not saved you, you'd be fifty years dead."

At the sound of steps in the hallway, he looked up. To his surprise Supervisor Aguila entered, followed by two of her marines and that shit of a captain, Torgussen. She stopped short, an eyebrow lifting in irritation and recognition.

She wore a black form-fitting pantsuit, her hair tumbling down her back in a dark wave. The familiar pistol hung at her side, and the utility belt with its pouches canted at an angle on her hips. A look of distaste marred her scarred features.

"What the hell are you doing in my chair?"

"Your chair?" Tam asked. "My chair." He gestured around. "My office."

"It's the Supervisor's. My space in Port Authority. Get out."

Tam chuckled, leaned back to allow quick access to his Talon. "There's been a change of management. From here on out, you may address me as Director. And as to your continued presence in Port Authority, that may well become a matter of discussion."

In the background, Torgussen looked like he was chewing nails. The marines were stony faced.

Aguila frowned, tapped her fingers on her pistol butt. "That will be a most interesting discussion. What have you done with Shig and Yvette?"

"I have them assembling census data. Port Authority isn't much, but it turns out to be the only game on the planet. It may appear hopeless at the moment, but I fully intend on organizing these clods into an efficient workforce. Can't order changes until I know who to assign where." He shifted just enough that his coat fell open so that it no longer impeded his draw.

"Dushane and Mosadek are not in their offices."

"Then they're about their duties. You should see these records. An absolute shambles. Hard to believe these people have managed as well as they have given the total lack of direction."

"And you're going to manage them? Think you'll run Donovan the way you and Shayne planned to run the Corporate Board? What did you do? Threaten Shig and Yvette with murder? Some sort of coercion?"

"Let's just say that they saw the light. As I would hope that you would. From here on out, things are going to be different in Port Authority. I imagine that, given your marines, you were able to dictate whatever terms you wanted. I come from a different world where the uses of power take on a more subtle and sophisticated orchestration."

"Ah yes, the fabled scorpion. Shayne's feared weapon." Aguila seemed to digest that, considered, and then burst into laughter. She turned, saying, "Tompzen, go check with Two Spot. Tell him I need to locate Mosadek and Dushane."

The marine saluted, pushed past Torgussen, and left the room. Aguila shot Tam a hard look. "God help you if you've harmed either one of them."

"Haven't touched a hair on their heads. Didn't need to. Both of them, it seems, are fully rational and understand just where their best interests lie. They even kept a lid on that silly kid Monagan, lest she demonstrate a lack of good sense."

"I'll bet." Aguila had an amused look on her face. "So you're planning on breaking the troublesome Donovanians to halter, are you? Going to try and capture the wind in a can?"

"Ultimately, Supervisor, everything boils down to a triumph of the will. I've made a study of social management. Fortunately for me, others have not only pioneered but mastered the process."

She smiled at that, the scars bending. "I know. According to your records, Lavrentiy Beria, Joseph Goebbels, and Hayden Keating served as your muses. Charming men, all of them. My implant reminds me that you kept a photo of Pol Pot on your wall as well. I've always found that odd since he didn't last as long as the others, nor was his vision as lofty."

"His goals weren't the heart of my interest; it was his meteoric rise and the immediate and complete transformation of his country that fascinated me."

"Tell me you're not looking to model Port Authority on what happened in Cambodia two centuries ago. The country never recovered the loss of its intelligentsia, culture, or pride."

"Of course not. You were the one who brought up the subject of Pol Pot. The lesson he taught me is to be circumspect in whom you eliminate. I'm more of a Hayden Keating fan. He used the security state with its algorithms, monitoring, and databases to identify and select 'enemies of the common good' for elimination or coercion. Without his ability to target and remove nationalists, populists, and so called 'adherents of the democratic process,' The Corporation would never have had a chance."

"Hayden was working with billions. You have what? Four hundred or thereabout?"

"Means I won't have to turn as many into fertilizer the way Hayden Keating did. He loved that, you know. All those 'disappeared' activists? Making their corpses into fertilizer solved so many problems. No bodies left lying around to be identified should the political winds change. And he got such a kick out of the knowledge that the people were ultimately consuming their own dissidents."

Tompzen appeared in the doorway, face as expressionless as a carved block. "Ma'am, Two Spot reports that Mosadek and Dushane are gone."

"Gone where?" Tam snapped, rising to his feet. "They were not given permission."

Aguila's lips quivered, making the scars along her jaw twitch. She turned to the marine. "Well?"

Tompzen, correctly, sussed out where the threat might lie and kept a wary eye on Tamarland as he said, "According to Two Spot, they've quit. Benteen, here, told them it was a coup, and he was taking over. That from here on out, Benteen was the government. Mosadek and Dushane told Two Spot that any and all complaints needed to be tendered to Benteen."

"Unfuckingacceptable," Tam muttered. Well, maybe it was for the best. As with Maniken, sometimes it saved trouble in the long run when examples were made of people. Mosadek and Dushane's elimination would have to be very public and milked for the greatest psychological impact.

"Private," Aguila said, "go find them. Bring them here. I want to get to the bottom of this."

"That's not your concern," Tam barked. "They're my people. Port Authority is out of your jurisdiction."

"You heard me," she told Tompzen, ignoring Benteen.

"Can't do it, ma'am," Tompzen told her. "According to Two Spot, they're really gone. Took an aircar about three hours ago and flew away. Mosadek, Dushane, and officer Monagan."

"They what?" Tam asked coldly. "Where'd they go?"

"Two Spot said they didn't say. Just said to tell the people what happened, and to say they wished them good luck."

As Tamarland's anger increased, Aguila couldn't contain herself. "Perfect. Absolutely perfect." She slapped her left hand to her thigh, the right continued to rest on her pistol.

To Tam she said, "Forget what I said. Keep the office for now. Oh, and God help you."

With that she turned on her heel, leading Torgussen and her marines out into the corridor. He couldn't miss her laughter as it echoed down the hall.

60

The word was all over town by the time Kalico exited the admin dome and walked down the avenue to Inga's. She found Talina's seat open and levered her butt onto the worn bar stool. A sense of wry amusement, mixed with worry, continued to bubble inside her.

So far the day had been shitty. She'd awakened to the news that Mary Ting was missing. The woman worked down at the farm, was one of the incredibly important tree tenders who ensured the young pines were watered and cared for where they grew at the interface of the Donovanian forest. Pines, with their chemicals, served as the first line of defense against the constantly encroaching native flora.

Quetzal tracks were found on top of Mary's. There had been signs of a scuffle. All that remained behind was one of Mary's shoes and the pile of her torn clothing. One of the reasons Kalico had come to PA today was to see if she could hire either Trish or Step Allenovich to track the killer down.

Then, at breakfast, Torgussen and Seesil Vacquillas had flown down to brief her on *Vixen*. The crew was on the verge of mutiny. Half wanted to space for Solar System. Half wanted to stay in orbit or make a home on Donovan. What were her orders? Worse, Torgussen had forgotten to deliver the last of the coffee he'd promised to Corporate Mine.

Which was when Lea Shimodi appeared to report a software problem in the program that modeled subsurface mineral deposits and that the mucking machine in the Number Two had broken a drive shaft. Operations were effectively halted until the machine could be extricated, repaired, and tested.

Letting the *Vixen* problem simmer on the back burner, she'd shuttled up to Port Authority and found the town in a flurry of upset. As she and her people had cleared the gate at the shuttle field, people were talking about something going on with Shig and Yvette. And that Benteen— who'd made a name for himself over a murder in The Jewel—was at the bottom of it.

Had that been one of the understatements of the year or what?

At least Torgussen had delivered the last of the coffee, but he did so with a visible reservation. Maybe he was finally figuring out what a valuable commodity the stimulant was going to be in the future.

But that still left her with the problem of what to do with *Vixen*'s rebellious crew.

"Just a beer today," she told Inga as the woman lumbered in her direction.

As much as Kalico wanted a whiskey, something told her that her interests would be best served if she kept her wits mostly un-muddled.

"That for sure?" Inga asked as she set a glass mug of IPA in front of Kalico. "Benteen forced Shig and Yvette out?"

"I got it straight from Two Spot. Benteen threatened them with bodily harm, told them he was taking over, so they loaded themselves into an aircar and left at around noon today."

"What's Benteen's plan?"

Kalico took a taste of the bitter IPA. "Says he's gonna turn PA into a paradise. Figures he's going to create a rank-and-file society where everyone fits the mold for maximum efficiency. Turn PA into a finely functioning machine."

"Sounds like Corporate bullshit to me." Inga accented the words with a hard scowl.

"You figure I'm going to take the bait? Fire back with both barrels about how it's the only way to maximize output, laud the sacrifice of the individual in exchange for the promotion of common good?"

Inga's slow grin bore a measure of conspiracy. "Once I would have, Supervisor. Since that day, you've shown a measure of personal growth and adaptation. You and your mine down there? You're no more Corporate than PA. You think we don't know what goes on? The plunder you're sharing with your people? Rewarding incentive and productivity?"

"Yeah, well how about we keep that our little secret?"

Inga snorted like a bull. "Seems to me there's not much of a secret to keep."

"Then how about we compromise and just say we're maintaining a fiction for the sake of appearances?"

"That'll work." Inga glanced out at the growing crowd. "So what's the real word on Benteen?"

"The scorpion is now in your midst. All I can tell you is that he's deadly, smart, and puts even less value on human life than a scarlet flier cares for an invertebrate. Don't underestimate him."

Inga shook her head. "If he thinks he's going to run roughshod over the rest of us, he's got another think coming."

"I'll tell you this once, so pay attention: Be. Careful."

Inga's expression sharpened. "I got ya, Supervisor. And thanks." A pause. "So, unofficially, where does Corporate Mine come down in all of this? You backing the scorpion's play?"

"Let's just say that we've been corrupted by your libertarian ethic. My people and I would just as soon see the status quo maintained. While we'd rather not take sides in PA politics, if Benteen manages to come out on top, he's going to come for Corporate Mine in the end."

"Nice to have allies." Inga gestured toward the beer. "That's on the house."

"Much appreciated." Inga wasn't known for drinks on the house.

Kalico glanced around the room, filling as it was with people. The crowd at the other end of the bar was growing, waiting on Inga to finish her talk with Kalico. "What I don't understand is why Shig and Yvette ran. When I showed up and made a claim on Port Authority, they stayed to fight."

Inga used her bar towel to wipe the scarred chabacho wood. "Different kind of a fight. You came with marines and a Corporate mandate. The scorpion comes on his own. Shig and Yvette know what they're doing."

"I sure as hell hope so." Kalico glanced around the room, saw the concern in the faces. "Anyone needs a place to run to, you pass the word. Corporate Mine will give them sanctuary."

"Is that right? If so, supper's on the house tonight, too." A beat. "You turned out okay, Supervisor."

"Yeah, well, that's another subject that I prefer we didn't let go public. After all, I have a reputation to maintain."

"Those are the best secrets to keep. The ones everyone else already knows."

"Then here's one that fits that category: The story is that the scorpion was trapped in Guanxing, that Boardmember Shayne had sent him down to blackmail a Chinese tech Supervisor who'd amassed quite a little empire and was one of Radcek's major supporters. Something went wrong; the Chinese Supervisor caught wind that the scorpion was going to try and flip him to Shayne's side. The man had better-than-average security, and he slowly began to cut off the scorpion's avenues of escape. Played him, like herding a sheep into a kill pen."

"So, what happened?"

"They supposedly maneuvered the scorpion into what should have been a dead end. When they closed the trap, nothing. The guy had disappeared. By the time the Supervisor's security figured out that Benteen had crawled into an electrical chase and traced his path though the guts of the palace, Benteen had made his final play. The security forces closed in on the power plant. Figured they had Benteen trapped in one of the subbasements."

"Obviously they didn't get him."

"Nope. That whole security force and half the city died in the explosion when the fusion reactor went suddenly fission. The official explanation claimed it was an industrial accident. Benteen showed up a couple of weeks later on Bali, said he'd never been in Guanxing."

"What kind of damage are we talking about?"

"A million and a half dead. Along with the tech Supervisor, his small army, and most of the assets that made him a threat to Boardmember Shayne."

"So, you're telling us we'd better not leave the guy feeling trapped with no way out?"

"That's pretty much it. Tamarland Benteen plays for keeps. He'll take the whole of Port Authority with him if he thinks he's going to lose."

apella burned in a fantastic orange ball on the western horizon; its rays painted the undersides of the clouds in the most remarkable patterns of reds, yellows, blues, and purples. The sandstone slickrock around Rork Springs glowed in a salmon color.

In the dying light of day, an emotionally distraught Trish settled her aircar onto the sandstone bedrock beside Talina's battered craft. Through the long flight, she'd tortured herself, figured that there was something she should have done, that she'd let Shig, Yvette, and Port Authority down. Not to mention herself.

"He would have killed you," Shig said softly as the fans spun down. "As a corpse your only value would be to Benteen. He'd use it as a symbol of his power and deadly ability. Alive you remind others that they have a choice, that Tam Benteen isn't invincible."

"Should have done something, Shig. Tal would have."

Yvette rose from her seat, placed a hand on Trish's shoulder. "You did exactly what we wanted you to. You were perfect. Talina? She'd have pressed the point. People who are alive today would have been dead. This might sound like heresy, but Tal's way isn't always the right way."

Trish caught her breath, the words having failed to soothe her guilt.

In the drainage below, the chime had changed pitch, now a symphony of rising and falling melody. Rork Springs was always pretty; now it filled her with wonder. The dome itself had taken on a reddish hue, and behind it the sheds and dormitory gleamed in the light. The solar panels had swiveled to take in the last of Capella's fading energy.

"Yeah, whatever. Well, guys, we made it. Welcome to our last refuge." Trish flipped the switches to kill the power.

Shig and Yvette turned to the luggage on the deck at their feet.

"Been a long time since I was here," Yvette noted. "Bet it's been fifteen years. Hansen and I spent a couple of weeks here. He was calibrating some of the equipment while I supervised the plumbing." With that she picked up her bag and stepped over the side.

Shig thoughtfully snared his own bag. "Never been out this far before. I begin to understand."

"Understand what?" Trish asked, plucking her pack from its restraints and slinging it over her shoulder before tugging her rifle from the rack. After a quick chamber check, she vaulted over the side, weapon ready, taking in all the surroundings.

"The lure of the bush," Shig told her as he clambered awkwardly over the side. "Beauty is sattva. And I saw an incredible amount of beauty today."

"Yeah, well, you enjoy all the sattva you want while you're flying above it," Trish told him; her trained eyes missed nothing as she searched for threats. "But the second you set foot back on the ground, you're in a world of shit." A beat. "They got a word for 'being in the shit'?"

"Dukkha. Ultimately, all is suffering," Shig told her. "At least until you can divest yourself of the illusion of existence."

"Illusion, huh? Just where in the process of being torn in two and swallowed by a quetzal does this illusion of yours come into play?"

"Right off the bat, actually. It's the first of the four noble truths. Things will happen to you in life that you really dislike. Being eaten alive, at least in my book, is right up there."

"Damn straight. You know why there was never a Buddha on Donovan? It's because not finding a Bodhi Tree, Buddha sat down under a mundo tree in search of enlightenment . . . and a nightmare ate him."

"You have the most remarkable ability to take the sublime, completely turn it on its head, and trash it."

Trish tapped a meaningful hand on her rifle, "Yeah, well on Donovan a full magazine trumps all the mystical teachings in the universe."

Satisfied that nothing was going to jump them and eat either Shig or Yvette, Trish checked Talina's aircar, noted the charge was up to ninety-six percent, and took a moment to shift the charging cable to her own car.

That's when she saw the ceramic fragments. Some sort of blue- on-white pieces. And then she fixed on the blood, now just dark drops in the shadow of Talina's aircar.

"Wonder where Talina is?" Yvette was asking as Trish followed the droplets of blood to the dome door.

"Hang on," she called. "Got blood here. Let me check it out before you go barging in to find a quetzal chewing on someone in the main room."

"Oh, you don't think . . ." Shig couldn't finish the thought.

"Welcome to Donovan," Trish growled. "When it comes to full magazines, I rest my case."

She eased the front door open and let it swing wide as she stared over the sights of her rifle.

The lights were on, which was reassuring, and the refrigeration was humming. Nothing looked amiss in the room; all the tables and chairs were upright. No sign of a struggle.

She could hear voices coming from the back hallway.

"Hey! Hello! Anybody home? Tal? You here?"

Within seconds a little girl appeared, maybe ten or eleven, dressed in oversized yellow overalls. "Who're you?"

"Trish Monagan. Where's Tal?"

The next surprise came when Dortmund Weisbacher stepped out of a doorway behind the girl, saying, "You really can put the gun down. Talina Perez is injured. I would have called, but it appears there's a problem with the radio. I call it imp-inspired sabotage."

Trish lowered her rifle, stepped all the way in. Yvette and Shig followed. "What do you mean, injured?"

"Something with the quetzals," Weisbacher said. "They sort of, well . . . mugged her might be the best way to describe it. She hit her head."

"And what happened to you?" Trish asked, taking in the fresh white bandage inexpertly applied to the man's forearm. She could see the discoloration from blood and disinfectant on the skin.

"Quetzal," Weisbacher told her, a curious gleam in his eyes. "Most remarkable. It's only a start, mind you, but given the basics, we've got an incredible amount of opportunity to build on. It won't be easy, visual patterns, variations of color, posture, and the way—"

"Let's get back to Talina," Trish growled, stomping forward. "Where is she?"

"Back bedroom."

The little girl darted off to take a defensive position behind the table and chairs as she warily watched Trish pass, then fixed uneasy eyes on Shig and Yvette.

"The kid looks like she's about to bolt," Trish said, figuring it had to be Kylee Simonov. "Yvette, keep an eye on her. Shig, come on. Let's take a look."

In the back bedroom, under a single light, they found Talina laid out in one of the beds. She looked thin, drawn, and, given the flickering of her eyes, lost in a REM state.

"Hey, Tal?" Trish said, settling herself on the side of the bed. "Wake up. We need to talk."

Trish gave the woman a hard shake, wary lest Talina come to on the attack. Nothing.

"The professor said she hit her head," Shig suggested. "Could you lift it while I feel around?"

Trish did, watching as Shig's fingers probed through the thick black hair in search of Talina's skull.

"A slight bump on the back of the occiput," Shig deduced. "Nothing that would indicate any kind of serious damage."

Trish lifted the sheet. "Fuck. She's been out of it for a while. They've got her in a diaper." Trish considered her friend. "Let me check something." She bent down, pried Talina's oddly bruised lips apart, and sniffed. "Peppermint."

"The quetzals are warring inside her brain," the little girl called from the door as she zipped in, and then off to one side as if to stay out of reach.

"You are Kylee?" Shig asked, stepping over and seating himself on the side of the second bed. "You've been living with the quetzals. What happened? How did you get here?"

"You're not taking me back." The little girl slipped along the wall like some feral creature as Yvette came down the hallway behind her.

"I wouldn't," Shig told her. "Not without your permission."

"Why not?" Kylee's voice dripped suspicion.

"Because, you are a new Tao. A new path. One specially tailored for this world. In my book, you're a miracle."

"What are you doing here?" Kylee demanded.

"For the moment we're in exile. Until this morning, we were the government. Now someone else has taken over."

"So you were in charge when they threw Rocket out? You were one of the ones who got him killed?"

Trish flinched at the anger in the child's voice. Her sense of guilt deepened. Shit, couldn't she do anything right?

"Wasn't my decision," Shig told the child, a sadness in his eyes. "Unfortunately, people don't always listen to me."

"What about Talina?" the little girl asked.

"She's one of the few who does. I know because she couldn't accidentally misinterpret my teachings the way she does if she didn't really know what I'm saying."

"That's backward." The little girl scowled at him.

"Sometimes backward is a way of finding our path forward."

Kylee was looking even more suspicious when Yvette said, "Kid, don't even think you can out-spar Shig. Seriously, what's wrong with Talina? What's all this business about quetzals? How's she injured?"

From the hallway behind, Weisbacher said, "It doesn't make any sense. The quetzals had her down. They both had their tongues in her mouth. Yes, she bumped her head, but not hard enough to keep her out for days. I think Kylee's right. That it's something molecular going on in her brain. Some chemically induced coma."

Trish muttered, "We've got to get her to Raya."

"As if that worked the last time we tried it." Yvette crossed her arms. "You know how that ended."

"Yeah. Raya's still fuming. I could fly her back in Talina's car while mine charges."

Shig studied Talina with thoughtful eyes. "We'll decide in the morning. Meanwhile, I think we should make supper, plan what we're going to do."

"I'll see what we've got." Yvette turned, leading the way out.

"Go on," Trish told Shig. "I'll sit with her for a while."

Only the little girl remained, her distrustful and weird blue eyes missing nothing as Trish stroked Talina's hair.

"She raised me," Trish said by way of explanation. "Kept me alive. I owe her."

"She's not like the rest," Kylee agreed. "It's okay. She's not going to die."

"How do you know?"

"'Cause Rocket told me."

"Thought he was dead."

"You don't understand anything, do you? He'd be even more alive if people like you hadn't hurt him." And with that, the girl turned and fled down the hall.

62

Down deep, Tamarland had to admire Mosadek and Dushane, while another part of him railed at their betrayal. Skipping town neatly saved them from any immediate retribution. Ultimately, however, they'd pay the price for their treachery.

Donovan was a small world, after all. Eventually they'd show up, and when they did, he'd deal with them in the most excruciating way possible.

He liked the notion of skinning them alive. The technique was ancient. Long incisions were cut about an inch apart, and then the strips were slowly pulled off the body with vise grips. As each strip was flayed away, the exposed muscle was sealed with a paste containing a measure of scorpion venom. He'd have to find a substitute here, given that the supply of scorpions on Donovan was nonexistent. Someone in The Jewel had said that a local plant called thorncactus burned like liquid fire in open wounds.

Maybe that would work.

As he contemplated, he heard boots thumping in the hallway and a burly, muscular guy entered. He appeared just short of his twenties, black hair, smooth-shaven face, and curious brown eyes. He wore quetzal hide over a chamois shirt.

"You wanted to see me?" Nothing in his tone hinted at deference.

Tam stood, a faint smile on his lips. "That would depend. Who are you?"

"Smit Hazen. Two Spot said that since Step turned in his resignation, you wanted to see me."

"What gives you the idea that Allenovich turned in a resignation?" He sure as hell hadn't told Tam. Not that it would be a surprise. Well, too bad for Mr. Allenovich. There would be no shortage of people to publicly execute.

"That's what Two Spot said." The guy crossed his arms.

Tam stepped up to him, taking his measure. The kid thought he was tough. Work-hardened. The kind who'd seen some hard knocks, survived, but had no formal training. "You will address me as Director."

"Sure."

Tam flashed a hard knee into Hazen's crotch, caught the back of the guy's head as it jerked forward, and shoved it down as his other knee rose to crush Hazen's nose. As a final thought, Tam kicked the man's feet out from under him and let him crash to the floor.

For a moment Hazen could only gasp and curl into a fetal position, one hand cupping his genitals, the other on his gushing nose.

"You can be hurt worse," Tam told him, "or you can pay attention. Which will it be?"

"Pay attention," the words came muffled.

"Pay attention, Director."

"Yes, sir, Director, sir."

"There, that wasn't so hard, was it? Now, if you are to be the head of security, what, exactly, does that entail?"

"I make sure the guards are on the gates, that nothing's missed, Director."

"How many of these so-called guards are there?"

"'Bout ten of us now that Tal, Trish, and Step are gone."

"Mister Hazen, from now on, if I give you an order, will you obey it? Or do we need another demonstration of my authority?"

"No, Director. I mean, yes, Director." He winced, peering owlishly past the hand that he used to clamp his bleeding nose. "I'll do what you tell me, Director."

"Good. Now, will your men take your orders?"

"Yes, Director. Or, I mean, I think. Depends."

"On what?"

"What do you want us to do?"

"Be my right hand. I am now in charge. There is no other appeal. There is no resistance to my authority. No matter what you might have heard, I was appointed by the Board. Yes, it was a long time ago. However, since I have yet to receive any notification from the Board that my authority has been rescinded, I remain in charge.

"All of which leaves you with a decision to make, Mister Hazen. You can serve me fully and completely, without any hesitation or reservation. You don't even need to think. Just follow my orders. Do that and you will receive ample compensation. New and better dwellings. Food, sexual companionship, SDRs, status, whatever you covet."

"Yes, Director."

"Should you choose, however, not to give me complete and immediate obedience, I shall shoot you dead. On the spot. Without any additional chances or options." He pulled his Talon, made a production of it as he clicked the safety off. "Your choice, sir?"

Hazen was staring up in disbelief, eyes fixed on the pistol's muzzle. "Don't shoot. I'll do as you say, Director."

"Good."

Tam holstered the pistol and walked back behind his desk. "Now, what I really need to know is who will buck my authority? Make trouble for me? I've got Dan Wirth and his people on my side. Aguila and her people are automatically hostile and considered enemies. Who else would I need to worry about? Anyone in your security staff, Chief Officer?"

Hazen sat up, his nose swelling, pain in his brown eyes. "Like I said, that depends, Director. My guys will do anything to keep the compound safe. Some might hesitate if they were asked to act against the people here."

"Your first order, then, is to find out where your people stand. You are authorized to shoot anyone who you think might compromise our agenda or refuse to take orders." Tam smiled. "See, that's one of the perks, Chief Officer. You answer only to me. Your people answer only to you. Any order you give to Two Spot, Dr. Turnienko, Dan Wirth, or anyone else, must be obeyed."

"I see, sir."

"Good. The next task is to determine which structure to use as a holding facility. There will be miscreants and malcontents in the beginning. People we are either going to have to incarcerate until they come to their senses, or eventually execute as examples to the others."

"Execute?"

"Harsh times, harsh measures." Tam propped his butt on the desk and crossed his arms. "There will be no more talk about the odds that the colony here will fail. I won't allow that to happen. I intend on making this colony self-sufficient if I have to kill half of the population to do it."

Hazen's eyes had taken on a worried sheen.

"I understand," Tam told him in soothing tones. "Making the transition will be difficult and not without cost. You, more than any of the others, will pay a terrible price. But, Chief Officer, you need to harden yourself. Understand that distasteful actions *will* be necessary to straighten this mess out. There may be privation, suffering, and what appears as injustice at first glance, but believe me, it's the only way to ensure that a human presence will endure on this planet."

Tam smacked his fist into his palm. "Damn it, there's so much potential, but only if we all act for the common good. Resources *must* be managed for the maximum potential return. The same with our labor. I've seen the statistics, our population is falling, which begs the question: Why isn't every female of childbearing age pregnant?"

"Well, it's sort of the women's—"

"Choice?" Tam cried in wonderment. "Because of a choice, the population can dwindle away into nothingness? How the hell do you think that's going to sound in another hundred years? 'Well, the women thought it would be inconvenient, so they failed to reproduce.'"

"Um, Director, how do you suggest . . . ?"

"All in due time, Chief Officer. First things first. Which leaves us at the detention center. Which building do you suggest would make a suitable prison?"

"Um, maybe the old repair shop out at the mine? The place is built like a fortress. There's those parts bays that could be turned into cells. But it's five miles out of town. Sort of far away, but nobody in their right mind would try and make a run for it out in the bush like that."

"What about the Wild Ones?"

"I don't follow, Director."

"Would they make a run for it?"

"Not without their kit, sir. Can't eat the plants. Take

their boots away, and it's a death sentence. And without a weapon they can't shoot a crest or chamois or fastbreak."

"As the Wild Ones come in, they are to be disarmed, detained, relocated to holding, and put into work details. It's a waste of manpower to have them wandering around out in the bush. I want them made productive."

"Doing what, Director?"

"For one thing a haul road around the fields so these damned trucks aren't rumbling through town every day. For another, I want this hodgepodge of cluttered property cleaned out and organized living quarters erected in their place."

"What about the titles?"

Tamarland considered. "All in good time. First we have to reeducate the people to what their real priorities are. Once we have instilled a more realistic understanding of what's good for them, we can tackle some of these other insanities."

"Yes, Director."

"You look skeptical, Chief Officer."

"Well, Director, the last time we had a Supervisor who tried this, it didn't work out so well."

"Clemenceau?" Tam arched an eyebrow. "I've seen the records. He suffered from a failure of the will. Nor did he employ his assets correctly. What's the point of making people afraid of you if you don't intend to apply that terror strategically and to obtain specific goals?"

"I see."

"No, Chief Officer, you don't. But eventually you will. Now, before you get on about your business, I need a list of families. Which ones might cause me trouble, and more to the point what are the names and locations of their children?"

"You're worried about the children?"

"Good heavens, no. But if one controls the health and welfare of the children, one controls the parents. Now, you have your first orders, Chief Officer. Please see to them."

Hazen swallowed hard, finally climbed to his feet, and said, "I'll get that to you immediately, Director."

Tam watched the man hurry from the room. After he'd gone, he asked, "So, what do you think, Tam?"

Then he answered himself: "Chances are Hazen's not going to cut it, and I'm going have kill three or four of them before I find the right subordinate who'll shut off his mind and just implement the orders."

But he'd still give Hazen a chance.

63

In the dream Talina walked with quetzals. Rocket matched pace on her right side. Her old nemesis, Demon, strode along on her left. For this task she carried an empty sack over her shoulder. They walked together down the length of the ballcourt at Copan, across the stones where Talina had been devoured. She wasn't surprised when Demon lowered its head, ran its tongue over the bloodstains, and flashed patterns of indigo, blue, and pink.

Talina stopped at the calabash tree, looked up, and considered the skull that rested on the branch. "In the old stories, it is the twins, Hun Ajaw and Xbalanque, who come and bring you back to life. But that's a story for a different time and a different world. Here I only have myself and the quetzals. One-and-many. A quality the Maya would have appreciated in their mystical concepts of Maker-Modeler, One-and-Seven. The many that make up the one."

The skull grinned down silently.

Talina removed the sack from her shoulder, shook it open, and reached up to lift the skull from the branch. That it could be so light shocked her.

The time she'd helped to lower Mitch's dead weight into the grave, he'd been so heavy she'd almost dropped him. And lowering Cap Taggart's body into his last resting place had strained the muscles in her shoulders and back.

The skull might have been made of air.

Carefully she placed the cranium into the sack, shifted it onto her back, and turned. She winked at Rocket and glared at Demon. About time the damn baby-killing monster had a name. She was getting too many of the beasts inside to keep track of.

Didn't matter that the great ballcourt of Copan was a couple hundred miles southwest of her home in Chiapas. Because she was in a spirit dream, the moment she climbed out of the ballcourt, she was on her old street. Walking down the cobblestones toward Mother's whitewashed-and-plastered house with its solar roof and cistern catchment. She wondered at the sense of contentment and belonging.

Such were the powers of *Way* and the spirit world. Had an ancient Maya shaman been hanging around Donovan, he would have told her that the realm of spirits was simply an inverse of the reality most people lived. A fact that wasn't lost on students of multiverse physics—or on the crews of the starships who inverted symmetry and traveled through parallel universes.

Stepping through the front door, she made her way to Mother's kitchen with its smells of cooking tamales, the incense-like aroma of steaming mole, and the tang of ancho in the air.

Talina crossed the Saltillo tiles and carefully laid the sack upon the scarred wooden table. She removed the skull and placed it next to Mother's sand bowl and the collection of shards from the broken burial pot.

Seating herself, Talina glanced at the quetzals who'd taken up places on either side. Next she carefully organized the broken shards, placing each according to the design. The images of One Death, Seven Death, and Blood Gatherer—not surprisingly—had remained in one piece. Hun Ajaw and Xbalanque she fitted back together, and then the image of maiden Blood Moon. But even as she did, the images changed, the lines and colors shifting.

Finally she organized the pieces that depicted resurrected One Hunahpu rising from the cracked turtle shell to become the Maize God. Only, to her surprise, as she labored to fit the pieces together, they didn't create the familiar male rendering of the Maize God who would lift the World Tree to hold up the Sky World.

The female rising from the cracked shell now wore a black suit; instead of the usual Mayan headdress, a small Donovanian quetzal perched atop her head. Two larger quetzals curled up from behind her shoulders. In her hands she carried a rifle, and at her hip the tripartite *Way* glyph was clearly visible.

"I don't understand," she said softly, and glanced at the skull.

Her mother's voice—so long out of time and place—

whispered from the skull's mouth. "This is the final choice. If you refit the broken pieces, it will be to create something new. Something dangerous."

"And if I don't want to?"

"Then you can drift away into the Dream and remain in Xibalba. But you will do so as yourself. The old Talina. The one locked inside this skull. Resurrection doesn't come without a cost. You will never be the same again."

"It's about saving the knowledge," Rocket told her from where he watched, his three eyes studying every move her hands made with the potsherds.

"Stay here in the kitchen," Demon told her. "How many times do you want to eat Allison's baby? Bury Mitch? Bury Cap? You put that pot together, you will be 'Other' for the rest of your life. A *thing* that is constantly apart."

She glanced again at the skull. Remembered the spit that had landed on her palm and how it smelled of peppermint. The way it magically had absorbed into her skin.

"Just because you reassemble the pot," Mother's voice warned her, "doesn't mean you'll ever find your way back."

"Wouldn't be the first time a person remade reality only to discover it didn't lead to any place they'd ever been before."

"Think *Freelander*," her demon quetzal told her. "You could end up just as lost."

Uncertain, Talina stared at the broken fragments of the bowl. If she reached out, took a first shard and fitted it to the second, she was condemning herself to finish.

"And if you get the order wrong," the skull reminded, "if you fit the pieces together and leave one out, you will never be whole again."

"It's got to be done in exactly the right order," Rocket insisted. "Even the little pieces."

"She's not that smart," Demon muttered as if to himself. "Since when has Talina Perez ever been about the details? This is delicate work. How can a woman who's spent her life as a hammer succeed at something this intricate?"

"Oh, go fuck yourself," Talina growled, reaching for the first two pieces.

64

Dortmund carefully checked his bandage. The wound in his arm was like nothing he'd ever experienced. It looked horrible enough to make him queasy. The damned thing ached, throbbed, and really hurt. The worst he'd ever been wounded in all of his days was a sliced finger when a knife got away while opening a package. That he'd been stabbed by an alien claw was still settling into his shocked brain.

Across the room, Trish sat before the radio. Dortmund had been listening in, first regarding the state of Talina's coma, and second, it appeared that the whole of Port Authority was in a growing ferment.

"Wasn't but a half hour ago that the scorpion walked in and told Two Spot to shut the radio down in the admin dome. I'm not sure that Benteen knows the hospital has its own frequency, or if he's going to want to shut it down even if he does."

Shig ambled across the room, leaned over Trish's shoulder, and asked, "Raya? What are you hearing from the people?"

"Confusion. Disbelief. Have to tell you, Shig. Most are down at Inga's drinking and talking about it. Kalico Aguila is staying over—including her marines. She's put two on guard here at the hospital in case things get out of hand. Others are standing guard at Inga's, the cafeteria, the foundry, Sheyela's, the food warehouses. Pretty much every place that's really important for the survival of the town."

"And to think I wanted to poison that woman back when she arrived here," Yvette said to herself as she listened from the old beat-up couch.

"So, after thinking about it," Trish asked, "what do you want us to do with Talina?"

"As long as she's stable, doesn't demonstrate any dis-

tress in her breathing, I'd say it's not worth the risk of a night flight, Trish. I'd wait until morning. Then fly her in. Radio ahead and I'll have Step and Dya ready. You can drop down at the main entrance. Step and Dya can evacuate Tal, and you can dust off for the back country again."

"I'll have to recharge. Not enough juice to make a round trip."

"Right. How about you drop Tal, dust off, land again at the aircar field, and take Step's unit while yours recharges. Given that PA is about to come apart at the seams, he's not going anywhere."

"Roger that. I'll give you a call in the morning just to make sure. And if Tal takes a turn for the worse, I'll just fly her in using the night gear."

"Okay. Sleep tight out there. And, by all of our lucky stars, hopefully you bring Tal to a quiet and boring hospital. If something goes wrong, and I'm overwhelmed by wounded, I'll wave you off."

"Roger that. Catch you in the morning." Trish thoughtfully replaced the mic and shut the radio down to monitor mode. She pushed back, stared thoughtfully at Shig and Yvette. "Well, that's that."

Shig chuckled to himself, wandered into the kitchen, and poured himself a cup of mint tea. "This will be most fascinating to watch."

Dortmund, still poking at his bandage, said, "I spaced with Advisor Benteen. It was bad enough just being in a room with him, and that was before we knew who he was. The very knowledge that he is Artollia Shayne's pet assassin and monster sends chills down my spine. You were wise to walk away, but it amounts to surrendering your people to a beast."

"Damn straight," Trish growled.

Yvette leaned forward on the couch, a cup of tea on the table beside her. "Dr. Weisbacher, is conservation biology an abstract?"

"Absolutely not. You know my record, my efforts at re-wilding. Each of those re-wilding compounds was built upon a sound theoretical background established by years of research and—"

"So is political science," the woman snapped, cutting him off in midstream. "You're a product of The Corporation's mind-numbing indoctrination, so I doubt that you'll understand this, but when it comes to Benteen, it's up to the people."

"What do they have to do with anything?"

Shig said mildly, "Like you, we are working from established theory. How does one run a libertarian society if the people are not responsible for their own governance?"

"You're leaving it to the people to appeal to the tender mercies of the scorpion? You should be there, directing them, showing them the way to resist."

Yvette said, "Had we stayed, Benteen would have turned us into tools. Used us against the people. One way, we'd have had to abet him in his takeover of the town. Become unwilling participants. The other way, he would have executed us to achieve the maximum psychological impact on the population. By leaving, we have dealt him the heaviest blow we could."

"Be giving him free rein?"

Trish seemed to stumble upon a sudden revelation. "Holy shit. I thought you were crazy when you just handed everything over."

"Doesn't mean we're not," Shig told her through a benevolent smile.

Trish laughed, looked at Dortmund. "You see, don't you?"

"Enlighten me," he told her dryly.

"Benteen's a Corporate animal. Like you. Raised in the system. He's expecting Port Authority to run like a smaller version of the Corporate machine. That's how the whole rest of Solar System functions. Everyone in their place. Following orders. Following the plan."

"And?"

Shig spread his hands wide. "Yvette handled the day-to-day administration. I acted as the liaison between disparate parties. Sort of the information broker, keeping track of who was doing what, teaching part time, keeping my thumb on the pulse of the community. Tal, and then Trish behind her, were the security. That's all gone."

"But who's going to take care of the people?" Dortmund repeated stubbornly.

Shig smiled. "That's the whole point."

"I still don't get it."

Yvette told him, "The fundamental underlying assumption of libertarian philosophy is that the people can take care of themselves."

"That's absolutely insane. Over a hundred years of Corporate government have proven that it's the most efficient, responsible, and compassionate evolution of population control ever invented."

"Key word," Trish told him. "Control."

"You don't know Benteen like I do."

"Actually, we know him better, but we can leave that argument behind for the moment."

"Your *people* need to be informed about the kind of man they're dealing with. If they don't do as he says, he won't hesitate to kill a couple dozen of them to make the point."

Shig's expression lined. "Yes, that's the risk they take by being free, isn't it?"

Dortmund took a deep breath, raised his gaze to the ceiling in supplication, and shook his head. "You're all lunatics. Just as infected with this place as that little girl and Talina."

Trish broke out in that irritating laughter again. "Yeah, well, join the club, Doc."

"I remain a rational human being. And as soon as I can get you to fly me back to Port Authority, I'm going to insist that Captain Torgussen ferry me back up to *Vixen*. Once there, I can write up my observations and either space back to Solar System with the ship—should they choose to leave—or await the next vessel to arrive here."

Kylee had crept into the room about halfway through the conversation. Wild thing that she was, she'd veered wide, keeping to the walls, and settled in the room's far corner. Now she said, "You can't go back."

"Of course I can. What do you know? Just like the radio. Trish plugged in the what's-it and it worked fine. Being here has had its moments, like actually communicating with a quetzal." He lifted his bandaged arm. "And you can see what that got me."

Kylee's oddly blue eyes narrowed. "You still don't understand, do you?"

"Of course I do. Some sort of symbolic quetzal gesture. Maybe like a bond. Some affirmation of communal acceptance. Perhaps even a status display, or a rite of passage."

"You're infected. Get it? That's what that blood transfer was all about. Right now, running around in your blood, you've got TriNA all through you."

Dortmund stopped, his heart skipping a beat. Disbelieving, he stared down at the bandage, felt that throbbing ache in his wound.

"Yeah," Kylee cried. "Now you're a polluted hybrid just like Talina and me!"

Dortmund swallowed hard, closed his eyes. As the implications filtered through his brain, he really wanted to throw up.

65

The small dorm room in the admin building wasn't the poorest of accommodations that Tamarland Benteen had ever endured, but it was pretty pitiful. He'd taken the lower of the bunks in the cramped room. The only saving grace was that he'd filled it with Allison Chomko. The naked presence of a warm and voluptuous woman to wrap himself around made all the difference. It also helped that she was a willing partner who actively enjoyed copulation.

He'd been intimate with enough high-priced courtesans back in Solar System to know when a woman was a trained professional. Allison wasn't, but she was both willing and dedicated, and that intrigued him. He frightened her, worried her, and despite that, she actively enjoyed sex with him.

He wondered if it was a curious psychological problem— something smacking of a bit of nymphomania. Or perhaps it came from a lack of nurturing in her youth that left her craving any kind of physical contact no matter with whom, or what their motives.

Then again, it might just be Donovan. People here lived with danger every waking moment of their lives. Maybe it was a new form of anxiety disorder, somewhat akin to how people lived in war zones where every minute might be their last. Or perhaps it was some need to punish herself because a quetzal had taken her baby from its crib.

Whatever. Her presence beside him made living in the admin dorm bearable for the foreseeable future. He certainly didn't want to expose himself by walking out on the street. Not until he had the locals firmly cowed and under control.

Tam slipped out of the bed, seeing a gray and dismal morning through the one small window.

"Time to get up?" she asked, rolling over and tossing her pale blond hair back. The way the sheet clung to her, the posture she unconsciously adopted, added to her allure, and she did it without thought. Nature might have programmed her specifically for his appreciation.

"We've got a busy day." He slipped his Talon into its holster and donned his suit coat. "Time to see if that moron Hazen can manage his people. His orders were to begin rounding up the individuals I have identified from the lists. I want them here by no later than ten."

Allison threw the bedding back, swung her feet over the edge of the bed, and studied him through a wary blue glare. "Rounded up? Like arrested?"

"You sound surprised." He offered his hand, pulling her up so that he could read her reaction up close. "All I have is me. No army, no police, no computer to run surveillance algorithms looking for dissidents. My security force is of questionable loyalty. My only chance for success lies in bringing in the potential ringleaders, figuring out where their weaknesses lie, and exploiting them to the best of my ability."

"You do know the kind of people you're dealing with, don't you?"

"People are simply humans, my dear. Chinese, Translunan, Egyptian, Cambodian, or station born. All remarkably and boringly the same. They share similar fears, weaknesses, and vulnerabilities. Pride is pride. Fear, terror, and pain are physiological reality. Even here in Port Authority. They can't help but value their children over all else. They will still dread imprisonment, torture, or execution."

He saw the faint wavering as her irises constricted. Caught the tightening of her jaw muscles. Saw the moment she realized just how far he was willing to go.

"It's all right, Ali," he told her. "It doesn't seem so at the moment, but it is in their best interest. Taking these potential ringleaders now, bringing them here, means that they can see the hopelessness of their situation. True, I might have to shoot one or more of them, but the rest will come to understand the new reality. In the long run that will save them more suffering than if I had to hunt them down one by one. The whole process of their surrender will be a lot less painful."

"Shit on a shoe, you really believe this."

"Not a matter of belief, love. It's just how people work. I've got to break their spirit, suffocate any hope of resistance before it can be born. At the same time, I've got to show them that I am indeed in charge, and any obstructionist behavior is doomed before they even consider it."

"That's it? Just beat them down?" He caught a flicker of amusement behind her voice.

"Of course not. Government must always offer the governed a path of least resistance. The realization that they might not like compliance, but it beats hell out of the alternatives. In return for their loyalty, they get to be part of a more efficient system. There will be rewards for those who pitch in on my side: advancement, power, and privilege."

"These aren't the same kind of people you're used to in Solar System. They'll make a fight of it."

"But not much of one. At heart they're just people." He lifted a finger to run along the angle of her jaw. "But what of you, my bird? If it came down to it, would you back me, or your people?"

To her credit, she held his gaze, really gave her response consideration. "If I betrayed you, you'd kill me in a second. So how about you don't let it come to that?"

He chuckled, seeing the fear behind her eyes. "You didn't answer my question."

"I don't want to be anyone's martyr. All I'm doing is trying to stay alive. If helping you means I can keep some other people alive at the same time, I'll do that, too."

He turned her loose, saying, "Then come on. I'll show you how one man can take over a whole colony."

When she'd dressed, combed out her hair, and nodded, he exited the door, walked down the hall, and collected binding cuffs from the armory. Then, at the radio room, he leaned in. "Two Spot? A word please."

The lanky youth nodded, stood, and walked over. "Morning, um, Director. What can I do for you?"

"Turn around."

"Sir?"

"Just turn around."

Tam cuffed him.

"Hey! What the hell?"

"Your days here are over."

"But who's gonna monitor the radio?"

"Absolutely no one."

Allison told him, "You're really playing with fire, Tam."

"First rule of governance, love. You've got to cut off the opposition's communications."

"But what about if there's an emergency?" Two Spot nodded toward the radio. "Maybe a medical, or someone goes down in the bush?"

"Then they go down. I'm playing for everything, and in order to win, I'm going to have to take some long risks. So, you see, it's my way or nothing."

He pulled out his Talon and placed the muzzle against the startled man's head. "Now, Two Spot, how do I disable the com system so that people with implants can't jabber back and forth and make trouble?"

Two Spot swallowed hard, shot a look of supplication at Allison. All he got was a slight shrug and her soft suggestion: "I'd tell him. He'll kill you otherwise."

Two Spot, as Tam had known he would, began to talk.

Ten minutes later, Two Spot was secured to a chair in the conference room and Port Authority was in total blackout.

All Tam had to do was collect his hostages and the real struggle would begin.

66

The hot cup of cacao seasoned with finely ground ancho chili reminded Talina of how special her childhood as an archaeologist's daughter had been. She sat in her mother's kitchen, the smell of warm sopapillas smeared in honey filling the air.

The cup she held was ceramic, not sialon or duraplast. Like all of their dishes, her mother had made the cup by hand. Formed it from local clay. She'd decorated the sides in traditional Mayan designs and fired the piece in a historically accurate kiln.

Mother's dedication to experimentally recreating the past had extended to food, too. Homegrown corn, beans, squash, peppers, chia, teosinte, several species of potatoes, yams, and amaranth had grown in the garden, and cacao and coffee trees crowded the surrounding walls. Monthly trips to the field resulted in bags filled with annatto, various wild fruits, medicinal plants, roots, and vegetables like tomatillos.

Not that they didn't eat more Corporate-distributed synthetic rations than either cared for. Mother didn't always have time to cook, and rejecting rations would have brought the dietary monitors knocking at the door to determine why Mother wasn't ensuring her daughter received the exact amount of nutrition and calories prescribed by Corporate nutritional tables for a child her age.

Even the house they lived in—what Mother called *la casita*—was special. Consisting of a whitewashed twenty-first-century adobe with a solar tile roof, the historic structure had originally been the groundskeeper's house just outside the Yaxchilan Maya ruins. As head archaeologist at the site, Mother had received a special permit to occupy the house and maintain its historic integrity.

Now safe in Mother's kitchen, Talina savored the warmth of the cacao radiating through the ceramic and into her fingers.

To her right, Rocket perched on one of the old wooden chairs, while Demon crouched across the table from her—the beast's three hard eyes like internally lit obsidian as they gazed at her.

How perfectly Maya that they should be here. *Way*. Transformation. Spiritual animal companions. Co-essences. Part of her soul, yet different. Implicit elements of her dream. Rocket, her friend and ally, diametrically opposed from Demon, who always sought to destroy her on his own terms.

And there, on the table between them, stood the recon-structed pot. Each potsherd had been perfectly placed right down to the tiny gray chips.

But what did it mean now?

The fragmented ceramics might have gone together in just the right order, but to Talina's unease, it was no longer the same pot. Or—more to the point—it might have been the original pot, but the designs painted on the slipped sur-face were now different. The *Way* glyph was twice as large as it had been before she broke the thing. And when she'd reassembled the pieces that depicted the Lords of Death, they'd come together in the images of quetzals: brightly colored, collars flared. Originally the image of the resur-rected One-Hunahpu was shown rising from the cracked turtle shell as the reborn Maize God; the depiction now was that of a dark-eyed, bare-breasted young woman with raven-black hair, wearing a black security uniform with a pistol at her hip. A small quetzal headdress rose above her head. Where originally the twin heroes, Hun Ajaw and Xbalanque, had been drawn, now Rocket stood on the right side of the cracked turtle shell in Hun Ajaw's place. Demon made threatening gestures on the left where Xblanque had been.

The *Way* glyph, once black on orange, now glowed in phosphorescent yellow-green light, as if it were illuminated from the inside.

"What did I do wrong?"

"Nothing," Rocket replied. "The pot could never have been put back together as it was. Look closely. Where you fit the pieces back in place, not even a line remains to sig-nify the repair."

She stared at the seamless surface, the burnish unmarred by so much as a hairline crack.

Transformation.

But into what?

She shook her head slowly.

"You hesitate?" Rocket asked.

"I don't know what I am."

"An abomination," Demon told her, a series of black patterns running along his hide. "A murderer. Call it up in your mind. Remember how it was? Your pistol leveled as you shot Sian Hmong down in the street? That's who you have become."

Talina could see it as if she were there, felt her pistol buck in her hand as her bullet tore a hole between Sian's breasts, blasted through her lower sternum, and took out the bottom of the woman's heart.

"What's to say that if I go back I'll ever know reality from the dream?"

"You would rather live here?" Rocket asked, his colors violet, mauve, and orange.

"Looking back at my life, it was right here. In this very spot. This was the happiest I ever was. Smell the air? Chocolate and the tang of chili. Do you know how long it's been since I've had chocolate?"

"This is illusion," Rocket told her softly. "A lie that you tell yourself. You really think this is your mother's kitchen? The Lords of Death laugh. Safe as you may wish yourself to be, you are still in Xibalba."

"That's not true." Talina pointed. "Look. See all of Mama's pots? The oven? The dent in that big kettle on the stove? She did that when she dropped it in the sink. The handles were too hot to hold, and she was pouring out boiling water."

Demon chattered, the white and iridescent red of amusement rolling down his flanks.

Rocket fixed his three eyes on Talina. "Step to the door. Look out. Blink your eyes three times. Then tell me what you see."

"That's—"

"Just do it," Rocket insisted. "Call it a test."

Talina put down her cup, stepped to the kitchen door, and looked out. "I see the garden."

"Blink three times."

"It's a trick," Demon called. "Come back. Your chocolate is getting cold."

"Blink three times?" She wondered at her sudden reluctance.

"It's an old shaman's trick I found deep in your memory," Rocket told her. "Humor me."

"He's deceiving you!" Demon insisted. "You're happy here. Why put it all at risk?"

Talina blinked once, twice, and on the third blink, the garden vanished. She was staring at the stone pavement. Beyond it stood the Copan ballcourt. She could see her bloodstains on the paving stones.

When she looked back, expecting to see her mother's familiar and comforting kitchen, a lonely, dead calabash tree stood there.

A sense of desolation washed through her—a hollow and draining emptiness. So terrible was the feeling that she raised her hands to her face, half certain she would feel the bony surface of her skull, the hardness of exposed teeth where her cheeks were supposed to be.

But her fingers encountered firm flesh, the triangle of her nose, and the softness of her lips.

Xibalba!

It didn't make sense. She'd repaired the pot.

"You need a guide," Rocket told her, appearing beside her. "In the stories of your people, when Blood Moon escaped Xibalba, she was led out by the messenger owls."

Talina studied every aspect of the ballcourt, every dressed-and-set stone, the empty temple above it, the leaden sky overhead.

"Kind of shy on owls."

Rocket turned a shade of black, patterned by angular chevrons in the infrared. A combination of sadness, frustration, and defeat.

"Yeah," Talina told him, "I know how you feel." A beat. "Pus in a bucket, you think I want to stay here?"

Rocket made a gargling sound of confusion, questioning why with his patterns of yellow, green, and pink.

"Because if I go back, what if I can't determine reality from the dream? I *would* have shot Sian. You get it? I really don't know what the hell I am. Human? Quetzal? That *Way* glyph says I've been transformed, but into what?"

Rocket snapped his jaws in a gesture of confusion.

"See, you think it's all well and good. But you were always a hunter, Rocket. Me, I'm a killer. Which is different. Just ask Demon."

Her old quetzal appeared from behind the calabash tree, flashing his hide in sky blue and orange patterns. "Yes, a killer."

Fixing on Rocket she added, "Which means that even if I find a guide, I may be going back as the worst possible thing: a monster."

67

Dortmund didn't sleep. The words *a polluted hybrid* kept repeating in his brain as he tossed and turned on the bunk. Adding to his woes, every time he'd start to finally nod off, and the outrage, confusion, and dismay would begin to fade into sleep, he'd roll onto his wounded arm.

Not only did the pain bring him rudely awake, but with it came the reminder of his infection.

What the hell am I going to do?

He had just become his own worst nightmare. The fact filled him with a despair so devastating he wanted to die. His paper entitled *Controlling the Genetic Damage of Hybridization in Re-Wilded Areas* had led to the culling of more than ten thousand zebras, wildebeests, bongos, rhinoceroses, and cheetahs. The action had left the evolutionists howling and enraged, but he'd had the Board behind him. Genetic purity had to be maintained to preserve the species in their original and natural condition.

And now I'm a hybrid?

Not that he believed in God—or in any permutation of a conscious universe that would act so capriciously—but it smacked of such a cruel irony it couldn't be random.

The mere thought of what his professional colleagues would say if they found out left his face burning. Let alone the joyous abandon of his bitter environmentalist enemies: "See! Weisbacher himself is now a living contradiction of his so-called 'moral imperative.'" And "Cull yourself, Weisbacher! Come on, put a gun to your head for the betterment of the general population."

Dortmund Weisbacher had always believed he could endure anything. That his bitter years battling in academia had prepared him for any kind of conflict. What it had not prepared him for was how to face the future as a living joke.

He couldn't countenance the idea of switching sides,

becoming an environmentalist. Would not see the glee expressed in his longtime adversaries' faces.

Nor could he ever go back and claim, with any moral authority, to espouse the conservationist cause.

A man could only take so much. Several times during the night, he'd hunched into a ball beneath the blanket and broken into muffled sobs lest any of the others hear.

Adding to his misery, any twinge, pain, irritation, or itch automatically had to be the insidious result of the quetzal infection. When he wasn't brooding about his lost virtue and purity, he trembled at the thought of what the alien molecules were doing not only to his body, but to his marvelous brain.

The mere chance that Dortmund Weisbacher might end up as sullen, vile, and uncouth as Talina Perez or that horrible waif, Kylee, filled him with dread. They'd told him that the TriNA changed the brain. And he need look no further than Talina Perez, lying in a coma as the hideous little molecules ate her neocortex.

That will be your fate.

Would he recognize the first invasive tendrils as they began to steal his intellect?

Alzheimer's, dementia, Creutzfeldt-Jakob disease, and so many other mental disorders had been vanquished in the last century that it was inconceivable to imagine that he might end up a vegetable. Not that it could get much worse, but in this benighted wilderness, thirty light-years from Solar System, he had no way to download his thoughts into a database for future access. All the wondrous implants in his head might be nothing more than useless metal and ceramic.

As that knowledge permeated his consciousness, a panic unlike anything he'd ever known possessed him. This was worse than just facing quetzals. Worse than the knowledge of impending death. This was the loss of himself. Of all that he'd accomplished, of all that he understood and had learned.

Vixen!

It was a survey and exploration ship. It had been designed to download from implants. That, now more than ever, was the key.

He blinked his eyes open, seeing the first graying of the windows. Morning was coming. He had to act. He might have been desperate before this, but it was nothing compared to the resolve that now pumped with each beat of his heart.

This was more than just mere survival.

Dortmund slipped his legs out from under the blanket. In the bunks across the room, Mosadek and Dushane slept.

Dressing quietly, so as not to disturb them, he emerged into a dreary and wet morning. Low clouds hung in the sky, and across the distance the drizzling mist seemed to drift down in rippling patterns.

The wet air carried the alien perfume of distant trees and vines. Was it just his imagination, or did his sense of smell seem better?

Quetzal molecules? Already at work in his nose? Just the thought of it sent him into a near fugue. He hurried along the side of the dome, headed for the doors.

Turned his head at a flicker of movement. What was that over behind the aircars? He'd swear he'd seen . . . No, had to be a product of the misty rain. Optical illusion. Nothing broke the pattern of the stone behind the vehicles.

Rounding the curve of the dome, he undid the lock and stepped inside. Ordering the lights on low, he crossed the main room, eased down the hallway, and into the sleeping quarters in the back.

In the faint glow from the hallway he could see Talina, no more aware of reality than a log. The urchin, Kylee, slept next to her under the blanket.

Gaze upon Perez, you wretch, for there lies your future.

His beautiful brain, turned into comatose mush. The thought sickened him.

Instead he turned to the bed where Trish Monagan curled on her side, breath purling between her lips. The spill of auburn hair made a swirl on the pillow.

You can do this.

Dortmund stepped over, made a face, and reached for Trish's belt. Lifting it from the end table where it had been carefully laid, he settled his fingers on the pistol where it rested in its holster. At the mere touch of the weapon, he jerked his hand back. As if the deadly thing were electric.

It's the only way. You do this, or all that you are, the endless years of study and struggle, everything you have been, is gone.

Taking a deep breath, he forced his fingers around the cold grip and tugged the weapon free. "Lights," he ordered, filling the room with brilliance.

Trish and Kylee jerked awake, both sitting up in bed. Talina Perez remained dead to the world.

Trish fixed immediately on the pistol that Dortmund pointed at her. She asked, "Have you lost your mind?"

"Not yet. Though I have come to the conclusion that it's inevitable. Get up. Get dressed. We're leaving. You are flying me to Port Authority."

Trish chuckled; the last thing he expected her to do. What the hell was humorous about the circumstances?

Trish climbed out of bed. Dortmund tried not to notice her young body as she dressed. Glancing out the window, she said, "Um, Doc? You noticed it's raining outside?"

"Of course. I came from the dormitory."

"Well, we're not flying anywhere." She turned to Talina, asking, "Hey, Tal? You with us this morning?"

Then Trish tried the woman's eyes, lifting a lid to find a vacant gaze. Something about Talina's eye seemed different, darker, larger.

Trish muttered, "Shit. But she's breathing okay. Maybe if we get enough soup into her."

"Officer Monagan, do you remember I'm holding a pistol on you?"

"You gonna shoot her?" Kylee asked. She'd slipped off the far side of Talina's bed.

"If she doesn't immediately move herself out to the aircar and head back for Port Authority, I will."

"Why Port Authority?"

"So I can get to *Vixen* where I can download my brain, save my thoughts and notes while I still can. Before the quetzal molecules turn me into a mindless wreck like Talina."

"Download your brain?" The woman seemed completely stumped and not at all concerned about the gun he held.

"From the implants. I need to place all of my thoughts

on record before the quetzal molecules begin to destroy them. *Vixen* has the equipment that can read and store my intellect for future reference and study."

Trish lifted a skeptical eyebrow. "And what makes your brain so fricking important?"

"Because of a lifetime of training and research. I have unique insights. This is the first Earth-like planet. Everything we're doing here is historic. Especially meeting with the first sentient extraterrestrial intelligences. As the leading planetologist in Solar System, my work here will become a benchmark. Generations of scholars will pore over every nuance of our interaction and failure on Capella III."

"See, that's the part I don't get." Trish straightened from Talina's bed. "You've only been here for days. Kylee tells me you don't know a bem from skewer, and that you'd probably walk under a mundo tree just to look at the bones."

"Enough talk. Now walk." He liked it. It sounded tough and witty. "Let's go. Or, damn it, I will shoot."

"Shoot me, and who flies?"

"How about I shoot Talina instead? Save her the misery of her infected body rotting away?"

Dear God, maybe he should. Though, eventually, her fate would be his. Would anyone have the mercy to end it for him? Or would they just keep his mindless corpse? A scientific specimen to be documented as it slowly deteriorated?

Trish growled, "I'll download your brain. I'm going to take a survival knife. Chop it out of your skull. Put it in a bottle in Cheng's lab with a label on the outside that says 'idiot.'"

Nevertheless Trish headed for the door, adding over her shoulder, "Watch the pressure you put on that trigger, Doc. It goes off at four pounds."

Dortmund was vaguely aware that Kylee was following cautiously behind, her alien-blue eyes taking in every move.

"Of course you wouldn't understand," he elaborated as they walked through the main room. "The reason downloading is so important? It's because I have a grasp of the larger context. I built the department of planetology at Tubingen. I first proved the Masterson hypothesis. Laid the groundwork for planetary exploration protocol, which Radcek—may he rot in hell—totally disregarded. The reason why my reports and observations matter is because of the intellectual framework I put them in. How they will fit into the research paradigm for the future."

They were outside now. The drizzle had slowed to a fine mist. The sky was lightening.

Trish stopped in front of the aircar, pointing up at the sky. "You really want to fly in that?"

"I do."

"What about Talina?"

"What about her?"

"Raya wanted us to wait until morning. This will break in an hour or two. Then we can load her."

"We go now."

"You're a real piece of work, aren't you, Doc?" And with that, Trish spread her arms. "So, go ahead. Shoot."

"What? Don't you see this pistol?"

"Yeah." An amused challenge lay behind the woman's green eyes. "But there's only two people here who can fly an aircar. Me and Talina. Tal's out of it. Which leaves me."

No wonder she'd walked out so easily. He couldn't threaten Talina anymore. It was just him and her in a battle of wills.

"You'd let me shoot you rather than fly?"

"Hey, I had to belly crawl for Benteen because it was that or he'd kill me, and I've been hating myself since. But you? I'm calling your bluff. You shoot me? Sure, I'm dead. But then what? Yvette or Shig will kill you for killing me. And then where's that sacred brain of yours? It's blown out of your skull in little tiny bits by a bullet. Unless, of course, you kill Shig and Yvette first. Which leaves you right where you started with Tal comatose and Kylee there to keep you company."

"Don't push me!" He gestured with the pistol in what he hoped was a threatening manner.

"For such a supposedly smart guy, Doc, you're really stupid."

Some part of his awareness cued up on the swelling stone on the backside of the aircar. It took a conscious effort to switch his attention from Monagan to the impossibility of flowing bedrock. For a moment his stunned mind couldn't process what he was seeing as the rock bunched and rose into a mound. Elongated. Impossible as it seemed, the living stone took on the shape of a quetzal. Three black eyes gleamed atop a towering, wedge-shaped head. The variegated sandstone patterns shaded into a bright crimson, the beast's collar flaring out in a dazzling sheet.

Dortmund gaped, felt his heart skip. Only the aircar separated it from Trish's back.

"What?" Trish asked, amused. "You look like you just stuck your finger in an electrical outlet. You're out of your league, professor. Now hand me the—"

He saw Trish's eyes widen as he shoved the pistol out and yanked on the trigger.

The thunderous bang, the way the gun bucked in his hand, absolutely terrified him. Almost made him drop the wicked thing. Eyes clamped tight, he jerked the trigger. Again. And again. Over and over. Like a thing alive, the pistol kept trying to leap out of his hand with each discharge. His ears rang from the thunder.

He continued to shoot until the gun clicked. Only then did he open his eyes, aware that Trish had dropped to the ground. To his amazement, the quetzal just stood there, having taken round after round.

In a fantastically fast blur, the alien beast turned and ran. Like nothing Dortmund had ever seen, it sped off across the sandstone, headed for the safety of the drainage. As it did it turned a glowing white, the legs seeming to vanish in their speed.

All Dortmund could do was stand there, panting for breath, knees locked, his hands trembling as they gripped the pistol. He couldn't swallow, felt like throwing up.

The impossibility of what he'd just survived, just done, left him rattled down to his bones. If he hadn't seen the sandstone turn into a quetzal, he'd never have believed it. The thing had been huge. How had it hidden like that behind the aircar?

And it had been about to grab Trish. The mouth had been opening, the thing had been on the verge of killing her. Would have eaten her alive before his eyes.

Trish's "Oh, fuck" brought him back to the here and

now. He glanced down, realized she was sprawled, her left leg at an odd angle.

She tried to rise, flopped back down on the sandstone. Her hair was hanging around her face; something about her posture looked broken.

His reeling mind finally fixed on the blood leaking out of her bent left thigh. How the hell had she broken her leg?

Some part of him heard the shouts as Shig and Yvette came running from the dormitory. The rain was picking up, washing Trish's blood from the leg of her coverall to stain the sandstone.

Then he lowered the pistol, stared at the weapon in disbelief, and the real horror began to set in.

68

Dan Wirth hurried down the main avenue toward Inga's. At the same time, he was trying to process what he'd just seen. Young Smit Hazen, Benteen's supposed head of security. Shot down in front of the admin building door. Benteen had just walked the guy out, Shankar Tallisvilli at his side. Allison had been standing in the doorway behind them.

"I will not countenance disobedience," Benteen had declared before the small crowd that had gathered in the street. "When I give an order, it will be obeyed. Promptly and to the letter."

His arm a blur, the scorpion had drawn, shot poor Hazen in the back of the head. The guy had dropped like a bag of bones. "Chief Officer Tallisvilli. You will immediately bring these people to my office." Benteen had handed the guy a list.

Tallisvilli—looking like he'd just swallowed a moldy prune—had gestured to four of the remaining security guys. All of them *Turalon* transportees. Weapons in their hands, they'd trotted off down the avenue.

Dan had watched Benteen smile as he turned to Allison, and dropping an arm around her waist, he'd led her back into the building.

So what am I going to do about it?

Damn it, it wasn't over between him and Benteen. Not by a long shot. But he needed more time, a chance to figure out how to take out that deadly son of a bitch without getting any more of his people killed.

The problem was, Benteen moved too fast, was always a couple of steps ahead. Every time Dan began to grasp how to deal with the wily scorpion, his adversary changed the game.

Dan's mood fit the weather: The day was overcast, clouds hanging low and threatening drizzle. The people he met on the street were subdued. Everyone was waiting, like the calm before the storm.

Dan had felt the like before, most notably in Hong Kong before the '46 riots. And whereas in those times Dan had prepared himself to exploit the chaos to his advantage, he was now on the other side. If Port Authority erupted into a war zone, it was going to play hell with his businesses. Might mean some of his best marks could end up dead in the violence.

He glanced around at the familiar sites as he passed the assay office and glassworks. In the last year it had hit home to him just how fragile life at Port Authority was. Everyone had their part to play, including the toilet-sucking family types like those three slits from Hell he had to deal with while building the damned school.

Who the fuck was Tamarland Benteen to come screw it all up by taking names, threatening livelihoods, driving Mosadek and Dushane—who at least had common sense—out into exile? Not to mention Dan's humiliation. It infuriated him. No one could just waltz into his life, take over, steal his woman, kill his best goon, and all the while Dan had to lick the fucker's ass and like it.

Intolerable.

Dan smiled in a failed attempt to humor himself. In this case survival meant creating new alliances. This would cost him. But better to slide into bed with an enemy you knew and could negotiate with if it meant taking Benteen down.

Vik Schemenski reported that he had seen the Supervisor enter the tavern. Dan loathed—absolutely loathed—having to do this. But he was nothing if not pragmatic—especially if this is what it took to win.

Call it the cap to a really shitty day. Dan hated waking up alone, and that ratfucker Benteen had sent one of his security guys after Allison the night before. She'd accompanied the guy to the admin building, probably shared Benteen's bed, and was by his side for the execution. Willing ally? Cunning survivor? Or desperately afraid for her life?

What was it about him and women these days?

He'd seen Allison's stunned and sick look when Benteen shot Hazen. A couple of years older, she'd still grown up with the guy. Clever as she was turning out to be at playing both sides, how was Dan to know that as Benteen's power grew, she wouldn't figure that life as the scorpion's woman wasn't a better bet than shilling at The Jewel? Especially in light of the fact that she'd changed over the last couple of months since she'd cut the drugs, like some switch had been thrown? He wasn't sure who Allison was anymore.

By the time he reached Inga's front door, the rain started in earnest. He nodded to two of the clay miners who sat on the bench out front, stepped in, and walked to the head of the stairs leading down into the tavern.

At the bar, Tompzen and Michegan, in full battle armor, but with helmets slung, stood at their places, guarding Aguila's back. The woman, characteristically, sat in Talina Perez's old chair.

Canny slit that she was, Kalico had canceled her people's R&R and sent them home along with the shuttle. Better to have them and the craft out of harm's way. She'd retreated to her dormitory with ten of her marines. The building wasn't the most defensible in Port Authority, but with tech her people could hold off a small army, and no one was going to mess with her.

He stopped a couple of seats down the bar from Aguila, just close enough that he could hear what she was saying to Inga. In doing so, he caught Kalen Tompzen's eye and gave the man a knowing nod. Tompzen was watching him warily, a trace of uncertainty rising behind his façade of an expression.

"So, what do you hear?" Aguila asked as Inga headed her way with a full mug.

The woman set the mug on the bar with a thunk. "Give that a try. As to what I hear? Benteen's going to make a prison out of the repair shop out at the mine. Word is that he's arrested two of the Wild Ones who came in to trade chamois hides and gold dust. Guess they're in restraints and piled into the back of a storeroom in the admin building."

"I've seen his people wandering around. Heard they're making lists." Aguila tried the beer, smacked her lips. "Wow. That's powerful."

"Yeah, I been saving that one for a time when people

needed a little more punch to the gut. I think that's now."
Inga rubbed the bar with her towel. "These lists, everyone's talking about them."

"Census." Aguila arched an eyebrow. "Can't begin
managing people until you know who they are, where they
live, and what they own. Not so long ago it would have been
one of the first things I would have done myself."

Inga mimicked the raised eyebrow.

Aguila took another sip. "I wonder how accurate the
census is. If I were a Donovanian, I'd be lying through my
teeth."

"Yeah, well, word is that Hazen's letting a lot of stuff
slide. That he's having second thoughts about being Chief
Officer. Rumor is that Wejee Tolland, Cal Umunga, and
Ko Lang slipped away in the night. Left word that they'd
trust themselves to the bush before they'd be part of Benteen's plans."

"That must have Benteen up in arms. His people are already dribbling away." Kalico fingered her beer. "I can only
talk to my marines on battle com. My town com's been dead
for hours now. Not a word. I thought at first that Benteen had
my personal frequency cut off. So I had Tompzen test it. Radio's down. No one's seen Two Spot. Something tells me that
Benteen pulled the plug on the public broadcast system."

That was news. Dan hadn't heard about the radio.

"Bet he's monitoring it, though. Waiting to hear what
the people say."

"Might be a psychological ploy. Keeping the tower
down is going to seriously affect the Wild Ones."

Inga cocked a skeptical head. "I would have figured
you'd have washed your hands of us, left us to sort it out.
You could always come back and pick up the pieces."

"This goes to shit? It's not just Port Authority going
down. It'll take Corporate Mine with it."

"So you could march in there with your marines and
shoot Benteen's ass at any moment."

"If it comes to that." She paused. "But if I take PA, I
won't give it back."

Dan perked up at that. By God's ugly ass, she was thinking the same way he was. All but the "not giving it back"
part.

And with that Inga headed his way, demanding, "What'll you have?"

"Beer. Whatever kind the Supervisor's drinking." He slapped a two-SDR gold coin on the bar.

Of course Aguila would be thinking ahead. She had already delegated most of her marines—in full combat armor—to protect the critical assets. That included the hospital with its labs, the foundry, Sheyela Smith's electronic shop, and the PA shuttle. She was right. Corporate Mine couldn't survive without Port Authority's technicians, medical staff, and artisans.

But then Dan had only made the mistake of underestimating Aguila once.

Accepting his beer, Dan raised it in salute to Inga, turned, and gave Tompzen a wink. "Private Tompzen. Good to see you looking so fit. I need to have a talk with the Supervisor." He lifted his free hand high, as if in surrender. "I swear, I come only as an interested party to the proceedings, bearing no ill will."

"Ma'am?" Tompzen asked. In all the world, only Dan could appreciate the man's uneasy dilemma.

She turned, gave Dan a distasteful wrinkle of the nose, and nodded. "It's all right, Kalen," she told her marine, and gestured to the adjacent chair. "Fancy seeing you. I would have figured you were squirreled away somewhere filling out your census form."

Dan took the chair. "Thought you might like an update. Benteen just shot Smitty Hazen for lack of vigor in the prosecution of his duties. Shankar Tallisvilli, one of the *Turalon* guys, is now Chief Officer, whatever the hell that means. I guess Smitty had too much empathy for the locals. Tallisvilli, he's more of a bootlicking follow-the-orders kind of guy. Not the sort to let any squeamish identification with the common folk jeopardize his safety and well-being."

"And what are you doing here? According to my sources, you're already under Benteen's thumb. Heard he even seduced your paramour."

"When you were cut up by mobbers, did I drop by to rub salt in the wounds?" Dan gave her a knowing glower. "We've had our differences, Supervisor. We worked it out. Mutual assured destruction. Masterfully played on your part, I might add. We both profit by not taking action against the other."

"And now?"

"Not that we'd ever be friends, mind you, but we seem to have a common problem. Before all of this came down, I tried to warn Shig, and the guy just didn't get it. Maybe you will."

The expression on her face might have been a reflection of some crawly feeling of distaste that was running across her skin.

She said, "I considered myself warned when I discovered the guy's identity up on *Freelander*. But for Shig, I'd have had my people put a bullet in him. How'd you miss him, given your supposed expertise at analyzing a mark?"

"Must be something about not having the historical implants, or maybe not being intimate with all the ugly facts when it comes to Corporate backstabbing. But let us not get too carried away with who knew what and when. We can cut each other's throats after the scorpion is no longer stinging both of us in the ass."

He kept his gaze flat and unemotional. She gave him the benefit of a wary smile. "Very well, state your proposition. But know right off the bat, I'm not marching in with my marines and gunning the guy down in that office."

"Yet." He filled in the word she'd throttled by the quirking of her lips.

He caught the faintest flicker of acknowledgment behind her eyes, and said, "I'll assume that your files are full of the guy's history. History can be rather flat. For example: It's one thing to read about the Hong Kong riots. Lots of dull statements of who did what and when. It's another take entirely if you were on the street watching fifty thousand people being blown apart, the body parts scraped up with front-end loaders, and fire hoses blasting the blood and guts off the pavement."

"That wasn't my jurisdiction."

"The point I'm making is that I've sat across the table from the guy. Not much scares me. Not even you, and believe me, with the possible exception of Perez, you might be the most dangerous woman I've ever met. Benteen?

What kind of cucking frazy does he have to be to send a shiver down *my* spine?"

"What's your endgame, Wirth?"

"I want it back like it was. So much so that I'd spend the rest of my life letting those witches Hmong, Oshanti, and Dushku chew my ass about that damn school."

"They're arrested," a voice called.

Dan turned in the chair to see Step Allenovich come tromping toward them. The big man was dressed in damp quetzal hide, his wide-brimmed hat slanted at an angle on his blocky head and dripping water. A rifle was slung from one shoulder; his rainbow-patterned jacket hung open, flashing colors. The man's boots were streaked with red mud.

"Arrested?" Aguila asked.

"Yeah." Step motioned the marines back as they moved to block his way. "Gimme a break. Shit's coming down, and I need to talk to Kalico."

Aguila gave her guards the desist signal. "Where you been?"

"Hanging out in places Benteen's goons wouldn't think to look. Soon as the arrests started, people have been slipping into the hauler shop on the north end of town. So far there's about thirty. More are coming. Everybody's armed. Getting ready to take back PA." Step unslung his rifle and laid it on the bar with a clunk. "Inga! Whiskey."

"Coming up, Step."

The big exobiologist turned, lips pressed thin. "Hmong, Oshanti, Dushku, Bernie Monson, Ruben Miranda, Mac Hanson, Pavel Tomashev, Lee Halston, those names ring any bells?"

"Most of the critical businesses." Dan frowned.

"The most influential people in the community," Kalico noted.

"Yeah, and Sheyela Smith, Pamlico Jones, Lawson, and Montoya are on the list but can't be found."

"They're at Corporate Mine." Aguila smiled wryly. "I've got them working on the aerial tram."

"When are they due back?" Dan asked.

"Couple of days." She lifted a brow. "So, Benteen has

taken a collection of the community's more prominent individuals. Where'd he take them? Admin dome?"

"For the time being," Step said. "But he had Muley Mitchman send for one of the buses that's parked out at the mine. Now, what would he need with a bus? Where would he want to haul a bunch of people to?"

"His new prison out at the clay pit." Dan filled in the pieces.

Aguila said, "So he's rounding up the potential ringleaders, going to make his pitch. Anyone who doesn't immediately toe the line is going out to the prison."

"That's clap-trapping crazy," Step growled. "That shuts down half the town's business. What's he think he's doing?"

"He doesn't care," Dan said softly. "He's bet the house on a single roll of the dice. Win it, or lose it all."

"Let me check something." Aguila squinted slightly, apparently concentrating on her implants, doing some kind of research. "Yeah, that's what I thought. Not good."

"What?" Dan asked, wishing once again that he'd been able to afford implants back in the day.

"I vaguely remembered that Benteen defused a revolt in Indonesia back before the turn of the century. Over the period of a week, he took a number of Min Tai See's ministers. Abducted some of them right off the street. Boardmember Shayne requested Min Tai See's support for a vote in the Board. Despite the abductions, he voted in opposition to her will. Made some sort of quip during the proceedings that while one could always find another minister, a person had only one sense of integrity."

"How'd that work out for him?"

"The scorpion left the murdered ministers in various public locations around Jakarta, Kuala Lumpur, and Singapore. New ministers were appointed, and within the week, Min Tai See's eldest son, wife, and two grandchildren were blown up in their penthouse apartment high above Kuala Lumpur. Boardmember Shayne reportedly asked old man See if children were as easy to replace as Ministers. His response isn't in the record, but he voted in her bloc thereafter."

Step lifted his glass of whiskey, slugged down a swallow, and said, "So, the lesson is, we move on Benteen, he might just go ahead and murder people rather than give up?"

"That's his profile," Aguila agreed.

"More than that, that's his personality." Dan fingered his glass of beer. "And he's got Allison as well as the rest of the people he's rounded up so far."

"Concern from the psychopath?" Aguila asked.

"Just because I'm a conniving, self-serving weasel in your eyes doesn't mean I'm stupid. It would really piss me off to lose her, bad enough that he's threatening my town. The son of a bitch beat me at my own game." Dan gave her his best winning smile. "As you know, Supervisor, I tend to obsess over grudges."

Dan saw Szong Sczui as the man came hurrying down the tavern's central aisle. The second they fixed on Step, the farmer's eyes showed immediate relief. Sczui lived in a fortified dome down on the southern edge of the fields and within spitting distance of the bush. Somehow he, his wife, and three kids managed to hang on out on the other side of the wire, thrive in fact, and produce some of the best harvests.

Now the man, rifle dangling from one hand, dressed in crest-scale-decorated quetzal hide, chamois, and heavy boots came thumping forward, only to be intercepted by the marines. Rain dripped from his outfit.

"Hey," he called. "We got a shitload of trouble."

"Step to the end of the line, old friend." Step turned, his whiskey in hand.

Sczui glanced nervously at the two marines, adding, "Where's the guards?"

"What guards?"

"The ones on the gates. I just came through the south gate. Not a fricking person in sight. Not even locked, just latched. So I trot along the western perimeter, and I find the west gate by the aircar field is unmanned. Like, abandoned."

Step made a face. "Shit. Hazen's dead. Tolland, Umunga, and Lang have skipped for the bush. That shithead Benteen's got all of whatever security that's left rounding up hostages. The stupid fool's left us wide open."

"Worse than that," Sczui said, making a face. "Mother and me." He always called his wife "Mother." "We got up this morning, figured to walk the kids in for school, and we don't get fifty meters, and we got quetzal tracks. Three sets. One sniffed around my tool shed, a big one. So what do I do? I get on the radio. Try to raise Two Spot. Nothing.

"So Mother and I go out with the rifles, trying to figure where they went. The tracks headed off up through Ruben Miranda's pepper plants. Like I said. Three. Trotting along side by side. Who the hell ever heard of three of those bastards running in a pack? They're supposed to be solitary. And now the damn gates are unguarded? And who the hell's monitoring the damn motion sensors?"

He paused, expression falling before adding, "Worse, it's raining. And it's gonna rain a whole lot harder tonight."

"Quetzal weather," Step said, already tense, his hand on his pistol. "We've got to get people on the gates."

"How long do you think they've been unmanned?" Aguila wondered, her own right hand dropping to her pistol butt. She must have accessed her battle com—a communications Benteen couldn't squelch, because she ordered, "Abu Sassi. Detail Miso to the south gate, Finnegan to the west. Put Paco on the east gate, and Wan Xi Gow on the north. Beat feet, people! We got a problem."

Step exhaled, grateful gaze going to Aguila. "Supervisor, anything I ever said about you, I take it all back."

"Good, because I still haven't forgotten that once upon a time you were going to crawl right up over this bar and blow my brains out."

Allenovich grinned. "Yeah, well, Tal stopped me in time, didn't she?"

"Wonder what else our new Director has let slip through the cracks?" Dan glanced back and forth. "Fact is, we really have to deal with him. Now. Before some really disastrous shit lands on our heads."

"Szong," Step told the farmer. "Get yourself and your family back to your place and button up tight. We'll blow the all-clear as soon as we've got this dealt with."

"Yeah, Step." The farmer fixed his gaze on Aguila. "Tell your people on the gates that they're appreciated, Supervisor. Mother and me, we got some sweet corn coming up. That's for you and your marines as soon as we can pick it. No charge."

No charge? Shit. Sczui's sweet corn was one of the most prized delicacies in PA.

The man gave a bow, whirled, and left no doubt of his haste as he headed for the steps.

"Three?" Step asked nervously.

"Maybe he saw the same quetzal's tracks in three places." Dan took a swallow of his beer, that old premonition of brewing trouble rising down in the pit of his stomach.

"Not Sczui. He's been too long in the bush and knows his shit." Step's gaze had tightened. "He says three, he means three. Something's up." He made a face, concentrating. Then said, "Damn it, com's still dead."

He started to walk away. Stopped. "Screw vacuum, if I go charging over there to sound the alert, Benteen's gonna fucking arrest me on the spot."

As he said it, Aguila went tense, hearing something in her battle com. Then she asked, "What have you got, Wan?" A silence as she listened. Then the woman's expression went firm. "Lock down the gate. Look frosty, people! Helmets on, weapons hot. Full tech."

Flashing her eyes at Dan and Step, she said, "Wan found the north gate open. Three sets of quetzal tracks. Fresh. Headed right through. Said there was blood in the road not twenty meters inside the gate. They're already inside."

"Dear God," Step cried through an exhale. "The whole town's wide open! I've got to get to the school."

With that he grabbed his rifle off the bar and left at a run, yelling, "Quetzals in the compound!"

Inga's erupted into chaos as people dropped everything and charged for the stairs.

69

Eight people? That's all that First Officer Hazen, and then Tallisvilli, had been able to round up? Tamarland studied them where they sat around the conference table, hands bound before them. Rather than worry, he saw various degrees of smoldering anger.

The three women, Hmong, Oshanti, and Dushku, seemed the least cowed. That was surprising given that all three of them had families. It amazed him when people didn't understand that he already held the keys to their defeat.

Bernie Monson, who ran the clay mine north of town, looked the most nervous. Mac Hanson operated the foundry. He and Lee Halston, the logger, both seemed irritated more than anything else. When he met Pavel Tomashev's gaze, or Ruben Miranda's, it was to see a seething anger.

"Too bad," Tam said aloud, arms crossed.

"What's too bad?" Oshanti asked, her hard black eyes showing not a hint of give.

"The number of you that I will have to kill."

"You're not very smart, are you?" Ruben Miranda asked.

"Smarter than you," Tam told him. "I'm not the one sitting in chains, unarmed, and awaiting execution."

He paused. Smiled. Gave them a moment to consider, then said, "But take a moment. Think it through. It doesn't have to end in death and mayhem. Actually, nothing much really has to change for any of you. We can come to an understanding here, and the choice isn't so tough. Not really."

"How's that?" Oshanti remained the prickly one.

"It's just a change of administration. Sure, Shig and Yvette were nice people, but they really didn't have the backbone needed to make this place thrive. Now, hear me out. By making some tough choices, we can raise the colony's chances for survival. You're here because I think each of you is smart enough to understand the advantages of a focused, top-down administration."

"With you at the top." Miranda snorted his derision.

"Oh, come on. Port Authority is run as a half-assed, inefficient, stumbling, and catch-as-catch-can disaster. Half the streetlights in the town don't work. The streets are paved with gravel. It's a disorganized mess."

"We like it that way." Halston lifted a shoulder in disdain.

"You should just leave now," Friga Dushku told him. "Save yourself while you've got the chance."

"Want to explain that?"

"Yeah," Tomashev told him insolently. "By now half the town is organizing down at the hauler shop. My bet is that people are headed home as we speak to get their rifles and stock up on ammo."

"They'll be coming for us," Hanson agreed. "My advice? You don't want to be here when they arrive."

"*Vixen*'s up in orbit," Monson said. "So, I guess there's no escape in that direction. I'd say your best bet is the bush. Maybe one of the abandoned research bases. Sort of a poetic justice in that."

"You're fucked," Oshanti told him.

In a lightning move, Tam drew his pistol. Oshanti was staring down the pistol's bore before she could blink.

"It would be a shame if your children had to grow up without their mother. But, you see, I don't give a damn about the little shits. Your life is as meaningless to me as a fly in a window."

He paused. "Do they even have flies here?"

The woman went pale, a faint sweat breaking out on her upper lip. She swallowed hard. "It's a good trade."

"What?"

"My life for the future of Port Authority."

"After you shoot Amal, you'll have to shoot me," Friga Dushku told him in an icy voice.

"And me," Ruben Miranda stated.

"All of us," Sian Hmong insisted, staring at him through stony eyes.

Tomashev said, "With us dead, you don't have a chance. The rest will string you up by the thumbs, and when you're half-crazy and screaming, they'll haul you off to the south and throw your ass under a nightmare's mundo tree."

"I don't need to shoot all of you, just a few," Tam told them. "Who's first?"

"Me." "I am." "Shoot me." "Me first," they all chimed in at once.

Clever ploy. Tam chose, picked Sian Hmong as the woman most likely to break. She shivered as he pointed the pistol her way. The woman took a deep breath. Braced herself for it, and nodded that he should go ahead.

Tam hesitated. The last thing he needed was a martyr.

"Nice try. But I have a better idea. You're all going to live. Wait. Amend that. You'll be alive if you can call it that. I think you'll spend the next year of your lives chained to a post in solitary confinement out at the mine. It's going to be your families who pay the price for your disobedience. Most of you have children. Spouses. Good friends. People you care about. Let's kill them first. One at a time, starting tomorrow."

"How's that?" Lee Halston asked, the first sign of uncertainty in his eyes.

"Tomorrow I will bring out one each of your children. You will watch them die. Be able to look them in the eyes, see that last moment of absolute fear as they plead with you to save them."

"Works for me," Amal Oshanti said, a wry smile on her lips. "You shoot a kid, you won't last out the day. Let alone get us to the mine and this new prison you think you're building."

"Brave words," Tamarland told them. What the hell? Even Halston was nodding, the resolve back.

"You don't get it," Bernie Monson told him. "People were suspicious about your census shit. The fact that you had those *Turalon* flunkies start arresting people? The rest of the town's alerted. Waiting to see what happens. You harm a single one of us, you'll never set foot outside of this building again."

"We're not Corporate," Ruben Miranda told him. "Me? I work on the other side of the fence. Farming. I wake up each day knowing Donovan can kill me. You come here, think you can run us the way the Corporation runs those mindless drones back in Solar System? We don't need you, *amigo*. We got each other."

"So shoot us," Tomashev said. "Best way to be sure you're dead by sundown."

"We have a saying," Dushku added. "On Donovan, stupidity is a death sentence."

"It's the prison," Tamarland decided. Damn it, they might have a point. Disappeared was a lot better than dead. It created uncertainty in the community.

He walked to the door, calling, "Chief Officer? I need that bus ready to transport prisoners."

"Yes, sir," Tallisvilli, standing by the door, called back. "Um, sir? Thought you might like to know. We've got people on the roofs across the way."

"Well? It's starting to rain. Maybe they're fixing leaks."

Allison had stepped out of his office, was listening, some deep knowledge smoldering behind her troubled blue eyes.

"Nobody fixes roofs with optically scoped rifles, Director." Tallisvilli slowly shook his head and turned back to the window.

"Tam?" Allison said. "None of your hostages so much as budged, did they?"

"It's the first move in a long game. They're still thinking they have a chance."

"So do you," Allison said. "Go to the radio room, Tam. Call Torgussen to set the shuttle down close to the fence. Get out while you can."

"You taking their side?"

"No." She gave him a sober gaze. "I'm just trying to keep the bloodshed to a minimum."

"What the hell is wrong with you people?"

"Try as you might, Tam, you can't trap the wind in a can. If you can get *Vixen* to send a shuttle, at least you'll have a chance."

"No one is going to attempt any sort of silly insurgency, let alone free my sulking future collaborators." He stepped back, nodded at the guard, and opened the conference room door.

Conversation stopped. All eyes went to him as he strode over, reached in a pocket, and laid a square lump of what looked like light gray clay in the center of the table.

"Anyone know what that is?" he asked mildly.

"Yeah," Monson said warily. "Magtex. Enough to blow this side of the dome off."

"Very good." Tamarland reached out again, using his thumb and forefinger to drive what looked like a small and decorative pin into the block's center. "That, ladies and gentlemen, is a detonator. A clever device that's keyed to my personal frequency. I need only send a command through my implants and you all go away."

He definitely had their attention now.

"That's insurance. Just in case any of your misguided friends try something foolish, like what they'd call a rescue. Oh, and please don't try to fiddle with it, even if you could get loose from your chairs. The slightest vibration could set it off. And, well, as the sign by the mine gate says, 'Caution! Explosives! Safety First.'"

He turned, seeing where Allison watched from the doorway.

As he locked the door behind him and headed for his office, she asked, "What if someone sneezes in there? Jars the table?"

"It's safe. It only goes off if I send the signal."

"And what if someone outside tries something?"

"Well, for the sake of those people in there, we'd better hope they don't."

70

Kylee watched from the relative safety of the other side of the table. For a girl who'd lived her life entirely among family at Mundo Base, it had come as a surprise when Mark Talbot appeared out of the forest. Then she had suffered her injury and the subsequent flight to Port Authority. Drugged as she'd been, she had never really absorbed the full impact of being around strangers.

Afterward, back at Mundo, the shuttle had come and Rocket had been murdered. Another shuttle had come, filling her world with unknown people she never really got to meet, and certainly didn't trust.

Corporate Mine had terrified her with its hundreds of foreign humans. She'd felt lost and bewildered. Now she was trapped at Rork Springs Base with more strangers.

Shig, she instinctively liked. Yvette was another story. The woman came across as cold and aloof, acting as if Kylee didn't exist. Trish had tried to be friendly, obviously cared for Talina, but Kylee remembered that Trish had backed the mob that wanted to kill Rocket back in Port Authority. Part of Kylee figured that Trish being shot was a form of divine retribution.

And then there was Dortmund Short Mind. The waste of skin. If that was the kind of person Solar System was all about, she wanted no part of it. How could anyone that old be that much of a fuckup?

"We've got compression on the wound and the leg splinted," Yvette said into the radio. "The femur's definitely broken."

"How much blood?" Raya's voice came from the speaker.

"It's still leaking."

"But not gushing?"

"No. It's slowly spreading on the bandage."

"Then the femoral artery is intact. Did the bullet go through the inside or outside of the thigh?"

"Kind of looks like straight through to me." Yvette pursed her lips.

"You gave her the drugs?"

"We did. Just like the directions on the medical kit instructed."

"Good. That's got her on a pain protocol. She shouldn't go into shock, but keep her hydrated. If she won't drink on her own, set up the IV. Then keep her immobilized, and get her here."

"That," Yvette said woodenly, "is a problem. We've got two aircars and no one to fly them. Looks like the rain's breaking up. Is there any chance that Step can fly out?"

"Yvette, we've got our own problems here. Step's not answering com. No one is. Benteen's making a mess of things."

"What about the shuttle? Can Manny pilot it out here? Pick up Tal and Trish?"

"I don't know, Yvette. Things are pretty dicey here. Kalico might be another option. She's here. I don't know what her role is, but she's in the middle of this. I'll just have to see. In the meantime, you've got my instructions. Keep Trish stable. We'll have someone out there as soon as we can."

"Okay, but hurry, this is—"

"Hey, I gotta go! Shit's hitting the fan."

"What do you mean?"

No response.

"Raya? Do you copy? What's going on?"

Silence.

Kylee watched the woman sigh, replace the mic, and stare vacantly at the radio.

Dortmund sat hunched almost double in one of the chairs, his face cradled in his hands, looking broken. Several times, Kylee had seen him sobbing.

Shig stepped into the room, turned, and locked the front door behind him. "Well, want the baddest news first? Or just the bad news?"

"What's the baddest?" Yvette asked.

"Quetzals are coming. Two of them. They're flashing all kinds of colors. Making no secret of their arrival."

"It was going to eat her," Dortmund murmured under his breath, refusing to look up.

True, it had. Kylee had seen the whole thing. She'd been at the window. None of the adults had heard her warning shout through the thick glass. She'd seen Trish fall at the first shot. And one of the last ones might have hit the quetzal. The thing had jerked, as if from an impact.

Shig ignored the worthless professor, saying, "But what may be the baddest news is that I count twelve bullet holes in Trish's aircar. Most are in the side, but one is through the instrument panel. I don't know if the controls are damaged or if the power pack took a hit."

"Oh, fine," Yvette said woodenly. Then she gave Shig an update on her talk with Raya.

"No rescue? PA is in an uproar?" Shig's brown face turned thoughtful. He walked over to where they had Trish laid out on the couch, a splint on her bullet-smashed and bandaged leg.

"I was trying to save her," Dortmund whispered hollowly.

"Trish's pistol holds fifteen rounds. That's one in Trish's leg, twelve in the aircar, which means that you might have put two into the quetzal." He smiled humorlessly. "Assuming they didn't just whizz harmlessly past."

Dortmund remained hunched in the chair, his head still buried in his hands.

"Waste of skin," Kylee repeated. From her vantage in the window, Dortmund had shot just about everything. She'd watched the quetzal freeze in its lunge for Trish, change color from crimson to yellow and black patterns of panic. It was turning to run even as Dortmund ran out of bullets.

And now other quetzals were coming?

Kylee climbed up to look out the window. The two approaching quetzals were most of the way up the slope from the valley bottom off to the west. If there were any good news, it might have been that instead of a burning crimson color, the quetzals were violet, mauve, and orange, the paler shade that indicated mild curiosity. The collars were down, and the patterns along their hides weren't communicating more than a casual conversation.

She turned. "These aren't the same quetzals that clod-brain here shot at."

Dortmund's pained voice insisted, "It had its mouth open, reaching over the car. Officer Monagan never saw it. The thing was hidden behind the car."

Shig ignored the man, walked over to the window to look, and asked Kylee, "How do you know?"

"None of these quetzals are panicked. See the light curiosity colors? How they're walking? If one of them was the one that was going to eat Trish, and got scared off, the colors would be intense, excited. He wouldn't be this calm."

"You're sure of this?" Shig fingered his chin as he stared out at the approaching quetzals.

"Well, duh." She gave him a sidelong glance. "Don't you know anything about quetzals? Two of them coming like this? Something's going on."

"I'll take your word for it. I didn't know quetzals traveled in packs. Thought they were solitary hunters."

"It's a lineage," Kylee told him. "Quetzals share territory with their relatives." She thought about it. "Doesn't make sense."

"What doesn't?" Shig, to her surprise, was hanging on every word.

"That a quetzal would hide behind the aircar, camouflaged, and try to eat Trish. Then, after being scared off, these two would just come strolling up the hill to see what's happening."

"They heard the shots?"

"Could be. Quetzals are curious. But if they'd seen what happened to the first one, they'd be wary."

Kylee chewed her lip, thinking it through. "Okay, time to guess here. Doesn't make sense that the one that was going to eat Trish would have talked to these two. They'd be upset, too. The local quetzals haven't made a single hostile move. They've been curious. Trying to figure out what we want. Following the pattern Talina started on the first day. Even with shit-for-brains, here." Kylee indicated the professor. "The quetzal that approached him? It tried to talk and ended up sharing blood. They know we're not here to kill them. They're still trying to figure out why."

"Sounds like a whole lot of guessing, kid," Yvette said warily as she stepped to the rifle rack at the door and pulled Trish's rifle from the cradle. Then she stepped to the window across the way to watch the approaching quetzals.

"Got a better idea?"

"Yeah, shoot these two dead from the safety of the dome, skin them, and start processing the meat," Yvette told her in return.

"You're as dumb as Dr. Short Mind here."

"You want me to give you a little lesson in how to talk to your elders?" Yvette asked from her window.

"It's all right," Shig soothed. To Kylee he asked, "If they're only curious, why did that quetzal attack this morning?"

"He's not local," Kylee said, feeling the sureness of it. "It's hard to tell sometimes with quetzals. I mean, I don't really know these guys yet, but I don't think I've seen the one that tried to get Trish this morning. I think he's new. It was in the way he patterned his colors. It was a statement of satisfaction mixed with triumph."

"Meaning what?" Yvette asked.

"Meaning he's not from here."

"He was an interloper? Just traveling through?"

Kylee considered, remembered the time Rocket had warned her and the family not to go into the forests around Mundo. All he'd said was, "Bad quetzals. Gone soon."

"What if that time back at Mundo, that was another bunch of quetzals invading Flash's territory?" she wondered, talking to herself. "Lineages in competition? Some sort of territorial dispute?"

"Why attack Trish if it was just passing through?" Shig asked. "It hid behind the aircar, knowing that someone would come. That quetzal knew exactly what it was doing."

"Yeah, almost like it was trying to make trouble, huh?" Kylee glanced at Yvette who'd hunkered down behind the window with the rifle. "Eat a human, and you can bet the humans will take it out on the local quetzals."

Shig looked worried. "Are they really that smart?"

Kylee pointed. "She's ready to kill quetzals. You tell me who's smart in this equation."

"I lost too many friends to those murderous beasts."

Yvette glared out at the closing quetzals. "If you ask me, the only good quetzal's a dead quetzal."

"You're one of the ones I'll destroy in the end," Kylee promised. "You'd have shot Rocket dead, too, wouldn't you?"

"In a minute, kid. And nothing I've seen this morning has caused me to reassess. Ask Trish."

Kylee studied the woman, filling every fiber of her memory with what Yvette Dushane looked like. She wanted to be sure that when she finally went to Port Authority, she'd be able to recognize her, no matter what.

"Meanwhile, what do we do about these two?" Shig asked, pointing to the quetzals who had stopped on the far side of the aircars and were now bent, inhaling the scent where the rogue quetzal had been hiding. A riot of colors and patterns ran down their sides as they recognized the intrusion.

"I say shoot them dead," Yvette called, raising the rifle and unlocking the window. All it would take was a push to swing it open, and she could shoot.

The woman was staring intently out the window. Shig, too, was glued to the sight. Dortmund, of course, could have cared less.

Since no one was looking, Kylee slipped to the door. Before anyone could stop her, she'd unlatched the lock, thrown it wide open, and was running. As she did she flapped her arms, yelling, "Run! Run! They'll *kill you!*"

71

With Tompzen and Michegan hot on her heels, Kalico cursed her way up the tavern stairs, burst out the door, and headed for the admin dome at a run. People were shouting, "*Quetzal!*" at the top of their lungs as they streamed out of Inga's. For Kalico's part, she had to get to the admin dome, find the siren, and alert the whole of Port Authority and the surroundings.

Rain was pattering down, light fading as the clouds thickened overhead. Perfect fucking quetzal weather.

"People, what have you got?" she demanded of her com.

"I've got marines on every gate, Supervisor," Abu Sassi's voice came through. *"The whole damn town was unguarded."*

"Any word on that blood at the north gate?"

"No, ma'am. Just blood. Some scuffed tracks . . . oh, and a pile of torn clothes, but they weren't bloody."

Torn clothes. Kalico bit off a curse, her memory going back to the first time she'd seen a quetzal kill. The damn beasts ripped clothes off the way a human peeled a banana.

She charged in the admin doorway, pulling her sidearm. "If Benteen so much as reaches for his shoulder holster, shoot him."

"Yes, ma'am," Tompzen said, taking point.

The three of them pounded down the hallway; one of the security guards gaped at them from where he stood before the conference room door, a rifle resting in his arms.

At the radio room, Kalico slammed the door open, hurrying in. "Where the fuck is the siren?"

"Try that one," Tompzen said, pointing at a large red switch on the wall.

Kalico flipped it, delighted to hear the blaring of the siren. She took a breath, picked up the mic, and keyed it.

"Attention. We have three, repeat, three quetzals in Port Authority. Lock yourselves down. We think one person's already dead. Repeat. Three quetzals in the compound."

"Halt!" Michegan barked outside the door. "Make so much as a move, and you're blasted meat!"

Kalico stepped to the door to see Benteen where he'd just emerged from her old office. The man's hand was hovering in front of his chest, perfectly positioned to reach into his coat.

Kalico told him, "Sure, with your implants, you could probably shoot me in the head before Michegan could blow you away. But she's in armor, her weapon hot. You won't live long enough to regret it."

"What the hell are you doing? What's that siren?"

People were banging on the door behind the now-terrified security guard down the hall at the conference room.

"You miserable piece of work," Kalico told him. "You've got three quetzals in the compound. *Three!*"

"So? Hunt them down and shoot them," Benteen said, a wary smile on his face. "They're just animals, after all."

With a crash, the doors to the conference room burst, knocking the guard into the far wall. People came pouring out. Among them Kalico recognized Hanson, Tomashev, and Halston.

"What the hell? Who set them free?" Benteen snapped, taking a half step forward.

"Freeze!" Michegan barked again, keeping Benteen under the muzzle of her rifle.

Meanwhile the hostages raced to the weapons locker and stripped out the rifles.

"Got three quetzals in the compound!" Kalico shouted. "Be damned careful getting home!"

"Roger that," Mac Hanson called over his shoulder.

Two Spot was the last to emerge, half stumbling down the hall, his hands in restraints.

"Kalen," she told her marine. "Cut Two Spot loose and get him on his radio."

"Yes, ma'am."

She pulled her pistol, flicked the safety off, and leveled it on Benteen. The guy hadn't shown so much as a flicker of emotion, but watched her the way a predator did its prey.

"On Donovan," she told him, "stupidity is a death sentence. Wonder how many are going to die because you're stupid?"

"How's that?" Benteen asked casually.

"You left the gates unguarded while your goons rounded up people."

"Hey!" the guard down the hall called. "We told him! We didn't dare object, Supervisor. Not after he shot Hazen down like that. He said follow orders, so we did."

"I rest my case." She let her finger caress the trigger, knowing how fast he was. "Dina, go put some cuffs on him. The scorpion's run his course."

Allison Chomko, looking pale, stepped out of the scorpion's office door.

"Ali! Get back!" Kalico shouted.

She had an image of the woman falling backward as Benteen made a flick of the fingers.

The flash and detonation were stunning, blinding, deafening.

Kalico stumbled back into the radio room, dazed, ears ringing. In the hallway, Dina Michegan's rifle was barely audible through Kalico's deafened hearing as the marine fired.

"What the fuck?" Kalico cried, sinking to the floor, dropping her pistol to press hands to her pain-shot ears.

Eyes clamped shut, she struggled through the afterimages of the flash.

For the moment her entire existence consisted of agony.

Then Michegan leaned over her, her helmet-amplified voice saying, "Benteen's gone. Made it out the back way. Are you all right?"

"Yes." The ringing was beginning to abate. She grabbed up her pistol, let Michegan help her up. "This is going from bad to worse."

72

I shot a woman.

How could a human being feel this miserable? He'd made his deal with Satan, picked up a weapon and threatened another human being. He'd forced Trish Monagan out there. Distracted her. And then he'd shot her.

The quetzal who'd caused the mess had escaped, and without losing so much as a single drop of blood. Or whatever its bodily fluid was called.

A waste of skin.

That's what that little cretin of a girl called him. Clodbrain. Dortmund Short Mind. And now, she, too, was gone.

He looked up through swollen eyes. He still sat in the chair at the table, his butt aching, back knotted and stiff.

Yvette Dushane remained at her post at the window. Shig stood just outside the front door, Talina's rifle awkwardly clutched in his hands, watching in vain for Kylee.

The kid had run off with the quetzals? How utterly insane was that?

He looked up as Shig stepped into the room, took two tries to rack the rifle, and finally managed to secure it. "No sign of Kylee."

"What the hell?" Yvette vented an exasperated sigh. "Not in any permutation of possibilities would I ever have anticipated that the kid would have reacted like that. It's nuts. She chose them over us."

"She places you with the ones who murdered her quetzal," Shig reminded.

"Never seen anything like it," Yvette said, refusing to relinquish the window. "She went charging out there, flailing with her hands, yelling, 'Run!' and then raced right through the middle of them. I thought one of them would snap her up, crunch her, and gulp her down. But no, they go trotting off toward the drainage in her wake. Following along like a bunch of clap-trapping oversized dogs."

"If she's still alive," Dortmund rasped to himself.

"I'd bet you a two-hundred SDR gold piece she's a pile of quetzal crap as we speak." Yvette's eyes thinned.

"How's Trish?" Shig asked.

"Not good. Fevered last time I checked. Leg's swelling, and the wound's weeping blood and pus." Yvette spared a glance for the young woman sleeping fitfully on the couch. "I gave her another dose of the pain drugs and antibiotics. Tried the radio again about a half hour ago. No response from Raya. Hell, the hospital could be smoking rubble for all we know."

"Have faith," Shig told her with a weary smile. "And Talina?"

"Still out."

"Not exactly the relaxing refuge we had hoped for, is it?" Shig asked, stepping over to the microwave to punch the button on the last cup of vegetable soup. "Tal's in a coma, Trish is shot, and Kylee's run off with the quetzals to who knows what fate?"

"And no telling what the toilet-sucking quetzals have in store for us." Yvette stepped away from the window long enough to place her hand on Trish's brow. "She's too hot."

"Not much we can do," Shig told her in an uncommonly placid voice. "I'm going back to try and feed Talina the last of this soup."

Dortmund had dropped his head back into his hands, letting the agony of the position in the chair be his penance. He was barely aware when Yvette stopped before him, saying, "What about you?"

"What about me?"

"You going to sit there torturing yourself?"

He looked up, wincing at the stiffness in his back. "I shot a woman."

"Yeah, you did." Yvette's expression showed no give. "Now, get up off your ass and make us a meal out of whatever's left of the food."

"I just want to die."

"Oh, for fuck's sake!"

"This is all Radcek's fault. This whole unmentionable disaster of a planet. I've been made into the very thing I've despised all of my life. And as soon as I take matters in hand to fix them, to save something for science, I end up shooting an innocent woman? How did this happen to me?"

He blinked, realization settling like a lead weight. "It's the quetzal molecules. It must be. That's what's changed me."

"You ask me," Yvette said disdainfully, "you're figuring out what it means to be remarkably book-smart and extraordinarily world-stupid. But that's not my problem for the moment. Get up and make us supper."

"I can't."

He started, wide-eyed, at the snick-snack of the rifle's bolt being cycled. Yvette had the gruesome thing pointed at his knee cap.

"What are you doing?" he shrieked, toppling the chair backward as he jerked to his feet.

"There, see," Yvette told him grimly. "You can get your sorry ass out that chair." With the rifle, she gestured. "Now, get over to the kitchen there and cook."

"But I—"

"I can blow your foot off. Give you a little taste of what you did to Trish. You see, I've always liked Trish. Known her since she was a girl. And, yeah, accidents happen. Doesn't mean I don't carry a grudge when they happen because of gross incompetence."

Dortmund stumbled over to the kitchen counter. "You wouldn't really shoot me, would you?"

"Professor, I'll tell you this once: You wouldn't be the first person I've blown a hole in. The difference this time is that I'll feel good about doing it."

Shit, she meant it.

Dortmund tried to get his heart to settle back in his chest. He kept fumbling with things, struggling to get lids off, pouring contents into the big kettle. Wondering what the hell he was making.

From the couch, Trish moaned, tried to shift, and kicked with her good right leg. In a weak voice, she said, "So sorry, Tal. Couldn't see you suffer . . . and Cap wanted me to do it. Could see it in his eyes . . ."

"Hey, easy there," Yvette said, retreating to the couch and bending over the wounded woman. "Trish, you've got to relax. You're hurt. We need you to rest."

Dortmund licked his dry lips, trying to concentrate on

what he was cooking. Not that they had a whole lot left. Some sugar peas, green beans, odds and ends from the garden. Barely enough to go around even with just the three of them. Trish sure wasn't eating, and soup was the only thing anyone had managed to get into Talina.

Which was a problem. Another of many.

From the corner of his eye, he saw Yvette inject more of the painkiller into Trish. What happened when that ran out? How long could a gunshot wound be left untreated? Dortmund wasn't any sort of medical man, but Trish looked way too sweaty, pale, and drawn to be any kind of stable. And the way that leg was swelling was just plain ugly.

He stirred his "stew" together and put it on the heat.

Tomorrow, before they could eat breakfast, someone was going to have to make a journey down to the garden.

Go to the garden?

To what fate? A really mad Kylee was out there with at least three quetzals. And one of them—if the kid could be believed—was a rogue that would have killed and eaten Trish that very morning.

Dortmund clamped his eyes closed. He couldn't count on Shig for protection. The man was just as fumble-fingered as Dortmund when he held a rifle. A scholar of comparative religion? Get real. Shig admitted that he'd rarely shot a gun, and the only times he had, it had been point blank. Point blank? What the hell did that imply?

Kylee made no secret that she had a score to settle with Yvette, so sending the woman would be like waving a red flag and asking for an attack. Dortmund going would be just as disastrous. Time and time again he'd proven he could not tell a quetzal from a sucking shrub.

"So, which one of us is going to try and make the trip?"

Whoever did, the odds were that they weren't coming back.

Dear God, we're going to starve to death here.

73

Xibalba had miserable leaden skies. Talina stared up at the sullen air and wondered what was wrong with her. The duality of her spiritual essence—what the Maya called *ch'ulel*—seemed to tear her apart as she stood alone in the Copan ballcourt. The Maya believed that the soul was composed of two conflicting entities, one wise, peaceful, and orderly, the other chaotic and violent. They had a word for that in Yukatec: *pixom.*

Is that why I am stuck here? Because I'm at war with myself?

Part of her nature was to protect, the other to destroy. A woman in eternal conflict.

"What the hell is *wrong* with me?" she screamed up at the dirty sky. And then, in a pique of anger, she stomped on the stones beneath her feet. The ballcourt floor drummed with the impact. She listened, amazed as the reverberations ran through the fitted ashlars and faded into the distance.

She felt the stirring. Knew instinctively that she'd awakened the Lords of Death from their repose beneath the ballcourt.

She saw the figure when he emerged into the ballcourt. For a single striking instant he looked like the ancient Maya depictions of the first lord of Xibalba: One Death.

An instant later the death god's appearance shifted, lengthened, and morphed into a blinding white quetzal. But something about it wasn't quite right. Talina raised a hand against the glare, squinted, and saw that the quetzal's head was nothing more than a gruesome wedge-shaped skull. The creature's joints were skeletal, and the flesh along its body hung in rotten strips: One Death as he would look in the guise of a quetzal? Or a quetzal in the guise of One Death? Which would it be? Or was it both at once?

The quetzal opened its spectral jaws, the serrations that

served as fangs looked cracked and broken. "Called me from the dead, did you?"

"Demon?"

"We are one and many. You killed me in the canyon. Then again in your house. But we waited. It was Whitey who finally figured out how to bring you down. Would have managed to kill you."

"Whitey?"

Movement from behind caused her to turn. Rocket, blazing in crimson, yellow, and black, trotted up to her side. "Whitey wanted to drive you mad. Turn you against your own kind through molecular manipulation. It's one of the more subtle ways quetzals fight," Rocket said softly, his tail flicking back and forth. "He couldn't have known until after he tasted you that day. You have too many other quetzal molecules from too many other lineages running in your blood. So you're a little of all of us. Our TriNA went into your reconstruction of the pot."

She cocked her head, right hand on her pistol. "So that meeting with Whitey outside Port Authority? It was a trick? Like, to sabotage my brain?"

"Wasn't a complete failure." The death quetzal snapped its skeletal jaws shut. Then added, "You're here. Locked away. Half mad, but it's better than nothing. They're on their own back there in the town. In your terms, it's war. Got to bring it to an end."

"Some of us are still learning," Rocket told her. "A few of us like humans."

Talina clamped her eyes shut, a slew of disparate thoughts rattling around inside her head: quetzal visions, quetzal thoughts. All struggling with her own soul and personality.

What was Talina Perez, and what was quetzal TriNA?

When she opened her eyes, it was to see the death quetzal, its shape merging into Whitey, Demon, the quetzal that had tried to kill her in her house. The same lineage. One displaced by Port Authority. How many of them had died at the hands of humans, all the way back to Donovan himself?

"Yes, you begin to understand," the death quetzal told her.

"Sometimes, when the hatred goes too deep," she told it, "there's only one way to end it."

She pulled her pistol, shot once, twice, three times. Seeing no effect, she lined the sights on the bony skull and triggered the pistol. The thing remained unscathed, a quetzal-shaped One Death.

This is only a dream.

Rocket told her, "You are the pot. You did the shaping, the fixing, the changing. You understand that, don't you? Whatever it is that you are, you are the vessel that holds us all."

"Me?"

Rocket flashed orange patterns of agreement. "Whitey and Demon, Flash, Diamond, Leaper, the Briggs and the Rork quetzals, all of their molecules are changing, seeking, building pathways in your brain."

"No wonder I'm dreaming I'm in Xibalba, that dead quetzals and skulls can talk. I'm insane." Talina allowed herself one last shot before reholstering her pistol. Of course she couldn't kill the death quetzal. The thing's TriNA lurked inside of her.

Made her wonder what the psychiatric professionals on Transluna would make of her. Probably write up a whole new category for the DSM-12.

"We win," the death quetzal told her. "Allison's baby? Gerry Hmong? Moshe Levitz? All the others we've tasted and tried to learn? You were the key who finally showed us the way to prevail. And we will, if it takes a thousand years."

They might at that; quetzals calculated based on an entirely different comprehension of time.

Talina took a deep breath, enjoyed a caustic laugh at her expense. Then she glanced at Rocket. "But that's only one lineage."

The little quetzal stared up from the ballcourt floor, his three eyes gleaming. "You begin to understand."

"Talina?"

She glanced up. There, atop the brooding temple above the ballcourt, sat an owl—one of the messengers of Xibalba. Like the owl who had led the pregnant Blood Moon from the underworld into the world of light. They were the guides, capable of traveling between the worlds.

"Talina? Do you hear me?" The owl's voice sounded disembodied.

She felt something, faint, a distant touch on her face.

"Follow the voice," Rocket said. "It will lead you back."

She glanced over her shoulder, could see her mother's kitchen. She took one longing step back toward it. Hesitated. She could smell the cooking tamales, the recado rojo, and chili-spiced cacao.

"Talina? It's important. We need your help."

She turned her attention back to the owl. Knew that voice. Someone familiar. A warm and loving friend.

She took one last look at the death quetzal, watched its form blend into the traditional image of One Death. It continued to watch with spectral eyes, calling, "You can't rid yourself of me. No matter how long it takes, I will drag you down."

"You got it half right," she told the apparition as she turned, leaped to the slanting wall, and climbed the ball-court's incline to the high temple. "You're trapped in here with me, but I'll screw vacuum before I let you drag me down."

She climbed with a greater sense of freedom. Above her, the owl took to wing, flying ever higher. Yes, she knew that voice: Shig.

She might awaken crazy as a rabid bat with all these quetzals inside her, but at her core, she had the pot. Carefully reconstructed. In one piece again.

Overhead, the owl flew, straight up, and into the light.

The light flared, almost blinded her.

Coming to, she lay on her back. Uncomfortable as hell.

Talina blinked, realized her bladder was full; she was desperately thirsty and hungry enough to eat a crest. Raw.

It took a moment to find her focus. She lay supine on a bed. The face swimming above hers sharpened into concerned brown eyes, a pug nose, and round cheeks.

"Shig?" she whispered hoarsely.

"Good to have you back. We're in somewhat of a mess. But I must say, what on Earth did you do to your eyes?"

74

Trish thought she could take pain. She'd been hurt before. Nothing compared to what she now suffered. Agony burned through her thigh, into her hips, and paralyzed her lower body.

It just fucking wouldn't stop. Somewhere life, happiness, and joy had slipped away to become this absolutely endless misery and suffering. Time had slowed to a near standstill. The suffering consumed everything.

If she could, she would have crawled out of her skin. Left herself just bared muscle and stinging nerve, and sighed as the faint stirrings of air blew cool across her wet and bleeding meat.

Another of the agonizing waves rolled up her leg, left her gasping.

She tried to flee. Tried to slip away into the dimness of memory. Recalled her childhood: Mother telling her that Daddy was dead. But that it would be all right. That they'd make it.

How they'd decorated the dome on the one-year anniversary of Daddy's death. Filled it with pictures of when he was alive.

Idly, Trish wondered where those pictures had gone.

Where anything but pain had gone.

She'd been twelve. Saw again the look on Talina's face as the young security officer in her natty new uniform said, "Trish, I'm so sorry. It's not fair. But your mother isn't coming back."

Trish had stood with Talina at the funeral where Mother's corpse was enclosed in a wrapping. Tal had told her that no one wanted young Trish to see what the skewer had done to Mom's body.

She'd never been able to really say good-bye.

She could see the red dirt being shoveled in on top of Mother's body, so clear it could have been yesterday.

Won't be long. Red dirt, just like that, will be shoveled on top of me.

"You're going to hang in there, kid," Talina's voice came echoing down. Was that from above? Or from the deep past? Things were so blurry—and just plain hurt too much to care about.

"Tal?"

"Yeah, Trish. Hey, I'm right here."

The heat burned even hotter in Trish's body. She tried to swallow down her hot throat. "So thirsty."

She felt a cup being placed to her lips, drank. Felt the soothing wonder of cool liquid as it hit her stomach.

"You're going to be okay," Talina told her.

Trish blinked, fought through the fog of pain, and fixed on Talina's face. The woman was smiling, looking worried.

"Tal? You all right?"

"Why wouldn't I be?"

"You gonna forgive me?"

"For what?"

Trish swallowed hard. So tough to admit. "He scared me. Knew he was going to kill me. I backed down. I just . . . I couldn't find the courage. Let him take it all. Failed you."

"What's she talking about?" Talina asked.

"Benteen. Corporate assassin." Shig's voice sounded distant. "Came on the *Vixen*. She's still blaming herself. Shouldn't. Good as she is, he'd have killed her before she could have pulled her pistol."

"Promise me you'll make Benteen pay." Tish swallowed hard. "He's evil, Tal. Don't just shoot him. Make him suffer."

"Sure, kid. I promise."

"Always tried to make you proud." Trish wished her mouth wasn't so dry. "Hated myself for what I did. Couldn't see you suffer."

"Hated yourself for not getting killed? That's nuts."

"No. 'Cause of Cap." Trish closed her eyes, remembering Cap as he lay in that hospital bed. "*. . . See the little wheel? With your thumb, spin it open . . .*"

"Cap?"

Trish struggled to organize her thoughts. "Sorry, Tal. So sorry. He asked me to. He knew. Loved you . . . We all did.

Love's such a funny thing, huh? Hurts so much when you might lose it."

"It's the fever, Talina. She's raving," Shig's voice came from somewhere above.

"We're going to take you out of here." Tal's voice sounded terse. A pause. Then, "Yeah, love's a funny thing."

"Didn't want you to suffer. Not after what you did for me."

Trish heard muffled voices. Tal's sharp. Shig's soothing, but she couldn't make out the words.

Then Tal was bent over her, the strength back in her voice. "Love you, too, kid. Gotta have you hang in there. Sounds like trouble back in PA."

"I got your back, Tal. Always."

Another pause.

"Yeah, kid. I know you do. We're going to put you under again. Next time you come to, it's going to be in hospital. You hear? You be there for me, Trish."

"I wasn't good enough." A sob caught in her throat as the pain spiked. "Lost you to a little quetzal. How fucked is that?"

"You didn't lose me," Tal's voice came from a distance. ". . . right here . . . will be waiting to . . ."

Then another of the searing, bone-blasting waves of pain rolled up her leg as it was jarred.

"It's raining." Was that Yvette? "And it's the middle of the . . ."

Trish struggled to place the fragments of speech.

". . . Just got out of bed yourself. You don't want to do this." Some part of Trish's mind thought it was Shig talking.

"She's gonna die. That's infection. Hell, she may be dead by the time I get her . . ."

"And God help us . . . crossing the Wind Mountains. Our luck, you'll . . . a peak. They'll never find . . ."

"Gotta get back." Yeah, that was Talina's voice. "Too much shit's coming down."

". . . About that little girl?" This voice sounded shrill. That fucking idiot professor? Had to be.

". . . Need to be worried about, it's that kid. She's half . . ."

For a moment, Trish's mind and hearing seemed to clear.

"Well, I'm not staying behind for her." Definitely Weisbacher.

"The hell you say. You made this mess. You keep a light on for her until I can get back. Now, move your shit and grab hold of the stretcher."

Trish yelped as she was moved. She tried to blink, saw blurry lights. Felt like she was floating. Another bash of pain left her scattered and panting. God, what she'd give for a drink of cold water.

"Tal?" she cried.

"Here." Trish felt Tal take her hand.

"Benteen . . . don't take him head on. He'll kill you. Make him . . . make him pay for what he did. Okay? Scared me. Shamed me."

"You just hang in there, Trish. You can take him down yourself."

"Love you. My best . . . I just . . ." Tried to find words in the haze. Couldn't.

Faintly she thought she felt rain on her face. Cool rain. Then blackness.

The pain lashed her again. Fainter now.

Trish let herself go. Felt her heart slow. Each beat ever more distant from the last.

Let herself drop into the empty black.

No need to fight anymore.

Just . . . let go . . .

75

Talina pulled the throttle back, sending power to the fans. Rain pattered down on the aircar's canopy; the wet topography flickered in blue-white flashes as lightning danced across the storm-torn sky. A blast of wind jolted the aircar, and Talina barely caught it in time to keep them on an even keel.

Shig and Yvette were giving her that uncertain and frightened look, faces made even more pale by the frequent strobes of lightning.

For Talina, the hits just kept coming. She'd awakened feeling weak, stiff, and vulnerable. Hungry as hell. Mostly naked and wearing a shit-sucking diaper, for God's sake?

She felt wobbly. A stim bar had given her a jolt of energy, and she'd scarfed down the dregs of the boiled vegetables.

Another gust of wind tossed the car. She looked back. In the dim cabin lights, Trish looked ghastly.

Trish? Damn. How could this happen to Trish?

Talina sucked a deep breath, fighting images that kept trying to crawl up from her subconscious. Xibalba, quetzal memories, her mother's kitchen, the expression on Cap's dead face where he lay on the hospital bed.

The aircar pitched again, hit sidelong by a blast of rain.

Concentrate. You're going to kill us all.

"Shig?" she asked, struggling to keep her mind on the flight, needing a distraction from the chaos of horrible thoughts in her head. "What Trish said back at Rork Springs. About Cap? I'm still trying to make sense of it."

Shig rose from where he sat beside Trish's litter, leaving Yvette to ensure that the wounded woman rode safely in the turbulence. Staggering, he made his way to the dash and clamped onto one of the grab rails.

"You heard what she said. Cap told her to turn the little

wheel. Come on, Tal. You knew the man better than any of us. You think he wanted to live like that?"

She fought back tears, a spear of grief and frustrated anger surging through her. "Damn it, no." A beat. "Why didn't he ask me to do it?"

"Because he loved you."

Talina shook her head, tried desperately to clear her vision of cobweb-like images that formed ghostlike behind her eyes.

"You all right?" Shig asked nervously.

"Seeing things."

He peered out into the blackness. "I can't see anything except storm. How the hell are you keeping us in the air? You're not even wearing night vision."

"Quetzal vision," she told him. "It's heavy in the infrared. We're following the terrain. Rork River is off to our right. The compass heading's correct."

Another frantic gust of storm hammered rain against the quivering aircar as it fought its way forward. Keeping on course took all of Talina's concentration.

In the next lull, she cried, "How could she do that to me?"

"Because she loved you."

Again she caught the aircar just before the wind pitched it sideways and out of control. Flying in this shit? It was asking for a disaster. Even Demon, locked away down in her gut, was huddling in fear, somehow realizing just how foolish and dangerous this night flight was.

Worse, Talina could feel her energy beginning to ebb. She struggled to peer through the windshield. The vibra-surface remained clear despite the downpour, but beyond that, visibility was limited to shrouds of falling rain. Just ahead lay Rork Pass, the high, torturous gap that led through this portion of the Winds.

As woozy as Talina felt, as slow as her reactions, any rage she harbored toward Trish was moot. Figured that it was Trish, especially after eliminating all the other potential suspects.

They'd no more than entered the narrow defile, jagged rock rising to either side, when the main force of the wind hit.

Talina's gut rose as the aircar was driven down. The effect was as if it had been hit with a hammer. She froze, terrified by the broken boulders that filled her vision.

"Hang on!" she screamed, and pulled at the wheel with all of her flagging strength.

76

Port Authority's worst nightmare: three quetzals, in the dark, in the middle of a storm, loose in the town. Were they still together? Hunting separately? Had they gone to ground in a building? Perhaps camouflaging themselves under or behind a piece of the parked mining equipment? Or worse, were they pursuing some more insidious plan?

Kalico hunched over the map, hands propped on the scarred old conference table in the admin dome, her feet braced. The last time she'd been here for a hunt like this, she'd been a spectator, disbelieving, struggling to come to terms with the impossibility that an implacable predator was hunting human beings within the town's walls.

Shig and Yvette had been here. Standing where she was. Directing as she was now.

More than anything, Kalico remembered there had been coffee. And she—smart-assed Corporate shit that she'd been—had let that cup go to waste.

"I'd give a hundred-kilo bar of solid beryllium alloy for that same cup right now," she told herself. "Cold, slimy, and black as it might be."

"What's that?" Dya Simonov looked up from the "quetzal map," a hand-drawn one-by-two meter rendering of Port Authority. It was stretched across the tabletop, each part colored differently, the town blocked into search zones.

"Talking to myself." Kalico accessed her military com. "Abu Sassi? What have you got?"

"We're lined out. Halfway through grid one, ma'am."

"Tompzen?"

"Still on the second block of the warehouse grid, ma'am. This is the shits. All this equipment from Freelander. *Each piece has to be cleared."*

"Get it right, Kalen. No matter how long it takes."

"Roger that."

One by one, she checked in with her other marines. The last time they hunted a quetzal in PA, she'd had twenty, with full tech. And the thing had still eluded them. Now she was down to nine, not counting the four watching the gates, and they had only half the manpower available that PA had had on that previous search.

This can go wrong in so many ways.

Looking down at the map, she mentally marked off each small section of the town. Damn, it was going slowly. Miso's team had barely gotten their search lined out and were only a quarter of the way through their half of the residential section. Every house had to be checked and cleared. Every potential hiding place probed. At the same time, drones were ensuring the roofs were clear.

"Look out!" a voice on the radio cried, the broadcast followed by shots. A scream faded in the background.

"Damn thing came out of nowhere!"

"Wye? Where are you? Wye, damn it. Answer me!"

"It was just there! Did you see it? Grabbed Wye, and . . . Oh fuck, no."

"Get it together, people." That was Step Allenovich's voice.

More shots could be heard over the radio.

"Report!" Kalico barked.

"Fucker just got Wye Vanveer." Allenovich's voice came through the speaker. *"My goddamned line's too thin! Everybody! Hold up! Don't go racing in after him. Don't want to lose anybody because of stupidity. I said, stop. Stay in sight of each other!"*

Kalico took a deep breath. If only they had more bodies on the lines. Half of the people who made up the search teams were essentially trapped in their businesses and houses. The usual guards hadn't been at their stations. People who normally would have been able to make the assembly points were hiding, praying, and most likely, dying.

Kalico slammed a palm into the table making Dya jump. "You're in charge, Dya. You've seen how I've been marking the cleared areas? Tell Two Spot to patch the military coms into the town net."

"What are you going to do?"

Kalico grabbed for the rifle she'd leaned against a chair.

"You heard Step. He just lost a man. He's short-handed. Last I looked there was still a night-vision headset in the locker. I'm going out there."

Dya gave her a measured, you're-crazy look. Not that the two of them had ever really been on the best of terms.

Kalico told her, "Keep the door locked. Something tells me this is about as far from under control as things get around here."

"Watch your ass."

"Watch yours."

Kalico swung her poncho around her shoulders, checked the load in the rifle's magazine, and closed the door behind her. At the locker, she pulled out the night-vision set and fitted it to her head. The ancient battery read sixty-two percent, and that was coming off the charger.

She strode out into the rainy night, flicked the headset on, and lifted her rifle to check the IR function in the optic. In the sight, blackness faded to a ghostly green.

"Two Spot? You hear me?"

"Roger that, Supervisor. What the hell are you doing?"

"Headed out for Step's line. Step? You hear me?"

"You out of your mind, Supervisor?"

"Where do you want me to rendezvous with your team?"

"We're held up. Block north of The Jewel. Got some nooks and crannies to peer at, and after losing Vanveer, don't want anybody too long out of sight."

She trotted down the main avenue, streaks of rain falling silver in the glow of the night vision. Water puddles were stippled with raindrops; the buildings on either side seemed to glow in a ghostly fashion, especially where their lights were muted in the goggles.

Have you lost any sense you ever had, Kalico? She now had time to take Allenovich's question seriously.

She was the most powerful woman on the planet, and here she was, headed into who knew what kind of disaster. Ready to step into a line and take the place of a man who had just been torn to pieces and eaten.

She kept her gaze roving, trying to call up everything she'd heard since setting foot on Donovan. Rifle hot. Safety off. Finger resting on the receiver just above the trigger.

Shoot fast. Don't miss. And don't—for fucking sake—
shoot anything or anyone but a damn quetzal.

Her adrenaline was up. Pulse pounding, she passed The
Jewel, glanced up at the roof lines as she hurried below
them. She could see the man in the street, one of Step's
team.

"Coming up behind you," she called. "Don't shoot."

He turned and she recognized Mgumbe. *"Roger that,
Supervisor. Step's halfway down the block."*

She made the corner, trying to see everywhere at once.
They had only seven people lined out on the street between
the avenue and the distant fence. Privates Tanner and
Michegan were spaced in the line where their tech could be
the most effective.

"Gotcha, Supervisor," Step's flat voice announced.
*"You're taking Mgumbe's position in the avenue. That's
got the best visibility. Your job is to keep in sight of Abu
Sassi's team across the way. They're waiting on us. As we
proceed you keep an eye on Mgumbe first, and the rest of
us second. It's your job to make sure no quetzal sneaks
around our flank and cuts back down the avenue to get
behind us."*

"You got it."

*"All right, people. Let's go. For Vanveer's sake, let's not
lose anyone else."*

A chorus of rogers sounded in Kalico's earpiece.

Swallowing down a suddenly dry throat, she signaled to
the closest man to her right on Abu Sassi's team, saw his
people move forward, disappearing between the buildings.
Allenovich's line of searchers did the same.

And then the immensity of it came crashing down on
her: It was the middle of the night, rain pounding out of the
sky. A thousand hiding places were on all sides. She knew
of two people already killed. Human beings who had been
alive that morning and now were digesting in quetzal gut
juice.

*And I'm out here in the dark. The only thing between me
and them is this rifle, and whether or not I can make a kill
shot on a charging quetzal.*

Muting her com, she whispered, "I'm a clap-trapping
fool."

Step by step she made her way, checking the rooftops, searching along the building fronts. She saw one of Abu Sassi's people climb the ladder behind Sheyela Smith's shop to check the flat roof before calling, "Clear!"

Three quetzals.

There'd never been more than one.

Which begged the question: What the hell had changed?

Like a popping string of fireworks, shots came from the warehouse district. Maybe fifteen or twenty. Then silence.

"Easy does it, people," came Step's calm voice. *"Keep cool. Eyes open and think."*

Damn. How did the man do it? Especially after just having a man killed?

Knowing a quetzal was close, Kalico was ready to jump out of her skin. She made her way slowly past the big square building where Toby Montoya kept his machine shop. And there, at the alley, she stopped, heart thumping ever faster until Mgumbe stepped into view on the other side of the building. Above, the drones would be checking every inch of the roof. The man flashed his rifle each way as he searched the shadows.

Only then did he give her a nod. She glanced to her right, seeing Abu Sassi's man clearing his alley. One by one, people appeared, waiting until everyone was accounted for. Then came the knocking on doors to check for anyone in hiding. Any unlocked door meant the building had to be scoured.

After what seemed an eternity they started forward again.

The further they drove the quetzals, the more desperate the beasts would be. In the end, cornered, what were the quetzals going to do? A massed rush? Hit the lines in three places? Did the thin lines have enough firepower to bring the beasts down?

Every nerve tingling, she whispered, "They'll do their best to kill as many of us as they can."

As if the gods of violence had heard, the rain really began to pound down. It battered on the hood of her poncho, blunting her hearing. Slashed down from the sky, cutting visibility.

She twisted around, searching desperately. One of the

damn things could be paces away, obscured by the hammering downpour. She'd never know. Not until that last instant when the giant head snapped through the curtain of falling water to crush her.

Sobering, wasn't it? To know that her life was no more valuable than any other man or woman's. For the first time in her life, she was completely inconsequential. Vulnerable. And the universe just plain didn't give a damn.

Fucked bitch that she was, half of her wanted to laugh—and the other half was desperate to break down and bawl.

A blinding white light flashed off to the west. Like a giant strobe it illuminated the falling streamers of rain in a million silver streaks. Cast the outlines of buildings in black silhouette. Burned pale against the low clouds and vanished in an instant.

It was immediately followed by a loud concussion, a blast that shook buildings and sent a tremor through the earth under her feet like a small quake. Sure as hell, that wasn't thunder. Explosion!

"What the hell?" was followed with a flurry of chatter on the com.

"Hey!" Dya's voice from the control room drowned them all. *"One at a time. Report."*

Paco Anderssoni's voice came through from the military channel. *"We just had a detonation at the fence about midway between north and west gates. Looks to me like a twenty- to thirty-foot hole has been blown in the chain-link, and what's still standing on either side isn't looking any too healthy."*

Wan Xi Gow reported. *"My battle tech shows that I've got an aircar coming in from the west. Don't know if it's related."*

"Don't shoot!" another voice broke into the net. *"We're coming in with an emergency medical. What the hell is going on down there?"*

"Yvette?" Two Spot asked.

"Roger that."

"Hey, my team." Step's voice cut through, hard and commanding. *"We got a problem, people. Somebody just took down the fence. And we've got three quetzals ready to rip us into pieces and swallow us chunk by chunk."*

"So what do you want to do?" Michegan asked.

"Keep to the plan. We stay in contact with Abu Sassi's team. Sweep forward until we hit the hole in the fence. At that point, we have to stop, people. We pass that hole, half of Donovan can slip in behind us."

"Roger that," Abu Sassi radioed back. *"We'll go as far as we can to keep the line."*

And what about all the people in the residential section beyond that? Kalico asked herself, thinking about the map, about the huge section of Port Authority they just didn't have the personnel to rescue.

She ground her teeth, searching desperately through the falling rain. As hard as it was coming down, a quetzal could be looming over her, its hide the same color of black as the night.

Catching sight of Mgumbe, she started forward, searching desperately for Abu Sassi's man. Where the hell was he? She was so focused that at first the pile of cloth in the middle of the street didn't register.

She was almost upon it before she recognized the torn overalls. A rifle lay in the mud off to the side. "People," she called, "Got another probable here."

Trying to see in all directions, she bent down, rifle up and ready, and carefully reached out. Water was filling the quetzal tracks where the beast had slid, turned, and grabbed its victim.

Kalico lifted the fabric. "Got a name stitched on the breast pocket. Says Dube Dushku."

Lightning danced above, the glaring flash of white light blinding before the night-vision filters kicked in, but Kalico could still see the rent fabric. How the quetzal had torn Dushku in half.

The thunderclap deafened, and Kalico let her tears mix with the rain running down her face.

77

Talina wheeled her aircar in a one-hundred-and-eighty-degree turn, lined up with the avenue, and set it down. Even as she was spinning the fans down, she turned, calling, "Shig, Yvette, you get one end of the stretcher."

Come on, Trish. Hang in there!

Port Authority seemed to flash into existence as lightning flickered in the black skies. The front of the hospital was briefly bathed in white; then darkness swallowed all but the light over the double doors. Rain pounded down around them.

Raya Turnienko was propping the doors open as Talina killed the power and swung her legs over the side. She barely had the strength to push herself onto her feet.

Rain battered at her head and shoulders as she forced herself to grab her end of the stretcher and lead the way. The world seemed to sway and spin with each step.

"How are you doing?" Raya asked her briefly, and then turned her attention to Trish.

"Lightheaded, half in the world of dreams."

"This is bad," Raya growled as she got her first glimpse of Trish's leg. She placed one of her diagnostic monitors on Trish's neck. "Operating room. Right now!"

Shig got the doors as they hurried down the hall. Raya—having produced cutters—was clipping off Trish's pants as they went.

Talina got a good look at her friend's face: slack, deathly pale, didn't look like she was breathing.

Tal bit her lip, fought the urge to reach down and touch one of the glassy eyes for a reaction. Didn't really want to know.

Memories flashed—times when Trish had been a kid. Lost, orphaned, in need of some sort of direction. "Listen," Talina had told the stunned and grieving girl, "I've got nobody. Why don't you move in with me until you get your legs under you?"

She remembered the sudden welling relief that had rolled through Trish's wounded green eyes. Was that the same person who'd thumbed Cap's drug monitor wide open?

I need you to pull through, kid.

And if she didn't?

No. Don't even think it.

"I need Dya!" Raya called as they burst into the operating room and slipped the stretcher onto the table.

"Where is she?" Shig asked, water running down his round brown face.

"Admin, running the quetzal search."

"On it," Shig said.

Yvette added, "We'll get her here if we don't get eaten in the process." That said, she and Shig were gone.

"That right?" Talina asked as she wobbled her way over to the medical cabinet. "They said three quetzals?"

Wasn't bad enough she was worried sick about Trish, her subconscious flooded with recurring images of Xibalba and quetzals. Damn it, she had to concentrate. Her best friend was hanging by a thread, her heart was breaking, her body was exhausted, and people were dying out there.

"Apparently so," Raya muttered as she ran her hands into the sterilizer. "What are you doing in my cabinet?"

"Stim shot. I've been in Xibalba for the last week being spoon-fed and peeing into a diaper."

"What's Xibalba?"

"The battleground where my psyche chose to fight for control of my mind."

"And how's that working? Last time you tied me to my own bed."

"How about you wait to whip and beat me until this quetzal thing is over? Save my friend's life. Then you can hammer the crap out of me in payback."

Raya nodded, glanced up, and for the first time, really got a good look. "Pus and buckets, Tal. What's wrong with your eyes?"

"Just woke up with them. We can creep-freak over my

new looks as soon as we get shit back in order around here." Talina found the stim, pulled a syringe, and loaded a healthy three ccs.

"Hey, you go easy on that stuff!"

"Yeah, what I'd give for a heaping plate of chamois enchiladas drowned in poblanos, refritos, and a couple of buckets of tea." Talina pressed the syringe against her forearm and hit the release.

"Absafragginglutely miraculous," she whispered as the chemicals hit her depleted system.

"Got a problem here!" a voice said in her com. *"Everybody hold up. Nobody moves until we clear this mess of haulers."*

"Keep Trish alive," Talina called over her shoulder. She hit the hallway, stopping only long enough to grab Raya's slicker off the back of the woman's office door. Then she was out into the night.

At the aircar, she retrieved her rifle, checked the load, and made sure her belt was tight, the pistol and knife loose in their sheaths.

"Okay, Demon," she told the quetzal in her belly, "it's war, is it? Let's go turn some of your relatives into steaks and leather."

Careful, Rocket whispered in her subconscious.

Quetzal vision. It had been shading into her eyesight for the last year. The eyes through which she now saw were remarkably clear. No wonder the damned things loved to hunt on stormy nights. She might have been walking down the avenue in broad daylight. Not only that, she needed only scent the breeze eddying through the rain to smell quetzal.

And blood.

And fear.

Should have been her and Trish walking down the avenue, headed into the jaws of danger. She half expected Trish's familiar voice to break into the com at any second, asking for a report, calling orders.

Damn it, kid. Stay alive! We'll deal with what you did to Cap later.

She passed a couple of people who'd been located by the search teams and were headed for their weapons to join the hunt. Caught up to the search lines just past Montoya's shop.

"Coming up behind you. Don't shoot," she called to the woman who stood in the middle of the avenue at the key position between the lines.

"Careful, got a quetzal somewhere close."

"Kalico? What the hell are you doing out here?"

"Trying to hold the line. How was Rork Springs?"

"Not much better than this. What the hell's happened here?"

"Benteen. You heard of him?"

"Yeah, Shig and Yvette gave me a brief history on the flight in."

"He pulled all the guards off the gates to arrest the town leaders. Left the gates open, and the quetzals came right in. If you were flying in, you saw that detonation."

"Yeah. What kind of lunacy—"

"Benteen. Fits his MO. He had to know he was screwed. Probably saw that my people had taken control of the gates. My guess is that he raided one of the warehouses. It's not like Port Authority is short of explosives. What better way to make an escape than to blow a hole in the fence in the middle of a quetzal hunt?"

"Deal with him later. Three of them, huh?"

"Just found Dube Dushku's overalls. They're killing people right and left. Doesn't make any sense."

"Yeah, it does. But you'd have to be a quetzal to understand."

"Tal? That you?" Allenovich called from his position on the line as they moved into the next cross street.

"Hey, Step!"

"You joining the line?"

"Sorry. Got other business."

"Manicure? Foot massage? Must be really pressing."

She chuckled, feeling incipient panic from the quetzal in her gut. "Yeah, got a bunch of quetzals to kill."

To Kalico she said, "Watch your ass, Supervisor. Don't let any of them slip past you."

"What do you think you are doing?"

Talina took a breath. "Steaks and leather. Paybacks are a bitch."

"You're not going in there alone!"

"Got to. They're not going to be expecting me." She grinned into Kalico's night-vision goggles. "Watch your ass."

"You're a fucking lunatic, Perez."

Talina gave a wave and trotted on down the avenue. The few still-working street lights cast cones of illumination through which the rain fell. The shadows behind buildings and in the recesses under machinery might have been liquid ink.

She could feel them, knew they were waiting.

Maybe there was more than one Lord of Death in Xibalba.

"Should have killed me when you had the chance, Whitey."

78

The heavy downpour had let up, the weather gods seemingly satisfied to surrender their wrath to a constant medium rain. Lightning kept flashing, only to be followed by hollow booms of thunder as the heart of the storm moved westward to pile against the Wind Mountains.

Distant rumbling filled the heavens as Talina slipped into the darker shadows of the new school building. The soft patter of rain covered any sound of her approach, but it did the same for any of the quetzals.

Flickers of memories, ancient hunts, the stalking of long-dead quetzals, tried to form. They battled with other images: times with Trish. She saw Cap's face looking up from the steps of her porch the night she'd found him there after his resignation from the marines.

Come on, concentrate.

The scent was stronger here, and she thought it might be Whitey. The squirming of her demon could have been confirmation. But then Demon, Whitey, and their companions, they were all part of the same lineage. Was a quetzal's scent as much a genetic constant as disposition and shared ancestral knowledge?

She could imagine how the beasts were working through the buildings. Shifting back to the north. Aware that the game had changed. That the humans were slowly closing the net.

"Shig?" she asked in her com. "Where's the search line on the east?"

"Past the shuttle field gate, working its way through the lumber yard."

Step's line was stopped cold at the blown fence. The other lines would have to swing around like a gate on hinges, pivoting around Kalico's position on the avenue at the corner of Montoya's shop.

Damn it, they hadn't trained for this. They had perfected the procedure of hunting from south to north in a single unbroken wave. This was altering the plan; people were having to search ground they hadn't developed a familiarity with and do it from a completely new direction.

Mistakes would be made.

Demon chattered with delight at the thought.

Talina listened to the com chatter for a moment more, fought with her worry about Trish, then blanked her thoughts.

She let herself become a hunting quetzal. They'd shared so many thoughts, so many memories of other hunts. She could see herself in their place moving, sniffing for . . .

A sharp pain in her gut took her by surprise.

"Scared you, huh? Just figured out what I'm doing?"

And in a flash of insight, she understood. Yes, that's how they'd react. That's what they'd do.

Stepping out from the school, she trotted across the street, slipped behind the Hmong house. She negotiated the obstacle course of children's toys, rounded Monson's dome, and slowed as she advanced warily.

Toys. Trish had come to her as a teen girl, past toys, but just suffering the first interest in boys. And of course, there'd been the school cliques, the anguish and drama. The time that Randy Jenks broke Trish's heart and she had wailed that it was the end of the . . .

Will you fucking concentrate?

A shift in the wind brought her the scent. Not Whitey this time. Different quetzal. One almost smoky in odor and tainted with the metallic tang of fresh blood.

Carefully Talina hunkered down behind a four-wheeled cart. The steady and slow pulsing of her blood, the feeling of rising tension, made her swallow hard.

You're still dehydrated. Still half starved. Got to be careful.

She caught a glimpse of movement. A quetzal head poked out from behind the curve of the old Micka dome. Abandoned now since most of the *Turalon* people had moved to Corporate Mine.

Talina settled her rifle, got a solid rest on the cart's sideboard, and steadied her sight picture.

Shit. Two heads.

Now both quetzals eased out onto the street, carefully searching for any threat.

Easy, Tal. She took up slack on the trigger.

Side by side, the quetzals crept out, clearly heading back south, paralleling the fence. Seemed that they not only understood the hole in the fence, but had recognized that the noose was tightening.

Peering through her optic, she watched as the red dot bumped slightly with each beat of her heart. She placed the spot of red right at the junction of the neck and shoulders.

The faintest pressure, and . . . Bam!

The rifle bucked in her grip. As the gun dropped back in recoil she was settling the sight for a shot on the second quetzal.

The bare eddy of breeze, the snatch of odor, the prickling at the back of her neck.

Run! Rocket's voice screamed in the back of her mind.

Talina leaped, turned, fired a panicked shot as a radiant mass of enraged quetzal launched itself from the Hmong roof.

Whitey's clawed feet hammered into the damp ground where Talina had been but an instant before. The beast crushed the cart in an attempt to kill its momentum.

Talina twisted her rifle around. Shot. Point blank. And turned and ran.

Behind her came a squeal of rage. She heard the remains of the cart being cast wide. Then came the hammering of feet splashing into the muddy street.

Tal pivoted, threw the rifle up, and fired. Hardly her best shot. Nevertheless, she saw Whitey's left foreleg jerking, flopping loosely, and the quetzal screamed.

At the last instant, Talina dove to the side. She hit face-first in a pool of muddy water. Lost her rifle. Scrambled and splashed her way under a junked backhoe, and pulled her pistol.

She fought to blink the gritty water out of her eyes. "Come on, you shit-sucking son of a bitch."

The only sound was the slapping of heavy feet, a shrill twittering. Whitey was leaving, hopefully dying.

Tell me I put at least one of those rounds into your guts.

Talina, adrenaline-charged, poked her head out, clawed

her way to her rifle, and pulled it from the mud. She stumbled to her feet, staggered out into the street. Saw nothing but tracks.

"Shig? I'm at Hmong's house. The quetzals are headed for the hole in the fence. Have Step's people on alert. I've got hits on two of them."

"Roger that."

Talina shook the water and mud from her gun. With a screwdriver she saw lying on the backhoe's deck, she ensured she didn't have a barrel blockage. Be a bitch to be blown up by one's own gun at the last moment when she was trying keep from being eaten.

With her weapon as serviceable as it was going to be, she trotted off in the quetzal's wake. Wasn't like it was hard tracking.

Nor did it take more than a hundred meters of warily stalking her way between domes, around tool sheds, past drying racks and clotheslines, before she found the first quetzal. She pasted her rifle's muddy stock to her cheek, stepping slowly forward. She was just back of the tail. Could smell the beast's blood and see the dark fluids leaking from the vents at the rear. The thing was wedged between Marsden's old dome and the Gatlins'.

Tal tensed as a door was opened, and C'ian Gatlin poked his head out, a bolt gun in his hands. "What the hell hit my house?"

"Quetzal, C'ian. Careful. There's two more out here, and we can't be sure this one's dead yet."

"Rude bastard," C'ian growled under his breath, stepped out into the rain, and used his rifle to blow a hole in the quetzal's pelvic girdle. "That'll keep it off its feet."

Even as Gatlin said it, a scream could be heard off to the south. A fusillade of shots followed.

"Stay inside until the all clear," Talina called. "And lock the door behind you."

"You got it, Tal."

"Steaks and leather," she said, taking the long way around his dome. Figured it was all right to leave the dead or dying quetzal behind her. Especially with that hip shot.

She picked up the tracks where they rounded Kashasvili's dome and followed the wreckage where the beasts were knocking stuff over and spilling things in their haste.

"Shig? Status?" she asked her com.

"Step here, Tal. Two of them just escaped through the hole that idiot blew in the fence. Did the mach-five sprint, running white hot, mouths open. Probably just until they crossed the ditch and hit the fields. If the rain hadn't petered out and let them run full bore, we'd have had them."

Quetzals couldn't run full-out in the rain. Open-mouthed, doing the ram-air thing, at high speeds they'd drown themselves.

"Third one's dead. He's blocking the space between Gatlin's and Kashasvili's old dome."

She sighed, becoming aware of the rage and sorrow felt by her demon. "Yeah, well, this time you guys started it," she told the beast. "Whitey had his chance. Instead of trying to make me crazy, he could have offered a truce. It's no longer just a matter of us protecting ourselves from predators. This raises things to a whole new level."

If the fastest always win, why do so many chamois escape?

"That a quetzal saying?"

The beast chattered in response.

Talina exhaled wearily, feeling the stim starting to wear off. Slogging through the mud, she turned her tracks for the avenue.

First things first. Check on Trish.

Too much to do. Pus and blood, what she'd give for a heaping plate of hot food and tall glass of Inga's best stout.

She was tramping down the avenue, half wondering how she'd gotten there. Saw Kalico, still standing at her station. "Coming in," she called, blinking, the world kind of wavering. "Don't . . ."

She vaguely remembered slamming into the street. The clatter of her rifle could be faintly heard in the distance.

79

How in the name of all of the cursed permutations of hell could things have gone so wrong? Let alone so clap-trapping fast?

Tamarland sat, arms tucked tightly to his chest. His butt was on a packing crate, his back to one of the big containers. Some kind of two-meters-tall shipping boxes stood on either side. Another crate was stacked atop it all, making a reasonable shelter.

Wasn't the first time that Tam had found himself soaked to the bone, hungry, and absolutely enraged.

For the moment, he could chalk one up for the Donovanians.

One minute he was fully in charge, sitting fat and sassy in the admin dome. He had half of the people he needed to firmly tighten his grip on Port Authority locked away in the next room, and the next thing he knew, that slit Aguila marched in with her marines.

Not to try and depose him. But because some of the local wildlife were loose in the compound?

That's what led her to take action? Quetzals?

If any upside could be found for the situation, it was that vile siren blowing, Tam had had freedom to roam the city. People had vanished from the streets—not that they'd been out in numbers before. He'd picked the lock on the magazine building where the clay pit stored magtex: the explosive they used to loosen clay. Just for good measure, Tam had used five sticks to take the fence down.

Well, hell, what kind of fools built a fifty-foot-tall fence in the first place? And there'd been armored marine guards on all the gates. Wasn't like they were just going to let him walk out.

Then, in the dark, he'd made the muddy slog through the rain-flooded perimeter ditch, had to veer wide around the gates where marines stood with their tech. But he'd made it to the shuttle field.

Now all he needed was Torgussen to send the shuttle down.

Vixen had been making dirtside runs once every three days. That meant that Wilson should be dropping out of the sky tomorrow at about eleven. If the shuttle followed protocol, they'd lower the ramp, unload a few personnel for a half-day's leave, and load up a couple of crates of vegetables for the ship's galley.

By this time, *Vixen*'s tanks should be a little more than quarter full. Not that it mattered. All Tam had to do was get back on board. Once there, he was back in his element. Could order the ship refueled from *Freelander*'s tanks, and they'd be on their way.

The last time, Torgussen had taken him by surprise. Turnabout was indeed fair play, and now it would be Tam's turn.

Torgussen was Corporate. He understood the rules, unlike these fricking maniac Donovanians. With a gun to his head, the good captain would do anything Tam asked him to do. Especially if the lives of his crew and the safety of his ship were at stake.

Tam made a tsking with his lips. Had to hand it to Shig and Yvette. They'd played him perfectly. Lulled him into thinking he'd grabbed the whole of Port Authority by its dangling balls. Skipping out the way they had? It set him up for failure in a way he could never have anticipated.

Who were these lunatics, anyway?

As rain beat on the containers around him, his thoughts went back to that last session in the conference room. He'd been looking right into Oshanti's eyes. The woman had known that he'd kill her as soon as look at her. And she'd known better than he that it would have destroyed him.

Who would have thought that humans had that kind of spirit in them? It almost reeked of the mythic stories about the past. Back before The Corporation had finally civilized and tamed humanity into an orderly and productive society.

If only he'd been able to get them to the prison, get them separated, play them against each other, and really make them suffer, he might have been able to beat, starve, and torture that stubbornness out of them. Sure as vacuum he knew all the psychiatric methods to destroy a person's sanity, break them, and bring them to heel.

If only I'd been given the time.

He'd understood that he'd lost the moment the conference room doors had burst open and his captives had broken out into the hallway. At the sight he'd triggered the block of magtex. And . . . nothing.

Who had unlocked their bindings? Rendered his bomb inoperative?

Not Tallisvilli. The guy wasn't courageous enough—let alone possessed of the initiative to have thought of it.

And then he remembered Allison stepping into his office, that half-fearful, half-triumphant look in her eyes.

"The guard at the door would have passed you, my love," he whispered. "You could have told him anything. He'd have believed you. Thought you were still on my side. And you knew the magtex could only be detonated through my implant."

What were her words? *I'm just trying to limit the bloodshed?*

He wondered what she had done with the detonator. Flushed it?

No matter. All he needed now was to get aboard that shuttle. Once he'd made it to *Vixen,* there were other bolder measures he could take.

80

Dortmund had never been alone. Ever. The closest he'd been to it was when he'd closed his office door to study or work on some paper. But even then it had been with the knowledge that people were passing on the other side of the portal. That he was surrounded by tens of thousands of human beings who were no more than a moment's walk away.

And he'd been connected through his implants, imbedded in the com net. At the merest thought, he'd be connected to anyone and everyone. Capable of accessing any kind of data.

I am totally isolated.

The reality of it felt crushing. Dortmund's heart began to pound.

He almost toppled the chair as he ran to the door and charged outside into the morning. The clouds were breaking, the damp air pungent with Capella III's magical and unique odors. Rays of brilliant light streaked out from the eastern horizon and rimed the patchy white tufts of cloud in silver.

The chime rose and fell down in the drainage, and a flock of scarlet fliers chased among the treetops rising above the narrow band of vegetation around the creek.

Trish Monagan's bullet-riddled aircar sat abandoned, a charge cable running to its power pack.

"Hello!" Dortmund bellowed.

The planet ignored him.

His was a pointless existence for a suddenly meaningless human being.

"Kylee!" he bellowed out, dropping to his knees.

"Please," he whimpered. Then he let the sobs come.

"If there is an empty corner of hell, I am in it."

With all of his heart, he wished for a quetzal to come and eat him. Could imagine it as he'd seen it the other morning. Like a mound of fluid rock, rising, morphing, a monster grown from stone.

It would loom over him, the terrifying mouth splitting open as it reached down to crush and rend his body.

How long did he wait? Fifteen minutes? A half hour? Maybe more?

In the end he couldn't stand it. His knees hurt too much on the unforgiving sandstone.

He fought his way to his feet, endured the pins and needles of renewed circulation.

His stomach growled. Empty as his soul.

Turning, he walked to the dome, grabbed up the burden basket, and trudged his lonely way down the trail to the drainage. Who knew what awaited him down there? Any of a thousand forms of lurking death.

But if a man had to die, he might as well do it trying to fill his belly.

He'd barely started down the trail, his attention on places where quetzals would hide. So, of course, he forgot to watch his feet. Or remember that the plants on Donovan moved. Which is why he blundered right into the thorncactus.

81

Someone slammed a door; voices intruded on Talina's dream.

She blinked her eyes open. Stared up at the overhead lights and familiar ceiling. Some part of her derived a morbid sense of amusement that she could instantly place herself. Knew exactly where she was: hospital, room seven.

The quetzal dream clung to her like old cobwebs. She gave a slight shake of her head, tried to rid herself of the afterimages.

As she did, she took stock of her body. Arms, legs, torso, all present. Nothing in a cast. No bandages. No sutures.

How the hell did I get here this time?

She sat up, found herself in a medical smock. The IV told her that while she had no physical injuries that she could either remember or find on her body, something bad had happened.

Okay, think, Tal. What were you . . .

Ah, yes. Hunting quetzals in the rain.

It came back to her. The flight through the storm, the hole blown in the fence. Three of the beasts loose in PA. The one she'd shot.

She sat up, pulled the IV from the back of her hand, and tried to come to terms with the horrible taste in her mouth. Spinning out of images of quetzals, gunshots, and mud came visions of food.

How long had it been since she'd eaten? No wonder her Xibalba dreams had been filled with tamales, enchiladas, chocolate, and carne asado.

She found her coveralls, washed and folded on the visitor's chair. After the mud puddle, someone had been a saint.

She was dressed, wondering which room Trish was in when Dya stepped in. "Hey, you're up."

"Yeah. Figured I was on my back long enough out at Rork."

"Where's Kylee? I've been worried sick since you came in without her."

"Last she was seen, it was running with quetzals out at Rork. Dya, I swear, I'll be out to get her just as soon as I can. Not only that, I think I know just the place for her. A place where she's going to be safe, and where you can go and see her."

For a moment, rock-solid Dya wilted, misery filling her face. A tear broke from the corner of her eye. "I just want my daughter back. This is like a never-ending nightmare. Never knowing if she's alive or dead, or hurt."

"Yeah, well, don't blame yourself. And don't go digging her grave yet. If anyone can survive Donovan, it's her."

Dya sucked a deep breath. A moment later, the iron-willed woman was back. "Well, that's something. I just want to bring my little girl home."

Just not quite yet, Dya. Tal said, "Listen. Gotta check on Trish, then I'm outta here. I've got things—"

Raya appeared in the doorway behind Dya, ordering, "Not so fast. Park your ass back on that bed. You and I have to talk."

Talina lifted her hands in surrender. "I'm sorry. Ever so sorry that I tied you to your own bed. I needed to get out of PA before I hurt anyone. Figured you'd call out the dogs to keep me here."

Raya stood like an avenging angel, arms crossed, a scowl on her usually sour Siberian face. "That's a first, you know. Never had a patient humiliate me that way before. However, let's set that aside for the moment. What I need to know is what the hell happened to you out at Rork Springs?"

Talina sighed, rubbed her face as she braced her butt on the elevated bed. "I had to fall apart. Then I had to put myself together again. The quetzals and I rewired my brain out there. I'm still me, but I'm different."

"How so?" Dya asked.

"I feel . . . alien. Part quetzal. Know things differently. The way I perceive time has changed. Sort of like I'm part of a telescoping series of events. Death's not the same. I am one and many all at once. The quetzal consciousness I call Demon is still down in my gut—a combination of quetzal molecules that hate me and want me dead. More so since I shot that one last night and wounded Whitey. Rocket, Flash, the Briggs and the Rork quetzals are all rolled into one and form a different part of my subconscious, one that rides on my shoulders."

"You know how that sounds?"

"Like I'm crazy? The thing is, I can shut it off. Use the quetzal sense when I need it. Like the ancient Maya concept of one and many. Right now I need to be human, so I'm human."

"Sooner, rather than later, I want you in the lab so we run a full analysis."

"You said Kylee's still out at Rork Springs?" Dya asked, expression again pinched with worry.

"Soon as I can get a charge in the aircar, I promise I'll be out to get her."

Assuming she's still alive.

Not that Dya needed to hear that.

"What about these quetzals Yvette says Kylee ran off with?"

"Different lineage than the ones here. And yeah, lineage is big when it comes to quetzals. The last time I had anything to do with the Rork bunch, they were really curious about us. My take, after living with their molecules, they've never really dealt with humans before."

"What about the one that attacked Trish?" Raya asked.

"Can't tell you. I was still locked away in Xibalba spinning fantasies."

Dya said, "Yvette told me that Dr. Weisbacher is still out there. Just in case Kylee needs him."

Talina laughed. "Now there's a piece of work. Hey, I'm so hungry I could eat a boot. How about we talk later, huh? I just want to see how Trish is doing and be on my . . . What?"

She glanced back and forth.

Raya, tough as quetzal leather, said, "She was already dead when you brought her in, Tal. Didn't want to drop that on you when you were headed out to battle quetzals. Dya and I tried. She'd been gone too long to bring back."

Oh, God no.

Talina closed her eyes, felt her heart drop like a stone.

"Sorry, Tal," Dya whispered.

"Yeah. Fuck." And the emptiness just kept growing.

For a weeknight, The Jewel was booming. Dan had started
the evening by announcing a free round on the house for
the searchers who'd put their lives on the line during the
quetzal scare. He'd had Vik pour liberal amounts of the
high proof to fuel the crowd.

As Dan watched the action at the tables, he had to wonder. Was it that they'd dodged the bullet again? That the
town survived? Or that the patrons who crowded to bet
their plunder at the tables and called for alcohol were just
fully aware that they'd made it while fourteen of their number had not?

Thirteen had died at the hands of the quetzals. Port Authority hadn't lost so many to a quetzal raid since the early
days nearly thirty years ago.

And then had come news about Trish Monagan.

The other draw that night was Allison. She looked radiant as she moved between the tables in her silver form-
fitting dress. Not that she hadn't always walked with a
slinky grace, but tonight she did so with a self-confidence
Dan had never seen before.

Men crowded around her, offering to buy her a drink, to
do her any service. The women in attendance offered Ali
any courtesy, gave her that slight nod of respect that he
wasn't used to seeing from them.

So, she's the fucking hero of the moment.

It didn't hurt that she had bandages on her left arm and
leg where Raya Turnienko had dug shrapnel out of her.
She'd barely avoided the brunt of Benteen's nasty little grenade.

Allison Chomko had been the person who'd dared to
sneak in and unlock the captives' chains. She was the one
who had reached over, took a deep breath, and pulled the

detonator out of a little block of magtex that Benteen had left as a final fuck you if things went off the rails. She'd been the one to drop it into the jar of acid Yvette kept in her office to analyze minerals.

And now she's home. Which means what for me?

That was the question. As the night had progressed, she'd shot him the occasional glance, sometimes accompanied by a slight smile. The way she looked at him now? He wasn't sure that he didn't prefer the old days when he'd kept her drugged on blue nasty.

Whatever she had in store for him, he'd find out. For the moment, the money and plunder were rolling in. "New shooter!" he called as Lawson crapped out on the table and Shin Wang raked in a stack of gold SDRs.

Fourteen people, including Dube Dushku, were dead. It lent a curious solemnity, and at the same time a sense of strength to the celebration. Calls for toasts were made. "Here's to Dube!" or "Let's drink to good old Willy!" And the cups were raised.

Nor was it just to the dead: "To Talina Perez!"

"Hooraw!" "To Tal!" "God bless Tal!" "Steaks and leather!" the shouts would come.

Sometimes Dan wondered about what motivated him. He stepped over to the bar, had Vik pour him a whiskey. Climbing onto a chair, he called, "Your attention!"

It took a couple of tries, but the room stilled, all eyes going his way.

"You all know that Officer Monagan had it in her heart to put me in my grave." Dan cataloged the various reactions to his remarks. "Fact is, ladies and gentlemen, her sudden death has left me with the realization that my life will be a lot less interesting. Here's to Trish Monagan. God bless you, girl, and ride the stars!"

"Ride the stars!" the voices cried in unison as glasses were raised and drained.

As he climbed down again, people slapped his back, shook his hand, heads were inclined in his direction.

"You surprise me sometimes," Allison said when he'd finally escaped the well-wishers and made his way back to the cage. She was giving him that look again. The new one. The one he hadn't been able to fathom.

For the love of pus, she wasn't going to make herself into some sort of adversary, was she? It would be a shame to have to take . . .

"Trish was a friend, you know." Allison smiled sadly, reliving something long ago in her past.

"Yeah. Little younger than you."

"You really sad that she's dead?"

"I don't do sad. Never have, never will. That doesn't mean I won't miss her. The kid had spunk." He gave her his boyish grin with the dimples. "And for an added benefit, all those marks out there drained their glasses and headed back to the bar."

"Forever practical?" She arched a blond eyebrow.

"Fucking A. What about you?"

"I do sad. Always have. Always will. But I do practical, too."

"So what does the hero of the hour think is practical now?"

"Forty-nine percent of The Jewel."

"Why the fuck would I give you forty-nine?"

"Because I want to be a player, not just one of the played. I'm not challenging you. You'd cut my throat in the middle of the night if I did. I want a contract for a bigger share of the responsibility and earnings. Pursue some of my own investments and projects."

"And what do I get out of it?"

"More of what you're getting now. And I shoulder part of the burden of running things." She ended with a knowing smile.

"You think I'm going to agree to this?"

"You will if I make it worth your while." She scanned the busy room, eyes on the marks as they gambled and drank. Angelina was leading Dan Morgan back to her room for a quick fuck. Dalia should be finishing off her john and back on the floor trolling for a trick any time now. Vik had a line in front of the bar. Roulette and craps were crowded.

"Worth my while how?"

"I think I'll take you back to the office, maybe sweep the desk clean of papers, and screw you like you haven't been screwed in years."

"Practical, huh?"

"Can't think of a better way to celebrate a new partnership."

He grinned in appreciation, wondering the whole time, *Yeah, Ali, but what does it mean?*

83

Trish's hand was cold, limp. The rigor had passed. She'd have to go into the ground soon. Another in the long and beloved line up on cemetery hill. Once again Talina would have to help lower someone she loved into the unforgiving red dirt. Try and still her tears as she shoveled soil onto a corpse who'd once filled her with joy.

Talina sat beside the gurney. It stood in a hospital room. The morgue was full. Not all of the quetzal victims had been eaten. Turned out that quetzals could only hold so much.

She held Trish's hand and stared down at her friend's pale face. A stranger's face, cold as it was and so different in Talina's enhanced infrared vision. The expression was slack, the sprinkling of freckles on Trish's nose in marked contrast to the washed-out tones of her bloodless cheeks.

Yes, a stranger's face. Someone Talina no longer knew. Not the precocious twelve-year-old Trish who'd come to her wide-eyed and hurting all those years ago. Not the wounded teen who'd shared her house through the long and questing years as she searched for a way forward in the wake of her mother's rape and murder.

"Never told you the truth about that," Talina told the corpse. "You really didn't need to know. Sometimes it would be better if we kept our secrets."

Better if Tal had gone to her own grave without knowing Trish's role in Cap's death.

With her free hand, Talina rubbed her brow, tried to make sense of it. Trish had been the one who dialed the drug feed wide open. Did it to keep Talina from a life of bondage where she'd struggle to care for a cripple?

"Love, Trish? Really?"

But the inert and decomposing flesh offered up no defense.

"I want to be in security with you." Trish's assertion

echoed in Talina's ears. What had that been? Four years ago? Three? Trish had stood defiantly, arms crossed under her breasts, one leg forward.

"Someone's got to have your back. Who else can you trust after Clemenceau?"

"What you did to Cap? Is that having my back? Cutting my feet out from under me over the Rocket thing?" Getting yourself shot by accident because you let some insanely stupid piece of soft meat get a hold of your pistol?

Or was it sharing cherries in this same hospital? Having Talina's back in the bush, putting her life on the line when Talina showed no more sense than God gave a rock with Whitey? Or hauling Talina's senseless and broken body out of that canyon?

The pain and grief rose to hollow out Talina's stomach and tie a knot at the base of her throat as Trish's grin floated in Talina's memory. All that passion and spirit, gone. Flicked off. Lost forever.

Maybe it was the time Trish had her first taste of coffee. Made a face, and said, *"And this is what all the fuss is about?"*

"Yeah, kid. That's the girl I knew." She squeezed the cold and limp hand. "For the record, you should know. You never lost me to any quetzal. I lost myself."

She sniffed, fought tears. "Should be me lying on the slab. Shouldn't have left you to carry all the weight. If I'd been here . . ."

What? She'd have shot this Benteen down? Been in her right mind without having the time to put herself back together? Become Whitey's molecularly programmed murderer?

Whatever. Trish would still be alive, that devilish gleam in her green eyes, her quick brain churning out quips. She'd have the promise of life before her—a chance at the compassionate lover she always wanted to meet, but never quite seemed to find. Hell, maybe she'd even manage to finally bring Dan Wirth down.

Not now. Not after Dortmund Weisbacher's bullet.

"Ah, hell, Trish." And the hole inside grew, ached, tried to overwhelm. Talina swallowed hard, feeling Demon squirm in her gut. Felt Rocket's invisible weight shift on her shoulders.

"I shouldn't have let things get so strained between us. My fault."

The bloodless lips remained still, damning Talina of any hope of redemption.

Reluctantly Talina released Trish's hand, carefully replaced it next to the dead woman's side. Stood.

Again she battled back the tears, tried to loosen the grief-knot at the base of her throat, and took a deep breath.

"You all right?" Shig asked from the doorway.

"Fuck no." Talina exhaled wearily. "After burying all the people I've loved, why the hell does it still hurt so much? You'd think I'd be used to it by now."

"Remember what you asked me? How you worried that you might be something else? Alien? No longer trustworthy in human company? As long as you still grieve, as long as you weep for those you love, you are still our Talina. In your center, whatever your Tao now, that single fact remains a shining light."

"Glad you've got faith. You don't know how I'm tempted to treat that son of a bitch professor. In my book that kind of stupidity and irresponsibility is a death sentence."

"One newcomer at a time. Right now we've got another problem that needs your attention: Benteen. He might have been careless enough to pull the guards off the gates and arrogant enough to blow a hole in the fence, but unlike Weisbacher, he may be the deadliest man you've ever faced."

"I want him. Made a promise to Trish. You understand that, don't you, Shig?"

"After what he did here that might be asking—"

"I mean it. Don't buck me on this."

Shig's eyes shone with worry as he shrugged in response.

"My word on that, Trish," Talina promised the cold corpse on the gurney. Then she turned and pushed past Shig, her heart like lead in her chest.

84

So, where the hell was the shuttle? Tamarland crouched in his hiding place, having waited out a whole day and a second night. He was hungry. He'd been able to slake his thirst by creeping around after dark and sucking up rain water where it pooled atop the shipping crates.

Everything hinged on that shuttle. He had worked out the permutations. Most likely scenario? Port Authority had radioed up that they had a mess on their hands trying to fix the gaping hole in their fence. It wouldn't have been unreasonable to have waved off *Vixen*'s usual crew rotation until the town could be brought back to some sense of normalcy.

Another explanation was that Torgussen had been apprised of Tam's escape. That the captain had chosen not to land planetside until Tam was captured. Which put a definite kink in the plans.

So, he'd begun working out the details on plan B. Sitting right across the way, gleaming in the morning light, was the Port Authority shuttle. The thing was occasionally piloted by a *Turalon* crewman named Manny Bateman. Tam had downloaded all the relevant personnel data into his implants during his short tenure as Director. All he needed was for Bateman to appear and head for the shuttle. Tam would manage to intercept the man and his crew as they approached the ramp. Bateman was the key. The guy was Corporate down in his bones, from *Turalon* after all. He'd fly the thing if a pistol was put to his head.

Plan C—should it come to that—would be the arrival of the Supervisor's shuttle from Corporate Mine. Tam hadn't a clue as to who the pilot might be, or what unknown hurdles taking that ship might entail. Not that it mattered. If he had to leave dead people in his wake, that was the cost of getting up to *Vixen*.

Short of armored marines, no collection of local security could stop him once he got on board. His implants, skills, and ruthless dedication to the task made any attempt at resistance hopeless.

He'd been in considerably tighter shit than this and survived, much to his adversaries' dismay.

A grim smile played across his lips. Paybacks were a bitch. He had a final gesture for Port Authority. He imagined the satisfaction he'd feel during those last moments when he sent *Freelander* plummeting out of the heavens trailing atmospheric fire. He'd threaten, cajole, or beat Seesil Vacquillas into programming it to impact in the middle of Port Authority.

"Artollia? I swear in your name that I will see that sight before *Vixen* inverts symmetry for Solar System."

Movement caught his eye. Three people. A man and two women. They emerged through the man gate and started across the shuttle field. Tam only needed to watch for a few moments before one of the cargo techs working a loader on the other side of the field called, "Hey, Manny? Where you headed?"

"Corporate Mine. They've got cable there we can use to fix the fence."

"Just like clockwork," Tam whispered to himself, straightening. "Torgussen, you son of a whore, I'm going to be knocking on your hatch within the hour."

Tam took a moment to dust the last of the dried mud from his cuffs. His shoes he'd carefully scraped clean over the intervening time.

He timed his exit perfectly, strolling along, pace as lazy as that of a man out for an afternoon stroll. To his amusement, the three seemed locked in a conversation, gesticulating, not paying the slightest heed to their surroundings.

From Tam's angle of approach and speed, he was coming in just behind them.

". . . Can hold together the sections of blasted wire," the man was saying.

"Thank God Kalico was gracious enough to loan us the materials until we can manufacture more on *Freelander*," the taller woman said.

Like a wolf behind sheep, he closed the distance.

Tamarland was behind them now, unconsciously matching steps with theirs. Something about Bateman bothered him. The way the man walked, he seemed to have a muscular roll to his stride. Not what Tam expected from a shuttle pilot and space dog.

The taller of the women had short hair, broad shoulders, a spring to her step. She wore a heavy quetzal-hide coat. The other woman was still a good five-foot-seven, her thick black hair streaming down almost to her waist. Only on Donovan. Any spacing regs back in Solar System would have insisted her head be shaven.

Tam enjoyed that surge of incipient success as he reached into his coat and laced his fingers around the Talon's grip.

Instead of reaching up for ramp control Bateman stopped, asking, "You ready, Tal?"

"Let's do this," the slim woman said.

Tam had his pistol out, leveled. "Please don't do anything rash. I need you to lower the shuttle ramp."

The three turned as if on pivots.

Tam started, stunned by the black-haired woman's eyes. Large, dark, and like nothing human that he'd ever seen. He might have been staring into pits of midnight that belied the laws of time and space.

"So you're Benteen," the black-haired woman said. "They say you're as heartless as a scorpion."

He caught himself, forced the old confidence back. "No sense in anyone dying. Open the ramp."

The woman called Tal actually stepped forward, closing the distance between them to less than a pace. Staring into her eyes was mesmerizing. "Far enough. Any closer, and I'll blow your guts out."

"It's been tried," she told him, a weary smile on her lips. Some part of him realized that even with the weird eyes, she was a handsome woman. Her face well-featured.

Tam was still absorbing her presence, had the flash of insight that here was a woman even more awe-inspiring than Shayne. That tickle of immediate danger barely had time to form before she blurred into movement.

His arm was wrenched sideways so violently the bone snapped under the impact. His Talon flew off to the side. She had him, lifting, pivoting. The world spun sideways.

The twisting of Tam's body felt like a physical blow. He was clawing for balance, turning in midair.

The impact on rock-hard clay stunned him.

Breathless, his nerves and senses in heterodyne, he couldn't breathe. Panic—electric in its intensity—paralyzed him. Pain wracked his body.

He couldn't so much as draw breath to scream as his coat was pulled off. His pockets were searched. His grenades, knives, and stun equipment stripped away. And then his arms were wrenched behind him and his own restraints used to bind them tight despite the agony of his broken arm.

The raven-haired beauty was leaning down, her alien eyes seeming to suck at his very soul. "You're in luck. People are feeling sorry for me. Most wanted to just put a bullet in your head. It was one of Trish's last requests that has a more just and fitting punishment."

"Whaaa . . ." He finally managed to gulp a breath as the world was closing down like a tunnel of darkness around his vision. It took all of his will to keep focus.

"What? Why, a little ride with me. But first, I've got business out west at Rork Springs."

"You sure you want to do this?" the big man asked.

Seeing the man's face, Tam recognized Step Allenovich's thick features. The other woman? Yeah, had to be Dina Michegan. One of Aguila's marines.

"Who . . . who are . . . ?" He was still battling for breath. Trying to win the struggle against his jangling nerves.

"Head of security. Talina Perez. Nice to make your acquaintance, you toilet-sucking piece of shit."

85

Kalico stared at the ruined section of fence where a crane was lifting bent and twisted chain-link as each piece was cut free of the tangle. Not to say that the fence had ever been a thing of beauty. It had, after all, been patched together out of ten-foot-tall rolls, five high, lifted and affixed to poles. The heights were additionally fortified by a hot wire that ran to the solar cells and the battery farm.

Without the hot wire, it would never have stopped a quetzal, especially a young one. The fact that it was guarded day and night meant that anything trying to climb it would be discovered and could be dispatched before it reached the top.

Bems, skewers, spikes, and sidewinders wouldn't have had a chance.

Shig stood beside Kalico, his hands and forearms tucked into his sleeves. A thoughtful look possessed his face as Lawson and his crew cut damaged sections loose with long-handled cutters and wrestled the bent mess over to where Montoya was trying to fashion a sort of roller that would re-flatten the wire into something they could once again piece together into some sort of barrier.

"I think I could have my people build a wire extruder." Kalico fingered the scar running along her jaw. "It's not like we're shy of the raw materials."

"Wire's way beyond the foundry's capability," Shig agreed.

"Chain-link can't be that hard; they've been making it for a couple of centuries."

"It's just getting the time to manufacture the machines."

"Any luck finding the two escaped quetzals?" Kalico asked.

"Took too long to come to grips with the chaos here. Not only did we need to run Benteen down, figure a trap, and contain him, but there were so many casualties. Funerals to attend. It's a shock, Kalico. It's been years since Port Authority has suffered a catastrophe like this. Trish was dead, Step needed to keep security together here. Look at the size of this hole. Our only protection until we get this fixed is an armed human presence. And Talina . . . well, she's hurting."

"What do you make of her now?"

"Something new. Both frightening and exciting at the same time. She represents an entirely new Tao. I can't wait to hear the whole story, all about her journey to Xibalba."

"I thought she was insane to head out into the darkness to hunt those quetzals like that."

"Everyone in Port Authority knows that she saved lives. Killed one, wounded Whitey. I suspect we're just at the beginning of understanding when it comes to Tal."

She studied him with a thoughtful sidelong glance. "So, tell me. Was it worth it? Benteen's short reign cost you thirteen people killed. Your fence is gone, the raiding quetzals with it. Benteen might be paying for his sins, but it all could have been avoided if you'd just shot the bastard the moment he stepped down off that ramp."

Shig's lips bent into that benign smile. "For as clever a human being as his reputation would have led you to believe, Tamarland Benteen really wasn't very smart, was he? That day when I met him at the shuttle, I told him everything he needed to know to survive."

"There're times, Shig, when I wonder if talking to you isn't just an excuse to hear my jaws flapping. I thought I asked you a question."

Shig gave her that maddening and knowing look. "Benteen was the price of freedom. It has to be paid every time a strong man, a pathological leader, or a messiah comes along. Port Authority is achingly aware of this again. So are you, Supervisor. It's a curious question though, isn't it?"

"Which question? We have a series on the table at this point."

"Whether the thirteen people killed by the quetzals were a smaller price to pay than if the people had marched on Benteen. But we shall never know. The universe is at heart random and chaotic."

"You're assuming I wouldn't have moved on him before

he could kill innocent people. I was contemplating just that when news came of the quetzals."

Shig was now beaming that irritating smile. "And what, my good friend, makes you think that all the lessons learned were only by Benteen and the people of Port Authority?"

"You think that I was part of your little educational experiment? Sorry. I still think your libertarian crap is just that."

Shig gave a modest shrug as another section of broken fence was cut loose to fall with a crash. "Of course you do. But I will keep your secret. Now, how about we retreat to Inga's? I'm having a terrible craving for a glass of her wine. I'll even stand you to a whiskey, and we will talk political philosophy."

She propped a hand on her pistol. "What makes you think I want to bore myself to death with that nonsense?"

"Because friendship is a most curious thing, isn't it?"

"Yeah, who'd have thought?" She chuckled as she turned and followed him back down the street. "What do you want to trade for a packet of coffee?"

86

"We're on final approach," Mick Wilson's voice came through the radio speaker and filled the room at Rork Springs.

The nightmare was coming to an end. Dortmund uttered a weary sigh of relief, rose from the chair, and limped his way across the floor to the front door. The pain in his leg continued to burn in excruciating agony. The calf had swollen to fill the confines of his pant leg.

He'd abandoned the burden basket down where he'd had his encounter with the thorncactus. The agony had been disabling, a fiery searing that left him screaming and stunned. More than once on his stumbling way back to the Rork Springs dome, Dortmund had considered lying down on the bare rock and surrendering to inevitable death.

But that hurt just as much as staggering along did.

So he'd made his way to the dome. Collapsed onto the couch, heedless of Trish Monagan's bloodstains, and let tears streak from his eyes.

Some deep part of his brain remembered that the thorns should be pulled out. And, of course, there was no one there to pull them. No physician, no nurse or trauma specialist. Just him.

He'd managed to wobble to his feet, searched drawers until he found pliers, and shrieked as he yanked each of the long, fire-laced thorns from his flesh.

On the verge of throwing up, he had pulled the last one, and was gasping for breath when his watery gaze had fixed on the radio.

Whimpering with anticipation, he'd staggered over, grabbed up the mic, and rejoiced when somebody named Two Spot had answered. He'd pleaded for rescue, only to be told that Port Authority had its own problems for the moment. And no, no one could be spared to fly out and get him.

Some part of his brain had kicked in at that point. He'd asked for the frequency monitored by *Vixen*.

"We're reading you, Dr. Weisbacher," Valencia Seguro's voice had responded.

"I need you to come and get me," he'd pleaded. "Can you send the scientific shuttle? Can you follow this signal? Help! I'm abandoned down here!"

"Roger that, Dr. Weisbacher. We've got the source of your transmissions pinpointed. We estimate four hours to ETA."

He'd talked to Seguro for twenty or thirty minutes, much of it babbling, explaining about his leg, demanding that they get him into the medical bay as soon as he was aboard. He was rambling on about quetzals when she informed him that Trish Monagan was dead. Of his gunshot.

Stunned, Dortmund had reluctantly signed off. It hit him that in Port Authority, they'd blame him. Hold him responsible for her death. He sat frozen, sick to his stomach with worry. Only to hobble for the door, desperate to await the shuttle.

He'd stepped outside when he saw the quetzal sniffing around Trish Monagan's bullet-riddled aircar. He stopped short, gaping in disbelief.

"No! Go away! They're coming to get me!"

Flat-footed, the quetzal leaped over the aircar. Dortmund barely managed to slam the door and lock it before the beast hit the portal with an impact that shook the dome.

Peering out the window, Dortmund stared eyeball to eyeballs with the creature. The most notable attribute was the single long bullet scar than ran along the huge wedge of skull right up to the ruined middle eye.

Okay, nothing friendly about this one.

Dortmund ran back to the radio, keyed the mic, and screamed, "I've got a quetzal at my front door!"

Seguro told him there wasn't a thing they could do about it until the shuttle arrived.

So he waited, leg burning so painfully he thought his flesh was melting, frightened half out of his wits, until Mick Wilson's voice assured him they were on final approach.

Giddy, almost dancing, he limped from window to window. Looking out, he could see no sight of the quetzal. But yes, there to the west—the setting sun gleaming from its hull—the shuttle could be seen banking around, losing altitude.

"Oh, blessed stars," Dortmund cried. "That's the most beautiful sight I've ever seen!"

And on it came, landing on the stone, thrusters sending heat waves to wrinkle the air. Then the ramp lowered and Security Officer Jace Ali stepped down, a rifle in his hands.

Dortmund threw the door open, hobbling out for all he was worth. Still, he kept throwing glances over his shoulder, expecting at any instant to see the bullet-marked quetzal streaking down to get him.

"Doctor? You all right?" Ali asked, taking him by the hand.

"Just get me off this fucking rock."

"Yes, sir."

The man helped him up the ramp, got him into a seat, and Dortmund Weisbacher experienced sheer, gut-sparkling exultation as the shuttle lifted off. Nothing in his entire life had ever felt so good as the g-force shoving him back into his seat.

"What now, sir?" Ali asked as they left atmosphere behind.

"I am never setting foot off *Vixen* again."

Then came the magical moment when the shuttle docked, and in an instant, Dortmund's implants all came back to life. He whooped in ecstasy.

Seguro met him at the hatch along with the medical officer and a port-a-med.

In the galley, after his leg had been treated, Torgussen appeared, drew a cup of coffee, and took a seat. Dortmund was shoveling a supper ration into his mouth, washing it down with draught after draught of ice tea.

"Good to see you again, Doctor. Glad we could be of service. What are your future plans?"

He studied the captain thoughtfully. "I think I'll be in my room and in the office for the most part. I have a lot of writing to do. If I do my job correctly, no one ever again will commit the atrocity that Radcek did with Capella III. I am the ultimate record of this evolutionary disaster. How soon do we return to Solar System?"

Torgussen gave him a flat stare. "We don't."

"Excuse me?"

"Crew voted. No one wants to take the risk of returning to Solar System another fifty years into the future. None of the other planets, asteroids, or resources have been systematically surveyed. By then, hopefully, Solar System will have figured out the problem and sent a ship with the right math."

"Unacceptable. I have to get my report back. I demand—"

"Is there something wrong with your hearing? Demand all you want. But, Doctor, you become too much of a pain in my ass? I'll dump you right back at Port Authority."

A place to which Dortmund could never return. All they'd remember was that he'd shot Trish Monagan. That she'd died because of him.

In that moment, his appetite died, his heart gone leaden in his chest.

"What if another ship never comes?" he asked weakly.

"There are worse places to be in the galaxy, Doc."

"In that, Captain, you are most certainly mistaken."

And with that, he rose and limped his way back to his personal quarters.

87

Talina wheeled the aircar around on approach to Rork Springs. Compared to the last flight Talina had made, this one was a joy. A perfect day for flying as she watched the remarkable landscapes and geology pass below. From the chaparral-like bush, to the Blood Hills, then the jagged immensity of the Wind Mountains, and now the remarkable greens and blues of the endless and dense forest.

The Rork dome, buildings, and facilities seemed to be all right. No sign of Weisbacher or Kylee. And what was . . . ? Yes, that was a quetzal carcass a hundred yards down from Trish's aircar. The thing had been stripped of most of the meat and organs. A flight of scarlet fliers burst from the bones, shrieking warnings and flapping off for the safety of the drainage.

She banked to the right, dropped down from the sky, and onto the reddish rock beside Trish's aircar. She set down without so much as a bump. Automatics couldn't have done better.

For a moment, all she could do was stare at the bullet-riddled vehicle beside hers. All the pain, grief, and disbelief broke out anew. She *hated* Dortmund Weisbacher, and now had to decide what to do about it. Her impulse was just to shoot him down on sight. At the thought, she made a face, thinking back to the day when she would have shot Sian down in the street. Fact was, from here on out, she had to ride herd on her first impulses.

"Kylee?" Talina called.

To Talina's surprise, the girl emerged from the dome, hair in tangles, her oversized coveralls scuffing as she trotted out.

The girl called out, "Can you believe that Dortmund Short Mind ran off and didn't even close the door behind him? What a dit."

"Tell me that dead quetzal out there got him." Talina indicated the corpse with her rifle.

"No such luck. That dead one? Tried to stir up the locals against us. Dortmund Short Mind grazed him with a bullet when he shot Trish. I acted as bait so the Rorkies could ambush him."

"Where is Weisbacher?"

"Called a shuttle down and flew off. That's when he left the door hanging wide open. I think it was a *Vixen* shuttle, had a picture on the side of what I think might have been a fox."

"Shuttle, huh?" Talina glanced up at the sky. "And where were you?"

"Hiding out with the local quetzals. Mostly they're nice. But different. Really curious. Half the time I was afraid they'd try and learn me the permanent way."

"Get in," Talina told her. "Or do you want to spend the rest of your life wondering if you're going to be swallowed just out of curiosity?"

"If you're talking Port Authority, I'll stay and take my chances."

Talina laughed at that, climbing back into the aircar. "Nope. Taking you back to PA would be like putting a time bomb in the middle of the town. I've got another place in mind. One where I think you're going to like them as much as they like you."

"What's Dya say about it?"

"Listen, kid. Dya puts on a brave face to the rest of the world. Because she's your mother, she thinks what happened to you is somehow her fault. She wants you back. The whole family does. But she knows Port Authority isn't the right place for you. I promised to put you someplace safe."

Kylee glanced away, seemed to blink back tears. "I can't see her. Not after Rebecca and Shantaya. After what I did. What I said."

"Your heart was broken. Makes you want to blame the world. And when that fades, you only blame yourself." Talina paused. "She knows that. And down in your bones, so do you."

The little girl started to climb in, hesitated. "It's not back to the mine, is it?"

"Nope. I mean it, I think it's the only place on the planet that will understand who and what you are."

"And if I don't like it?"

"Then we'll leave."

Seeing Kylee safely seated next to her, Talina powered up the aircar.

As they rose from the ground, Kylee asked, "How's Trish?"

"Dead."

"Sorry." The little girl frowned, pursed her lips into a scowl. "We going after Short Mind?"

"Depends on what he says when I catch up with him."

"In that case you'll shoot him the moment he opens his mouth."

They turned west again, sailing off over the endless forest.

"Where are we going?" Kylee asked.

"To the Briggses. Chaco and Madison's. They've got kids. Including Tip. And they've got friendly quetzals."

"I'm tired of strangers."

"Yeah, well, see, the thing about strangers is that they're only strangers until you get to know them."

"Why do adults say things like that?"

"'Cause mostly it's true."

88

The way they had trussed Tam Benteen up, he might have been a mummy fit for one of the museums on Transluna. They'd allowed him to dress in coveralls before he was bound with his broken arm behind him. Hurt like a bastard, but while he tried to play up the injury, neither the hard-eyed marines nor Talina Perez seemed to care in the least. And that was before they immobilized him with a body restraint and strapped him to a wheeled dolly.

That they'd paraded him out of the admin dome like a roll of carpet, through the fence and into the shuttle field, had given him hope. Word was that the town was all for standing him up against a wall and blowing his body apart with explosive rounds. He'd heard the shouts and calls for his death.

"It's not going to be that easy," Talina Perez had told him, something cold and dangerous in her voice. "And, well, most of the folks around town are feeling sorry for me. You see, I promised Trish I wouldn't just shoot you. You remember Trish? Perky young woman you threatened to pistol whip with her own weapon?"

"Oh, her," Tam told her with a smile. "Bit of a disappointment, actually. Silly little slit. And that was the best Port Authority could do?"

He'd watched the woman's alien eyes change, darkening. A chill had run through his bones. "Not even close," she'd whispered in an otherworldly voice.

He hoped she'd lose it, shoot him dead in a moment of rage.

Come on. Get it over with. Don't drag this out.

He'd come to grips with the knowledge that he was going to die. Like Artollia, he'd gambled. Lost. Unlike Radcek back in Solar System, these Donovanian maniacs couldn't dissect his brain. And if they tried to imprison him, it would only be a matter of time before he escaped.

Nor was torturing people to death one of the Donovanian's acceptable means of punishment. They liked things direct. So, what was the hangup?

Or so he asked himself right up to the moment they wheeled his bound body to the A-7 shuttle. A feeling of disbelief, hope, and amazement filled him as they pushed him up the ramp. It turned to euphoria as Allenovich and Michegan strapped him into one of the seats. Perez seated herself, across from him, her pistol in hand.

He couldn't believe his luck as the craft lifted, accelerated like an arrow from Donovan's gravity well. There was only one place they could be taking him: *Vixen*!

"Going to hand me over to Torgussen?" he asked mildly, controlling his features. He didn't dare allow Perez even the slightest hint of his relief. Once he was aboard *Vixen* it would only be a matter of time. How stupid could these people be?

"Got a special room ready for you," Perez told him, her gaze unfocused as she listened to something in her com.

To mollify any suspicions the woman might have, he said, "I have to say, looking forward to spending the rest of my life in the holding cell aboard *Vixen* isn't the least bit enticing. Better to have shot me back at Port Authority."

"One of the suggested alternatives was to drop you in deep forest. Maybe under a nightmare's mundo tree. Me, I had a better idea. Didn't take much to sell it to Shig, Yvette, and the rest. Heard that they raised a glass to me in toast when it was announced in The Jewel."

You fool. Scary and alien you might be, Perez, but you don't have the cunning of a twelve-year-old if you're going to let me loose in Vixen.

"*Five seconds to hard dock,*" the pilot's voice came through the ship's com.

Tam counted the seconds down, felt the thump as the shuttle settled and heard the clang as the grapples clamped. Gravity had changed, the shuttle's lights might have momentarily gone runny. Power flux from *Vixen*?

Step Allenovich and Dina Michegan unbuckled from their seats, Michegan checking the hatch. "Powered up. Got pressure. We're good to go."

Allenovich reached down, unbuckled Tam's restraints,

and lifted him onto the dolly. Perez used the straps to bind
Tam tightly to the frame.

"Don't you think you're overdoing it a little?" he asked.
"I've got a broken arm. We're on a ship. What do you
think? I'm some sort of magician?"

They ignored him. But he was used to their disdain.
With *Vixen* back under his command that would come
back to haunt them sooner rather than later. It was all he
could do to keep from giddy laughter as they wheeled him
to the hatch and bumped him over the threshold into . . .

He blinked, staring in disbelief at the dimly lit waiting
room. Lines of chairs, some strewn with trash, stood in
rows to one side. A single light panel flickered in the roof.
The floor looked filthy, streaked. The very air had a stale
and moldy taint.

"This is . . . *Freelander*!"

"Welcome aboard," Perez told him in a wary voice.

"This way." Michegan produced a hand light.

Allenovich wheeled Tam's dolly across the room and
into the dark hallway, Perez following behind.

Tam struggled to focus, trying to memorize the route as
he was rolled down stygian corridors, the way illuminated
only by hand lights. What the hell were they planning? Just
going to leave him? That was nuts. He'd have the whole
creep-freaking ship to himself. It was like handing him . . .

He lost the thought as they wheeled him past the hatch,
and into the hallway with the spooky script-overwritten
walls and ceiling. He gaped at the thousands of lines of
writing as they they passed. Felt a shiver ghost its way up
his spine.

I remember. They're all odes to the dead.

Like a blow it hit him that maybe they were going to
shoot him in the room with the eerie dome of bones. Add
his to the macabre temple of death. Death? Damn straight,
the ship reeked of it. Being shot was one thing. Having his
body left in the shadow of that gruesome shrine?

Get over it. Dead is dead.

And then Michegan stopped before an open hatch, saying, "This is it."

Two of Corporate Mine's engineers—from his previous
visit Tam placed them as Strysky and Bogarten—were

waiting beside the hatch. Some piece of equipment rested to one side. Something with cables and what looked like a powerpack.

Perez released the straps that held Tam onto the dolly, and together she and Allenovich lifted Tam, carried him, bucking and kicking, into what was obviously the astrogation center. The place was illuminated by a couple of light panels. What looked like two dessicated skeletons lay on the floor, the limp remains of uniforms conforming to the bones. Callously, they dropped him onto a bed, an action that shot pain through his broken arm.

"There's the hydroponics you requested," Strysky said, pointing across the room to where plants grew in a series of vats atop com consoles.

"What the hell is this?" Tam demanded, his heart beginning to pound. "This is insane!"

Allenovich said, "You wanted to be the boss. The guy at the top no matter what the cost. After what you did to us at Port Authority? You ask me, you're getting off easy. But then, I never could say no to Talina."

Perez placed a pack on the bed beside him, saying, "There's a knife in the side pocket there. Given your skills, shouldn't take you more than five, maybe ten minutes to wiggle around, pull it out. After that, it's only another few minutes, and you'll be free. Then *Freelander*'s all yours."

With that, Perez, Allenovich, and Michegan each flicked him his or her own wave of farewell before following the mine engineers from the room.

Tam gaped, taking in the furnishings, seeing the silent command chairs, the dead consoles, piled as they were with duraplast crates, and the curious, home-made hydroponics. The two skeletons on the floor—though nothing more than piles of bone—mocked him.

A hollow thump made him start. Looking back at the hatch, it was to see it being fitted in place. The sound of a welder could be heard, bead glowing red along the seam of the door as it was welded shut.

He'd never known panic like what possessed him now. It burst through his chest, liquid, paralyzing.

Thrashing, heedless of his broken arm, he threw himself at the pack. Found the knife. Dropped it. Finally got it.

By the time he'd managed to cut himself free and stagger to his feet, the door had been sealed.

Tam stood, staring in disbelief. The red beads of weld were fading, darkening to the same gray as the metal.

Tam blinked. Swallowed hard. His heart was hammering at his chest, his legs turned to rubber.

Stumbling back to the bed, he sank down, fought back a manaical laugh.

"Oh, Artollia, if you only could see me now."

The silence was like that of a tomb. The air seemed to eat his words. Suck them away into nothingness.

He saw the first flicker. A shadow of a person, it passed like smoke through a corner of the room.

Tam jumped when something brushed along his arm. He cried out, seeing nothing there.

The skeletons on the floor were watching him through vacant orbits in their shattered skulls. Seemed to be grinning.

"Leave me alone!"

Without the ability to tell time, he didn't know how long it had been since he was sealed in. Minutes? Hours?

He threw his head back and began to scream.

Inga's tavern appeared to be having a slow night when Kalico descended the stairs, Private Tompzen behind her. She had that feeling of nagging premonition. Like she'd forgotten something, left a light on, or a door open that should have been locked.

She'd just ridden her shuttle down from *Vixen* where Torgussen had finished his preliminary survey of Capella I. The captain had determined to work his way out from the closest to the farthest planets.

Cap I, it turned out, was a hot and dense little ball with liquid-metal lakes on the Capella-ward side and eerie lava tubes, weird caverns, and fantastic spires on the dark side. If it were unique for anything it was the harmonic singing the planet made in Capella's solar wind and a flip-flopping gravitational field.

Hitting the tavern floor, Kalico called greetings to some of her people, who were on their scheduled rotation to PA for R&R. Things had been going well at Corporate Mine. Maybe too well.

Was that the source of the feeling of incipient disaster?

In all her time on Donovan, she'd become hardened to trouble. Just last week Ituri and Ghosh had barely avoided a core meltdown at the smelter. Something gone wrong in the shuttle reactor they'd cannibalized from one of *Freelander*'s birds.

Not that she shared their superstition, but they both insisted that anything that came down from *Freelander* was haunted. Or at least spooky. Sometimes, when she was around the equipment, she could almost believe it—and more than once had sworn she sensed a presence, caught a fleeting glimpse of something from the corner of her eye.

Left her wondering how Benteen was doing up on the ghost ship. Talk about a living nightmare.

"Enjoy the moment," she muttered to herself as she picked out Talina Perez sitting at her barstool.

She walked up, gave Inga the high sign for a glass of whiskey, and seated herself next to Talina. "How's it going?"

"Last of the fence was installed today. Been a fricking long couple of months. Lot of people are going to sleep better tonight." Talina glanced at her. "What's new on your end?"

Kalico had never grown used to the woman's changed eyes, or the fact that her cheekbones were more pointed now, giving her face an almost diamond shape.

"Just got back from a briefing on *Vixen*."

"See Weisbacher?"

"Just a glimpse. He sticks to his quarters, doesn't interact with the crew. Lives in a self-imposed exile. Almost furtive, like a rat."

"Some people never put the pot back together."

"Where's Dya? Thought she'd be here."

"She's headed out to the Briggses place tomorrow. She and Madison have been talking on the radio. Word is that Kylee's finally willing to see her mother again. Meanwhile, Su's holding down the fort."

"Kylee settling in out there?"

"She and Tip are like entangled photons, that's the second son. Madison reports that they're inseparable. There's also a rumor going around that the kid's tight with a young quetzal."

"What do you make of it?"

Talina waited as Inga placed a plate of quetzal steak, a roasted clove of garlic, broccoli, and chili-simmered refritos before her.

"Inga, bring me a plate of that," Kalico said. "I haven't had a decent meal in two weeks."

"Coming up."

Kalico tossed out a ten SDR coin, adding, "Put Tal's bill on mine."

"What do I make of Kylee?" Talina shrugged. "She's still carrying a grudge. My hope is that Chaco and Madison can work her through it. Hopefully like I did with Trish after her mom died."

Kalico watched Talina's expression go slack. But it was

nothing like the wrenching of the soul she'd seen reflected in the woman's eyes the day they'd buried Trish.

After the quetzal rampage there'd been too many funerals.

"Attrition." Kalico remembered how nonsensical the term had sounded the first time she'd read it in a report as *Turalon* came hurtling in-system.

"This new quetzal Kylee's supposedly hanging out with? Maybe it's got some of Rocket in it?"

"Different lineage," Talina said. "I got a taste of that line when I was bringing Cap in. It never made much of an impression. Not the way Demon's line, Rocket's line, and the Rork quetzals have."

Kalico studied the woman. "What do they want, Tal?"

"Mostly they want to know what we're doing here. How to deal with us. And then there's Demon's line. They want us dead. The more of us, and the bloodier, the better."

"Last I heard there has been no sign of Whitey, as if anyone but you could tell one quetzal from the next."

"He'll be easy to recognize. I left him with a broken left front leg. I got at least one shot into his body, too. For all we know, he might be lying dead under some aquajade tree out there."

"That's too good to be true. Maybe after the raid, they gave up?"

Talina shook her head as she cut a slice of steak. "Quetzals don't work that way. Think long term. Generations. And Demon has occasionally let it slip. They think the raid was a success."

"Demon? They? Is it one or two?"

"One and many all rolled into one. Forget it. You'd have to think like an ancient Maya shaman. What you and everybody here need to know is that they think we're all at the beginning of this thing."

"How about down at Corporate Mine? What do they want? I'm having people killed."

"Everybody thinks I'm a quetzal expert? Kalico, I've got a faint glimmer of how these beasts think, and it's really different than we do. And the parts I think I know, it's probably because those are the few parts of quetzal logic that make sense to my Earthly primate brain."

"Haven't had any urges to shoot Sian Hmong lately? You know, you were the hero after the raid, but some people still worry about you."

"That include you?"

"Sure. But not in the way you probably think. I worry that you're too hard on yourself. Especially after Trish's death. You were in a fricking coma out there. Not your fault that that idiot Weisbacher shot her."

"Right. Not my fault." Talina's alien eyes narrowed, as if she was completely aware that she was lying to herself.

"That's exactly the attitude that worries me. Like you blame yourself for not always being at the heart of things, keeping people safe. You're setting yourself apart, Tal. You're not a pariah. These people need you."

"*Pixom*," Talina said.

"What the hell is peeshom?"

"Two souls in the same body in constant opposition to one another. That's me."

"That's all of us." Kalico leaned back as Inga set a steaming plate and two fingers of whiskey before her.

"Eat in health, Supervisor," the burly woman said before trundling down the bar, her towel over her shoulder.

They were silent as they ate, Kalico watching the woman from the corner of her eye. Why did she always have to worry that, like a grenade with the pin pulled, Talina was ready to detonate?

And Trish Monagan's death had really taken something out of the woman.

The sense of premonition continued to grow, almost like an itch under her sternum.

"Here comes Shig," Talina said without so much as a lift of her head.

Kalico turned, expecting Shig to be barreling down on them. Instead he was just stepping off the bottom steps clear across the room.

"How do you do that?"

"What? Know that Shig's coming? I just know. How about you? Want to know something?"

"Sure."

By then Shig was there, breathing heavily. "News just came in."

"The Buddha's bones were found beneath a bunch of tentacles under a mundo tree?" Talina asked mildly.

Shig scowled at her. "Don't be crass. Two Spot just got a signal from *Vixen*. They had a ping on their photonic com. There's a ship out there. Way, way out there. Like almost a light-year. But it's ours. And it's headed our way."

Kalico took a deep breath. "And just when we thought it was getting boring around here."

EPILOGUE

Second Elder had been observing on the day the young biped arrived. She was brought to the lineage grounds by One Quetzal Woman in one of the flying boxes. This new one was young, with a different coloring than the familiar bipeds. The hair was yellow, the skin more pale.

Of particular interest, wherever she went, she left quetzal knowledge. It could be smelled on the breeze, in places where she placed her feet, and more particularly where she squatted and left water.

She had come to live among the strange creatures who had settled on the edge of Water Runs in Black Canyon.

On the very first night the girl had sneaked out. She'd explored all around the dwellings where the bipeds sheltered. Third Elder had followed her, and where she'd made water, had tasted the scent of many quetzals from four different lineages.

That knowledge stunned the entire lineage. What could it mean? The mystery of the yellow girl only deepened.

On this morning, Third Orange—who had yet to achieve elder status—stalked the young biped and Brown Boy. Brown Boy had been born here. He left the lineage alone, and sometimes food-shared, as did the rest of the local bipeds—a sign of ritual respect to the lineage that demonstrated the bipeds weren't entirely barbaric.

To have been chosen to make contact with the yellow girl was an honor for Third Orange, given that the number came from his birth order. His color name had been granted because he agreed to attempt this most daring plan.

Third Orange now crept through the aquajade and scrub mundo, each step placed warily. His flared collar picked up the morning sounds of chime, of the distant scarlet fliers, and the whisper of breeze in the leaves. Most of all, it absorbed the gentle laughter, the rising and falling of the bipeds' curious vocalizations. It seemed to be such a limited means of communication.

The alien bipeds amazed Third Orange. Since entering the forest, they'd remained unaware of his presence. Heedless of how close such a large predator could stalk.

It's so easy. Charge from behind. Snap the jaws shut on one, stun the other with a blow from the tail.

The bipeds had entered the clearing now. This was the place.

Third Orange—flashing all the patterns that insisted he was not a threat—stepped out into the clearing where the yellow girl and Brown Boy had caught a crest in a snare.

"'Bout time you got here," the golden-haired girl said, turning and staring right at Third Orange. "You following us for a reason?"

Third Orange stopped short, a flash of blue tinged with yellow and black slipping down his hide before he could cover it with a shade of black that betrayed frustration.

Brown Boy watched him with unconcerned eyes, and then went back to removing the crest from the snare.

The yellow-haired youngster stepped forward, apparently unconcerned, and then, to Third Orange's total surprise, she bowed low, extended her arms, and let out an incomprehensible squawk. Awkward, clumsy, and impossible as it seemed, she was imitating the nonthreatening posture of a young quetzal.

Third Orange couldn't help the violet, mauve, and orange flash of curiosity.

The yellow-haired girl giggled and cried out, "Way ahead of you." Then she straightened, walked up to Third Orange, and pointed at her chest. "Kylee."

She pointed at the Brown Boy who was watching from where he'd finished with the snare. "Tip."

Third Orange knew the sounds associated with the boy from years of observing the bipeds.

It was impulsive. He flashed his name.

"Orange Three?"

Her vocalizations meant nothing to him. Out of frustration he flashed a momentary black and vented his irritation and confusion. How could she understand him, and he hadn't a clue of what her uttered noises meant?

"You sound like a flute," she said. "That's what we'll call you." She pointed at herself again. "Kylee." Then the Brown Boy. "Tip." And at Third Orange. "Flute."

For once the ancestral memories and knowledge had nothing to offer. Only Fourth Elder, who had once tasted One Quetzal Woman, had been this intimate with one of the bipeds before.

Which was when Kylee stepped right up to Third Orange and said, "Let's see just who you really are."

And with that she opened her mouth, her two curious blue eyes challenging and twinkling in the light.

Third Orange's reaction was instinctive. His tongue shot out, was probing her mouth. The softness of the biped's tongue and cheeks, and the tiny line of her teeth surprised him. To his amazement her fluids teemed with information.

To absorb it would take time. To understand it, even longer. But to Third Orange's surprise, he had done the unimaginable. Even more to his amazement, the bipeds were more than just clever animals.

Kylee walked over, took the crest from Brown Boy's hands, and laid it before Third Orange. He would remember the vocalizations, would eventually know what they meant.

"Only members of a lineage share food. You eat this. And from this moment on, Tip and me, we're part of your lineage."

"You sure about this?" Brown Boy—Tip in his own language—asked.

"I'm sure. He won't be Rocket, but I'm willing to share him. You'll see. We'll be great friends. But I got to get back now. Dya's coming. And I don't know how I'm going to do this."

Third Orange watched Kylee and Tip as they vanished down the trail back toward the settlement.

He stared down at the crest, and in one quick gulp, swallowed it.

Even as the flood of quetzal knowledge was absorbed by Third Orange's brain, the images were stunning. Beyond anything his ancestors or lineage could have expected.

Memories of quetzal and biped. Miraculous visions. Curious new emotions no quetzal had ever experienced.

And there, down deep, much to Third Orange's horror, he suddenly lived the black darkness of pain, grief, guilt, and an abiding rage.

The question was begged: *What kind of terrible creature has come among us?*

Tanya Huff
The Peacekeeper Novels

"Huff weaves a fast-paced thriller bristling with treachery and intrigue. Fans of military science fiction will enjoy this tense adventure and its intricately constructed setting."
—*Publishers Weekly*

"Anyone who has read any of Huff's previous books featuring Kerr . . . knows of her amazing ability to combine action, plot, and character into a wonderful melange that makes her books a joy to read."
—*Seattle Post-Intelligencer*

AN ANCIENT PEACE
978-0-7564-1130-5

A PEACE DIVIDED
978-0-7564-1151-0

THE PRIVILEGE OF PEACE
978-0-7564-1154-1

To Order Call: 1-800-788-6262
www.dawbooks.com

Cries from the Lost Island
by Kathleen O'Neal Gear

Set against the glory and tragedy of ancient Roman Egypt, a novel that brings to bring to life the greatest love story of all time...

Sixteen-year-old Hal Stevens is a budding historical scholar from a small town in Colorado. A virtual outcast at high school, he has only two friends: Roberto the Biker Witch and Cleo Mallawi. Cleo claims to be the reincarnation of Queen Cleopatra. She also believes she's being stalked by an ancient Egyptian demon, Ammut, the Devourer of the Dead.

But when Hal and Roberto find Cleo murdered in the forest near her home, it appears she may have been telling the truth. Her last request sends them journeying to Egypt with famed archaeologist Dr. James Moriarity, where it quickly becomes clear that Cleo has set them on the search of a lifetime: the search for the lost graves of Marc Antony and Cleopatra.

But they are not alone in their search. Cleo's murderers are watching their every move. And not all of them are human...

Available in hardcover March 2020

978-0-7564-1578-5